Dear Reader,

Welcome to Silh...
to Mother with L...
celebrating motherhood is a tribute to the many
complex facets that make up a mother's role.

Mary in "More Than a Mother" by Curtiss Ann
Matlock profoundly shocks her family by
demonstrating that mothers are people, too—women
with lives of their own, women who don't exist solely
in relation to others! In "Neighborly Affair," Carole
Halston's heroine decides to bypass marriage and
move directly to single motherhood—until she learns
that basic biology doesn't begin to explain the
miracle of family. In Linda Shaw's emotional
"Jilly's Secret" we compellingly see that indeed
biology does not define motherhood—it is caring
and commitment that create the loving bond.

This collection celebrates the mother in us all—the
caring, nurturing being within who comforts in times
of sorrow, is a companion in joy and inspires us to
meet and exceed our goals.

Wishing you all the best,

Isabel Swift
Editorial Director

to Mother with Love '92

Curtiss Ann Matlock
Carole Halston
Linda Shaw

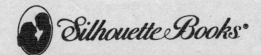

Silhouette Books®

Published by Silhouette Books New York

America's Publisher of Contemporary Romance

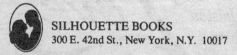

SILHOUETTE BOOKS
300 E. 42nd St., New York, N.Y. 10017

to Mother with Love '92
Copyright © 1992 by Silhouette Books

All rights reserved, including the right to reproduce this book or
portions thereof in any form whatsoever. For information address
Silhouette Books, 300 East 42nd Street, New York, N.Y. 10017

ISBN: 0-373-48239-6

First Silhouette Books printing May 1992

All the characters in this book are fictitious. Any resemblance to
actual persons, living or dead, is purely coincidental.

The publisher acknowledges the copyright holders of the
individual works as follows:

More Than a Mother
Copyright © 1992 by Curtiss Ann Matlock

Neighborly Affair
Copyright © 1992 by Carole Halston

Jilly's Secret
Copyright © 1992 by Linda Shaw

®: Trademark used under license and registered in the United
States Patent and Trademark Office and in other countries.

Printed in the U.S.A.

Contents

*More Than
a Mother*

CURTISS
ANN MATLOCK

A Note from Curtiss Ann Matlock

Curtiss Ann Matlock is my real name, not a pen name. Who would choose such a pen name? I was named Curtiss Ann after my grandfather and grandmother, Curtis and Anna Wentworth, of Elizabeth City, North Carolina. As a girl, I positively hated my name. It sounded coarse and boyish and painfully different. I spent hours listing names I would love to have—lovely, feminine names like Laura and Nicole and Charlene. I quite passionately insisted I would legally change my name to one more beautiful and girlish when I was of age. I'm sure this hurt the feelings of my mother, but she never got angry and simply patiently predicted that someday I would be very glad to have so unusual a name. I did not believe that for an instant.

As I said, my roots lie in North Carolina, and I'm very much a Southern belle. I'm not certain why, because in actuality I've lived all over the country, from Florida to Alaska, as has my mother. Still, the Southern woman heritage runs deep and is passsed down through the women of my family. It's an attitude about being a woman, who is always feminine, even while capably doing a man's job, and about pride, which keeps our heads high though our pockets may be empty, and about manners, which demand we be sweetly cordial, even when telling someone to eat frogs and die. It's about appearing soft, yet being made of steel. And it's about speaking with a Southern accent, which vibrates with color and emotion.

Pronounced in the Southern way, my name is Curtissann, the first and middle names slurred together and with the *t* touched on ever so lightly. All my family and close friends say my name that way, even those dear ones who are Yankees. Though if my mother is reproving me, she pronounces the *t* quite clearly and with a hint of genteel shock, which makes me immediately contrite for my misdeed.

Of course, you know by now that I eventually, just as Mother predicted and most likely prayed, did grow to appreciate my name for its uniqueness. Besides, by the time I came of legal age, I was already married. Changing my name to Laura or Nicole or Charlene would have proved very confusing for a lot of people, not the least of those the young man whose class ring I'd worn since I was a junior in high school and whom I'm still with today.

I've also come to recognize my name as a link to my grandparents and, in some inexplicable way, to a heritage from which I came and which helps define who and what I've become. All of which eventually reflects in the stories I write—from writing about towns like Minnett Springs to people like Ellen Louise Minnett, whom I drew from memories of my grandmother, Anna.

Curtiss Ann Matlock

Chapter One

The interior of the house didn't need painting, but Mary needed a change. At least, that was what she thought: a simple little change to lift her spirits. As a mother facing the empty-nest syndrome, it was normal for her to be a little blue, a little confused.

She'd tried rearranging the furniture, which had always helped in the past but didn't now. She'd considered buying new furniture—draperies, too—but that was just too foolish when all of the furnishings had been the very best when first bought, remained classically stylish and like new. As it was, painting a house that didn't need it was stretching her good sense, so she pronounced to everyone that the walls were *so* in need—the brand of paint used only fourteen months ago, when everything had been painted for Ellen's wedding, just hadn't held up. Then, of course, there'd been that time last winter when Alanna had stuck the damper of the fireplace. And the furnace had had that silly spell. And Dani Lee had gone through that period of cooking along with the Grand Gourmet on television and managed to set off the smoke alarm each time. Once the fire department had even responded.

These were good, sensible reasons, and the general consensus concerning Mary Minnett Lunsford was that she was as sensible as saddle shoes and as dependable as the sunrise. Mary had always agreed with the description, had even taken pride and comfort in the fact.

If she'd truly understood herself as a changeable human being, if she had known all the commotion that was going to result from having her house painted, she never would have done it. It's very well for a woman not to understand herself sometimes.

Mary wasn't happy with the painter when he arrived thirty minutes ahead of his appointed time.

She was up, showered and dressed, had breakfasted, started a load of laundry, removed a stain from Dani Lee's jacket and finished a skirt for Alanna—all pretty much a normal routine. Mary liked routine and was as punctual as Christmas, and she wished the painter had arrived at eight, as he was supposed to have done, because she had counted on a full thirty minutes alone to read from a most marvelous book about the Rio Grande Valley.

Hearing the vehicle in the driveway, she set aside the book and went to the bedroom window. Parting the miniblinds with two fingers, she peered down at the curved driveway in front of the house. Sure enough, a van with the Miller Brothers Painting Contractors logo on the side sat there. Apparently an eight o'clock starting time meant nothing to these people. A dark-haired man in white, paint-splotched coveralls alighted and looked uncertainly from the front door to the one around the side.

While her mind hurried down the stairs to the door, Mary raised the blinds and let her hand pause on the window handle, hesitating while her mother's voice echoed inwardly, *"One doesn't holler out the window, Mary!"* That was one of those nebulous codes of conduct she'd learned somewhere along the way. It went with the ones that forbade a lady—and secretary of the Ladies Circle at that—to wear shorts downtown or smoke on a public street. Still, calling out the window right then appealed to her sense of expediency and, just a mite, to a spark of rebellion, too, though she was only vaguely aware of the rebellion part.

She jerked open the window. The already sultry air of an August morning hit her in the face. "Excuse me!" she called softly; Alanna was asleep in the next room.

The dark head turned, looking for her.

She unlatched the screen and poked her head out. "Up here...please."

The man's face came up. They gazed at each other, each of them with their own sense of surprise.

"Good morning," he said.

A magnificent, infectious smile spread across his face, but Mary resisted smiling in return. She resisted the surprise, too. "Good morning. Mr. Miller said you wouldn't be here until eight o'clock." She spoke crisply.

He blinked several times, then said, "I could go away and come back in—" he glanced at his watch "—twenty-five minutes. Or I could wait out here in your driveway. Whether I start now or at eight, you won't pay a nickel more or less."

And so she felt foolish. And she thought how he wasn't what she had expected. For one thing, she'd spoken with Fred Miller about the painting. Fred was at least sixty but looked seventy and as if he kept a lemon in his mouth all the time. This man was...well, he appeared to be a man who had sunbeams in his pockets.

Not responding to his suggestions, she said, "Mr. Miller told me there would be two of you."

"Shorthanded today. One of the fellas broke his arm yesterday, and another called in sick this morning."

"Oh, I see."

Mary brought herself up short with the thought that she didn't need to be carrying on an entire conversation with him through an upstairs window.

"You can bring everything through the front door. I'll come and unlock it."

She passed Dani Lee coming out of the bathroom. "Did you get the mustard stain out of my jacket, Mom?"

"Uh ... yes, dear," she said, hurrying on to the stairway. "It's downstairs in the kitchen. Don't let your sister come down half-dressed—the painter's here."

Her sneakers made a muffled staccato beat on the carpeted stairs and squeaked a bit on the polished oak of the entry hall. She opened the door to see the man bending, setting two cans of paint on the porch. He straightened, and their eyes met, and the sense of unexpectedness washed over her again.

He was handsome. Very. Deeply tanned, with the kind of features that were both mature and ageless. Quite a bit of gray shone in his rich, dark and curly auburn hair, and small lines shot out from his eyes. The most luminous blue eyes Mary had ever seen. And they were regarding her in the strangest fashion. *As if he were glad to see her.*

"Please come in," she said, feeling a silly smile bloom.

The man stepped inside. The scent of paint and faint manly after-shave came with him. Old Spice, Mary thought with a sudden, sweet memory washing over her. Her grandfather had worn Old Spice. Now all the men in her family seemed to prefer colognes from Europe that cost an arm and a leg.

She shut the door, then turned to see the man looking around. His gaze circled to rest again on her. Suddenly she felt acutely aware of herself. Of her khaki trousers and pink cotton shirt, so very comfortably worn—ten years worn, to be exact. Of her hair, streaked with gray, that she'd hurriedly stroked five times that morning and pulled back to tie at her nape. Of her skin that no amount of modern beauty cream would return to the first bloom of youth.

The curious way he looked at her made her wonder if there were toothpaste on her cheek, or if the fly of her trousers was unzipped. She glanced toward the hall mirror but saw only a faint shadow of where it had been. She and Dani Lee had removed the mirror last night in preparation for painting.

"I'm Jim Pettijohn," the man said and held out his hand.

She shook his hand, saying, "Hello, Mr. Pettijohn. I'm Mary Lunsford." His hand was warm, and he held on to hers.

Withdrawing her hand, she brushed it quickly across her cheek. "I'll show you what I want painted," she said, discreetly fingering her trouser fly. Everything seemed okay.

She walked him through the downstairs rooms, pointing out the elaborate cornices, the turned spindles on the banister and the fancy trim everywhere. The trim that was already white would be repainted white, of course, so that shouldn't be much problem. He pointed out places that were heavy with paint and should be stripped; she agreed. Assuming it would be convenient for him, as well as for her family, she had prepared the downstairs to be painted first, and he readily agreed that whatever suited her suited him. She wasn't certain of the colors she wanted, but had been assured by Fred Miller that she could be shown samples, and again he smoothly agreed.

"I have all the colors you picked as possibilities out in the van," he said. His Southern drawl was distinctive, with an inflection she couldn't quite identify.

He was an easy, breezy sort of man. He smiled a lot, though she sensed this more than saw it; she didn't look directly at him. Quite suddenly Mary felt very shy. It came as an unsettling realization to find herself noting his strong hands and the forearms that stuck out below his rolled sleeves. And it was further unsettling to notice a fluttering inside herself.

In the solitude of her kitchen, Mary put on an apron, poured herself a cup of coffee, turned and leaned against the counter. Her gaze came around to the shiny black glass of the wall oven. Cautiously, feeling like a misbehaving five-year-old, she stepped close to the oven and stared at her shadowy reflection.

Turning her head, she saw clearly that there was no toothpaste or jam on either cheek. She bared her teeth and saw nothing caught between them. Solemnly she gazed at the face staring back at her. A plain face, the face of a mother in her forties, she thought, oddly feeling no connection with that person. It was happening again and again these days—she couldn't seem to recognize herself.

A movement glimpsed through the panes of glass on the door sent Mary pivoting away from the oven and over to the refrigerator.

It was Ellen, of course, who came through the back door. Her eldest daughter had been married more than a year to an executive at her grandfather's bank and had a small apartment only two streets away, but she spent more time here than there. The truth was that most of Ellen's friends worked, leaving her with no one to talk to. She said her apartment was so small as to be boring, but Mary knew it was more a case of Ellen not caring much for any type of housework, and if she wasn't in her own home she couldn't mess it up too much. And to be fair, Mary thought as her daughter kissed her cheek, Ellen was pregnant with her first child, and she was nervous.

As Mary brought a bunch of spinach from the refrigerator and dumped it in the sink, she saw Ellen rubbing her stomach.

"I'm beginning to feel like a blimp. I swear, Mother, I'd be happy to have this baby right now."

Ellen was a beautiful woman, with chestnut hair, pale skin and full lips, which now, and eighty percent of the time, were formed into a pout. Ellen had pouting down to a science. Mary had long ago learned to look beyond the habit, but right now she thought drearily that it seemed more than she could bear.

She sighed. "You probably won't say that when you have to be getting up at night with him—or her."

"Well, Todd's going to help me with that. I'm not solely responsible for creating this child," Ellen said as she took a plate from the cabinet in order to help herself to the breakfast Mary had prepared and left on the counter for her daughters to serve themselves. "Oh, good! You made waffles!"

The hundreds of nights when Ellen had been a baby merged into one in a flash across Mary's memory. Mary had walked the floor at night with Ellen while Daniel slept on; most women of her era had been expected to do that—or had it been that Mary had held Ellen to herself?

Dani Lee burst through the swinging door from the dining room. "I can't believe I got up early and I'm still running late," She grabbed the jacket Mary had cleaned from the back of a chair. "Did you bring the paper in, Mom?"

"No, dear, I forgot."

"Oh, Mom! You know the Websters' dog likes it."

"If he's gotten it, read your grandfather's paper down at the bank. And have some breakfast—you have plenty of time."

"I want to get to the computer before Nick does. Granddad Lunsford has promised a bonus to the one of us who makes the most profit on our investments by the end of these last two weeks."

Granddad Lunsford was the girls' grandfather on Daniel's side of the family, and it was very clear that Dani Lee favored that side. She was dark, as her father had been, slim and dynamic, certain of where she was going, which was up, and how to get there. Mary was constantly amazed at how fast her little Dani Lee with the Buster Brown haircut had grown into a competent adult.

"That jacket does nothing for you, Dani Lee. Mustard just isn't your color," Ellen said as she moved gracefully over to the table with her heaped plate. Even nearly five months pregnant, Ellen moved like a model.

"Oh, can it, Miss Fashion."

"All right, but that jacket doesn't go with your rising executive persona."

"Mom, don't forget to take my teal suit to the cleaners. I left it on my bed—and can I borrow a ten?"

"I won't forget the suit." Mary gave her daughter the money along with a bag packed with some breakfast and saw her out the back door just as Alanna entered through the swinging door.

Each of her daughters was special to Mary—Ellen because of being her first and very much like Mary herself in appreciating traditional values; Dani Lee for being second and, like Mary, very dependable. And then Alanna, fair haired and bouncy, her last child, and a surprise, because she seemed to be what Mary was not—

impetuous and unreserved. Alanna had always been the easiest to get along with, and for this Mary found an extra tenderness in her heart.

Alanna bopped to the counter and picked up a sausage link, saying gaily, "That painter is sure a cutie."

"For goodness' sake, Alanna, you're a pure embarrassment sometimes," Ellen protested. "I bet you've already been throwing yourself at him. Mother, you really must do something about this child."

Mary glanced up from the sink where she was washing spinach. "I think it's a little late to do anything about your sister. We'll just have to hope for the best."

"Well, you probably shouldn't let her move off to Wichita. She can't seem to control herself from making eyes at anything in pants—left alone, she'll be pregnant in two months."

"There's been no report of making eyes causing pregnancy," Alanna quipped as she curled her graceful bare legs into a chair at the table. "And I do not make eyes at *anything* in pants—only *handsome* men in pants."

To which Ellen replied loftily, "I saw that guy outside getting stuff out of the van, and I didn't see anything in him to write home about. He's just some old housepainter. The world's full of them. My heaven, Alanna, he's old enough to be your father."

"So? I think he looks an awful lot like Mel Gibson, don't you, Mom?"

"Umm . . . who's that?"

"Mel Gibson—that actor in that movie Dani Lee brought home last Saturday. Jim looks a lot like him—ruggedly handsome. Ooo-wee."

"Oh, maybe," Mary said and dumped spinach on a cloth and began to tear out the stems. She thought, yes, just a little bit. But Jim Pettijohn had more flesh, and curlier hair, and certainly more gray.

"Jim?" Ellen raised an eyebrow.

Alanna nodded. "I introduced myself—manners, dear sister." She laughed. "He's got a really cute rear end."

Ellen shook her head. "You're so crass, Alanna."

"I know—let's all go in and have a look. Then we'll take a vote to see if we all think he has a cute butt."

"Well, *I*," Ellen said emphatically, "have more taste than to go around surveying men's rear ends. And Mother is far beyond your juvenile games."

"Okay, maybe Mom isn't interested, but you can't convince me, Ellen, that *you* don't notice other men from time to time—taste or no taste. You may be married and pregnant, but you're still a woman."

It was the way both women spoke that raised hairs on the back of Mary's neck. They sat there, talking not only as if Mary weren't even there in the room, but as if she had no voice to speak for herself. As if she didn't count as a woman. And as if she were simply *incapable* of being interested in men!

Before she knew it, she'd said, "Yes, my dear daughters. All sexual urges are reserved for the young and vanish when a woman reaches thirty."

She didn't actually say it *to* them. She simply spat out a tart statement, as much to the spinach as to anyone.

But they heard, and fell silent.

Mary looked up from the spinach to see both daughters staring at her with the surprise and suspicion of offspring who'd just heard their mother mention sex in connection with herself.

"And I *do* think Jim Pettijohn is handsome," she said.

A rap sounded at the swinging door, causing all three of them to jump.

Jim Pettijohn poked his head in the room, sweeping them all with his gaze and his grin. With those vibrant blue eyes resting on Mary, he said, "Ah . . . I've made up samples of those colors, if you'd like to come look."

He gave no sign as to whether or not he'd heard their conversation. As to whether he'd heard Mary say she thought him handsome. But she knew with mortification that he surely had to see her red, hot face.

Jim Pettijohn had spent twenty years as a journalist and, before that, eight years of wanting to be and studying to be one, so he had keen powers of observation. He was an excellent listener and totally without shame in doing it. He was, quite proudly, an ace snoop; life was highly interesting that way. And then, too, there were his almost infallible instincts, upon which he'd learned to rely heavily, above anything the "facts" might have screamed at him. His old boss used to say Jim could tell whether a man was a thief or an honest soul just by shaking hands with him.

On first sight of the Lunsford home, Jim knew a lot about its inhabitants. The house was located in the elite section of Minnett Springs, Kansas, brick with white trim, dating from the twenties and still screaming substance. A bright red Mustang convertible and a sporty blue Datsun were parked outside the garage, a garage with chauffeur's quarters above, no less, though they were unused these days. All of this said the Lunsfords were old-family wealthy, or at least quite comfortable.

Jim had once lived in a house much like this one, though it had belonged to his wife. As for himself, he'd been born a poor boy and had had to learn the manners of the upper class. He'd thought the learning fun.

Mary Lunsford lived here with her three daughters, grown women all. Though there was a man dominating a number of the family photographs on the table behind the couch, no man lived in the house—no man's shoes anywhere, no sports magazines or clothing, no scent of a man. And Mary Lunsford didn't wear a wedding band. Plain old instinct told Jim she was a widow.

One of the daughters was almost the total opposite of her mother, dark headed, slim as a rail and in high gear—tossing him a hello as she raced through. Type-A personality, Jim judged, just as he was himself. Or had been. He'd made a deliberate effort to change and had succeeded.

The daughter he thought was the youngest was pert, pretty and flirty. She flashed him a smile and took time to introduce herself as Alanna and connect with her eyes. She was going to move down to Wichita and begin college at the end of the month—he learned that when she was talking on the telephone in the living room, reclining on the couch and swishing her bare legs in the air in order to catch his attention while she was at it. Also during this conversation he learned that she'd agreed, reluctantly, to work in an uncle's insurance office while she went to college, that she'd caught the eye of some guy named Kirk, that her sister Dani Lee—the dark-haired one, he had no doubt—was going away to Columbia University this year. He also gathered that some group called the Metal Hairs were "boss." Being a man in tune with the times, he knew that meant they were great.

Along about ten o'clock he learned that only two of the daughters lived here. The third, the pretty pregnant one who walked like a tired model in a grand sulk, was married and lived quite close, because she'd walked over. However, she still continued to keep a bedroom here, which he learned when he overheard her whining to her mother.

"You aren't going to turn my room into a guest room or anything, are you, Mother? Just because I've moved out doesn't mean I don't like having my room here."

"You can have that room as long as you want, Ellen," Mary Lunsford said in a soothing voice.

"Well . . . we could need it someday, Todd and I. Or if I ever get mad at him and have to come home."

"You can always come home, Ellen, but I don't advise you ever to leave Todd."

"Do I have to have it painted that peach color?" the pretty one whined, still going on about her bedroom. "We've always had white, and I like it. It's so clean and crisp."

"We'll leave it white," her mother answered almost automatically as she mounted the stairs.

All the painted walls and ceilings and a lot of the trim were done in white, but this time Mary Lunsford had chosen misty apricot for most of the walls. He'd known she would. He'd known as he mixed it that it was the perfect shade for her. And he wasn't too surprised that she'd picked the smoky blue for a few places. Smoky blue had subtle pizzazz, like Mary Lunsford herself possessed. Oh, her pizzazz was well hidden, buried deep down, and most people wouldn't recognize it. But most people weren't as perceptive as Jim Pettijohn, which perhaps reflected a lofty opinion of himself, though he tried not to let himself get a swelled head.

Mary Lunsford was a punctual woman—he'd certainly seen that right off—and a no-nonsense, straight-arrow type of person. No foolish bouffant or faddish clothes for her. Her hair, the color of sunshine streaked with silver, was pulled straight back and tied sensibly at her neck. Her clothes were the epitome of practicality.

Her tastes ran to traditional, classic... and very, very classy, he thought, standing with his spackling knife in hand and sweeping his gaze over the dining room. She was also shy; she tended to keep averting her eyes from his, and she did it because she liked him. He'd known that even before he overheard her say she thought he was handsome. It was true he hadn't truly caught the mention of his name, but, in his experience, when three people shared that same embarrassed expression it was because they'd been talking about the person who'd popped onto the scene. So where did he find the pizzazz? Oh, that was in her eyes, which were as green as spring leaves and just as glistening.

Jim had liked Mary Lunsford the instant he'd laid eyes on her.

He'd just pounded the lid into place on the paint can when Alanna came up. He saw her bare legs first.

"Breaking for lunch?" she asked with a fresh-as-the-morning smile. "Come and join me. I make a mean sandwich. Take your choice—turkey or seasoned beef."

Jim smiled but shook his head. "I have an errand to run."

She cajoled, "But you have to eat. And we can sit out by the pool. Relax. You know."

He looked at her and was reminded of his young, golden-haired niece. He was a little grateful to her for that; sometimes he missed his family.

Again he shook his head. "I'll have time to catch lunch. Thanks just the same."

If it had been her mother doing the asking, he would have stayed—and gladly. Living as he did in a small studio apartment, with only a two-burner for cooking, he would have enjoyed eating something fixed by a woman's hands. And he would enjoy talking with Mary Lunsford.

Though this pretty young thing's attention did his ego a world of good, he felt no temptation. He smiled and bade her goodbye, and felt a little sorry at her disappointment.

As he drove out the driveway, he saw Mary walking far down the sidewalk. She moved leisurely, like a woman enjoying herself. For an instant he felt a stab of jealousy aimed at nothing more than circumstances, which kept him from walking with her.

Mary walked slowly, taking pleasure in the familiar neighborhood. She knew this route well, must have passed along it hundreds of thousands of times, because she'd grown up in the white house only four doors down from the one she now owned. Daniel had lived in the big Victorian house on the corner. They'd played together as elementary-school children, gone steady as teens. It had been expected for them to marry, but they'd loved each other no less for that. Daniel had left her a widow ten years ago, and she'd at last forgiven him.

Once Mary had dreamed of seeing the world as an airline stewardess, and for a while, at sixteen, when her father had given her a camera, she had considered being a photographer of faraway places and events for magazines. When she'd been thirteen, she'd been all packed for a Girl Scout trip to San Antonio, Texas, when she'd come down with the three-day measles. She and Daniel had gone to Mazatlán for their honeymoon, but she'd always wanted to see San Antonio. The only other thing besides marrying Daniel that Mary had considered doing was traveling. Seeing places—like the deserts and the

Grand Canyon and where hairy goats roamed the mountains in Afghanistan. And most of all San Antonio.

That dream seemed to be coming back to her these days, haunting and taunting, now that it appeared beyond her. She had the money, but she wasn't so young, though she wasn't old, and it didn't seem there should be an age limit for travel. But then she didn't really want to go alone, and there were the girls to consider. And she'd never done anything to prepare her for just up and changing around her entire life.

She rapped lightly and entered the house where she'd grown up, and in which her mother, Ellen Louise Minnett, had lived for almost fifty years. Mary's father had been dead fifteen years, and Aunt Fran had shared the house for the past five, though Aunt Fran spent a lot of time in California with her eldest daughter. She was there now.

A few years ago Mary's eldest brother, William, had suggested that his mother and Aunt Fran move into one of those fancy condos he was building; it would need far less upkeep, and it would be convenient to shopping and the hospital. Their mother had thrown the biggest hissy fit this side of the Mississippi.

As Mary walked along the hallway, she found it hard to picture not being able to come here, to find her mother—as always, impeccably dressed, usually in a pastel color, and complete with her pearls—in command of all around her.

For an instant Mary did imagine telling her mother that she was going off, alone, to San Antonio. Her mother would be surprised. Then she imagined telling her mother that she was actually a bit *relieved* that her daughters were moving out. No, she would do better to mention San Antonio.

Mary had just taken a swallow of her mother's delicious coffee—her mother made the best coffee in the entire world—when her mother said, "So I told Odelia you could step in early as president, and all of us in the Circle would understand."

Mary choked, grabbed an ivory linen napkin from the glass-topped table and spewed the superb coffee inelegantly into it. "Me?" she croaked when she could draw half a breath. She hadn't been paying close attention to what her mother had been saying and saw this as her punishment. *For not paying attention to your mother, the fine is one year as president of the Ladies Circle.*

"Why, of course," her mother said. "It's been understood for some time that this coming year would be *your* year. Everyone knows that, though we'll have the elections as always in December. And I didn't speak out of turn in telling Odelia you would take over early—I simply told her I would ask you, and that you couldn't possibly do it this month, but probably wouldn't have any problem at all in doing so at the September meeting." She smiled. "I was just your age when I took over the presidency—you were sixteen. Remember? You got to vote for me."

Right there in front of Mary's eyes, her mother's face blurred into an image of her own, and Mary's life stretched before her, an exact replica of her mother's. Shaken, she looked away.

"Odelia is simply tired," her mother rattled on. "She had that surgery, you know, and I don't think she'll ever be the same. Either Rose or I would have taken over for her months ago, but for some reason Odelia didn't seem to take to that idea. But she's always taken to *you.*"

"Mother, I don't know about this," Mary said.

Her mother looked at her.

"It's not a good time." Mary was ashamed of the timidity in her voice.

"Well, of course, not right this minute. I said that. But next month, with Dani Lee off back East and Alanna down in Wichita, you'll need this. Believe me, I know."

"I'll be needed to help Ellen with the baby." Mary wondered why it was so hard to simply come out and say no. Because she'd lived a lifetime trying to please her mother, that was why.

"That's four months away yet, dear, and we'll all be here to help Ellen with the baby. You'll still have plenty of time for the Ladies Circle." Her mother reached for the silver pot and began pouring them more coffee.

"I don't want to do it," Mary said, not very loudly.

To which her mother replied, "Oh, but you'll enjoy it! Not that it can't be a trial at times, but mostly it's a lot of fun—and challenging, too. When I was president the first time, the Circle saw to the building of Spring Park. It was my idea to begin with, and it's still there for people to enjoy. That gives a person a great sense of satisfaction."

"I really don't want to do it."

"Well, I guess Odelia could carry on until you took over at the beginning of the year. We can all help her."

"Mother, I meant I don't want to be president *period.*"

"Oh, don't be silly. Of course you do. And it'll be a great excuse for you to buy a bunch of new dresses, dear. We'll shop together. It'll be great fun. And you must get something done with your hair, Mary. A woman of your age shouldn't wear it long and stringy."

"I really don't want to."

"I've never understood what you have against visiting a beauty salon, Mary. Some of my most enjoyable and relaxing moments are spent down at Susie's."

"Not my hair...I meant I don't want to be president. I really don't."

"Why ever not? What else will you be doing with yourself with the girls off on their own?"

It was on the tip of her tongue to say she was going to San Antonio, but she said instead, "I'm not certain. But I'm not going to be president of the Ladies Circle."

Averting her eyes, she thought, I won't live my life like yours. I *can't!*

Her mother said, "I'll tell Odelia you can't take over right away, that you have to think about when would be the best time."

Mary closed the door behind her and fairly stalked away from her mother's house. She had held in her frustration because she hadn't wanted to hurt her mother's feelings, but the sidewalk took a pounding now.

She was at a loss to understand the complicated relationship that existed between mothers and daughters. She was a grown woman, but she felt like a ten-year-old with her mother. Sometimes she felt ten years old with her own daughters. Where did being a daughter end and mothering begin? Where did mothering end? Maybe it never did.

Her mother's image filled her mind, and again came the unsettling picture of herself following that pattern. She pictured herself years from now in the house, living alone because she wouldn't give another man the time of day, or with one of her daughters, since she didn't have a sister. She would never go for one of William's condos, either, because her daughters would have hissy fits. She imagined herself doing all the things her mother did: sitting in the same seat at church that she'd sat in for thirty-plus years, playing bingo with the local church group on Wednesday afternoons, walking with two or three friends every day, cleaning the entire house the first day of spring and the first day of fall, presiding over various functions of the Ladies Circle, going to luncheons and fund raisings and parties and political rallies—her mother was a born leader and should have run for some office.

Her mother's life was a good life, a rich life, a rewarding life. But no matter how similar they were, Mary was not Ellen Louise Minnett. And she wanted a different life.

For the first time Mary could see that. Her life to this point had been almost a carbon copy of her mother's, and it had suited her, at least mostly. But it was growing more ill-fitting with every passing day.

Only when she heard a loud clunk and a male voice say, "Whoa," did she realize she'd slammed the front door and apparently startled Jim Pettijohn into knocking over his pail of paint.

"I'm sorry, Mr. Pettijohn."

Bending over and dabbing with his rag, he said, "It's okay. A bit more paint on this tarp certainly won't hurt— that's what it's here for."

She returned his smile with a small one of her own, then very discreetly, as she passed on through the dining room, she took a look at his buttocks. It *was* a nice, trim behind for such a broad-shouldered man, she thought. She would vote with Alanna on his cute butt.

Chapter Two

Though Jim was in Mary Lunsford's house from morning until evening for two solid days, he saw her for only a few brief encounters.

"It looks very nice, Mr. Pettijohn," she said that first afternoon. "You're doing a wonderful job."

"Thank you. I enjoy it." He'd always found something relaxing about painting; he seemed to have a natural talent for it.

The next morning, when she brought him a glass of lemonade, Mary said, "It must be tiring doing this all alone."

"No... I'd say it's peaceful."

The only reason he didn't have a helper that day was that he'd deliberately discouraged Fred Miller from giving him one. He liked working alone, and he especially didn't want to work with Fred Miller's nephew, Odell, the only helper available and a man who talked like a broken record—on and on.

Also he was hoping to get more time to talk to Mary Lunsford. This, however, appeared an uphill battle. No matter how friendly he tried to be, she kept herself out of his way. And it didn't seem that she was ever in the house alone. Ellen—in his mind he called them all by their first names—ensconced herself on the family room couch to watch television and called out to her mother about every ten minutes. Alanna breezed in and out all day, and then there was Grandma, who'd swept in the second morning like a queen ready to make her white-glove test. She did actually wear white gloves.

Late that afternoon, as he was cleaning up, Mary came down the stairs with a basket of laundry, and he hurried to help her because it seemed much too much for her. She wasn't a speck over five foot four, and she had small bones.

"Let me help," he said and took it right out of her hands.

"Oh! Thank you." She blushed beet red, and he felt like both a gallant gentleman and a fool. She might just as well have slapped him for his forwardness.

For a rare, unguarded instant her gaze met his. She brought her hand up to smooth at her hair, and he had the wildest urge to grab her and kiss her. This time he was the one who quickly looked away.

He hadn't expected to feel like this about a woman ever again. Not at all.

And he certainly didn't expect to run into her, quite literally, that evening at the bookstore.

He was so intent on the books on the sale table that he didn't see another person bending down, studying some books stacked on the floor, until he almost stepped on her.

"Oh! I'm sorry," he said, registering immediately that the person he'd bumped into was a woman. Next he found himself looking down into a familiar face, one he had to struggle to place.

Surprise hit him across the chest.

"Mrs. Lunsford." He reached out to take hold of her arm to keep her from falling over. Pleasure washed over him.

She stood, her eyes wide. "Well, hello, Mr. Pettijohn. I'm sorry... you look quite different when you're not in your painting coveralls. I didn't recognize you at first."

"I didn't recognize you, either." In his mind, he attached her to the brick house, and it felt strange to be talking to her here now, like this. Strange and pretty good.

She recovered herself and averted her eyes from his. Two bright blotches appeared on her cheeks. She was holding a book about Texas, and he recalled seeing similar large coffee-table books lying around her living room.

"Are you interested in Texas?" Adopting a casual stance, he propped a hand atop the book-covered table.

"Yes. This one especially caught my eye. And you? Are you looking for something special?"

"The Rocky Mountains, I guess."

He moved, and so did the stack of books where he'd propped his hand. He grabbed frantically at several as they slipped toward the floor, and so did Mary.

"Thanks," he said, feeling like some clumsy teen.

"Sure..." She patted a book in place. "I'm addicted to the sale tables. I'll sale myself right into debt here."

"I always look at these tables first," Jim agreed.

"You're not from Minnett Springs, are you?" she asked, then seemed embarrassed to have done so.

He grinned. "My accent gave me away again. No, ma'am. I'm from Georgia." Crossing his arms, he tucked his hands up under his armpits to keep from knocking anything else over.

"Oh."

"I have a great addiction to books, especially spy novels and armchair travel books."

"I do, too," she said warmly. "I've been reading a lot about the Southwest lately."

"Mom!"

Ellen, followed by Alanna, came up behind her mother. She cast him a bare glance, while Alanna said, "Hi, Jim! What a nice surprise. What are you looking at in here—any of these?" She bounced over beside him and looked at the books next to him on the table. "Oh, a book on Corvettes? Are you interested in them? I love them!"

"I was just browsing," Jim said and shifted away.

"Mom," Ellen prodded, "we really need to go. My feet are tired, and I'm hungry."

"Yes, dear, all right." Mary's eyes met his for a brief second. "It was nice running into you, Mr. Pettijohn."

He nodded. "You too. And I'll see you in the morning."

"Bye, Jim," Alanna said pertly.

"Goodbye."

He pretended deep absorption in the table of books as the three women went to the register, but he sneaked a glimpse of Mary as she left the store. She didn't look back.

He sighed deeply and stared unseeingly at the book in front of him.

Jim Pettijohn knew himself well, and he knew he was falling in love with Mary Lunsford. There was no question about that, no railing that it was impossible in such a short time. The question that *did* need asking was, did he want to pursue it?

Mary awakened reluctantly. She stared at some gray splotches on the wall for several seconds before realizing they were Spackle and that she was lying on the living

room couch, which was sitting in a jumble of other furniture in the middle of the room because of the painting.
She'd sat there to look at the Texas book in the luxury of
an empty house, and now she vaguely remembered leaning over, intending to close her eyes for a few minutes.

Someone had tucked the fringed pillow from the easy
chair under her head and laid the cotton throw from the
back of the couch across her legs.

She sat up slowly, heard movement and looked around
to see Jim Pettijohn. He'd been out to lunch when she'd
come into the living room.

He must have sensed she was awake because he turned,
paint brush in hand, and smiled. "Have a nice nap?"

Embarrassed, she ran her hands over her hair, saying,
"Yes . . . I'm sorry to have been in here in your way."

Oh, dear, she'd been sleeping right in front of him! It
was nearly as if she'd been naked.

Already returned to his painting, he said, "No trouble."

She was trying to get her legs untangled from the cotton throw and set properly on the floor when the cold
dawning knowledge of who had put the pillow beneath
her head, the throw over her legs, crept up her spine.

She stared at him—at his back as he carefully painted
around a windowpane. "Did you put the pillow under my
head?"

"Uh-huh . . ." He examined his work, then dipped his
brush in the paint can, saying, "You looked a little uncomfortable with your head on the arm of the couch that
way—good way to get a stiff neck."

And he'd covered her up, too.

"Uh . . . thank you," she said faintly, mortified not only
that he'd done it, but that she'd asked about it.

He cast her a fleeting nod over his shoulder. "Sure."

She put the pillow back in the easy chair, folded the throw and replaced it on the back of the couch.

"I'll finish this woodwork in a few minutes, and then I can put the furniture back in place in this half of the room before I leave today," he said. "But I wouldn't re-hang any of the pictures until tomorrow if I were you."

"Okay. That's fine. There really isn't any rush."

He tossed her a grin. "Oh, I'm not rushing. Slow and steady gets it done right in about the same amount of time. And at the same price."

She stood for a moment watching him paint. His motions were smooth and easy, very graceful, as if he enjoyed what he was doing. It came to her sharply that they were alone in the house.

"Mr. Pettijohn, would you like to take a break and share some iced tea with me?"

He turned and looked at her, and there was that grin again, in all its magnificence. "That sounds great. My arm could use a rest."

Suddenly Mary felt as if she were the one with sunshine in her pockets.

She dug out a pine tray from a back kitchen cupboard, put their two tall glasses of iced tea on it, along with the pitcher, then decided to add a plate of her snickerdoodle cookies. Whirling around to the oven glass, she smoothed her hair and wished it did something other than stretch back from her face, and that it was without gray streaks. She bit her lips to bring color to them—it worked in novels. With shock, she realized she was imagining what it would be like to kiss him.

Silly Mary. What in the world are you doing?

Offering a hardworking man refreshments. The polite thing, after all.

*Polite, my Aunt Fanny. Lust is the more accurate
word.*

Perhaps . . . She had resisted temptation for three and
a half days, she thought defensively.

Then she thought of how he'd put a pillow beneath her
head and a cover over her legs. The thoughtfulness of the
act, the tenderness of it, sent a wave of emotion over her.
No one had done anything like that for her in a long, long
time. It was always she who looked after others. Not that
she was complaining, because she liked doing it. But
having someone looking after her was a very sweet novelty.

She wasn't fool enough to think he was interested in
her, she told herself. She was simply going to enjoy his
company. And it was natural, after all, to be attracted to
a man.

She felt the importance of this feeling, since she hadn't
been in the least attracted to a man in a long, long time.

"Please, call me Jim...Mary," he said when she came
back. His tone was deferential, but not at all shy.

He wouldn't sit on the couch, because of his paint-
splotched coveralls, so Mary joined him in sitting on the
tarp on the floor over by the windows.

"Here—let me help you with that, Mary," he said,
taking her tray and setting it on a table made of two paint
cans.

They were both doing a lot of smiling at each other.
The room was bright, with the wide windows bare of
drapes and blinds. It was like being outdoors, wild and
free. Except for their voices, the only other sounds in the
house were the loud ticking and timely chimes of the
mantel clock.

He thanked her for the tea and waited for her to sip hers before he began. He bit into a snickerdoodle and grinned. "These are good."

She felt almost absurdly pleased. "Did you find any good books on the Rocky Mountains last night?" she asked.

He shook his head. "Nothing very interesting."

"I have a couple you may like. I'd be glad to lend them to you."

Oh, that grin! "Thanks."

"Have you been in Minnett Springs for long?" she asked. The brightness of the windows added to her boldness.

He shook his head. "About four weeks."

She wondered about that, and about why he was here. She didn't think he'd come especially to work for Fred Miller. And she wondered about the obviously expensive gold watch on his arm. There was something about him that made her feel he wasn't exactly what he appeared to be, but it wasn't her place to pry.

Their eyes met, and Mary found she couldn't look away.

"I'm traveling," he said. "Seeing the country."

"Traveling?" She didn't know anyone who simply traveled.

"Yep," he said. "Traveling."

In the following few minutes, Mary came to realize that Jim Pettijohn was not a shy man, that he enjoyed talking about himself as well as his philosophies of life, and that he could do so in such a way as to make a person wish he would go on and on forever.

He told her about leaving his job as an executive with CNB News out of Atlanta ten months earlier, after a close friend's death made him realize the foolish emptiness of his own life. After his wife had died five years ago, he'd thrown himself into his work at such a pace that he'd figured he would soon be following his friend to the grave, and without really ever enjoying life, or even knowing fully what it was about.

So he'd quit his job, turned over all his finances to an accountant, given his house over to his brother and all but one of his suits to the Salvation Army, bought a nice truck because he liked some comfort, packed what would fit in two suitcases and started off on his "odyssey," as he termed it. He'd chosen his direction out of the city by closing his eyes and stabbing the map. And since that time, he'd supported himself along the way by picking apples in Indiana, working a loading dock in Minnesota, herding sheep in North Dakota and being a stable hand in Nebraska.

"I've had a devil of a good time," he said, clearly quite pleased with himself.

Mary gazed at him in wonder and not a little envy. "What about your family and friends? Do you have children?"

"I have a big family who all have one another, and no friends who truly needed me. And no children. Amy died with our first child."

Mary gazed at him. "My husband died ten years ago."

For long seconds they looked at each other and shared an unspoken understanding. Jim had loved his Amy with every part of himself, and he knew that Mary was the kind of woman to love her husband the same way.

"And now it's your turn," he said. "Have you always lived here in Minnett Springs?"

"Yes," she said, her shy reserve seeming to take her away from him. "There's nothing much to tell, really."

But he regarded her expectantly, and she slowly began to tell him. Her parents' house was just four houses down on the same side of the street; her family was descended from the founding father of the town; she'd married the older boy who lived on the corner—Daniel—and had raised three children in this house. Except for her honeymoon trip to Mazatlán, she'd never traveled farther than Kansas City.

She raised her eyes to his, and they were the distinctive color of Kentucky bluegrass, shimmering in the light pouring through the curtainless windows. "Have you ever seen San Antonio, Jim? I've always wanted to see San Antonio."

He grinned. "Yes, ma'am," he said in his best Georgia drawl. "I've seen San Antonio a couple of times back when I was working for one of the networks." He sat up straight and assumed a commanding position. "San Antonio, Texas, is experiencing the worst flooding in its history. The governor is calling out the National Guard."

With delight, he watched her eyes widen. She rose up on her knees. "I remember seeing you! On television."

"I did a lot of on-camera spots for about five years and sat in as temporary anchor of the nightly news a couple of times," he said.

She sat back on her heels and laughed. "A celebrity painter. Right here in my living room."

Jim liked hearing her laugh, and for an instant, while she wasn't paying much attention, he enjoyed looking at her.

Thoroughly relaxed now, she poured them each more tea, and they spoke of other things. He told her that he was staying in one of the small studio apartments in the renovated old candy factory, and she revealed that as a girl walking home from school she would pass that factory and be given lemon or cherry drops, or whatever they were making on the day. Did he know that the building right next door to the factory was one of the oldest brick buildings in the county? He asked if she had old pictures of the town, and she promised to show them to him. He told her that he was planning to write a book about the places and people he met on his travels, and that he would have to get her picture for his book.

She laughed at that and averted her eyes, smoothing her hair. He sensed that she thought herself plain, and he was sad about that, because he hated for her to think so little of herself.

And she was far from plain, he thought emphatically. Her skin had a translucent quality, her voice a lilting tone that made him want to hear her keep talking. He imagined how she would look with her corn-silk-and-spun-silver hair let loose from its band and falling down around her face. He imagined running his fingers through it.

Desire for her came to him like a breeze out of the South, all warm and sultry and promising.

"How long do you plan to stay in Minnett Springs?" she asked.

"Well, I promised Fred Miller I'd finish this job, so until then, for sure. My lease on the apartment is up at the end of the month." But he thought meeting her might just have radically changed all his plans.

"And where to from here?"

"I've been thinking about spending the winter down around the Mexican border."

"I envy you," she said quietly.

They stared at each other, telling each in that silence that they liked the other. And he sensed that beneath this woman's pale, quiet exterior lay live embers of passion just waiting to be coaxed to a roaring flame.

"Mom?"

Footsteps sounded, and Jim glanced around to see Dani Lee coming toward them through the hall.

"Dani Lee. You're early for a change." Smiling nervously, Mary jumped to her feet.

As if she'd been caught misbehaving, Jim thought, rising more slowly.

"I took off early," Dani Lee said, glancing curiously to Jim and back to her mother. "Clea's coming over in a little bit, and we're going to go over our clothes."

"You've met Jim Pettijohn, haven't you? Jim, this is my daughter, Dani Lee."

Jim and Dani Lee nodded at each other and said they'd met. Dani Lee's expression resembled that of a lioness who suspected her territory was being invaded.

And Mary looked faintly guilty, too, as if sharing conversation and tea fell in the same category as illicit sex. She averted her eyes and bent to pick up the tray.

A napkin slipped off and floated to the floor. Jim retrieved it, handed it to her.

"Oh . . . thank you."

For an instant their eyes met again. Blushing, Mary almost dropped the tray. A glass fell over, and she hurriedly righted it. "My, I'm all thumbs," she said breathlessly, carefully keeping her eyes on the tray.

Jim wanted to grab her and kiss her.

"Painting this house is a pretty slow job on your own, isn't it?" Dani Lee said and gestured at the elaborate ceiling trim. "With all the crown molding and stuff."

Jim got the hint. "Too many painters simply get in each other's way. But I'll have help with the stairway and the kitchen, and after that there's only the bedrooms upstairs. They should go pretty quickly." He turned his attention to Mary. "I enjoyed the tea and conversation, Mary."

"I did, too," she said, a warm smile flitting across her face before she turned away with her daughter.

Mary kept her eyes averted as she stuck the dishes in the dishwasher and wiped the tray. *Silly Mary. Your thoughts about Jim Pettijohn are not written across your forehead.*

But she felt as if everyone would know her feelings and therefore know her foolishness. And she certainly didn't want to reveal this side of herself to anyone, most especially to her children. Dani Lee had always been too good at reading her. She was so much like her father.

"This guy sure did fall into a good job when he came here," Dani Lee said, her words muffled because her head was stuck in the refrigerator. She turned, holding a half gallon of milk and a plate of carrot cake.

"This guy?" Mary asked and handed her a plate and fork.

"The painter, Mom." Dani Lee propped a hand on her hip. "He knows a good thing when he sees it—cool, air-conditioned work, you treating him to afternoon tea."

"There's nothing wrong with friendly politeness, Dani Lee."

"He's supposed to be painting, Mom. That's what you're paying him for. He's not supposed to be sitting around like company."

"He's entitled to a break, and so am I. And I don't think I have to explain myself to you—and neither does Jim."

Mary wasn't certain who was more shocked by what she said—Dani Lee or herself.

The telephone rang, and Mary turned to get it. It was Clea for Dani Lee, and Mary handed her the receiver, took her tub of gardening tools from the cabinet and went out through the patio door.

She went far out to the flower garden edging the back fence, knelt down and began pulling tiny weeds with a fury. She could have told Dani Lee that Jim Pettijohn was a fascinating man. A man who'd had a career in television news, who'd been on television and behind the camera, too. A man who had dared to give it up in hopes of finding a more rewarding life. He was something, Jim Pettijohn was.

Silly, silly Mary.

She was having a mid-life crisis, she thought. That was it. Women had them, too, just like men. She'd read a long article about it just last month.

She was feeling old when she wasn't, not quite, and lost right here where she'd lived all her life. She was wanting things that had passed her by.

Making a fool of herself over a man.

She had not made a fool of herself! She'd shared tea and conversation. That was neither foolish nor a crime. No matter how Dani Lee had looked at her—and, oh, how cruel it was when a mother's child disapproved of her, thought her foolish.

She thought of Jim and his happy eyes. *It was what she felt inside that scared her.*

She'd looked into his eyes and felt familiar stirrings of the sort she'd battled and put in the deep-freeze after Daniel had died.

Sitting back on her heels and gazing up into the tree limbs, Mary drifted back in time to her beginning with Daniel. Her children would die now to know of them in the back seat of Daniel's Ford Galaxy, the one his father had given him on his sixteenth birthday. They'd fogged the windows so badly, they'd had to dry them with his T-shirt.

She took up the trowel and began digging the ground, thinking how all of that belonged to yesterday, when she'd been young.

Anything with this Jim Pettijohn or anyone else was impossible.

Why?

Well, because . . . her children needed her to hold together and be there for them. They didn't need her going all crazy over a man. And because going crazy over a man wouldn't help in this confusing time. And because it was just impossible, *period.*

She would not make a fool of herself.

Mary hadn't reappeared by the time Jim had replaced the furniture where it belonged at the front of the room, so he used up more time moving furniture from the back half, where he intended to paint the following day. He dawdled around, respackling a few cracks and taking his time to straighten his equipment.

When she still hadn't appeared by quarter to six, Jim hesitated, then went through the house to the kitchen, where he heard voices. The door was open, and he saw Dani Lee and Ellen sitting at the counter.

They both caught sight of him and gazed at him with about as much welcome as they would give a rat.

"I was looking for your mother," he said. "Uh . . . thought I'd tell her I was done for the day," he said and glanced around for her.

"She's not here," Dani said.

Jim could see that. "Well, please tell her I'll be a little later tomorrow, but not to worry."

"All right."

Jim allowed the door to close quietly and went out to the van. He kept an eye out for Mary, wondering where she was, and felt sharp disappointment not to see her again.

It hurt a little that she hadn't come to tell him good-bye.

As he was getting into the van, Alanna sped into the driveway in her bright red convertible and stopped with a jerk.

"Hi!" she called and waved gaily.

She hopped from the car and bounced toward him, a big grin on her face. Returning her smile and friendly greeting, Jim thought again of his curly-haired niece, and how if she wore a skirt as short as Alanna was wearing he would give her a spanking. This young lady needed taking in hand, he thought, yet he admired her open friendliness.

She came around to his open window and asked, "Done for today?"

"Yep."

"Then how about you and I go for pizza?"

Jim, who prided himself on rarely being surprised, sure was in that instant. "I thank you for the offer, but no thanks," he said and looked away to start the van. He really didn't want to hurt her feelings.

When he looked at her again, she was assessing him. "I'll go dutch," she offered.

She thought maybe he couldn't afford it, he realized, amused. He shook his head. "Thanks, anyway."

She shrugged and smiled. "Your loss."

Jim drove away thinking about Mary. He knew without a doubt that he was in love with her. That monumental realization didn't frighten him; it was his nature to determine these things quickly. But now he had to figure out exactly what he wanted to do about it, and that was a little more difficult because it involved weighing pros and cons about his future.

Chapter Three

When Jim hadn't arrived by eight o'clock the following morning, Mary was a little surprised. When 8:25 rolled around, she became a little annoyed. And by nine o'clock she was telephoning Miller Brothers Painting Contractors, her mind alternating between indignation— Didn't this man realize she had more to do than wait around for him?—and worry— Maybe he'd had an accident—and calm reasoning— Fred Miller did have other jobs to be attended to.

Just as she pressed the last number, the doorbell rang. Slamming down the receiver, she hurried to the door, calling out, "I'll get it!"

She jerked open the door. Jim, in his paint-splotched white coveralls, stood there, grinning at her.

"Good morning, Mary."

The flush of excitement that rushed over her was highly annoying. "I'd begun to think you weren't coming," she said, turning her back to him and walking away. "I was just calling Fred Miller."

"Well...didn't Dani Lee and Ellen tell you I'd be late?"

She pivoted around. "No."

He gave a puzzled frown. "I told them yesterday before I left to be sure and tell you I'd be late today. I had to take the van to the quick lube this morning. I'm sorry. I guess I should have called you."

"No...there was no need. I knew you—or someone—would get here eventually." She felt ashamed of herself and said crisply, "I'll get out of your way and let you get to work."

He had come to paint her house, she thought as she walked up the stairs. He would be out of her life as soon as the job was finished. She should be polite to him but not overly friendly. It would serve no purpose—and she wasn't going to allow herself to be foolish.

Mary spent most of the day upstairs, working on dresses for Dani Lee and Alanna in her sewing room, and reading her new book about Texas in her bedroom. Once she looked around her room and realized Jim would be painting it, would be seeing her bedroom.

Again and again the memory of the pleasant time she'd spent with him yesterday beckoned. She thought repeatedly of taking him a cup of coffee or a glass of tea. But she wouldn't allow herself that. *It was silly... this attraction.* When he began whistling, she got up and shut her door. It would have been good if she could as easily have shut out the feelings that tugged at her heart.

Jim saw Mary only three times that day, and he could almost have counted on both hands the number of words she said to him. In addition to her few terse words that morning, she said a cool, "Fine," at noon when she came down and he told her he was going to lunch. He'd been hoping for a lot more than "fine"; he'd been hoping she would ask him to lunch. His disappointment grew deeper late that afternoon when she again came downstairs and he told her he was quitting for the day.

"Fine" was her only word again.

She held open the door and waited expectantly for him to walk through it. Jim, carrying a paint can and a bucket of brushes, felt as pushed right out as if she'd planted a swift kick on his behind.

On the step, he turned hopefully. "I'll have help to-morrow to paint the stairway."

She simply nodded to indicate that she'd heard. His hope turned to ashes, he turned away to the van and heard the door shut behind him.

He sat in the van and stared at the white door with its curved fanlight, wondering what in the world he had done to anger her. She'd been as cool as a February north wind, totally unlike the openly warm woman who'd brought him tea the day before. Today she'd acted as if the closeness they had enjoyed yesterday had never been. Or as if she regretted it.

And that thought was like a bee sting, surprising and painful and maddening.

He left the driveway with a roar. She wanted to be cool? Well, he would be an iceberg!

Jim was distinctly cool and businesslike when he arrived Friday morning. As Mary held open the door, he passed through without a glance and said, "We're going to do the stairway and kitchen cabinets today. We'll be setting up scaffolding here, so you may want to use your back stairway."

Mary craned her neck to see a man unloading some big metal things from the back of the van. She looked back at Jim, who was measuring the stairs. He hadn't grinned at her, and as he studied the walls he totally ignored her.

It was one thing for her to be cool to him, she thought dismally, and quite another for *him* to be cool to *her.*

Cool was exactly what she wanted between them, she reminded herself. It made it that much easier for her not to be foolish.

She took herself off briskly to the kitchen to make fresh coffee before the men started in there, and dropped the glass pot in the process. Dani Lee gave her a kiss goodbye, but a minute later burst back through the door and announced that the Websters' dog had chewed the morning paper and Alanna had put a dent in her car and she was going to kill both. Ellen arrived in tears because she had the hives. And right then, with Ellen still crying, Hazel Skinner telephoned to say she'd broken her leg and would be unavailable to clean house for at least six weeks.

After finishing cleaning up the broken coffeepot, playing arbitrator between Alanna and Dani Lee, and soothing both Ellen and her hives, Mary made herself a cup of tea and carried it to her favorite chair in the den, only to discover the cat had peed in it. The capper was the arrival of her mother, who breezed through the house with her critical eye.

"Those colors, Mary," she said. "I'm not certain about them. I told you that blue was too drastic a change."

"I wanted a change, Mother. That was the purpose of painting."

"You'll get tired of that blue."

"Then I'll have things redone again."

"You'd go through this again so soon? It's such an upheaval."

"Mother . . . let's go shopping."

Her mother stared at her. "You want to go shopping?"

"Yes. And I want to get my hair done."

Her mother continued to stare at her. Ellen piped up, "Oh, yes, let's go shopping. And I'll have my hair done, too!" The very mention of a beauty salon and shopping could cure Ellen of anything.

Sharply aware of Jim's whistling, Mary grabbed her purse and herded her mother and daughter out the door. Fleeing, she thought, then hurriedly redefined it as a prudent retreat. It was best that she avoid being in the house all day long with Jim Pettijohn, who was barely speaking to her and had apparently sewn his sunshine tight inside his pockets.

If she wasn't around him, she couldn't make a fool of herself over him.

Mary might have left the house that day feeling as limp as a worn-out dishrag, but something magical happened during those hours, and she returned as fresh, lovely and purposeful as a brand new linen towel put out for company.

"I simply can't imagine what has come over you, Mary," her mother said a number of times that afternoon.

Mary didn't know what had come over her, either, except that it had begun in Susie's Clip 'n' Curl, when she'd watched a transformation take place in the giant mirror. She resisted analyzing her feelings; it was simply enough to be experiencing the uncommon sense of being beautifully alive.

With joyous glee, she began pulling shopping bags and string-wrapped boxes from the trunk of her mother's Oldsmobile, handing some to her mother and Ellen to carry, too. She, sane and sensible Mary Lunsford, had gone on the biggest shopping spree of her entire life.

"Mother, if you wear this hat around here, I'll just die," Ellen said.

"You said you liked it on that girl in the poster."

"That girl was Alanna's age and a rodeo rider, Mom."

"Well, I'll need it if I want to learn to ride a horse."

"Did you really mean that?" her mother asked. "Oh, dear, I'd hoped you were joking."

As Mary struggled excitedly to the house with all her purchases, thoughts of Jim filled her mind. She threw open the door. The hallway was bare, of course, all traces of scaffolding gone, the walls a fresh, blushing apricot, the scent of paint lingering. The deep blue in the dining room drew her eye. She liked it. She liked it fine.

As she ascended the stairs, she wondered what Jim would think of her hair—or if he would think anything at all. Oh, how she wished to see him that moment! How awful that she would have to wait all the way until Monday! *Silly, silly Mary.* Yes, but maybe silly wasn't so bad a thing. Perhaps sometimes it took silly to truly live life.

They placed all the packages on Mary's bed. Her mother cautioned her that the dresses should be hung up immediately, kissed their cheeks and left. Mary and Ellen went through the bags, separating out Ellen's things. Mary took the plastic off one of the dresses, held it up in front of her and did a pirouette in front of the mirror. White, with a high neck and cutout shoulders, it nipped in at the waist and then fell in soft folds. Mary moved again and felt a lot like Marilyn Monroe.

"It's amazing how styles come around," she said to Ellen. "I had a dress almost just like this one when your father and I were first married. It was my very favorite. What do you think?"

Happily she turned to her daughter. But Ellen's sour expression stopped her in her tracks.

"I think that doesn't look much like a dress a grandmother would wear," Ellen said.

Mary looked down at the dress. Perhaps it was subtly sexy, but surely not risqué. "Why not?"

"It just isn't something Grandmother would wear."

"No, maybe not—but your grandmother is sixty-eight years old. And she thought it looked very nice," Mary added in a small voice.

Ellen shrugged. "I have to get home. Todd promised to be on time for dinner tonight."

Mary's heart dipped. She knew her daughter was irritated with her, but she didn't fully understand why. Ellen had grown more petulant as the afternoon had gone along. Mary had tried to buy gifts for Ellen, but her daughter had refused. It seemed Ellen, who had nagged Mary for years to do something about her dowdy appearance, wasn't at all happy now that Mary *was* doing something.

"I'll drive you," Mary said. "You've been on your feet enough this afternoon."

"No. I'll walk. I have to control my weight, or it'll be forever until I can fit into anything that isn't a tent." And she marched out the door.

Ellen was jealous, Mary thought with a pang of guilt. It seemed a most farfetched idea, but the more she thought of it the more it fit. For the first time in all the hundreds of shopping trips she'd gone on with her daughter, Mary had paid more attention to herself than to Ellen.

She sat on her dressing bench, the guilt growing. But she couldn't quite understand why she should feel that way.

Then she lifted her gaze to the mirror and experienced surprise anew. Tentatively she touched the softly waved hair that now framed her face, the wisps of bangs. Pleasure rushed over her as she gazed at her glowing image. That woman in the mirror was *alive*. And that woman no longer seemed such a stranger.

* * *

It was dusk when Jim pulled to a stop in the Lunsford driveway. He noted nervously that Alanna's red convertible sat outside the closed garage. He surely hoped Mary was home, but he would rather her kids weren't. He picked up a small box on the seat, got out and went to the door.

He looked down at his gleaming white sneakers, smoothed his blue-striped cotton shirt. He rang the doorbell and wondered if Mary would rebuff him with the cold shoulder.

Alanna opened the door. Her hair was wet, and she wore a big terry shirt over a bathing suit. For a moment she stared at him without recognition, then surprise followed by curious pleasure crossed her face. "Well, hello, Jim." She drew the door wide. "Come on in. It's awfully nice to see you."

"Nice to see you, too." He stepped inside and cleared his throat.

She gazed at him expectantly, a small grin playing on her lips.

"Is your mother home?"

Her smile faded. "My mother?"

"Yes . . . is she here?"

She nodded slowly. "She's in the kitchen. I'll get her."

Waiting there in the hallway, clutching the small box, he felt about as welcome as a door-to-door salesman. He gazed in the direction of the dining room and listened, hearing the sound of the swinging kitchen door and approaching footsteps. But the woman who appeared from the dining room was a stranger.

Mary! It *was* her. She'd had her hair cut just above her shoulders and softly curled. It shone in the lamplight. And Mary smiled in warm, maybe even eager, welcome.

* * *

That Jim had come to see her—come "calling," bearing sweet French mocha as a gift—was a stunning thing for Mary to absorb.

Her heart was dancing as she prepared the French mocha and felt Jim's intense gaze from where he leaned against the end of the counter. He shifted his stance every few seconds. Occasionally their eyes met, and her heart danced a little faster. It seemed the sunshine had burst from his pockets to overflow on her.

"We don't have to have the mocha," he said as if suddenly thinking of it, "if you don't care for it."

"I like it—I usually have some around here."

They smiled at each other.

The swinging door burst inward, and Alanna whooshed into the room. "Excuse me..." She ducked her head into the refrigerator, pulled out a fruit juicy and went over to the family room couch, barely three yards away, to plop in front of the television.

Mary poured their mocha and handed Jim his. Their eyes met and danced together. Then Mary erupted in chuckles.

"What?" he asked, his eyebrows quizzical, though he smiled that wonderful smile.

"You look so different when you're not in your coveralls."

He looked down, touched his shirt. "Good or bad?" His eyes sparkled.

"Good."

Her eyes met his, and a sensual charge jumped between them. Mary averted her gaze to fill a plate full of cookies.

"I like your hair," Jim said as she pushed the plate toward him.

"My hair?" Mary touched her hair. His words and look nearly took her breath.

"Yeah. Looks great like that."

"Thank you," she said faintly, awkwardly. She glanced over and saw Alanna looking around at them. "Let's go out by the pool," she said.

They sat by the pool and tried to see the stars, but it wasn't easy to see any in town. Still, Jim pointed and told her about the constellations; studying stars was one of his hobbies and one reason why he really liked the vast Great Plains region of the country. Stars were easy to see on the plains. Mary recalled being interested in stars back in her teens and listened to him now with rapt attention.

They'd been outside for about fifteen minutes when Alanna came out. "Thought I'd swim a bit more," she said. "It's such a nice night." She plunged in, swam the length and back, then stopped on the side of the pool to get her breath only three feet from Mary's toes.

Mary felt as if her youngest daughter's eyes and ears had become a movie camera.

She tried to ignore Alanna's chaperoning, but that was difficult with her splashing and interrupting comments. "You two should come in—it's a great night." And, "Gosh, the sky's clear." And, "Mom, did you remember the chlorine today?"

Finally Mary suggested, "Let's go back in for another cup of coffee."

They stayed inside to sit at the kitchen table, where Mary could still see Alanna through the large window, but she and Jim could carry on a private conversation. Alanna, apparently miffed, soon abandoned the pool and stomped noisily up the back stairs to her room.

Jim asked again about the old pictures of Minnett Springs, and Mary brought several very old albums from the desk in her den. Many of the pictures were of herself and Daniel as children, and she found herself speaking about her husband—he'd been an avid swimmer and had built the pool, and, no, she'd never loved anyone but Daniel. Jim said he and Amy had been married six years, and Mary could tell he'd adored her.

When Dani Lee arrived home, she helped herself to the mocha and joined them at the table without being asked. Alanna came into the kitchen for a glass of milk and sat down, too. Both were polite but stiff, and the way Dani Lee spoke wasn't so much conversation as a third degree. Mary thought her daughter would do better to change her major from business to law. Highly annoyed, Mary fantasized about kicking both girls' shins.

Jim, however, seemed to take them in stride and answered all the questions they put to him, staying until nearly ten o'clock. Mary saw him to the front door, then stepped through it and closed it behind her because Dani Lee and Alanna had followed and were lingering in the living room. She imagined their ears stretched out a mile.

She and Jim stood there for a long moment, he down on the first step with his hands tucked into his denim jeans pockets, she up on the stoop with a hand on the cool porch pillar. The scent of the honeysuckle bush beneath the dining room window filled the air; crickets chirped once, twice, then sang merrily, and intimacy swirled around them. Mary had the crazy urge to throw herself into Jim's arms and roll with him onto the grass.

At last Jim said, "I enjoyed myself tonight. Thanks."

"I did, too."

His eyes held hers and she felt foolish, but wonderfully so.

"Mary... would you like to go to dinner tomorrow night?"

Her mouth went dry. "To dinner?" she said hoarsely. He nodded.

"Oh, Jim, I don't know."

She looked away from his questioning gaze, and her head reeled. She kept thinking about rolling in the grass with him; it seemed no more farfetched than dinner. He waited, requiring her to speak, to make some explanation.

"Perhaps you'd like to come to dinner here instead," she suggested. She wasn't likely to make such a fool of herself, then.

"I'd like to take you out, Mary. Just the two of us," he said pointedly, "without the chaperon committee."

Again his eyes held hers.

It wasn't easy to get the words out, then they came with a rush. "I'd love to."

Her heart seemed to open right up and flow with joy when his grin lit up the night.

He jumped up and kissed her cheek before she knew what was happening. Then he was striding away to his truck. "I'll be around for you about six-thirty—okay?"

She nodded, then called, "Where are we going?"

"That Italian place out at the west end of town—Milo's." He gave her a thumbs-up and got into his truck.

As Mary watched him drive away, she touched her cheek where he'd kissed it.

Then the enormity of what she'd done washed over her.

A date? With a man she hardly knew? After all this time?

Mary put a hand to her mouth as panic washed over her like Niagara Falls. She had no idea of how to behave on a date at her age. And she had no idea of what she would say to her daughters about this, either.

* * *

Mary held the sweet anticipation of her date with Jim to herself that night. She didn't want anything her daughters might have to say about it to spoil her happiness. Which, of course, was being silly on her part. She was making too much of it. There was no reason for them to be upset about her little date. Still, she thought the wisest course would be to tell all three girls at once, get it over quickly in one shot. She waited until the following morning, just before Dani Lee was leaving for a tennis game and after Todd had dropped off Ellen on his way to play golf.

She had just pulled a batch of brownies from the oven, a favorite of all three girls, though of course she wasn't trying to bribe them. Her news seemed to fit providentially right into the conversation. Alanna said she had a date with the fabulous Kirk Overton that evening, so not to expect her in until late. Dani Lee said she was going to a gathering of the gang at Clea's. Ellen said she and Todd were joining the Arnolds for dinner at the country club. And then Mary said she was going to dinner with Jim.

Ellen paused with a brownie halfway to her mouth. "You're what?"

"Going to dinner with Jim Pettijohn—you know, the man who's been—"

"We know who he is, Mom," Alanna broke in.

"Oh, Mother, you're not. You *can't* be serious," Ellen said.

They all stared at her, demanding an answer.

"Yes . . . yes, I am."

"You hardly know the man, Mom," Dani Lee said in her best condescending tone.

"I know him enough." Turning, Mary took refuge in the mundane act of clearing up the baking dishes.

"I can't believe this! My own mother is carrying on with a guy," Alanna muttered loudly and with as much disgust as if she'd been told that Mary planned to run naked down Main Street.

"I don't think I would term this carrying on," Mary said. "I'm not planning to have an affair with him. I'm simply going to dinner with the man. What is the problem?" By the look on their faces, she thought she shouldn't have mentioned the word affair. It appeared to have given them ideas.

"The problem is that you know only what this man himself has told you. And he could be lying," Dani Lee said, as if she were the mother and Mary the child. "You can't believe all that stuff he said about being an executive with CNB News and leaving there to travel, Mom. Nobody would leave a good job like that. At least, no sane person. You simply can't go out with a man you know nothing about. He could be some con man who goes around fleecing old widows out of their life savings, or some crazy lunatic who could kill you, or worse."

Gazing at her middle daughter, Mary wondered what in the world could be worse than being killed. And that term "old widow" stuck in her mind, too.

Then Alanna said very sarcastically, "Oh, Jim isn't someone like that, Dani Lee. He's just hungry for something else."

Ellen asked sharply, "Where are you going for dinner?"

"Milo's."

Ellen groaned. "All our friends go to Milo's. They'll all see you having dinner with the man who's painting our house."

"I think that's quite enough," Mary said in the quiet voice that always got their attention.

She looked at their disapproving, scolding faces. Their words, tones and expressions were as painful as stones hurled at her.

"Is that what you think of me?" she asked. "That I have so little brains, so little intellect, as to not know how to conduct my life? That I am some poor, doddering *old* widow, Dani Lee—or that the only thing about me that could possibly interest a man is the prospect of easy sex, Alanna? Do all of you think you have more experience than I do when it comes to judging a person's character? My heaven, how did I get along without the three of you choosing my friends all these years?" She turned her gaze on Ellen. "And I am ashamed to think my daughter is such a snob that she speaks of a housepainter as someone beneath her respect. I am ashamed you would give a hoot what others say about the mother you're supposed to love."

"Oh, Mom," Dani Lee said, "we're just trying to point out the craziness of all this."

"Craziness, is it now? Well, I thank you very much."

"Yes, it's crazy!" Ellen cried. "You're a mother who's about to become a grandmother! You don't need to be getting involved with some man from who knows where!"

"You are going out this evening, Ellen," Mary said, holding her calm. "I don't see how my sitting here at home or not will have any effect on you and my unborn grandchild."

"You could have gone with Todd and me to the country club, if you'd said you wanted to," Ellen wailed.

"We would have stayed home with you, Mom," Alanna put in, "if we'd known you wanted us to."

"Oh, darlings, I don't want any of you to stay with me. I want to go out to dinner with Jim. A simple date. That's all."

Ellen grabbed her purse. "There's just no talking to you. You're determined to be foolish over this man—though heaven only knows what you see in him." And she left, slamming the back door behind her.

Alanna whirled away and up the stairs.

Dani Lee said, "I hope you think about this today," picked up her bag and tennis racket and left.

Mary gazed at the remaining brownies and wondered whatever was happening to her life.

Half an hour later the summons came from her mother.

"I don't know what you can be thinking, Mary, in considering a date with this man at this time. Ellen is beside herself."

Mary sat facing her mother, who sat in her imposing, high-backed chair and gazed at her with a stern, unrelenting expression that demanded an answer. For an instant Mary felt ten years old again.

"I haven't set out to intentionally upset my children, Mother. And I can't imagine why this single date, inconsequential as it is, should cause everyone to get up in arms. It in no way affects anyone but myself."

"I disagree. Anything you do affects your daughters, me, your extended family—even your community."

Now Mary felt she had the weight of the world on her shoulders. "It's just a dinner date, Mother. I'm not joining the Foreign Legion or anything."

"Don't be flippant." Her mother stared at her for a long second. "It isn't unusual for your children to feel shaken, threatened, by your interest in this man, who is

a complete stranger. We don't know anything about this
Jim Pettijohn's people, nor what his past has been, other
than what *he* has said. Now is not the time to get flighty
over a handsome man who travels from town to town,
Mary. Your children need you."

"Well, Mother, Jim may be a stranger to you—you
haven't even met the man. But I've met him and feel I
know enough to have dinner with him. And I'm fully
aware of the needs of my children. I'm here for them. My
wanting to enjoy Jim's company in no way affects that."
Mary rose. "I've always been there for my children and
always will be, but my *children* are now *adults*. They have
lives apart from mine, just as I have a life apart from
them."

"Mary, I am surprised at this foolishness."

"Why are my desires and longings considered foolish?"

Her mother gazed at her with cool, condemning eyes.

"Mother, this is just a simple little date—it doesn't
deserve all this commotion."

"Then let it go and attend to your responsibilities."

"Mother, I am very aware of my responsibilities to my
daughters. I will always be Ellen's and Dani Lee's and
Alanna's mother, and they will always be my daughters,
but they are no longer *children*. And for the first time in
a long while I find myself a woman facing many choices.
Choices I never, ever had, Momma..." The endearing
address burst from her lips with emotion. "Wonderful
choices. I have the freedom of money and health and
time to do anything I wish. I'm thinking a lot about that.
I love and respect you, Momma, but I can't quite see
myself living the rest of my life in your pattern—filling
my life with the Ladies Circle and bridge and social
causes and events. And, oh, Momma...I'm attracted to

Jim Pettijohn. I can hardly believe it, but I am. He makes my heart get up and dance. If that makes me foolish, it seems a good kind of foolish. And something that I don't want to miss. It isn't anything that changes how I feel toward my children, toward you or any of my family."

She gazed at her mother, silently begging for understanding. For approval and acceptance, because the human need for those things knows no age barrier. And because she was still a daughter to this woman.

But her mother remained unrelenting. "As your mother, it is my duty to insist that you stop this foolishness before it can go any further. Before you end up doing something you'll regret forever."

Mary's heart cracked. "Just as my daughters will always be my daughters, I will always be yours—but I am no longer your child to order to do this and that."

Her mother gazed at her like a stone-cold statue.

Mary said a quiet goodbye and walked out through the hallway she'd walked as a child taking her first steps. And she had a sense of once again taking first steps. She wondered if she were making a misstep now and was about to take a hard fall. Well, if she was, she thought, she would simply have to get back up again and go on.

At this age, she thought drearily, falls were a lot more painful.

Chapter Four

Mary was ready a full thirty minutes before Jim was supposed to arrive.

She gazed at her reflection in the full-length mirror and felt amazement, fear and sheer joy, each emotion overlapping and tangling with the other inside her chest.

A palm to her neck, she felt her pulse beat beneath skin that was as silky smooth and flawless as that of her daughters. She'd never before realized this. She ran her hand downward over the dress that fit both her body and her spirit perfectly; it was like wearing a breath of summer. She turned her head and watched the movement of the pearl-drop earrings Daniel had bought her for her twenty-fifth birthday. In all the years since, she'd rarely worn them. They'd always seemed to overwhelm her. But now, suddenly, they suited her.

A woman full grown into loveliness. But it wasn't pride she felt—it was gratitude to be so healthy and attractive and *alive*. And no longer such a stranger to herself. The fine lines around her eyes, the skin around her waist that was no longer as firm as when she was twenty, the thin white streaks highlighting her pale hair, suddenly seemed like badges of honor, evidence of life lived, making her a woman worth knowing.

She blinked rapidly and wished her daughters were there with her, sharing this time. But they remained furious with her. Alanna had said a terse goodbye that afternoon. Both Ellen and Dani Lee had called to inquire whether or not she'd changed her mind about the date.

She'd told them no, and now worried that she was making a terrible mistake.

Oh my, she couldn't cry! She certainly didn't want her mascara to smear.

Why in the world this one date was so special she couldn't say. She thought of how she'd told her mother it was a small, unimportant thing and felt a stab of guilt because the statement had been a lie. If it was so unimportant, everyone wouldn't be up in arms over it, and she wouldn't have dug in her heels as if set in concrete.

Jim arrived five minutes early. Mary ran downstairs and stopped with her hand on the doorknob, her heart pounding. It surely wouldn't do to run outside to meet him. To practically throw herself into his arms! But it seemed silly to stand right at the door waiting for the bell to ring.

She opened the door just as he stepped up on the stoop.

His eyes widened in surprise, and then his marvelous smile slipped across his face. "Hi."

"Hi." She lowered her gaze to his pale striped shirt, a fine cotton of European styling, and his red print tie, then to his maroon suspenders. "I love suspenders," she blurted and immediately felt gauche.

But he grinned in pleasure and touched them. "Holdover from my office days. It was just too hot to go whole hog with a jacket, though." His gaze warmed. "You look beautiful."

"Oh . . . thank you."

They stood there staring at each other like two adolescents. Two alive hearts pumping hot blood.

"I'll just get my purse," Mary said and turned back into the house, trying to walk without shaking.

"And maybe a sweater, too," Jim suggested. He waited for her just inside the door, watched her reach into the hall closet. She was awfully pretty. His chest got a hard knot in it, and he guiltily shifted his gaze from her bare shoulders. But he found himself looking at her waist and the way her hips swelled below, and imagining what she looked like beneath that fabric.

Then she was coming toward him, smiling, and he forgot everything else, except smiling back.

He was helping Mary into the pickup when Alanna in her red Mustang sped into the driveway and came to a screeching halt. Mary froze, half in and half out of the seat, and stared at her daughter. Puzzled, Jim swung his gaze to Alanna, who got out of the car, slammed the door and glared at them. If looks could kill, he figured he and Mary would be about six feet under in a second.

"Alanna..." Mary said quickly, with a trembling smile. "I'm glad to see you before I left. Did you need me for something?" Her expression and voice echoed apprehensive hope. Jim wondered what was going on.

Alanna shook her head and stalked away to enter the house without a word of reply. Mary stared after her, and the desolate expression on her face got to Jim. Anger flared at Alanna's rudeness to her—this woman who was her mother and who was fragile and could be easily hurt. This woman he was already thinking of as his.

She flicked him a glance and slipped over into the pickup seat. She was plainly embarrassed, and she kept her face averted. He slipped onto the seat beside her, thinking the best way to ease the moment was to get going without calling attention to what had just happened.

He put his hand on the key, then paused. "Do you want to go in and speak with her?"

She looked at him, then at the house, and for a really rotten few seconds he thought she was going to say yes and leave him then and there. Then she shook her head. "No." And she sounded firm.

He started the truck out of the driveway, and then his keen curiosity got the best of him. "What's the problem?" A nagging instinct told him the problem was him.

She glanced at him. "My daughters aren't very happy with our date."

"Oh." He'd kind of thought this might happen.

Mary sighed. "I've hardly dated since my husband died."

"Could have fooled me," he teased, and his chest expanded when he got a smile out of her.

"You can feel awfully full of yourself, Jim Pettijohn, to have gotten me to go out with you."

"I feel full of myself and humble, too, to be taking a woman such as yourself to dinner." It was amazing how much seeing her smile could affect him. "I'm sorry about causing trouble between you and your daughters. Is it me personally, or just any guy you were to go out with?"

"Oh, they have plenty against you personally. Ellen doesn't like you because you have no pedigree and are just a common housepainter—and a roaming one at that. Dani Lee doesn't trust anyone who would profess to leave an upscale professional career—translated to mean lots of money—to ramble around the country. And Alanna, who has wrapped men from six to ninety-six around her finger since she was born, has her nose out of joint to find you paying attention to her mother and not to her."

Jim sighed. "It appears they each have a pretty good case against me." A sinking feeling settled over him. In his week of working in the Lunsford home, he'd certainly come to know the tight relationship Mary had with her daughters. What chance did he have with her?

"Well..." she said and gazed thoughtfully out the window. "I do think they'd be a lot happier if you were someone from town, who everyone knew, a stable banker or lawyer or doctor, or even a pharmacist from Elmore's Drugs. And it might possibly help if you were sixty, totally bald and very wrinkled, with a great potbelly."

"I'm getting a thin spot in the back," he said, "if that will make everyone feel better."

She smiled and then sighed. "I think their reaction would be the same toward any man—or anyone or any-*thing*—that took my attention away from them. You see, when my husband died my girls became my whole world. Of course, even when I had Daniel, my daughters were just about everything to me. Daniel took a back seat many times, because that's how it is with a mother when she has to split herself between her husband and her child. The needs of a child must be met first, above all else. Daniel and I talked about it a number of times, and he agreed that he, too, would put the girls' needs before mine, because he figured as an adult I could manage to fend for myself." She smiled. "I loved Daniel for that— if any of this is making sense to you."

He nodded. "It makes sense. I was almost a father, you know. And I've had a mother and father—and sisters and a brother, and nieces and nephews."

She shook her head and said softly, "It's not the same until you have your own children, until you live with them for a while. No one can explain it with words. They can tell you how once you've brought that child into the world, you are never a single being again. And how a part of your heart walks around in another body. And how it's sealed there by the nights you hold that body and walk the floor to quiet the cries, the times you kiss a hurt to make it better, and the times you ache because you can no longer kiss and make it better. About how you listen in the night for them even while you're asleep, and how even when they might be at school or at work, you know the instant they need you, and you get in your car and drive to where they are to find out you were right. A person can tell another about all that, but until you experience it you simply can't understand.''

He pulled the pickup to the curb and turned to her. She looked at him with surprise.

"You want me to take you home?" he said. "I could take you up on that home-cooked dinner you offered.''

He didn't in the least want to do it, and he was powerfully, if a little guiltily, glad when she shook her head and gave him a small, tender smile.

"No. My girls are grown women now. They're starting lives of their own, as they should. The only thing they need to realize is that I, too, still have a life that has to go on.'' She shyly looked away. "And I didn't wear this dress for dining at home.''

Jim, feeling like he'd captured the homecoming queen, shifted into gear and drove them to Milo's, where he'd called earlier to reserve a quiet table.

Not only was this Mary's first date in years, it was easily one of the most romantic nights of her life.

Jim had had a special vase of three red roses placed on their table, which was situated by the corner window and looked out at Clyde Larson's meadow. He'd also arranged for the best wine the restaurant offered to already be chilling. Milo himself, clearly getting a kick out of such unusual requests, waited on them with a mixture of his down-home friendliness and what he believed to be the panache of a high-class waiter.

Mary had the sensation that she'd entered another realm where she was no longer a mother, a daughter, a widow, or even the secretary of the Ladies Circle. In every way Jim made her feel like a fascinating and desirable woman. And after they'd lingered over their meal, when Jim suggested a drive out around the lake, she readily agreed. Feeling very much a modern-day Cinderella, she hated for the special evening to end.

The night was silky around them, the sky above like diamond-dusted black velvet, with a giant glowing topaz of a full moon casting its magical glow on the earth below, as if it intended to rival the sun with its light.

"Oh...slow down!" Mary laughed as she ran along the beach, her hand in Jim's, both of them acting like little kids on holiday. She'd left her stockings and heels back in Jim's pickup, and the cool sand pushed up between her toes. It had been so long, longer than she could recall, since she'd walked barefoot in the sand. Longer still since she'd held hands with a man. She drew back as he led them toward the water.

"Not afraid of a little water, are you?" he teased.

"Not of the water," she said, "but what could be in it."

"Nothing there that isn't there in the light of day."

"Maybe not, but it looks a lot less inviting."

They laughed together and, giving in, Jim turned down the beach.

Was he after something with all his courtly romancing of her—something as basic as getting her into bed? The thought crossed her mind a couple of times, but she decided it was definitely a compliment, if he was. In any case, he was making her feel as she'd never before felt, for she was a woman such as she'd never before been.

She savored the hand-holding, the sensual awareness that vibrated between them, the way she felt when he looked at her, the sound of his voice. Perhaps they had only known each other for a mere six days, but they were easy, familiar, together, as people who'd known each other for a very long time.

"I definitely think you should follow up on the idea of a book about your travels," Mary told him. "It would be a bestseller."

"You sound very certain of that," he answered, chuckling.

"I am. Many people have done it, you know. There was a man who sailed around the world in this little boat, and people who've flown around the world. And there was that man who walked around America. All of them wrote books about it that became great sellers. And you have a way of describing things that makes them so vivid. Especially the way you told me about that horse bucking you off." And she laughed, imagining it again.

"You don't have to get such a kick out of it." And he laughed, too.

He stopped and gazed down at her, and the laughter died in her throat as a spiraling heat rose up from her stomach. Quickly she turned and started walking again, extremely conscious of his warm hand closed around hers, his intent gaze, the power of him beside her.

"I envy you your traveling," she said softly. "Daniel and I used to talk about taking trips. We planned to take one of those Caribbean cruises someday—the ones where you rent a private yacht and sail for a week or two to all the different islands. And I always wanted to see San Antonio. But Daniel was always so busy...and then I had the girls to look after."

"Why don't you go now?" he asked.

"Why? Oh...I don't know." She often dreamed of traveling to all the places she read about, but the dreams seemed too much of an impossible fantasy.

"You could come with me," he said lightly.

"You? Oh, wouldn't that set well with everyone!"

"Doesn't have to set well with anyone but you."

His oddly serious tone sent a nervous vibration through her. She looked away at a dark fallen tree trunk. "We'd better turn back. I don't think there's a way around all those logs."

The path back up to where they'd left Jim's truck was deeply shadowed by trees, and Jim kept hold of her arm and placed a hand on her back to guide her. Mary was so aware of him that she could almost hear his heart beating.

He opened the passenger door for her, and she glanced up into his face as she was about to slip into the seat. His eyes held hers.

As she gazed at him, his eyes dark orbs in the silvery light, her breath stopped in the back of her throat. She wanted at once to have him kiss her and to run like crazy away from him.

He kissed her, and she didn't run. She held on to him.

The fire that exploded between them seemed to take them both by surprise. They broke apart and, quivering, Mary laid her forehead on his chest, which rose and fell with his shallow breathing. It was the first time she'd kissed a man in ten years.

"Oh, Jim," she whispered.

And then he was kissing her again, deeply, passionately, and she was kissing him in return, with all the hunger of a woman long denied.

On the stoop, they looked at each other. Mary held her breath and wished for him to kiss her, saw the consideration in his expression. He kissed her quickly, said goodnight and whirled away. As if fleeing, Mary let herself into the house. She leaned against the closed door and listened to Jim's truck go off into the night and had the sensation that her heart was going with him.

A light had been left on in the living room, but no one was there. No one was in the kitchen, either. Upstairs, light shone from beneath Dani Lee's door.

After checking first on Alanna and finding her asleep, Mary went to Dani Lee's door. She heard the murmur of the television on the other side and knocked.

"Come in."

Mary opened the door. "I'm home." She smiled, hoping for any sign of warmth from her daughter, any encouragement to talk about her evening. She was bursting with excitement and joy and wanted to share it.

Dani Lee, propped on her pillows, said, "Okay," and turned her gaze back to the flickering television screen.

"I had a very nice time," Mary ventured.

Dani Lee slowly looked at her. "I'm glad, Mom." Her voice didn't sound overly glad, however.

Sharply disappointed, Mary bade her good-night.

She hung up her white dress and gave it a last touch, reliving the look on Jim's face when he'd arrived. His look had made her feel worth a million dollars. His kiss...his kiss had scared her to death. What a goose he must have thought her when she'd broken away, shaking like a leaf and babbling something about not getting carried away.

But he'd said, very quietly, "Me too, Mary."

She washed her face and gazed at her lips, wondering how it could be that they showed no signs of the fire that had burned there when he'd kissed her.

In bed, with the lights out, she stared at the patterns the streetlight made on the wall and thought that she was very glad to have gone out with Jim Pettijohn. She was sorry to have hurt her daughters and her mother, but she would have been sorrier to have missed this special night. And in due time her mother and daughters would forget all about it—while Mary would carry the sweet memory forever. She thanked God for the kiss, and then, quite timidly, she wished for a few more before Jim Pettijohn left town. It didn't seem too greedy a desire.

The following afternoon Jim called to ask Mary to go fishing.

Ellen, clearly appalled, asked, "Are you going out with him again?"

Mary said simply, "Yes."

Over the following days, she went out with him again, and again.

During the day Jim painted the rooms upstairs and, closely chaperoned by Ellen and Alanna, he and Mary said little to each other. Though Mary figured anyone seeing them would know exactly what they were saying with their eyes.

Monday night they went for hamburgers and afterward to the bookstore, where they pored over the sale table and on to the travel section, not leaving until the store closed. They walked hand in hand along the older streets of the downtown square area. Once Jim pulled her behind the tall bushes at the courthouse and kissed her hungrily, taking her breath and her good sense. Tuesday night they returned to Milo's, where again the small vase of roses awaited Mary. Later they went to the lake, this time sitting out a warm drizzle in Jim's truck, listening to an oldies radio station and indulging in enough heavy petting to fog the windows. Wednesday they went to the Chinese Dragon, and afterward to the library, where Mrs. Beesley had to shush them three times. In the shadows of an old oak in the library yard, Jim kissed Mary breathless.

The days and nights were at once the best and very close to the worst of Mary's life. The best was with Jim. The worst was with her daughters.

All three of her daughters continued to be vehemently opposed to Mary's seeing Jim, and they took no pains to hide their disapproval from Jim when he was at the house. He would say hello, and they would go the other way with their noses stuck in the air. They spoke as little as possible to Mary, except to criticize almost anything she said or did.

Alanna's and Dani Lee's attitudes could best be described as superior. They clearly considered their mother stupid for not acting her age—whatever that meant—and for not seeing that this man was simply after sex and money. Mary found this poor opinion of her worth hard enough to take, but Ellen's vehement anger was like a knife to her heart. Ellen was simply furious at Mary for no clear reason. Passionate jealousy, Mary suspected. And her eldest daughter's attitude conveyed the clear message that until Mary came to her senses and totally rejected Jim Pettijohn, Ellen would withhold her love.

Mary recalled the times when Ellen had spent all day on the couch watching television, or simply tagging around after her, until Mary had thought she'd go mad. But now that her eldest wasn't there, Mary missed her terribly.

And then there was her mother, who insisted, "You have to stop this nonsense, Mary."

"Is it nonsense to be attracted to a man?" Mary asked. "Was it nonsense for you to be attracted to Daddy?"

"Oh, Mary, you can't equate this man with your father. And there is a right time for these things—as well as a right man. Now is not the *time,* nor is this the *man.*"

"I believe I'm the one to judge whether Jim is the right man, Mother. And I'm not certain as to there being a right and a wrong time. These things can't be planned like the correct day to have one's hair done. They just sort of happen, and one must take advantage of opportunities as they come."

"Mary, you're being talked about!"

"That's nothing new in this town. Around here, Ardith Lufkin going up to the Quick Stop at midnight for the first edition of the Sunday paper is interesting gossip. No one wants to consider that maybe she's simply got insomnia."

Fixing Mary with a stern gaze, her mother said, "And just where do you expect this opportunity to lead you?"

"I don't require it to lead me anywhere."

"You are not behaving as the daughter I raised," her mother said icily.

Mary could have said that that daughter had done a lot of changing over the years, but she didn't think to say it until after her mother had gone.

Not quite certain how it had come to pass, Mary found herself at total odds with the people she loved most. The entire controversy seemed ludicrous when she tried to understand it.

As the days went by she began to believe that what was most troubling to her daughters and her mother was that she was persisting in doing something they didn't want her to do, thereby hurting their feelings. And she began to wonder whether she persisted in seeing Jim Pettijohn for much the same reason—they were hurting her feelings and she was striking back.

Well, perhaps it was that, a little bit, she admitted to herself with proper shame. But there was much more to it, the main thing being that she was crazy about Jim. She could not call what she felt love, for love, as Mary saw it, could not happen within a week's time. That was too implausible an idea to be believed; it might happen in the movies, but not in real life.

However, she couldn't deny being totally infatuated with Jim. And she would not willingly let this special time pass her by. Most importantly, she was daring to follow her own heart and mind. She was finding out exactly who Mary Minnett Lunsford was, which was something she could not give up even for those of her own blood whom she loved so dearly.

The painting probably could have been finished on Wednesday, but Jim decided the elaborate trim in the hallway needed a second coat, and Mary decided the small alcove off the kitchen should be painted, too. Both decisions led to the job lasting into Thursday afternoon.

That evening they went for chicken-salad sandwiches at Conroy's Sandwich Shop. Afterward they went to the library, but were too restless to remain quietly looking at books, and Mrs. Beesley's expression clearly showed she didn't want to have trouble with them again.

They walked around the courthouse square and then went over to see the old candy factory where Jim was now staying. Standing there on the sidewalk, with her hand in his, staring at the building where his apartment was, Mary wondered when Jim would leave, now that he'd

finished painting her house. He'd told her the day they'd
shared tea that he would be leaving soon after he'd finished painting her house, that his lease was up at the end
of the month, which was only a week away. But he hadn't
mentioned anything recently about leaving, and she
didn't want to ask. She didn't want to think about it.

He squeezed her hand, and she looked up into his eyes.
They were luminous in the light from the street lamp.
Desire, like droplets of water in a hot skillet, sizzled be-
tween them.

"Do you want to go up?" he asked.

After a moment she nodded, and together they walked
across the street, through the heavy oak door, up the
white enameled wrought-iron staircase and along a short
hallway. The urge was strong in Mary to turn and run.
She was a mother, a traditional homemaker. She was not
a woman who slept with men she'd known only for days.
But the desire to be with Jim was stronger than all of
those realities.

Large factory windows made up the far wall of the
apartment, and both moonlight and light from the street
lamps lit the room with a silvery glow. Remaining beside
the door, Mary could easily make out the couch and
chairs, the long bar separating the kitchenette area, the
ceiling fan turning silently, even before Jim switched on
a lamp. When he did she saw in amazement that it was a
lovely, inviting room. A pale plush carpet covered the
middle of shiny oak flooring; antique coffee, soft drink
and ice-cream emblems decorated the warm brick walls.

She felt Jim's gaze, his questioning. When at last she
looked at him, the desire she saw in his beautiful eyes
made her pulse hammer. He came to her, took her in his
arms and kissed her. And kissed her. And kissed her

again, until her mind was reeling and her legs were melting.

When at last he moved his lips to nuzzle her neck, she gasped for breath and held on to him. "Oh, Jim...I...I don't have birth control. And I can still get pregnant. At least, I think I can." She was shaking so hard, her words came out shaky, too.

He lifted his head and grinned at her. "I have protection," he whispered.

"You do?" she said breathlessly.

"I confess, Mary. I've thought about this for a few days now."

"Me too." She squeezed her eyes closed, self-consciousness washing over her. She felt as if she were naked before him, totally defenseless, all her emotions hung out for him to see.

"Oh, Mary." He kissed her lovingly, tenderly, as if she were a prize hard won and much valued.

They made love on his pullout bed, on crisp sheets, the lamp off, silver light, like an ethereal glow, falling through the windows and casting intimate shadows around the room, the ceiling fan whispering above and sending cool air across their bare, heated bodies.

"Oh, Mary...Mary...your skin's like velvet."

"Oh, Jim..." He was hard muscled. So very much a man. But she couldn't speak those thoughts aloud.

He caressed her breasts, stroked down her stomach, slowly, reverently. She quivered with his touch, with both anticipation and fear and self-consciousness. She wasn't a fresh young girl any longer, and surely he could see that in the silvery light.

But when she looked into his eyes she felt as if she were the most beautiful woman on the earth, and when he touched her she felt as valued as a china doll.

I love you, Jim. I love you. Her heart was flooded with the emotion, but she couldn't say the words, for in this moment she was so turned around she couldn't trust herself.

And then fiery passion swept over them, and they gave in to it, savored it. Mary had loved Daniel and had experienced the passion that comes only with loving. This was the same, only more, because now she was so much more totally a woman capable of loving and being loved.

Jim lay with Mary in his arms, enjoying her velvety skin and flowery, female fragrance and, most of all, her silky hair.

"I love your hair," he whispered, running his fingers through it. "It's like mixed threads of spun gold and silver. I'm glad you didn't cut it real short."

She moved her palm across his chest, as if she enjoyed touching him and making him wish she would do it all night. "I love your Old Spice."

He chuckled, and she did, too. Then he sighed and said before he realized, "Oh, Mary... Mary." He loved her name.

"I like to hear you say my name," she whispered.

"Mary, Mary," he said. And it seemed natural to add, "I love you."

He felt her stiffen. Her face came up, and she stared at him wide-eyed. He'd known she would be surprised.

"I do love you, Mary," he said and cupped her cheek.

She averted her eyes. "Oh, Jim... you don't have to say that."

"I *want* to say it. I love you."

"We've known each other less than two weeks, Jim."

"I didn't know there was a certain time schedule for love," he said, amused. "And since I didn't know, I just went ahead and fell in love. And what's more, I think you did, too.''

Her eyes flashed up at him. "I do care for you. A lot...I mean..." She blushed. "I couldn't have done this unless I cared for you. But I..."

He saw her fright and stopped her words with a kiss, then pulled back and looked long into her beautiful eyes.

"I love you, Mary, and I want to marry you."

Chapter Five

A declaration of love and a proposal of marriage didn't make sense to Mary's logical and sensible nature. Jim wasn't unprepared for that, for he knew Mary better than she believed he could.

He said to her first protest, "Of course I'm serious. Do you think, with us lying here like this, now's a time for teasing?"

She jerked the sheet higher. Her expression highly distrustful, she said, "Love at first sight is a fantasy. It doesn't happen in the real world."

"It happens in my world," he said, "and I guess mine's as real as anyone's. I don't fall in love every day, Mary. You're only the second woman I've loved in my entire life, puberty included. Amy was the first, and I fell in love with her in one night and we married ten days later. I never changed my mind about her. I knew I was in love with you the day we had iced tea on your living room floor, but I didn't tell you because I was afraid of scaring you away."

She scooted up against the back of the couch, carefully keeping herself covered with the sheet. She was so modest, and he found that highly erotic. He scooted up beside her.

"You're such a romantic," she said with a soft grin, and he thought he was gaining ground.

"I know I love you," he said, "and I believe you love me."

"Oh, Jim, I'm crazy about you," she said shyly, then gazed at him for long seconds. "But I don't know if I'm in love enough for marriage."

"You are. Take my word for it."

She smiled, lifting her chin. "Just say I was in love with you . . . just listen a minute. Even supposing I'm in love, that doesn't mean it would make sense to get married. We know almost nothing about each other—except that we're quite different."

"We'll learn after we're married. That's the fun part." He kissed her temple and down to her neck, savoring the softness of her.

She pushed him away. "Jim, be serious. Where would we live? You're on your odyssey. Are we going to travel around? For how long? Forever? What about my house? And what about children? Do you expect me to have children? I'm not certain I could go through becoming a new mother at my age—I'm not even certain I could get pregnant. And what about . . ."

He held up a palm, stopping her speech. "Okay. I've thought about this—I really have. I can afford to respectably support us both. You have no worry there. The only thing I would find hard to give up right now is my traveling. I want to do that, and to do it with you.

"Think of it, Mary! You and me together, traveling, going anywhere we want, whenever we want. There's so much to see in this world, so much to learn and understand about it. And we could do it together. We can travel until you want to come home—to your home. If you want, we'll live there. If you want another house, we'll get another house. I really don't care. If you want a baby, I'll do my best to give you one. If you don't, I'll do my best *not* to give you one. We'll work out pesky little things like who gets which side of the bed and the first shot at the shower in the morning as we go along. Now see what a flexible fella I am?''

Her face turned all soft and warm, and she put her palm to his cheek. "Oh, Jim." He loved it when she said that. "You're flexible, but perhaps I'm not quite as much." Her shoulders sagged, and her hand dropped away. "And there are my daughters. I doubt very much that they'll take to this idea."

This, he knew, could prove to be a great hurdle. He took her hand in his and said softly, "Your daughters are grown women, Mary. It isn't like I'd be stepping in as their father or anything."

She nodded. "But they are and always will be my daughters. My family. I have to think of how my relationship with them would be affected." She paused. "Whenever I feel it necessary, my daughters will come first with me."

For the first time, Jim felt fully threatened. He forced patience into his voice.

"They would come to accept me when they saw how happy I made you. You don't have to answer this minute—think about it, talk to the girls about it."

"Oh, Jim." She gazed at him with tear-filled eyes and a trembling smile.

"You're not saying no?" he asked.

She shook her head. "No, I can't say no."

But she hadn't said yes.

He pulled her against him and felt her sweet tears on his chest. He hadn't expected her to jump right in with both feet, he reminded himself. He was lucky she hadn't given him a firm, sensible refusal.

"You think about it for a few days, sweetheart," he said huskily. "And while you're thinking, remember this." And he kissed her deeply, seeking to seal her to him.

It was early, just past ten, when Jim brought Mary home. Holding tight to his hand, she switched off the porch and hallway lights, leaving them in the dark.

Jim pulled her against him, kissed her neck and whispered hoarsely, "I don't want to leave you. I don't suppose you could slip away tomorrow night during Dani Lee's party?"

Mary found thinking hard, but she replied at last, "No, darling. I'm the one in charge."

"You won't forget me by Sunday morning, will you?"

"Kiss me again just to make certain," she said and wrapped her arms tight about his neck.

He kissed her, hard, and she returned it.

"Now get gone before Dani Lee or Alanna comes and catches us."

"Are you ashamed?"

"Oh, Jim . . . How could I explain to them? And this is *our* time. I don't want to share this with anyone."

"I'll call you tomorrow. Remember—I love you."

Mary wanted to say it but couldn't. Jim didn't press. She made herself let go of his hand and stood watching his truck taillights pass out of sight.

Trembling, she closed the door, then felt lost, uncertain of what to do.

She, sane and sensible and conservative Mary Minnett Lunsford, had just thrown out all the rules she'd lived by and made love with a man she had met only eleven days ago. A man she had dated for only one week!

She stilled, wondering if she were going to be hit by lightning or something.

Feeling she had to sit or fall down, she moved to the
living room couch and sat in the dark. She recalled Jim
putting a pillow beneath her head there—only last week,
when she'd known him not even three days.

She was heartily glad none of her daughters was home
to see her right this minute. She certainly didn't feel like
a sane, competent mother. She felt like a full, ripe
woman. A woman who was confused, frightened, ec-
static.

Would her lovemaking with Jim show on her face?
Surely it had to. How did a mother act around her
daughters so they wouldn't guess?

Oh, the passion, the love, they had shared! It was too
wondrous to describe. She thought she ought to feel
guilty. After all, she'd let her guard down and done
something she'd never, ever thought she would do. But
she felt too marvelous to feel guilty and kept finding
herself smiling giddily and wanting to get up and dance
around the room. Again and again she heard Jim's voice
in her thoughts: *I love you, Mary, and I want to marry
you.*

Me? He wants to marry me?

He had to be crazy to propose it; she had to be crazier
to even faintly consider it. They barely knew each other.
And there were her daughters . . . oh, yes, there were her
daughters.

She looked around the shadowy room. If she married
Jim, she would share it with him. Would he want to
change the furniture? What if their tastes were vastly
different? Oh, she would die if he liked bright, bright
colors and varnished plastic!

"You're not saying no?" he'd asked.

No, she hadn't been brave enough to turn aside his
outlandish proposal, nor to embrace it, either. So she'd

ridden the fence, which called to mind her mother's admonition that people who rode the fence often got splinters in their behinds.

Her mother! Her mother would say she'd lost her mind!

Quite suddenly the need to see her mother swept over her. She rose and hurried out the door. Eleven o'clock was early for her mother, and Mary formed the wonderfully familiar mental picture of her mother in the wing chair in the den.

Her steps slowed as she recalled their argument. Had that been only six days ago? It seemed an eternity.

But it didn't matter now. Mary needed to talk with her mother.

"Am I to suppose that now that this Jim Pettijohn has finished painting your house, you have time to visit me?" her mother said right off the bat.

She sat, regal in a red robe, in her wing chair and poured coffee for Mary from a china pot sitting nearby on a rolling tray.

Mary, her heart dipping, took the coffee and said, "Yes, he's finished." She held her tongue on defending herself, half out of guilt because she had truly been preoccupied with Jim and had not spent any time with her mother, and half out of futility because she knew it would do little good to point out that her mother had been at least partly to blame for their rift the past week. Ellen Louise Minnett had never admitted to being even a smidgen at fault in any situation that Mary could remember.

She flicked her gaze over her mother's trim figure and wondered if her mother had ever known inner confusion. Had she ever had doubts about the choices she'd made in her life? Mary had never seen evidence of that. But then she herself had rarely shown her doubts to her daughters, either. That, she thought quite clearly, was a mistake.

Inwardly reeling with confusion, Mary sat calmly drinking coffee and, with the television droning in the background, conversing on everyday things. Aunt Fran was having such a splendid time out in Los Angeles with Cousin Patsy that she'd extended her stay another week. Dani Lee and Alanna were arguing over clothes for their respective trips to college. Ellen was tired, and the hot weather made her cranky.

Then her mother said, "So are you still carrying on with this Jim Pettijohn?"

Mary only then realized that she'd been staring at the swirls on the carpet, lost in thought. She jerked her head up and found her mother gazing at her with a thoughtful, knowing expression. It was suddenly as if her mother had read every thought she'd had—and those had all been about making love with Jim that evening.

"Yes," Mary said, "and he's asked me to marry him."

Her mother blinked and elevated her left eyebrow. "Well." She reached for the pot to pour them each more coffee. "So are you going to?"

"Oh, Mother!" Mary plunked her cup and saucer on the table. "How in the world can I marry a man I met eleven days ago?"

"I imagine you do it the same way as when you've known him eleven months, dear."

Mary, amazed at the levity, stared at her mother.

"I assume he's waiting for your answer," her mother prompted.

"Yes . . ." Mary sighed, took up her cup, then set it down again. "I just don't know what to say. If I tell him no, he'll go off—and I'll never see him again. But we barely know each other. Our lives are so different. *We're* so different. How can I say yes?''

"The same way you said yes to Daniel.''

"I never said yes to Daniel because he never asked me. We just sort of fell into agreement over the years. And besides, when Daniel and I got married *you* had planned our marriage for years. And I didn't have three daughters who might possibly hate him. And neither was I forty-two years old and set in my ways.''

"It sounds as if you don't want to let this man go, but you don't want to commit to keeping him, either.''

Mary wasn't certain she cared for that description, nor her mother's tone. "You make him sound like a fish. And I don't know why I came over here thinking you'd help me. You've made it very clear from the beginning what you thought of my involvement with him.'' Feeling like a fool and hating it, she tossed aside her napkin, a silly nuisance of a thing, and rose.

"Sit down—Mary, please. I'm sorry.''

Somewhat astounded, Mary sat.

Her mother said, "It's just that you've never asked for my advice before. Oh, I've given it, often, and you've usually taken it, too. But you never *asked* me for it before.''

Mary absently picked up her napkin and fiddled with the corner. "Well, Mother, I'm asking now. I realize you were never taken with Jim, and I'm not promising to follow your advice, but I value your wisdom. And I need your help in thinking this out.''

"It isn't that I wasn't taken with Jim Pettijohn. As you pointed out, I didn't know him.''

"You certainly haven't liked me seeing him.''

"No, I haven't," her mother said. "But not for the reasons you may think. And since you've *asked,* I have license to explain. Plain jealousy is one of the reasons, though I'm highly ashamed to admit it. But I've sensed you slipping away from me for months. Suddenly you weren't listening to me at all. I know you never expected such foolish weakness from me, but there you have it. I've been afraid of losing you."

"Oh, Momma, you could never lose me. You're my mother. I love you."

"Sensibly said, but common sense has little to do with those silly emotions," her mother said, gesturing. "Let me get to the other reason I criticized this romance, a very good and well-founded reason. It was and remains my observation, my dear daughter, that you've been restless and lonely for quite a while now and were at a point to have an affair when you met Jim Pettijohn. You thought this would be a fun romance. An exciting little fling with a man who was passing through town, with whom you could feel daring. You were using this man to kindle life inside yourself, with very little thought to what might happen to him. You never counted on this man falling in love with you—or on falling in love yourself. And now, when you're in over your head, you want to cut and run."

Tears welled in Mary's eyes. Her mother had spoken so sharply—but so astutely. So much of what she said was true.

"You're wrong when you say I thought this would be a little romance," she said, forcing the words past the lump in her throat. "I didn't *think* about any of this. I went on feelings all the way. I didn't know I was so lonely, Momma. I didn't know until I saw Jim Pettijohn and some great longing stirred inside me. It was the longing to love and be loved as a woman. Not as a reliable mother or dutiful daughter loves and is loved, but as a full, desirable woman. I felt that with Jim and just followed my feelings where they led. I never thought beyond each day."

"And now, darling? What do you feel now?" Her mother's tone was tender.

"Confused and scared to death," Mary admitted.

Her mother chuckled, which Mary didn't find appropriate, and said, "I'm assuming you do care for Jim."

"I'm crazy about him. I think about him all the time, and my heart races when I see him. But I don't know if it's real love, and I keep thinking, how can it be real in less than two weeks? And what about the girls? They haven't been too pleased with our dating. I know they won't be overjoyed at the idea of us getting married and taking off."

"I don't believe that at this point your decision should rest on your daughters' reactions," her mother said practically.

"No...I have to decide first."

"By this taking-off business—you mean traveling? He's traveling around, isn't he?"

"Yes, and I like that idea. I've been wanting to do that for some time."

"I did notice all those books, but I'd hoped, as I did about your learning to horseback ride, that it was just a phase."

"Up through the teens these things are called phases, Mother. When you're an adult they're called passages." Mary gazed again at the carpet.

"How long will he wait for your answer?" her mother asked.

"I don't know." She recalled that he'd told her, *You think about it for a few days.* "I don't think very long.

He's the most wonderful man, but I wouldn't say patience is his long suit. And put yourself in his place—he declares his love, offers me himself and his whole world. It's got to be a blow to his pride for me to not jump at the chance.''

She thought of his adorable smile, his tenderness, his strong steadiness about everything. His passion. Then she thought of her daughters. And all of them seemed to be calling to her at once.

''Darling...'' her mother said, bringing her back to the moment. ''There's no way I can tell you what to do this time.''

Mary experienced a sinking feeling, and she realized that deep inside she'd come running to her mother for exactly that—so her mother could, as she had in the past, direct her life now.

Her mother smiled tenderly and said, ''In these past days I've learned a few things, too. So I've vowed to quit running your life and, by heaven, I'm sticking to that. You and I are very different, so my decision wouldn't be the same as yours.'' Her mother reached out and took her hand. ''I'm trying to let you know that whatever you decide is fine, though I suppose I'm making a very clumsy job of it. But what I mean to do is make up to you for letting you think I wouldn't stand by you when I was upset with you over Jim Pettijohn. I was wrong to do that— and I never meant that. You'll always be my daughter, and I'll always love you.''

''Oh, Momma,'' Mary said, smiling through her tears.

''However,'' her mother said as crisply as an army commander, ''you must discuss this with the girls. Tonight, even. Tomorrow at the latest. It'll be a great help to you.''

And Mary had to chuckle. Thank heaven her mother could still give orders.

When Mary awoke, she looked across the bed and thought of waking to find Jim there. When she opened the medicine cabinet, she tried to imagine Jim's shaving cream, bottles of after-shave and deodorant sitting there. Half of her things would have to go to make room.

When she entered the kitchen she wondered if he were a morning person, or if he preferred to sleep in. Would she have to adjust her schedule to accommodate his?

She looked at the telephone and half expected it to ring, Jim calling to say that sanity had returned to him with the light of day and that he hadn't meant a word of what he'd said the night before. But the telephone didn't ring, and the memory of his hard, male body against hers brought a blush to her cheeks. She enjoyed it for long seconds, living again the rising heat, the scents and sounds.

Marry him? Did she want to do that? So many things to consider.

Her daughters weren't the least of those, she thought. She would have to talk to them. But not today, no matter what her mother said. She'd better be certain Jim didn't change his mind. And besides, this entire weekend didn't seem a good time.

Actually, no time seemed good.

Restless in the extreme, she plunged in, cooking a breakfast meant for a king—or three queens. She hoped all her daughters would join her this morning. She needed them around her, and she'd long ago learned the power of good food to bring about good moods.

Wrapped up in her thoughts, she didn't hear Dani Lee enter the room until her daughter said, "Momma."

"Good morning, honey," Mary said readily, cheered that Dani Lee had approached, instead of turning the cold shoulder, which she had done so much of late. But as she took in her daughter's expression, her mother's intuition sensed a problem.

Dani Lee poured herself a cup of coffee and pulled a stool to the counter, where Mary was placing sweet rolls into a baking pan. "Kinda nice to have the house to ourselves again," she said, and Mary felt her keen appraisal.

"Yes," Mary agreed diplomatically and didn't find it a lie. She would just as soon be with Jim elsewhere than her house. She put the pan in the oven.

"You're making the works for breakfast," Dani Lee said.

"Uh-huh," Mary said, feeling slightly self-conscious. "We'll need strength to spend the rest of the day getting the house ready for tonight's party."

Dani Lee's going-away party had been planned for months, and even though Dani Lee had been miffed with Mary the past days, she'd still fully expected her mother to carry on with the party.

However, a glance at Dani Lee gave Mary the inkling that something was wrong about the party.

"The party's still on, isn't it?" she asked. "When I spoke to Bud Griffin yesterday, he said you'd been in on Tuesday to finalize the hors d'oeuvres." Since she and Dani Lee hadn't been talking much, and since Dani Lee hadn't been home overmuch of late, opportunities for party planning had been scarce.

Dani Lee nodded. "Yes...everything's set. Except for us getting everything ready here."

"Did you get the lights to string out on the patio?"

"Alanna picked them up yesterday."

"What about tables and chairs?"

"Mike and Nick are bringing them this afternoon." Dani Lee spoke solemnly, as if this party were her execution.

"Is something wrong, honey?" Mary prodded after a long, quiet minute.

Dani Lee took a deep breath. "Oh, Mom, now that the time is almost here, I'm not certain I want to go halfway across the country just to get my degree. I could just as well get that up at Kansas U."

Ah, Mary thought, beginning to understand. "Well, of course you could," she agreed. "But you've been so set on going to New York. Where it's all happening, you've said."

"I know," Dani Lee said sadly. "But it's so far away."

Mary gazed at her daughter, hurting for her. "Would you like me to fly out with you, honey, just to get you settled?" She thought of Jim and how he would be left still waiting, and wondered what he'd say to that.

But Dani Lee replied vehemently, "No! I told you that before—I'm not a child, Mom. If I can't handle going out there alone at my age, then I shouldn't be going. Besides, I don't mind going out there alone. It's . . . oh, the whole thing!"

"You don't have to go to Columbia, Dani Lee. The University of Kansas is a very fine school."

"But everything is set," Dani Lee said with a wail very much like her older sister's. "The plane ticket, all my classes, a part-time job with Blackstone and Company, which Granddad went to a great deal of trouble to get for me, my rooming with Clea—not to mention all those clothes you made me and the party tonight. It's certainly too late to call that off. And what would I say to everyone?"

"You'd say that you were having a staying-at-home party, and everyone would be thrilled," Mary said practically. "The plane ticket can be cashed in, your classes canceled, the job turned down. As for Clea—she'll be disappointed, but she'll get over it. And you can wear the clothes I made you up in Lawrence just as well as back in New York."

Dani Lee's bottom lip trembled. "You wouldn't be disappointed in me for not going?"

Mary shook her head and grabbed her daughter to her. "I love you, sweetheart. Whatever you decide is all right with me. Always remember that I'm proud of you simply because of who you are. You're my daughter, and you're the best. You have what it takes to go to Columbia, if you want to. But you don't have to. There's an awful lot to be said for attachment to home state and family."

Propping their foreheads together, they grinned at each other, each sniffing back tears.

"Oh, Mom...I just feel so...scared. Silly, huh?"

"No, darling, not at all. It's fear of the unknown, very human and sometimes quite wise."

Mary set the mixing bowl in the sink, then looked again at her daughter.

"You can go out and try it, Dani Lee, because if it doesn't work out you can always come home."

Dani Lee gazed at her for long seconds in which her lips turned upward in a trembling smile. "Thanks, Mom," she said, kissed Mary's cheek, then turned shyly away to set the table.

Mary thought of her own mother, who'd given her much needed assurance last night. It occurred to her that her mother had said much the same thing as she had to Dani Lee.

But then Jim's voice echoed in Mary's mind: *If you want, we'll live at your house. If you want another house, we'll get another house.*

She couldn't imagine living anywhere but this house; it was home. But how would Dani Lee feel about coming home to a house Jim was sharing, as well?

And more, how would all of them feel about her taking off to see the world with Jim?

Mary didn't have to telephone Ellen. For the first time in four days, Ellen came to share breakfast with them—Alanna said it was the aroma of sweet coffee cake that brought her—and for the first time in a week, they all sat at the table together. Mary credited her delicious breakfast with helping to bring about the congenial mood. That, she thought, and Jim no longer being in the house. It was as if her daughters equated his no longer painting the house with being totally out of Mary's life, too. As if the two went hand in hand, which seemed a rather odd assumption. Perhaps her daughters were just, as she was, sick of the conflict.

Whatever the reasons, within ten minutes of gathering, everything seemed back to normal—the arguing and loving teasing and sharing of plans. No one mentioned Jim Pettijohn. No one asked where he was, or if perhaps he might join them for the party. And no one made so much as a whisper of apology to Mary for having hurt her feelings the past week.

She listened to her daughters' chatter and tried to imagine how it would be if Jim were sitting there among them. They'd had her to themselves for so long, they weren't of a mind to share her. That was the plain and simple truth.

It came to the tip of her tongue to blurt out the possibility of her and Jim marrying, but she decided she wasn't ready to witness a volcanic eruption there in her dining room.

She just wasn't ready to tell them, because she didn't see any way at all that she could say yes to Jim, and she wasn't ready to face that. Not today. Today she wanted to remain the spirited woman who had been asked, not the staid woman who'd said no.

Mary was busy with her daughters all weekend. Friday night she was occupied with Dani Lee's going-away party; then on Saturday it was a trip to Wichita to view the apartment where Alanna would live while going to school, and on Sunday afternoon it was a baby shower for Ellen. Jim felt their Sunday breakfast date at the Red Barn Waffle House was something of an inconvenience sandwiched between all her other commitments. With surprise and chagrin, he recognized pangs of jealousy. She'd been his for days, he told himself, but this weekend she had commitments to her daughters. Getting possessive wouldn't bring anyone happiness—and might just prove some kind of point as to why she couldn't marry him.

That worry—that she was going to say no to his proposal—had grown during the days when he hadn't seen her, had only spoken to her in quick conversations on the telephone. And seeing how nervous she appeared now, he wondered anxiously if she were going to tell him just that. He knew, as she spoke about her daughters and what had gone on with them, that she hadn't told the girls about his proposal. Was she worried about what they would say, or did she simply not want to tell them because she'd made up her mind not to marry him?

She put her hand over his. "What have you done with your weekend?" she asked softly.

He smiled. "Went out and met some of Fred Miller's rural relatives, fished in their pond, read about Colorado silver mines—and thought incessantly about you."

"I thought about you, too." She averted her eyes, and his chest tightened. The attraction remained like lightning between them, but he sensed her pulling away from him.

"I also called a friend back in Atlanta about a job."

Her eyes widened. "A job...but I thought..."

He gestured. "This job would fit right into my traveling, would legitimize it and help me look a little less like a bum to your family." She frowned at that, but he went right on. "Starting next Saturday I'll be doing a network radio spot once a week about places and people around the country, wherever I happen to be at the time. Charles Kuralt made a career of doing that, so I don't know why I can't get a little mileage out of it, too. I'll start with ten-minute spots, and if it turns out well I'll work up to twenty- or thirty-minute segments."

"What a marvelous opportunity," she said and gazed at him with such admiration that he felt faintly guilty. It wasn't any great thing; commentators had done much the same since the beginning of time, and his expertise was in the media, after all.

He picked up his coffee cup and drank deeply. She did the same, and the silence between them seemed quite loud.

At last he said, "Did you sound the girls out about us getting married?" He immediately wished he hadn't said it; he knew the answer. He guessed he'd been foolishly wishing he would be wrong, and besides, someone had to say something to bring the subject out in the open.

She shook her head and averted her eyes.

At that moment Jim knew he wasn't coming out ahead.

She glanced around self-consciously. "Let's go for a walk, so we can talk. I'll have to be getting back to the house soon."

Mary knew she had to come down off the fence, even if she fell down. She had to set things straight. It wasn't fair to Jim not to.

They walked hand in hand along the neat sidewalk beneath the warming August sun. Jim's hand was hot around hers. Mr. Cole drove by, called a greeting and waved. Mary waved back. She was having trouble formulating what she had to say. She dreaded losing both this man and the person she'd become when she was with him.

"It must be nice to live in a place where you know almost everyone," Jim said.

"It is—most of the time," she answered.

He looked at her, and she looked at him. Then he indicated a bench beneath an old elm on the courthouse lawn, and they went to sit.

"What is it you want to tell me, Mary?" he asked, getting directly to the point as was his nature. It seemed one more example of how different they were.

She gazed at him and blinked, directing her tears not to come. "Jim, this whole thing is just going too fast for me." She faltered. "You're such a decisive man. You know what you want in five seconds. But look at me—it took me five minutes to decide on my breakfast order this morning, and there wasn't that much variety."

He chuckled at that, and her heart cracked.

"I know we're opposites in many ways, Mary," he said gently, "but that's why I'm so attracted to you. Our differences complement each other."

She sucked in a trembling breath, wondering how to explain without hurting his feelings. He was a dear, sweet man, even if his suggestion bordered on insanity.

She touched his arm. "Jim...I care about you. You've made me feel like I haven't felt in years. Maybe in my life. But I just can't jump into marriage. I'm sorry."

She felt his gaze, but she had to look away because she didn't want him to see the tears in her eyes. The silence hung painfully between them. She waited for him to speak.

"Mary, can you say you *don't* love me?"

Surprised, she looked at him. That she didn't love him? What was he driving at? His eyes, his beautiful sky-blue eyes, searched her face, and she lost herself for an instant in them.

He cautioned, "Answer yes or no. Can you say, cross your heart and hope to die, that you *don't* love me?"

"No," she said hoarsely, honestly. "I'm not saying that. But I certainly don't believe people can fall in love at first sight—or even in a week. Oh! I don't even know what I feel, what I—"

He broke in. "Can you say you *think* you love me? Yes or no."

"I can't think *any*thing at this point!"

"You're evading."

"No, I'm trying to be honest. And sensible. You'll thank me for this someday, because I prevented you from doing something impulsive that you would end up being sorry for."

He said, "You couldn't have made love to me the way you did the other night and not love me."

"It may be blunt, but I imagine any woman would re-act to you the way I did. You know what you're about in bed, Jim Pettijohn!" And she thought how it had been so long since she'd made love to a man. Then, embarrassed at both her words and her thoughts, she got up and headed for the sidewalk, the urge to run and hide propelling her along.

Jim came up beside her. "You're not being sensible," he said angrily. "You're just being scared. You know you'd love to marry me and go away with me."

She stopped. "Maybe a part of me would like to do that, Jim. But at times in my life I've also wanted to fly out of a tree or to be a movie star. I've had sense enough to know that neither of those things was likely to work out for my good."

"Nothing wrong with being a movie star."

"Oh!" She stalked faster, passed the windows of Corys Department Store. He was making this so much harder than it needed to be!

He caught up and stepped in front of her to make her stop, and she felt trapped, panicky. His gaze caught and held hers.

"I love you, Mary. I do."

She shook her head. "You love the woman you *think* I am. But the woman you've been with isn't the true me. Mary Lunsford doesn't go around going to bed with men she's only known for days. And she doesn't go around marrying them, either."

"Mary Lunsford has a heart capable of falling in love. And she did."

"I just can't make the commitment," she said. "Ellen is pregnant, Dani Lee is nervous about going to Columbia and Alanna doesn't know enough to be nervous about going away for the first time. They need me. And

I've been a widow for ten years. I don't mean to hurt you, but I'm not certain I want to be married, Jim. I've accommodated my daughters for so many years, and I'm finally getting my life back to myself. My daughters will always need me, sometimes at the most inconvenient times—there's no way you can understand that."

He looked away, and his jaw tightened. Then he faced her again. "There are no guarantees in life, Mary. I learned that with Amy. There are no guarantees, and every day given to us is precious. I couldn't be more certain about how I feel about you four weeks or four months from now. This is something I know."

"But I don't."

Their eyes locked in battle. Then Jim stepped back to let her pass. She'd walked five steps when he called after her.

"Then I'll just have to convince you!"

She whirled around to see him grinning at her. Thoroughly flustered, she hurried away to her car.

Jim telephoned Mary that evening.

"I'm sorry for getting worked up this morning," he said.

"Oh, Jim."

His heart did the little flutter that it always did when she said that.

"Mary, I just wanted to tell you that I do understand what you're saying. I *do*. But I'm not giving up on us just yet."

"You're not?" Her voice was breathless.

"Nope. I'm in love with both the sane and sensible Mary Lunsford *and* the Mary Lunsford who is crazy enough to fall in love at first sight. And I'm staying around to see if I can convince you to see things my way."

Chapter Six

She hadn't considered that Jim would stay. He'd been ready to leave Minnett Springs when he finished painting her house; he'd told her that the day they had tea together. His deal with Fred Miller was to finish her house, and then he had planned to be off toward the Rocky Mountains or down toward the Rio Grande, whichever struck him at the time.

But now he said he would stay—for her.

Mary was thrilled. She really was. But she was also put right back where she'd been—in a quandary about what to do. Jim still wanted to marry her, which continued to give her the choice, which she'd already agonized over and made, darn it! She almost wished he would just go away so she wouldn't have to think of it anymore. Almost but not quite.

"So he turned the tables on you," her mother said when Mary told her. "Oh my, this is shaping up better than a soap opera!"

"Thank you, Mother. It's great to know I'm giving you some entertainment. What in the world has come over you?" As soon as the words were out of her mouth, she recalled that her mother had said the exact same thing to her.

"Perhaps watching you has gotten me thinking about my own life, dear. I may be a grandmother, but I'm still a woman. Judge Hubert has been holding the church door open for me for two years. I think he's been waiting for encouragement for more."

Mary gaped at her mother, then laughed aloud. "Then you'd better be darn certain you don't start something you can't finish, Mother."

Monday morning the florist brought Mary a colorful bouquet of daisies and carnations. The attached card read, *I love you, Mary. Please marry me—Jim.*

That afternoon's mail brought a card from Jim. Somewhere he'd managed to find a valentine! She opened it to read, *Mary, Mary, marry me.*

And that night, Jim, dressed impeccably in a starched shirt and a tie, showed up at her front door with a basket of food. He had fried chicken, potato salad, olives, a whole apple pie and a bottle of chardonnay.

"What is this?" Mary asked, amazed.

"Dinner," he said.

"But..."

"I thought dinner in might be a nice family thing to do." Looking past Mary's shoulder, he said, "Would you like to join us? I brought enough for us all."

Mary turned to see Alanna and Dani Lee at the bottom of the stairs, gaping at them. The next instant both their expressions turned cool. "We have plans," Dani Lee said icily, and both she and Alanna turned away.

"Ah, excuse me," Jim said and whipped an envelope from the basket, extending it toward them.

"What's this?" Dani Lee hesitantly took the envelope.

"A brief personal profile. Please feel free to share it with Ellen and your grandmother."

And on that note, Mary urged him into the dining room, closed the sliding doors and whirled around at him. "Your profile?" she said hoarsely.

"Yep. So everyone can get to know me better. And I have one for you, too," he announced, pulling another envelope from the basket and holding it toward her. "I went into much more detail on yours, and some of it I'd just as soon remain private—like the part about the tattoo on my rear."

"You have a tattoo on your...?"

"I was after a news story, I swear. You'll see it when you marry me." He grinned. "Mary, marry me."

"Oh, Jim."

She took a breath, then opened her mouth to remind him that it was impossible, but he stopped her with his mouth on hers, and the kiss was just too sweet to refuse.

That evening, propped in her bed, Mary read the profile Jim had written about himself, typed, five pages, single-spaced. He was indeed a gifted storyteller, she thought. Several times she laughed aloud, and once, at the part about loving and losing his wife, she came close to tears. When she'd finished, she sat with the paper in her lap and looked around the room lit only by the bedside lamp.

Jim had written that he liked to watch television in bed, even to fall asleep with it on. Mary didn't. He generally liked to stay up late and sleep late in the morning. Mary was the opposite. He liked jazz. Mary hated it. He liked pizza with everything, even anchovies. Mary's stomach rolled over at just the thought.

Her gaze fell to the bottom of the page, and she read again what he'd typed in red ink: *I love you. Please marry me, Mary.* She squeezed her eyes closed and felt a flood of emotion. There could be no other man like Jim Pettijohn on this earth, and to be with him brought sunshine into her life.

A light rap sounded at her door. It was Alanna. "Mom, may I borrow your new white dress for tomorrow night?" she asked shyly. "Kirk's parents have invited me to a dinner party at their house."

"Of course, sweetheart."

Alanna pulled the dress from the closet, sized it up against herself, then swished back and forth to watch the flowing skirt swirl. Her gaze came up and met Mary's. "It'll fit, won't it?"

"You'll look lovely in it," Mary said.

Alanna continued to gaze at her. "I never thought we'd wear the same size."

Mary chuckled. "We're close, though it's arranged better on you."

"Oh, Mom..." Alanna moved to sit on the bedside. Mary waited while her daughter searched for words. "I'm sorry," she blurted, tears coming to her eyes.

"Whatever for?" Mary asked, immediately concerned.

Alanna began to cry in earnest. "For the way I've treated you about Jim! I'm really sorry, honest." Her tone dropped. "I was jealous, Mom—because of Jim looking at you and not at me. Oh, I'm so embarrassed. How rotten to be jealous of your own mother! And then I couldn't stand thinking of you paying more attention to someone... you know, outside of any of us. You've always been here, just my mom. And then I saw you in this dress that night, and you looked so...beautiful. My mom looking almost like one of those women on television who advertise perfume. I guess I'd just never really looked at you."

Mary smiled tenderly and touched her daughter's cheek.

Alanna smiled, too. "I like Kirk a lot, and I can understand how you must feel about Jim."

Mary hugged Alanna fiercely. "Thank you, darling." She held on to her daughter and thought of Jim and Dani Lee and Ellen.

Then she drew back. "Just how much do you like this Kirk?"

"Oh, Mom, really! Don't get worried about it. Yet," she added with a little minx smile.

Tuesday morning Mary awoke at the crack of dawn. She lay there for long minutes and looked at the empty side of the bed. It might work out very well if Jim enjoyed sleeping late, she thought, because she could rise early and have the time she needed by herself, just as she always did.

She could pick the anchovies off the pizza.

But the jazz... Maybe he could listen to that when he was by himself, or through earphones.

Ellen was there later that morning when Carter's Pharmacy arrived with a delivery. "Mother... someone has sent you a present." Her face pinched, she handed Mary a small silver-striped box. "It's from that Jim Pettijohn, isn't it?"

"I haven't opened it, Ellen."

"Well, aren't you going to?"

"Yes, later." She didn't care to do it in front of Ellen, because suddenly Mary felt she might cry if Jim had written another proposal.

"Oh, Mother, won't you look at what you're doing?" Her mouth a pout, she stormed around the kitchen table, took hold of a chair.

"What am I doing, Ellen?"

"You're making a fool of yourself with this man."

It flashed across Mary's mind to tell Ellen that she had already broken off with Jim, but then, as it had turned out, that would be hard to claim. And besides, her romance with Jim was her own private business. She said instead, "How is that?"

"Oh, Mother! You're never here anymore. You're always off with *him!* Sunday morning I called to invite you to breakfast with me and Todd, and Dani Lee said you were off with *him*. Good grief, Mother—breakfast?"

"If you had called me the night before, I would gladly have joined you and Todd for breakfast," Mary said. "It is the polite thing, even with one's mother, to plan ahead."

"So now you have to plan to fit us into your schedule just so you can take time away from Mr. Pettijohn! Well, I, for one, am not highly impressed with that man. I never was. I don't care what he wrote in that... that résumé he gave Dani Lee and Alanna last night. I don't like him, and I don't trust him."

"What is it you don't like about him, Ellen?"

"I just don't like him. That's all. He thinks he's so smart. He's...well, he's not your type. He's not at all like Daddy was."

Mary looked at her daughter for long moments. "Your father has been dead a long time now, Ellen, and I think I'm quite a bit different than I was when we were married."

"Maybe so, but that doesn't mean Jim Pettijohn fits with you."

"Well, I believe I'm the only one who can judge that. There *are* times in a mother's life when she is not answerable to her children. This is one of them, Ellen."

They gazed at each other for long seconds. Seeing the anger and pain in her daughter's eyes sent a sharp pain through Mary's heart.

"I can't understand how you can put this man before us—your own flesh and blood!" Ellen cried. "I just can't!"

Mary went to Ellen, saying, "I'm not putting him before you, darling. I love you. You're my daughter."

But Ellen pulled away, shaking her head. "Everything's changed since he came!" she said vehemently. "You're not the same as you were."

"Ellen," Mary said, searching her heart for the words, "all people change. It's part of living. You're certainly not the same as you were five years ago, are you?"

"No, but I still care about this family!"

"And I do, too. Just because I'm interested in Jim doesn't change that."

But Ellen insisted, "He's changing you. He's changing everything, and you're letting him!" And she ran from the house.

So Mary knew, as she'd known all along, that Ellen would make it a matter of choosing between them. That was how Ellen saw it. And Mary felt as if she were being torn apart in a tug-of-war between her children, Jim and her own needs and desires.

Slowly, with shaking fingers, Mary untied the ribbon of the silver-striped box. Nestled inside was a bottle of Knowing perfume. She drew out the blue card and read, *I want you to know how much I love you. Marry me, Mary.*

Her heart swelled and tears overflowed. Knowing was her favorite perfume.

That afternoon another valentine card arrived in the mail, and again Jim had written, *Mary, Mary, marry me.*

Mary held the card to her chest and thought perhaps Ellen would come around eventually. And then she wondered how long eventually would be, and what would happen in the meantime.

That evening Jim telephoned. "Did you get my presents?"

"Yes. I sent you a thank-you card."

"Will you go for a walk with me tonight?"

"How can you persist in this?" She couldn't fathom that his pride wasn't dented, his patience thoroughly tried.

"Because I know what I want, and that's to be with you. Just walk with me. That's all I ask—tonight."

"I'll walk with you," she said.

Wednesday morning her mother came through the kitchen door fairly bursting with amusement. "Mary, dear, have you looked over at the Websters' house this morning?"

"No? What is it?"

"They're having their house painted."

"Oh?" Mary went to the front door.

"Yes...and there's a message on this side of the house for you."

"A message?"

Highly curious, she stepped outside, and there, up on the gable of the Websters' house, was written, I love you, Mary. Marry me. The lettering was plain and bold in blue gray against the white clapboards of the house.

"Oh, my heaven!" Now this was going just a bit too far! She definitely didn't want Ellen reading this—she didn't want her neighbors reading it! Mary flew across the driveway and through the hedge, scanning the workmen's faces, looking for Jim.

"Don't know any Jim Pettijohn, ma'am," the young workman on the scaffolding said. "Some guy came by here a few minutes ago and paid me ten dollars to write this." He grinned. "No skin off me—I'll be painting over it."

"Well, paint over it *now!*" And she marched back to the kitchen.

Her mother was chuckling merrily and said, "He's carrying on quite a marry-me campaign, isn't he?"

Mary glared at her. Jim must indeed be having himself a grand time, she thought. And spending a ridiculous amount of money.

The marry-me campaign continued over the following days. The bookstore delivered two colorful, glossy books, one about the Rocky Mountains and the other about Texas. Alanna found balloons with an attached envelope tied to the mailbox. A box containing a world globe showed up on the front stoop, and the pizza parlor delivered a large pizza with pepperoni slices formed into the shape of a heart. There came a calendar with question marks written on the dated squares, a video documentary about the Grand Canyon, the latest edition of the Rand McNally road atlas and an empty photograph album with the names Jim and Mary printed in gold on the front, and with each day's mail delivery came another valentine. Along with each gift and each card came a hand-written message, which was, written in various ways, *I love you, Mary. Please marry me.*

By Friday morning Mary had the urge to stay in bed and pull the covers over her head. She wondered how long Jim would continue this nonsense.

A man like him didn't come along every day, she told herself, amazed at his persistence, his ingenuity, his pas-

sion, his tenderness. And his audacity! The evening before he'd dared to tell her that he *knew* she wanted to
marry him. He knew it, he'd said, and he was simply
trying to help her do what she wanted to do. That got her
back up. She'd lived enough of her life doing what other
people expected of her—she didn't need Jim Pettijohn
telling her that he *knew* what she needed and wanted!

She had the opportunity of a lifetime here, she
thought, recalling Jim's magnificent smile, the offer he
was making her, the way he kissed her. He had awakened in her things she hadn't known existed, and though
she was all alone, she blushed, recalling what it had been
like making love with him.

But there were her daughters to consider. Alanna
would be all right, and she thought now that Dani Lee
would eventually come to accept him. But Ellen...her
firstborn, a part of her own flesh. What if she lost Ellen
forever?

And always there remained the choking fears, which
she could only partially give name to—the fear that it
wouldn't work out, that she would have her heart broken, that it would turn out to be a great mistake. The fear
of stepping out of the safe little world she had known all
her life.

That morning remained quiet, unusually so. While
Mary divided her time between Alanna and Dani Lee,
helping them with their packing for the coming week, she
waited to find out what Jim would have delivered that
day. What he might possibly *do.*

As noon came and went and no gift appeared, she felt
a sharp disappointment. Had he given up? Couldn't he
have tried a little harder? she thought, irritated, then immediately contrite. Jim had given her every opportu-

nity; it was her own fears that had held her back. Her own fault!

And, she countered, her own good sense! Yes, she was glad he had stopped this nonsense. It was time they both stood with two feet on the ground.

But then the tears came. She tried to stop them, hurried herself downstairs so Alanna and Dani Lee wouldn't see them and ask questions that she couldn't begin to answer. She didn't even know why she was crying.

A knocking at the door finally helped her to get herself under control. When she opened it to find the florist delivering long-stemmed roses—three enormous bouquets of them—she was shocked both speechless and tearless.

She slowly sat on a chair and gazed at the roses sitting on the dining room table. Two of the bouquets were large, canary-yellow blossoms arranged in green vases, each accented by a pale yellow bow. One was for Alanna, one for Dani Lee.

The third bouquet was larger than those, with crimson blossoms in a large heavy crystal vase and accented with a red velvet bow. Her name was on the attached envelope.

The roses captivated her eyes while their scent swirled around her. She inhaled deeply, luxuriously, and felt the sweet scent penetrate her very marrow.

Never had she thought to be in love with a man again, and certainly never had she imagined a man chasing after her. Not a man like this.

Slowly, almost reverently, she reached out to remove the card attached to the ribbon. She opened it and read the words, *I love you, Mary. Will you marry me? Jim.*

A slight difference, but her mind recorded it at once. It was the first time the proposal had come in the form of a true request.

When he'd first proposed, Jim had said, *I want to marry you.* Each time since, he'd written, *Mary, marry me. Please marry me. Marry me, Mary.*

She pressed the card to her chest and thought how silly of her to think this made a difference. A difference no one would understand. Not really a difference . . . of course not.

Losing herself in emotion, she gazed at the roses, inhaled their drugging scent. When her mother arrived, carrying another bouquet of roses, white this time, that had been sent to her by Jim, Mary wasn't surprised. She doubted that anything Jim Pettijohn could do now would surprise her.

Her mother placed her bouquet with the others on the table. Their eyes met, and they chuckled softly. Then, together, she and her mother sat and stared at the four bouquets crowding the dining room table.

There came the patter of feet down the stairs, and Alanna's voice calling, "Mom!"

"In here," Mary answered softly.

Alanna breezed in through the arched entryway. "Mom, do you think I should . . ." Her words trailed off and she froze, her gaze fastened on the flowers. "Oh my! Aren't they beautiful! What is all this?"

"Jim Pettijohn," her grandmother said merrily. "These are for you." And she pushed the vase forward.

"For me?" Alanna cast Mary a quizzical glance, then read her card. She looked at the bouquets again. "But why?"

"Good grief! Where did all the flowers come from?"

They all looked over at Dani Lee, who'd stopped in the entry.

"Jim Pettijohn," Mary's mother piped happily and gestured. "These are for you."

Mary watched Dani Lee read her card and wondered what Jim had written to her mother and daughters. Dani Lee scowled in deliberation, then looked in wonder at Mary. But before any questions could fly, Ellen burst through the swinging door from the kitchen. "Look what I just got!" she said, and not at all happily. She saw all the others. "Oh my..."

"Just add yours to the rest, Ellen, dear," her grandmother said.

Ellen plunked the vase of yellow blossoms she carried on the table and sank into a chair, her expression incredulous.

The fragrance from all the roses seemed to hold Mary in some kind of calm, floating spell. She inhaled deeply, automatically closing her eyes and forgetting all about everyone but Jim.

"Mother, what is going on?" Ellen demanded, jarring her.

Mary's eyes popped open. Ellen's face was a mask of fury, her mother's was speculative, Dani Lee's anxious and Alanna's tender, and all were staring at her.

"An old-fashioned proposal from Jim Pettijohn," her mother said. "He wants to marry us."

All of them began to babble.

"Mother!"

"Are you going to?"

"You can't really consider this."

"Of course she can. It's so romantic!"

"No—it's disgusting!"

"When?"

"Mother?" Alanna said, and they all looked at her.

Mary breathed deeply. "Nothing has been decided..." she began, then was interrupted by the doorbell.

Alanna ran quickly to answer it, then returned and whispered excitedly, "Mom...it's for you."

From Alanna's face, Mary knew it was Jim. Her heart beating double time, she moved into the hallway. He stood there, just inside the opened doorway.

He still wanted her, she thought. He'd been trying so hard to win all of them. He'd been trying so hard.

She stopped in front of him.

"Did you get my flowers?" he asked, a nervous grin twitching his lips.

She nodded.

"I come bearing a last gift." He held out an envelope.

"Oh..." She couldn't get any more words out, and she blinked rapidly to clear her vision.

"Please open it."

She took the envelope, opened it with shaky fingers and drew out a pale blue card. On it was printed, *Good for one week at the Menger Hotel in San Antonio. Will you marry me?*

Slowly she lifted her gaze to his. His eyes glimmered with hope and fear and love and promise. And suddenly she knew what she wanted. What she had to do, be it wise or foolish.

"Yes," she said.

The next instant she was in his arms, and he was swinging her around and around. "Oh, Mary...Mary... Mary!"

When at last he set her on the floor, the others gathered around them. Self-consciously, Mary wiped the tears from her face and looked anxiously at everyone, wondering as to their reactions.

"My congratulations," her mother said, stepping forward first and foremost. She kissed and hugged Mary, then fixed Jim with her regal gaze. "You are a piece of work, young man." And she allowed him to kiss her cheek.

Then Alanna and Dani Lee were both kissing and hugging her at once. Alanna was exuberant. "Oh, Momma, I'm so glad for you."

Dani Lee said a quiet, restrained, "Congratulations, Mom."

But Ellen was gone.

"Where's Ellen?" Mary asked, knowing in her heart that her daughter had fled.

"She . . . she left," Alanna said.

Mary looked at Jim. "I have to go after her."

But he stopped her. "Let me go."

"No, she won't listen to you."

"Let me try," he said and started out the door.

When she would have gone after him, her mother put a hand to her shoulder. "Let him try, Mary."

"Their apartment is up on Crowder Street," Mary called and pointed.

Jim saw Ellen far down the sidewalk, stalking away, her arms moving like pistons at her side. He called her; she looked over her shoulder and continued on.

He ran to catch up with her, but when she broke into a run he slowed, not thinking it a good thing for her to be running since she was five months pregnant. She'd gone inside her apartment when he arrived. He knocked, then stood back and called out, "Ellen!"

"Go away," she yelled back, her voice floating through an open window.

"Not until you listen to me!"

The window came down with a loud thump.

Jim moved to the door, he leaned near and spoke just below a yell. "I love your mother. Doesn't that count for something?"

No sound from inside.

"I will make your mother happy. I promise. And isn't that what counts? You're married—did your mother get all mad at you when you married Todd? Did she back out of your life because of it? From what I see, she hasn't only held her arms open but has kept your room ready for you. Can't you do that much for her?"

Again he paused, but no answer came.

"Look, Ellen..." His voice was growing hoarse. "I'm not out to be your father, and I'm not out to take your mother away from you. I just want to be a part of your mother's life—of all your lives. We love each other, Ellen."

He waited five minutes but the door never opened. With great reluctance he walked back to Mary's house, dreading telling her that he'd failed.

The look of pure despair on her face tightened his chest. *Would she back out now? Would this change everything?*

Dani Lee appeared with a tray of iced glasses. "Couldn't find any champagne. Will Coca-Cola do for celebration?"

A smile spread slowly across Mary's lips. Eyes shining, she took his hand. "That will do wonderfully, sweetheart. Thank you. Thank you so much."

Chapter Seven

Mary sat alone in the family room, drinking a cup of coffee by the light of a single lamp.

She and Jim were to be married the following morning, Sunday, right there at the house. Reverend Beecham was fitting them in between his early and late services, because directly after the ceremony Dani Lee needed to catch her flight to New York.

Mary, her mother and Alanna had spent long hours since Friday afternoon not only helping Dani Lee finish her preparations for going off to Columbia but preparing for Mary's wedding. Though Mary had argued against it, Alanna had insisted on postponing her move down to her apartment in Wichita.

"I have a whole week until classes start, Mom. I don't need to hurry. And if I wait, I'll have Grandma's help all to myself."

"Everything will work out, Mary," her mother insisted when Mary began to worry out loud. "Everyone has their lists. Follow them!" In her great commander tradition, Mary's mother had written each of them a list of things to be taken care of—even one for Jim, who'd been left in charge of many of the wedding plans. "I believe he's proven he's quite capable," she said.

Poor Jim, Mary thought. He was just beginning to discover what his life would be like, a lone male in the midst of females. The one son-in-law in Ellen Louise Minnett's life. Jim had teased that maybe he would have been better off if Mary's mother had continued to dislike him. She didn't now; she adored him.

Once they'd given him a chance, they'd all come to adore him. All except Ellen.

An iron weight settled on Mary's heart as thoughts of Ellen filled her mind. She recalled carrying Ellen in her womb, recalled giving birth, recalled her daughter's first steps and first word—which hadn't been Dada but Mommmm.

Her life would be perfect at this moment, she thought, if only Ellen would give her approval.

But Ellen had refused to talk to any of them—even, though it was hard to believe, to her grandmother, who'd stalked down to Ellen and Todd's apartment and gotten so mad as to lose her decorum and smack her purse into Ellen's bedroom door. A bedroom door that remained closed.

Mary had done what Jim had said he'd done—talked to Ellen through the door. Dani Lee had done the same, and Alanna had given it a shot. Alanna had ended her plea by calling her sister a stupid nincompoop. Yet even that had received no answer.

Todd had promised he would speak with her, and Mary put her hope in his corner, though it was now eleven o'clock on Saturday night and Mary had received no word from either Todd or Ellen.

Mary heard her daughters' voices, and the back door opened.

"We thought maybe you'd be up in bed, Mom," Alanna said and jumped over the back of the couch to plop down beside Mary.

Dani Lee came around to sit on the ottoman. "What's wrong, Mom? Too excited to sleep?"

Mary nodded. "I can't seem to stop my thoughts. Did either of you happen to stop at Ellen's?"

Alanna and Dani Lee exchanged glances. Dani Lee frowned and looked down at her knees. "Dani Lee tried again," Alanna said, "but Ellen won't budge."

Mary sighed. "I walked down earlier, but she wouldn't see me."

Dani Lee, always the most practical one, said, "She'll get used to it eventually. She won't be able to stay in that room and miss the annual half-off sale at Corys, that's for sure."

They all exchanged grins.

"It's pretty exciting, isn't it?" Alanna said. "Getting married."

Mary nodded and said, "Yes . . . and scary, too."

Dani Lee gave her an understanding smile. "Remember what you told me about going to Columbia?"

"What's that, dear?"

"Go out and give it a try. If it doesn't work out, you can always come home. And we'll always be around to help."

They fell together, the three of them, and the mother heart inside Mary fairly burst with pride. "Thank you, my darlings . . . thank you," she whispered.

Jim jerked loose his tie and swore, then peered into the mirror and tried again.

He'd never felt more alone than he did that morning, getting ready for his wedding without anyone there to help him. He'd called his mother, his brother, one of his sisters and a couple of friends last night. His mother was irritated that he wouldn't wait for her to fly out, but she'd long ago learned that he had his ways. Though if he'd had his way, he would have married Mary on Friday afternoon. He'd made the concession to her family to do a small ceremony on Sunday.

He looked at his watch, jerked off the tie and went to fortify himself with another cup of coffee. Thinking of Mary, he got a tightening in his belly. He would be glad when all this wedding business was over and Mary was his wife and couldn't change her mind—at least, not quite so easily.

His gaze strayed to the neatly made couch, and sweet memories of their lovemaking filled his mind. Anticipation of the night ahead came to him as full and ripe as a Georgia peach. By golly, that woman did something for him! He chuckled. Mary couldn't understand what she meant to him; he knew that. But he would convince her in the days and weeks to come.

A knock at his door startled him almost out of his pants. Quickly he went to open it, and there stood Dani Lee and Alanna, both as pretty as a spring morning, smiling with shyness and excitement.

"Mom sent us," Dani Lee said.

And Alanna added pertly, "We're your support group—and valets. Where's your tie?"

They didn't like his tie, so he brought out the only other one he owned. Dani Lee tied it, while Alanna buffed his boots.

"Hold still," Dani Lee commanded. Jim thought she had Mary's nose.

"How's your mother? She isn't about to back out, is she?"

Dani Lee shook her head, and Alanna said, "Mom has a terrible time making up her mind, but once she has, she won't be moved. You're stuck with her now."

"Stop grinning like that," Dani Lee said. "You're wiggling."

"What about Ellen?"

Dani Lee's eyes came up to his, and she shook her head.

Alanna said, "Ellen is the most like Mom—she's made up her mind not to accept you, and it'd be easier to move a mountain than to move Ellen."

"I think it's this pregnancy. It has her hormones all out of kilter," Dani Lee said. "She'll come around when that baby comes—because she'll be hollering for Mom to hold her hand."

Jim hoped Ellen came around, and the sooner the better because he knew the situation was tearing Mary apart. He'd sent to Ellen the same bouquet that Dani Lee and Alanna would be holding during the ceremony, and he'd included a special note, though he wondered if maybe a note from him would do more to hurt the cause than help. Still, he'd done all he could.

He slipped into his coat, and Dani Lee brushed invisible lint from his shoulders. Alanna drew something from her purse.

"One of the roses from the bouquet you sent Mom," she said. "For your lapel."

They gave him a critical going-over, then pronounced him ready.

"Got your shaving kit?" Alanna asked.

"More importantly," Dani Lee said, "do you have your credit cards? If you have them, you can always buy whatever you forgot."

But Alanna held up her hand. "You can't buy the ring—do you have it? And the license?"

He patted his pockets. The precious license was tucked in the breast pocket of his coat. In order to be prepared when Mary came around, and as an act of faith that she would, he'd applied for their marriage license first thing

Monday morning. And right after she'd told him yes on Friday afternoon, he'd wasted no time in getting her down to the courthouse to complete all the legalities.

"Got everything," he said briskly. "Let's go."

There were people he'd never seen before at Mary's house. Taking his arm, Ellen Louise introduced him around to various relatives, whose names all blurred together in his mind and who stared at him and Ellen Louise as if both of them were from another world. He did have the impression that Ellen Louise didn't ordinarily behave so breezily.

Then suddenly Dani Lee was tugging on his elbow. "Mom wants to see you." She looked very worried.

Jim's heart beat double time as he went up the stairs and triple time when he rapped on her door. The door opened, and Mary drew him inside. For a long second he stood there looking at her. Her hair fell in soft waves around her face. Her dress was of some white silky fabric that flowed over her curves and was dotted with green and blue flowers, colors that brought out the green of her eyes. Eyes that shone up at him.

"Mary..." He drew her to him, and she came fluidly, returning his kiss.

When they drew away, they smiled at each other.

"Guess you aren't going to change your mind," he said.

Her smile slipped. "No, but you might want to—and I won't hold you to this if you want to back out." She paused. "Oh, Jim, I can't leave here after our wedding. I can't go off on our honeymoon and leave Ellen with things this way. She's upset, and it could cause problems with the baby. Todd says she's hardly eaten these past days, and with Ellen that's a sure sign of a serious problem. I simply can't leave her."

It was a disappointment, a great one, and Jim stood there, trying to get past his first response, which he recognized as decidedly selfish.

"It's what I've tried to explain, Jim. I'm a mother."

He gazed into her anxious eyes and slowly felt a warm assurance come up from deep inside him. "Yes..." he said. "You're a mother, a daughter, and the woman I want for my wife. Shall we get on with it?"

The ceremony was held on the back lawn. Reverend Beecham stood in the shade of the giant elm, Mary beside Jim in front of him. To her right and a step behind stood Dani Lee and Alanna. Mary turned her head to smile at them, and they smiled back with encouragement. Jim's sleeve brushed her arm, and she thought she detected him shaking. He turned his head and gave a small grin.

Reverend Beecham cleared his throat and began, "We are gathered here in the sight of..."

He followed the words Jim and Mary had hastily written the day before, a very standard ceremony but with small changes they felt were applicable, such as Jim promised to be sensitive to Mary's children, and Mary promised to be sensitive to Jim's need to travel. She thought her part was a lot easier than his—she had a great desire to travel, too.

With a glance at Jim's profile, she thought how fortunate she was, and how she would have a lot to do to give to him all that he'd already given to her.

Yes, she was fortunate, and her life was almost perfect. If only Ellen had come, and she stole another glance at Dani Lee and Alanna, hoping against hope that Ellen would appear.

Suddenly Jim said, "Stop... wait."

Shocked, Mary looked at him.

"Let's move the ceremony down the street," he said.

"Move the ceremony?" Mary said, with Reverend Beecham and Dani Lee and Alanna parroting after her.

Jim nodded, his eyes intense. "Let's move it down to Ellen's front yard and start over."

She stared at him, trying to comprehend.

"It will only take a few minutes," he said. "We don't need to bother with taking those flower stands and stuff."

"Oh, Jim...you are a piece of work." And she turned to the small group assembled behind them. "We're moving the ceremony down to Ellen's. Please join us."

Everyone was stunned, of course, but Mary's mother called, "What a splendid idea!" Just as if people got married practically out on a public street every day.

Declining to ride, Jim and Mary strode down the street, with Dani Lee and Alanna running and laughing ahead. Within minutes everyone had taken up their positions on the grass that was Ellen and Todd's postage-stamp-size front lawn. Jim told Reverend Beecham to wait a few minutes, and the reverend looked impatiently at his watch.

The front door opened, and Todd appeared. Mary slipped her hand into Jim's, and he squeezed, giving her an encouraging smile. Reverend Beecham cleared his throat to begin, and Mary's heart dipped.

Then a murmur swept the people behind her, and Mary looked around to see Ellen walking forward. She was dressed for the occasion and carrying her bouquet!

Mary's heart filled with joy and pride as she watched her beautiful daughter, as regal as her grandmother, take her place beside Dani Lee and Alanna. Her gaze met Mary's, and she gave the barest of smiles.

Joyously, Mary blinked back tears and looked at Jim.

"You can get to it now, Reverend," he said.

The reverend wasted no time. He rushed through the words, conscious that he had a church service to get to, and in short order he pronounced Jim and Mary husband and wife. Jim kissed her much more fully than she would have liked right there in front of her daughters and her mother. Blushing and out of breath, she turned to face the cheers and laughter.

Her eyes met those of each one of her daughters.

Alanna's lively eyes said, "I love you, Mom, and this is great!"

Dani Lee's calm eyes said, "I love you, Mom, congratulations."

And Ellen's misty eyes said, "I love you, I'm sorry, and this is embarrassing!"

Mary looked over the small gathering and found her mother, who raised an eyebrow, standing back several feet from everyone and waiting expectantly. Drawing back, Mary threw the bouquet directly at her, and Ellen Louise Minnett caught it neatly.

Then again, oblivious to those around them, to the two cars that had stopped in the street and the six neighbors who had come out of their houses, Mary and Jim came together in each other's arms.

Jim whispered, "I love you, Mary."

"And I love you, Jim," she answered.

And then she kissed him, right there in front of her daughters, with all the passion in her heart.

Epilogue

A year later, the photo album Jim had sent to Mary with their names embossed on it was filled.

One of the first photos was of all of them after the wedding, there on Ellen's front lawn. "I could just die!" Ellen had said. Then there was a photo of Mary beside the San Antonio highway sign. A bigger copy of that one hung on their bedroom wall. Then there was a photo of Mary and Jim holding their new grandson, Toddy, Jr., and another of Jim diapering Toddy. "Can we tie him down?" Jim had said.

Another photo, from the past spring, was of her on a mule going down the rim of the Grand Canyon, and another was of Jim speaking with an old man who still trapped in the high mountains north of Santa Fe. Still another showed Jim signing an autograph for a plump redheaded woman who was a regular listener to his radio program, and one was of him holding up a copy of his contract to do the show for two more years.

Then there was that photo of both of them in front of a little doughnut shop in Texas that had topless waitresses, evidence to Mary's mind that they were truly seeing a varied America. After one look at the waitress in that doughnut shop, she'd gotten up and left. Jim had remained inside for five more minutes. "Had to get the doughnuts," he'd said.

One of the photos toward the back of the book was of Mary's mother and Judge Hubert at their wedding. On the last page were one of Dani Lee on Wall Street, a

family portrait of Ellen, Todd and Toddy and a snapshot of Alanna studying, which no one believed.

Pressed in tissue paper and taped inside the back of the
album was a red rose from the bouquet Jim had sent her
that day. Sometimes Mary sniffed it and found it retained, still, its sweet scent. In those moments she would
recall how she'd felt when he'd sent them. Like a woman
in love.

*   *   *   *   *

My information for writing about mothers and daughters comes from myself as a female, daughter and mother, and from dear friends who have daughters. My husband, Jim, and I have only one child—a son—who views me only as Mom, and, of course, never as a female. Jim and I had our son after we'd been married nearly nine years. Though a child was something of a surprise, he certainly was very much a *wanted* one. I'd prayed for four years for a child—morning and evening I'd begged, cajoled, nagged and pleaded with God for a child.

What a shock when he came. My husband and I had built a life of just ourselves, doing what we wanted, when we wanted. Sleeping late on Saturdays, lazing around watching Charlie Chan movies on Sunday afternoons. Suddenly we had to get up every few hours all night long (and, contrary to popular belief, some children never outgrow this—they simply learn to leave their grouchy parents alone), and we had to spend a great deal of our time rocking, soothing, washing spit and diapering a bottom. One day I tossed up my hands and spent the entire day in the rocker that had once belonged to my grandfather, doing nothing other than holding and feeding my son. I remember clearly that I wore a ratty white T-shirt, a pair of shorts, and hadn't combed my hair. I sat and rocked my baby, and I treasure that memory.

I read all the childcare books and watched every baby expert who came on *Donahue*. I wanted to do it all right and nearly had a nervous breakdown trying. Our son was about three years old when I realized there simply is no "perfect" way to bring up a child. Now that he's fifteen, I'm beginning to believe that all we as parents can do is give direction and love, love, love, and let the child bring up himself.

And I often wonder, who brings up whom? Before I had my son, I was decidedly impatient and, I admit, very spoiled. Then along came a little person who needed me to care for him and teach him about life and love. And in the process of trying to do that, I was the one to learn about life and love.

Neighborly Affair

CAROLE HALSTON

A Note from Carole Halston

I grew up a south Louisiana native in a rural community twelve miles from the small town of Ponchatoula, where I attended high school. As a child, the big event of the week for me was the trip to town on Saturday. For a quarter my brother Shelby and I could watch a feature Western like *The Durango Kid* (my favorite), Looney Tunes cartoons and a segment of an adventure series.

Another highlight of our summers was the much-anticipated arrival of the bookmobile. Shelby and I would meet this mobile library up the road at the Stickers' house. We'd be pulling a wagon loaded with all the books we'd read over the past two weeks. We would drop off that load of dreams and then replace it with a new supply of written adventure and entertainment.

When I was twelve, my family acquired a television set—an Emerson—and a whole new door to adventure was opened up. It was the height of luxury to sit in our very own living room and watch *Sugarfoot* and *Cheyenne*. Before that, such rare pleasures could only be enjoyed in the living rooms of a few of our more fortunate relatives and neighbors. Today's deluxe screens and crystal-clear color images can't compare with those first glimpses at boxed wonder.

I loved school, and did well enough to win a full academic scholarship to Southeastern Louisiana College in Hammond. And it's a good thing I did. Although by today's standards my school expenses were minimal, I couldn't have afforded to attend college without the financial help. Choosing a major was easy. I just followed my natural love of reading and writing, which led straight to English.

After graduation, a teaching assistantship at the University of Georgia in Athens financed two more years of study. Once I earned my master's in English, I returned to Louisiana to teach. It was there that, through a colleague who was a sailing enthusiast, I met Monty, my Yankee husband for the past twenty-two years. Back then, Monty was a bearded "young salt" living aboard a sailboat that he'd sailed down the Mississippi River. En route to the Virgin Islands to work in the charter-boat trade, he breathed life into my own latent urge to travel and experience romance and adventure outside the pages of a book.

Although I'd been slated to go to Auburn University the next fall to pursue studies toward a Ph.D., I went off to St. Thomas instead and worked a slew of odd jobs—front-desk clerk, shop saleslady, bar cashier. Six months later—with a tropical tan and notoriety for having been fired from every job I'd taken—I returned to the States to live on Merritt Island near Cape Kennedy. There I worked as a cocktail waitress, serving drinks to TV newsmen covering the space launches.

Back in Louisiana after a year's hodgepodge working holiday away from academic life, I was about to get back on track when Monty showed up. He was on his way north to spend the fall and winter in New England and was looking for a travel companion. The temptation was more than I could resist. We got married, regarding it as a temporary measure for as long as the adventure lasted. (It still is.) Our wedding reception was a shrimp boil with long-necked Dixie beer. We spent our first year of marriage working at a ski lodge in Vermont. For the next ten years, we lived aboard boats and performed a variety of jobs.

Eventually we settled down. Now we live in a house near Lake Pontchartrain in close proximity to New Orleans. Monty is a boat captain offshore. And here I am—full-time romance writer, part-time potter. Still without my Ph.D. and still without regrets over that road not taken.

Carole Halston

Chapter One

Catherine didn't really mind keeping her Saturday appointment with Billy Wheeler's father. He commuted to New Orleans and didn't get home until six o'clock on weekdays. Then the poor man had to fix supper for himself and his three children. A month ago Billy's mom had packed her bag and left, which was, of course, the reason Billy had suddenly become a problem child and was disrupting Catherine's first-grade class.

He was a cute, bright little tyke. His third-grade sister was just as cute, just as bright, and reportedly just as unhappy since the desertion of the mother. The other sibling was preschool age. Catherine would never understand how a mother could just walk away from her children like that.

Here was another instance—all too common—where children were innocent victims. It wasn't as ugly a case as some. At least there wasn't physical abuse. Another little boy in Catherine's class, Ted Anderson, would have been far better off to have had both his parents abandon him. His father was a drunk and his mother a battered woman, no longer able to cope. Ted had come to school with bruises and lacerations from being brutally beaten. With the backing of her principal, Catherine had filed reports to the proper agencies and been instrumental in having him removed from his home, if it could be called that, and placed in foster care.

Teaching wasn't an eight-to-four job on Monday through Friday. It involved more than lesson plans. By this time of the year, late March, Catherine was emotionally attached to all her small students, including Billy Wheeler. So for Billy's sake, she cheerfully got dressed in her schoolteacher apparel on a Saturday morning to drive to school and confer with his dad, lend what moral support she could and offer advice.

There was no unwillingness on her part, but there was some reluctance. It had nothing to do with the fact, not publicized, that Catherine didn't intend to return to the school next fall, after ten years on the faculty. Billy's dad was a man; therein lay her problem.

During the past few months—since Christmas, to be exact—Catherine's thoughts tended to go off on embarrassing tangents in the presence of men. It wasn't exactly absentmindedness, but a disconcerting ability to follow two tracks of thought, one that made her blush.

The trouble had started with her having decided, during the Christmas holidays, that she didn't have to be some man's wife in order to be a mother. Something must have clicked in her brain, affecting the way she looked at men, regardless of who they were. It didn't matter whether she knew them well, knew them slightly, or encountered them as total strangers.

She saw them in their reproductive capacity. That was the most delicate way of stating it. She sized up every man who crossed her path as though she were conducting a survey of the male population in search of a man to father the child she longed to have. Her cheeks stayed flushed with shamed inner amusement.

Goodness knows there was no lust involved. Would that there were. Then she might be able to take the natural, easy route to motherhood, plain old sex. Instead Catherine was resigned to dealing with endless bureaucratic red tape and making whatever financial sacrifice was necessary to either have a child by means of artificial insemination or else adopt one. She fully expected that before she ever held her own baby in her arms, she would empathize even more than she already did with those desperate women who stole infants in shopping malls.

Until she was ready to proceed with her plan to be a single mother, Catherine saw no point in even gathering information. Conscience demanded that she devote all her usual attention and energies to her teaching. And fortunately she was able to do that.

Today she had no fears about letting Billy down. Even if she did ogle his dad, as she was determined *not* to do, the caring, knowledgeable educator in her would still function.

Now you behave, Catherine Baker. Keep in mind who you are and who that poor man is, she admonished herself as she exited from the back door of her house.

Bob Wheeler had poured out his troubles to her on the telephone, and she was genuinely sympathetic, but she knew she was overdoing the "poor man" sentiment in the interest of self-control.

Her car was parked under a carport that had apparently been built as an afterthought, after the driveway had been located along the property line. Enough distance separated the carport from the back door that Catherine could get soaking wet in a downpour without an umbrella. Until recently, she hadn't been particularly conscious of the inconvenience or particularly aware that her next-door neighbor's driveway ran parallel to hers on the edge of his property line.

Until recently, her next-door neighbor hadn't been Graham Macaulay. He drove his big super-cab pickup truck as if it were a sports car. The sight of it parked abreast of her car reminded Catherine that she'd been awakened late last night by the sound of him roaring into his driveway and racing the engine before he killed it. There had been the slam of doors, plural, and the high-pitched voice and laughter of a woman.

Catherine smiled, remembering the fuzzy thought that had surfaced before she'd gone back to sleep: *the darned man could supply a sperm bank*. What a quirk of fate for Graham Maculay to take up residence next door now, of all times.

The grown man was as *physical* as the strapping high school boy had been. He hadn't married and was apparently still going strong, living up to his considerable potential as a womanizer that he'd shown in adolescence. He even turned the charm on her when he passed the time of day with Catherine in neighborly chats.

All that wasted virility was a shame, she reflected, picking her way along the stepping stones that led to her driveway. He could father dozens of cute little auburn-haired, blue-eyed babies for childless women such as herself to mother. Catherine's smile became wistful as she imagined a big hospital nursery filled with infant replicas of Graham.

Then the door opened and he walked out with a shapely brunette about his and Catherine's age, early thirties. For a split second Catherine was annoyed at the intrusion. Then she blinked hard and snapped back to reality, murmuring, "Oh, dear. This is nice." Graham and his overnight guest had emerged from the back door of his house. They hadn't spotted Catherine yet. The reason they hadn't wasn't that they were too wrapped up in each other. Catherine wasn't an expert about such things, but she thought there might be trouble in paradise.

Graham gave the impression that he was hustling the brunette from the premises, and she appeared to be in a sulk. Catherine was tempted to turn around and pretend that she was returning from somewhere, not departing. But he raised his head, glanced over and saw her. It was too late. From the expression on his face, he was wishing that he'd waited another minute or two to leave; exactly what she was wishing herself.

To her surprise he looked embarrassed. Catherine would have expected him to take the situation in stride. Surely it wasn't a first for him to encounter a neighbor when he had a girlfriend in tow.

During the time that Catherine lived next door to him, she, no doubt, would soon become blasé about such scenes as this. With luck, that wouldn't be more than three or four months. She hadn't broadcast her intentions, but she would be putting her house on the market as soon as the school term was over.

By now she'd reached her driveway, and Graham and the brunette had reached his. There was no avoiding speaking.

"Good morning," she called over pleasantly.

"Hi, Catherine," he said, sounding faintly embarrassed. "You look as though you're off to school."

"I am off to school," she replied. "But don't let me confuse you. Today *is* Saturday."

"Saturday just means that I work for myself, instead of punching a clock," he declared.

The woman with him apparently sensed, as Catherine did, that his words carried a message for her. She spoke up in a pouting tone of voice, "All work and no play makes Graham a dull boy."

"Well, have a nice day, to coin an original phrase," Catherine put in quickly before he could reply. They could finish this discussion in private in just a few seconds, after she'd made her hasty departure.

"So long, Catherine." The embarrassed note in his deep, resonant voice was more pronounced.

Graham had found the scene damnably awkward. He liked Catherine Baker and wouldn't do anything intentionally to offend or embarrass her. If he'd had his way, Brenda—he couldn't even remember her last name—would have been long gone from his house by now.

In truth, he hadn't really wanted to bring her home with him last night. He'd gone to the yacht club at Cal Bordelon's invitation to have a few beers. Cal, Graham's long-time buddy and present employer, was divorced and on the make. He had started buying drinks for Brenda and two women friends of hers at the bar. Brenda was Cal's pick, but she had latched on to Graham.

When he'd gotten up to leave, she'd asked him for a ride, and then, in his truck, invited herself to spend the night with him, using more than words to state the invitation. She'd all but stripped him of his jeans on the short drive from the yacht club to his house.

Graham hadn't had any problem performing, last night or this morning. Not that much performance was required. He'd just provided a male body. More and more, that seemed to be the case. Maybe he was just burned out on sex.

This was definitely a one-night stand. He couldn't wait to be rid of Brenda. Her little-girl pouting had gotten old very quickly. Graham was making himself a promise, here and now, that he intended to keep: the next woman he slept with would be someone he wanted to wake up with. And taking her to bed had to be at least partly his idea. He wasn't going along with being hustled into bed like some stud.

"I guess we made her day," Brenda remarked as Catherine was backing out of her driveway.

"I doubt that." Graham had the passenger door of his truck open and stood waiting, trying to hide his impatience.

"She has that look of a schoolteacher. I'd have guessed she either taught school or was a librarian."

Graham didn't answer. He helped her climb up onto the high seat, keeping his thoughts to himself. Brenda wouldn't be flattered by them. He supposed Catherine did look like a schoolteacher, but he liked her looks better than Brenda's, and he also liked her personality better, based on a superficial acquaintance with both women.

The preference came as somewhat of a surprise to him. Even more surprising was his lack of any doubt that he'd have enjoyed Catherine's company last night more than Brenda's, and been glad to skip the sex. It hadn't crossed his mind before now that he might like to get to know Catherine better.

Slamming the truck door shut, he glanced out toward the street, where she was driving off in her staid sedan. He remembered her only vaguely from high school as a mousy girl who wore glasses. Now she wore contact lenses, and while she hadn't bloomed into a beauty, she was attractive, with dark brown hair, deep blue eyes and a pretty, fresh complexion.

Graham didn't see any reason why she shouldn't have gotten married. Out of curiosity, he'd pumped the real-estate agent who sold him his house. The woman knew the history of everyone in town. What he'd learned about Catherine made him respect and admire her. After high school, she'd gotten her teaching degree, taken a job in a local school and lived at home to share with her elderly father the responsibility of caring for a bedridden mother. By the time her mother passed away after years of being an invalid, her father's health was bad, and Catherine had taken care of him until he died a couple of years ago.

For all that background, Graham couldn't detect any hint of the martyr. She gave every indication of being happy and purposeful. He'd picked up on her wry sense of humor.

"I thought you were in a big hurry." Brenda had rolled down her window.

"I am," Graham said, coming back to the present and realizing that he was standing there gazing out at the street and thinking about Catherine. He walked around to the driver's side.

Among other things he meant to accomplish this weekend, was an essay for his English course. Graham was enrolled as an undergraduate at L.S.U.N.O., the New Orleans' branch of Louisiana State University. After a hitch in the navy and a succession of different jobs around the globe, he was finally getting around to earning a college degree. It would take him a while since he also held down a full-time job and had just bought a house he planned to renovate and resell for a profit.

Maybe he'd write the English paper this afternoon, he reflected, swinging up into the driver's seat. Then if he saw Catherine around, he could ask her to proofread it for him. It would be a good excuse for a casual get-together with her.

Graham grinned, starting up the engine. How many years had it been since he'd needed to invent an excuse to propose getting together with a woman?

"Well, you certainly look in a better mood all of a sudden," Brenda commented.

Following her conference with Bob Wheeler, Catherine braved the Saturday crowd at a discount store. She needed some toiletry items and she also wanted to buy bedding plants from the store's garden shop. Though not an avid gardener, Catherine liked flowers blooming in a yard. Her favorite annuals were begonias and impatiens, and she loaded up a shopping cart.

The realization that she was planting them partly to spruce up her yard and make it more attractive for prospective buyers that summer brought a pang of sadness. Her house had been her parents' house and her home for her entire life. Selling it wouldn't be easy for her, she knew, but she wasn't going to dwell on that in advance. Catherine lived one day at a time, and today was much too pretty a day for moping.

Graham's pickup was parked in his driveway when she turned into hers, but there was no sign of him. Evidently he was indoors. Catherine remembered his remark that morning about working for himself on Saturdays. He'd mentioned that he meant to fix up the house. It was rundown. Old Mrs. Jenkins had lived there as far back as Catherine's memory went. Seven or eight years ago she'd died, and the house had been rented out. It had been put up for sale around Christmas—an eventful season this year in more ways than one. The house had sold. Graham had turned out to be the new owner and had moved in with no more furniture than he could carry in the back of his pickup truck.

For selfish reasons Catherine hoped that he would get around to painting the outside by summer to add to the well-kept look of the neighborhood. On that thought she went inside to have a quick lunch and change clothes.

A half hour later she was transporting her bedding plants and gardening tools to the front yard when the mailman delivered her mail. She walked immediately toward her mailbox at the edge of the street, noticing that a small red car was driving past very slowly. Behind the wheel was a pretty young blond woman. She put on the brakes and leaned her head out the window to call out to Catherine, "Excuse me. But do you happen to know where Graham Macaulay lives?"

"I certainly do," Catherine replied with a smile, mentally shaking her head. Now she knew why he had been in such a rush to take the brunette home. He was expecting more female company. "He lives right next door there." She pointed.

"Thanks a lot."

Catherine got her mail out of the box, looked through it, and opened up the most interesting envelope. It was a card with a note from a friend. She read and ripped open a couple of bills next. The rest was junk mail that she could look at later and throw away. Her curiosity satisfied, she walked toward her porch to deposit the stack.

In the meantime, Graham's visitor had parked in his driveway, gotten out and gone up on the front porch. He had come out, evidently in response to her knock, and the two of them stood there in conversation. At the risk of being nosy, Catherine couldn't resist a second glance. He didn't appear to be overjoyed. Perhaps the blonde had gotten lost on the way to his house, and was late arriving.

It was none of Catherine's business. She just wished that they'd go inside and leave her to do her gardening in peace. The sense of being conspicuously present out in her own yard was somewhat irritating. Catherine was darned well not going inside herself so as not to seem a snoop.

Fuming a little, she got to work. It was a lovely spring day. The sun felt warm, and yet the air was crisp and fragrant. Catherine concentrated on enjoying being out of doors, but the sound of voices drifted over from Graham's porch, spoiling her pleasure. His was a low rumble, and hers was cajoling and insistent. Were they going to spend the rest of the day out there? she wondered.

Exasperated, she glanced over, and he took that same moment to look over at her. Catherine could tell somehow that he hadn't just noticed her. He lifted his hand in greeting, and she nodded and waved.

Okay, I give up, she thought, dropping the small trowel that she'd been using to loosen the soil along her bricked walkway. But apparently she'd held out long enough because Graham was finally taking the blonde inside. Oddly enough, he left the front door wide open, but Catherine didn't puzzle over the fact.

She breathed in a deep breath and relaxed.

Minutes later she was down on her haunches with the trowel, happily planting a border of spry little waxy-leaved begonias, when she heard voices again on Graham's porch. *Good heavens, that was quick,* she reflected, and was immediately appalled at herself; if she wasn't careful, she would turn into a nosy neighbor and start peeking out from behind the curtains.

Fortunately her back was to his porch. Unfortunately she wasn't deaf and would have had to press her hands over her ears not to follow the conversation. The visit was apparently over. Graham was escorting the young blonde out to her car and seeing her off. She wasn't going voluntarily, it seemed, and sounded no happier than the brunette had been that morning. Catherine couldn't help hearing words, not just tones of voice.

"You're a real brute, Graham. I drove all the way across the causeway to look you up."

"I wish you'd called first. I could have saved you the drive."

"It's such a pretty day. I just never figured you for a guy with his nose to the grindstone. Life's too short not to stop and smell the roses."

Please. Take your debate somewhere else and let me plant my begonias, Catherine pleaded silently.

"Well, I'll see you in class Monday night," Graham said. "So long, Tina."

Mercifully the rest of the parting exchange was drowned out by the car engine. The disappointed Tina drove away. Catherine blew out a breath and sat back to take a rest.

"My face is a little red."

Graham's rueful remark was her first clue that he hadn't headed back into his house, as she'd assumed he would do. Instead he had walked over into her yard.

"If it's any consolation, my ears are burning," Catherine replied. "I didn't know whether I should clear my throat or cough or stand up and announce that I'm not hearing-impaired. Nor am I doing research on a book about the life of a bachelor," she added.

He sat down on her steps, so blatantly masculine in his dark T-shirt and jeans that she didn't dare gaze at him for fear of refuting her last disclaimer. She busied herself by extracting a bedding plant from a nearby plastic tray.

"I apologize," he said.

"There's no need for you to apologize," Catherine stated. "You haven't done anything to apologize for. At least not to me."

"I was polite to Tina. She was the blonde who was just here," he explained unnecessarily.

She gave him an astonished look and saw that the expression on his face matched his tone, sheepish and defensive. "I heard you call her by name. Whether or not you were polite to her is none of my affair. No pun intended. If you acted like a 'brute' with her, as I heard her accuse you, that's between you and her."

"I wouldn't want you to think that I was a brute to women. Because I'm not. But neither am I under any obligation to drop what I'm doing and spend the day with a woman who's picked me out as her male companion for the day. I never thought I'd say this, but women's liberation has gone a little too far for my liking," Graham declared.

Catherine was sitting back on her haunches, holding her trowel in slack fingers. "I believe you when you say that you were polite to Tina," she assured him.

He went on with the same note of frustration. "She's in one of my classes—I believe I've mentioned that I'm finally getting around to going to college."

She nodded and quickly put in, "You said you'd decided you want to be an architect."

If Graham had gotten her message—*Shall we talk about something else besides your women problems?*—he ignored it. "That's right. Well, Tina is in my English class that meets on Monday nights. We've talked and once or twice gone to a fast-food place after class with a group, but I've never asked the woman out. She shows up here uninvited and makes no bones about the fact that she wants to—" He broke off, finishing his sentence with an apologetic gesture.

What woman wouldn't *want to* with him? He oozed sex appeal, sitting there with his broad shoulders slumped and his knees straddled open. Catherine wasn't even immune to it herself, especially not now when she was so tuned in to male sexuality. Her sympathies were all for Tina.

"You must have encouraged her. As pretty as she is, and with her figure, I doubt she has to chase after men who don't show any interest in her."

He tugged at his T-shirt, which molded his muscular chest, and shifted his position on the step, looking disarmingly guilty, like a small boy in one of Catherine's first-grade classes who'd been called on the carpet for tormenting a little girl.

"Okay, so I probably did send out signals," he admitted honestly. "I'm a friendly kind of guy."

"You were born with a natural talent for flirting, and you've developed it," she stated. "If you don't want women to come on to you, don't send out signals." *End of subject.* Catherine resumed her gardening, which meant scooting a few feet closer to him. She was working her way toward the steps.

"I guess I'll have to learn to be standoffish. When you've played the mating game as long as I have, it gets to be second nature. Even when you've lost interest in the game, so to speak."

"I'm afraid I don't relate to your problem, since I don't play the mating game. But maybe you can find a support group," Catherine suggested flippantly.

"There probably is one." The amusement in his voice took her by surprise, and she glanced up to see a smile tugging at his lips. "Support groups are the in thing these days, aren't they? You know, I really like your sense of humor," he added before she could answer.

"It comes in handy," Catherine said, disconcerted by her rush of pleasure. She felt sorry for the Tinas in the world, who couldn't possibly resist his charm when he smiled crookedly like that and looked at them with a glint of warm interest in his blue eyes.

"If it's not being too personal, why don't you play the mating game?" he asked.

"Why?" She was taken aback by the question. "I tend not to play games that I'm not good at. I never showed much aptitude."

Curiosity was plain on his face as he waited, encouraging her with his silence to elaborate. It was a brotherly kind of curiosity, not especially flattering. Catherine knew what he was wondering: had she had any experience with sex or was she still a virgin? She decided to eliminate the mystery without mincing words. Some part of her had the urge to shock him with frankness.

"To answer the question you're too polite to ask, no, I'm not a virgin," she said. "I was 'deflowered' in college and didn't enjoy the experience at all. The earth definitely didn't move. Since then I've given sex a couple of other tries and haven't been in the least tempted to become promiscuous. I've concluded that I'm probably your classic case of a frigid woman." Catherine held up her hand as he started to speak. "Don't look so sympathetic. Contrary to popular belief, there is happiness without sex. Let me add that I'm aware of the male credo that a frigid woman is a sensuous woman who hasn't had the benefit of a good lover."

"I happen to believe that."

"Of course you do. And I'm sure you have better credentials than the majority of men do."

He smiled and shook his head. "I never dreamed, when I walked over here, that I'd end up having this conversation with you."

"Neither did I," Catherine admitted, smiling back at him. "But maybe we've cleared the air. I won't be keeping track of your women visitors, Graham. The more the merrier, as far as I'm concerned."

"There aren't going to be a lot of women visitors for you to keep track of," he assured her.

Catherine tried not to look dubious, refraining from pointing out the he'd had two in the space of four hours. "I'd like to ask a nosy question," she confessed.

"Ask away."

"Don't you worry at all about the health dangers of being sexually active?"

"Sure. But I'm very careful to protect myself."

"I'm glad to hear that."

"I've always been careful," he volunteered. "I started supporting the condom industry when I was a teenager to make sure I didn't knock some girl up. There aren't any little redheaded kids running around who can call me daddy."

Catherine opened her mouth to say "That's good," but the hypocritical words stuck in her throat. She was remembering her vision that morning of a hospital nursery full of his babies. The words in her heart were, "What a shame."

"Did I say something that touched a sensitive spot?" Graham inquired.

"No." Inherently honest, Catherine immediately retracted the lie. "Well, yes, you did touch off a memory. But it's gone now." She smiled at him, and the concern in his expression eased.

"Well, as pleasant as this is, sitting here and visiting, I'd better get back to work," he said, making no move to rise. "I'm tearing out cheap paneling on the walls and ceiling tile off the ceilings. Once I accomplish that, I'll be able to put up drywall.''

"It sounds like you're planning to do a first-class job," she commented.

"I am. It's going to be a nice house when I get finished with it." He got to his feet. "The reason I came over was to ask a favor of you. I wonder if you'd proofread an English paper for me."

"I'd be happy to."

"Will you be home this evening? I could bring it over. Then we could go out and get something to eat."

"No, I'm sorry. I won't be home. I'm going out for dinner." Catherine had a date with Dale Stanton, a man she'd been dating on a regular basis for the past six months. "I could proofread the paper for you right now," she offered.

"I don't have it written yet. I was going to write it later this afternoon, but now I'll just wait until tonight." He looked and sounded disappointed.

"Then I can read it tomorrow sometime."

"How about in the morning? You can come over and have coffee. I'd like to show you my house, anyway, so that you can appreciate the 'before' and 'after' condition."

Catherine took a moment before answering. She was taken aback that he'd followed up so quickly with a second spur-of-the-moment invitation. "What time?" she asked.

"Whatever time you get up."

"Say, nine o'clock?"

"Nine o'clock. I'll pick up some doughnuts. What's your favorite kind?"

Catherine told him, searching for a tactful way to state what was on her mind. "If you have a late night, I can always take a rain check. Just leave me a note on my back door. Or on yours."

He grinned ruefully, immediately comprehending. "I'm not planning to go out tonight. If I do, I'll be coming home alone."

"In case you have a change of heart, feel free."

"It won't even be a temptation. I wouldn't miss out on our coffee date."

Catherine raised her eyebrows to convey her skepticism and also to conceal her pleasure, the normal pleasure that any woman would feel.

"I mean that sincerely," Graham said. "It's not a line of bull. I thoroughly enjoy talking to you and would like to know you better. As a person," he added.

"Not in the biblical sense. I understand," she said dryly. "And I'm truly flattered by your interest."

"Come on, Catherine. Give me the benefit of the doubt. You may find that there's more than meets the eye."

It wasn't easy to let the last earnest remark slip by, but any retort would be too revealing. Unless she were a masochist, why would Catherine want to look beneath the surface and discover that he was not only virile and good-looking and personable, but also had high ideals and steady qualities that would make him a good husband for some lucky woman?

"We were in classes together in school," she reminded him. "I know that you're bright. And I don't doubt that you have some depth to your character. To return the compliment, I enjoy talking to you, Graham. Honestly. Don't forget—jelly doughnuts."

"I won't forget."

His blue eyes were much too keen and thoughtful for her liking as he studied her face for a brief moment. Then he raised his hand in a casual salute and turned to stride away across her yard, whistling a cheery tune.

Catherine gazed after him appreciatively. He was well worth watching from the rear view, too. The dark cotton knit of his T-shirt pulled across his wide shoulders and tautly muscled back as he raised a hand to scratch his head in an absent motion. His walk had just a hint of male swagger.

She sighed, thinking of how thrilled a sixteen-year-old Catherine would have been if Graham Macaulay had asked to come over to her house and have her read his English paper and afterward take her out for a hamburger. Why not admit it? The thirty-two-year-old Catherine was more than a little thrilled and sorry that she'd had to say no.

Her regret had nothing to do with the fact that her date for the evening, Dale Stanton, a widower in his late forties with grown children, had had a vasectomy. An evening with Graham would be equally nonproductive in fulfilling Catherine's all-important need to be a mother. He wasn't the least interested in having an affair with her. He simply wanted them to be friendly neighbors.

In the unlikely event that Catherine could entice him into bed with her, nothing would come of it. He would practice safe sex and take no chances with getting her pregnant.

Chapter Two

Graham was listening for Catherine's knock at his back door. It came on the dot of nine o'clock. He'd been expecting her to be punctual. Though he hadn't given the matter any thought, the way she knocked fit his expectations, too. The sound wasn't loud and assertive, neither was it timid nor reluctant.

It was exactly right for her, a brisk, efficient tapping that said "Here I am. This was your idea that we both agreed upon." His gut response was to pat himself on the back for having come up with a damned good idea.

With a smile on his face, Graham opened the door to welcome her.

"Good morning, Catherine. You look fresh as a daisy this morning," he declared. His English professor would call that a trite expression, Graham knew. But a compliment was definitely in order, and *fresh* was a keynote of Catherine's appearance as she stood on his doorstep, dressed in dark blue cotton slacks and a pink blouse. He gave her an approving once-over from head to toe.

"Good morning, Graham. You look well rested, too," she said, giving him a polite inspection. Her voice had the humorous undertone that he found so appealing, and her expression mirrored the friendly message that her lie detector was fully operative.

"Come in," he urged, and she stepped inside. Graham got a waft of a delicate flowery scent. He inhaled deeper and commented appreciatively, "I like your perfume."

"It's not perfume. It's cologne and dusting powder," she corrected him. "I had a shower this morning, and I may have been a little too liberal. I hope you don't need a gas mask."

"No, it's not that kind of scent," Graham assured her. "It's very nice and suits you."

"Your after-shave lotion has a nice spicy scent and suits you, too." She returned his compliment and glanced around the kitchen, her gaze seeking out his coffee-maker.

"It works. I haven't lured you over here under false pretenses," he said, meaning to put her more at ease. But his tone came out slightly too genial.

"That thought would never occur to me," she replied.

Graham was taken aback by a tinge of something besides irony in her voice. Was it regret?

"Never let down your guard with a guy like me who likes women," he advised only half jokingly. "Even when we talk a good story of reform, we might be wolves in sheep's clothing."

Catherine arched her eyebrows and gave him one of her frank, skeptical looks. He could feel the beginning of a relieved, sheepish grin, but then her gaze traveled over him in a brief but thorough examination that started at his hair, still damp from his shower, and ended at his sock-clad feet. He wiggled his toes in reaction, as all one hundred and ninety pounds of his big, six-foot frame stirred pleasantly to life underneath his clean T-shirt and clean pair of jeans. And underneath his clean pair of jockey shorts, too.

"I think I'm safe enough," she said with that same touch of wistfulness.

"If you are, it's only because I respect you and would rather be friends with you than try to get you into bed."

She smiled and retorted lightly, "Who said chivalry is dead? Shall we take the guided tour while the coffee is brewing?"

"First, I want to finish this conversation, if you don't mind. Chivalry has nothing to do with what I just said. I was being honest and aboveboard. Why shouldn't I find you physically attractive?" He gave her an approving head-to-toe inspection, similar to the one she'd just given him, to prove his point. Pretty pink color bloomed in her cheeks.

"No reason other than the fact that I'm not at all sexy. Put me beside that brunette you brought home with you Friday night, or next to Tina, and no man is even going to notice that I'm there. Now could we just drop the whole subject?" she requested. "I didn't come over here to celebrate Be Kind to Catherine Day."

"Damn it! I'm not being kind!" Graham objected. "And you're selling yourself short. Yesterday morning I had the chance to compare your looks with Brenda's— she's the brunette. I like yours better. Admittedly it took me a little by surprise," he added truthfully.

His words were more than a surprise to her. There was sheer amazement on her face. And an odd thoughtfulness. "You may need glasses," she murmured.

"No, my vision is good. I can see even at a distance that your hair has a healthy sheen. It isn't frizzed and gummed with hair-styling gels or spray." Graham reached and picked up a lock of her dark brown hair, becomingly and simply styled in a kind of in-between length, not short and not down to her shoulders. "It *feels* nice, too," he observed. "The way hair should feel."

"I'm glad it passes the touch test. Which goes to prove that an old-fashioned brushing is still a good aid to beauty." Catherine moved her head, pulling the glossy strands free of his fingers. Graham lowered his hand, aware that his work-toughened skin tingled.

"I could go on and tell you other things I like about your appearance," he said.

"Then, please, don't let me stop you," she urged facetiously. "I've always wanted to be more conceited."

He smiled and shook his head. "There's no danger of that if you make it this hard for a man to pay you a few sincere compliments. I wasn't bowled over by the sight of you, but I thought you were attractive when I saw you the first time after I'd bought this house. On closer inspection, I find that you have pretty hair, pretty eyes and pretty skin. Or I should say complexion," he amended. Before he could stop himself, he dropped his gaze down to the vee of her blouse.

"You're making me blush. I haven't felt this self-conscious in years," Catherine confessed with embarrassment.

"You *are* blushing." Graham touched a fingertip to her flushed cheek. It was not only warm, but soft and fine-textured. He took his hand away reluctantly.

"It's a shame you couldn't have said all those nice things when we were both sixteen years old," she reflected. "You might have made a huge difference in my life. I had the same hair, eyes and skin. The same figure, too, which was the reason you never noticed my hair, eyes and skin."

"Haven't you put on a few pounds since high school?"

"A few," she conceded. "I'm not quite as thin."

"You've added an extra inch or two here and there where it counts," Graham stated objectively, with a downward glance at her small breasts and slim hips.

"Do you mind not taking my measurements with your eyes?" Catherine demanded, folding her arms across her chest.

"Sorry, I didn't mean to make you uncomfortable," he apologized, a wronged note in his voice. It wasn't as though he'd undressed her with his eyes, a skill that wasn't easy for him not to put into practice. "I'll just get the coffee started."

"Good. I'm dying for a cup of coffee and have my mouth all set for one of those doughnuts in that box."

"I'm sorry. I'm not a very good host, keeping you standing here." Graham apologized again as he moved over to the coffeemaker. He sounded like he felt, dissatisfied and annoyed with himself, but also a little annoyed at her.

"It's partly my fault. I don't play the female role very well, and that puts you on the defensive. You can't help flirting. It's second nature to you. Compliments roll off your tongue. I'm sure you are sincere, in your own way," she added hastily as Graham turned around, frowning with his irritation. "And despite the way I act, I'm thrilled deep down. Honestly."

"Compliments don't roll off my tongue," he denied. "I'm no flowery-talking Casanova."

"I didn't mean to sound critical. I was simply being analytical." She sighed. "Maybe I should just take my doughnut home with me in a napkin."

Graham ignored that suggestion. "Let's set matters straight between us and go from there. I like you a lot and want us to be friends. You can relax and treat me like a brother because I won't make any advances. You have my solemn promise."

"Why should I hold you to a promise like that?" she inquired. "I'm not a nun, for heaven's sake. I haven't taken any vows of purity. Make all the advances you want. I might enjoy them. If I didn't, I could fend you off."

He stared at her, baffled and irritated, and yet amused in spite of himself. "I should have known better than to try to predict your reactions," he remarked, smiling and shaking his head. "There's nothing simple about the way your mind works."

"If it's any consolation, I find my own reactions around you contradictory," Catherine confessed, smiling back at him. "My mind and body are in conflict."

"Well, go with whichever one says that I'm a decent guy who wants to be a friend and good neighbor."

"They both say that." She sniffed. "Doesn't that coffee smell wonderful?"

"It smells like coffee, all right," Graham agreed, giving up on reaching an understanding with her at the outset. He wasn't making any headway. Her answers were truthful—he didn't doubt that—but they were like riddles, hiding as much as they revealed. For all her directness and forthright nature, she was a puzzle to him.

He wanted to keep turning up clues and figure her out, and the interest wasn't purely intellectual. Graham didn't want just a mental exchange. He was starting to find her more and more physically appealing, somewhat to his consternation.

"I'll show you the rest of the house," he said. "But maybe we'll skip my bedroom, unless you'd like to reconsider and put me on my honor not to make a pass."

"I doubt that you'll be struck by any powerful carnal urges," Catherine replied. "But if it will relieve the pressure on you, well, then, consider yourself honor bound to be a perfect gentleman."

"The pressure?" Graham queried.

She sighed. "Do I have to explain? You obviously feel some burden of responsibility on behalf of the male gender."

"Are you saying that my male ego won't allow me to take any woman into my bedroom and not try to get her into my bed?" he demanded. "If you are, you're wrong. Yesterday Tina wouldn't leave until I'd shown her the inside of my house. Good Lord! You didn't think—" Graham broke off in astonishment. "We weren't in here more than fifteen minutes!"

"I didn't time you, but it didn't seem very long," Catherine admitted, her cheeks pink. "The fact that you apparently weren't interested in taking Tina to bed only proves my point that I didn't make very well. She was, I gather, willing."

"That's stating it mildly," he put in. "I think I see your point now. Tina was too easy, whereas you're more of a challenge?"

Catherine made a little pained face, nodding. "You may be bored with homecoming-queen types and ready to show some attention to a wallflower, for a change of pace."

"You may have been a wallflower once, but the label doesn't fit now," Graham scoffed.

"Once a wallflower, always a wallflower," she said lightly, but in seriousness. "And it's too late to be charitable and give me a romantic thrill, as you could have once. I'm past the stage of believing in romance or needing it. Nor do I have any problems with sexual frustration. Yesterday when I told you that I was frigid, I wasn't challenging your male prowess." Her expression was odd as she added, almost to herself, "Or at least, not consciously."

"I don't like your whole theory about my behavior one damn bit," Graham protested. "But it does make some sense. I've begun to wonder lately if my sex drive wasn't slacking off. The interest in women just hasn't been there."

"Now that we know what we're dealing with, we can go from here," she said.

"Yes, but where? Nothing's changed."

"For starters, I'm hoping we'll go into the next room. At the risk of seeming greedy, I'd like to get the house tour behind us and sit down to a cup of coffee and a doughnut. Then we can deal with the future on a full stomach."

Graham smiled and gestured toward the door. "After you. I'll make it a short tour. You won't have to stumble over furniture."

Aside from the kitchen, the only two other rooms with furniture were the living room and his bedroom, and they were furnished with the bare minimum.

He wasn't as brief as he had intended to be. Encouraged by her interest, he found himself going into enthusiastic detail about his renovation plans. By the time they'd reached his bedroom, he was speeding up the tour.

"And this is my bedroom," he said, walking past the door. "It gets recarpeted, like the other two bedrooms, and also gets a fresh coat of paint."

Catherine stopped and looked inside. "It's going to be a really lovely house," she remarked in a strangely regretful tone of voice.

"You said that you were only in this house once or twice during all the years that you lived next door," Graham reminded, thinking that it was unlikely that she could be suffering an attack of nostalgia.

"Yes, and both times I was only in the kitchen."

"Speaking of the kitchen, are you ready for that cup of coffee?" he asked.

"Definitely."

Despite the alacrity of her answer, she gazed a second longer at his bed and then collected herself. Turning to see that he was watching her, she smiled and looked flustered.

"When you're having intercourse with a woman, are you at all conscious of your capability to become a father?" she asked.

Graham had been prepared for her to make a dry, humorous remark to cover her embarrassment and was completely taken aback. "I think more in terms of making love, not 'having intercourse,'" he replied. "And I try not to let any thoughts of becoming a father intrude."

She nodded and had nothing more to say on the subject. He let the small incident pass, finding it rather mystifying. From her abstracted air, he wondered if she still weren't dwelling on it in the back of her mind as they returned to the kitchen and had coffee and doughnuts.

Over second cups of coffee, she read his English essay. The topic was Ambition. Graham had taken the approach that with each stage of life, from childhood to retirement, human ambitions change. He'd used himself as a case history so that the essay sketched in his background and laid out his own past, present and projected future goals.

"This is well written," Catherine said when she'd come to the end. "I see a few spelling and punctuation errors, but that's all." She used the pencil that he handed her to circle several words and insert commas.

"What about the content?"

"It's good. So is the title, 'Behind Schedule.' Do you have any regrets that you've taken longer than most men to sow your wild oats?"

Graham was surprised that his immediate response wasn't a denial. Until now he hadn't thought he had any regrets.

"I don't regret that I saw a lot of the world and had my share of adventures. But I guess it does bother me a little that I'll be pushing forty before I can take on the responsibility of a family," he reflected.

Catherine didn't question his reasoning. It disturbed him that he was disappointed when she didn't. She asked him what parts of the world he had seen during his hitch in the U.S. Navy. He told her and answered more questions about his travels after his discharge and his work experiences.

She gave him her rapt attention, and Graham found himself drawing word pictures for her and recounting anecdotes and mishaps that would amuse her. He talked on at greater length than he might have otherwise, enjoying the play of expressions on her face and finding her prettier by the minute.

"Enough about me," he declared finally. "Tell me about yourself."

"There's nothing for me to tell that you'd want to hear," she replied. "I went to college at S.L.U. in Hammond, got my teaching degree, lived at home with my parents and taught first grade."

"I understand that your mother was an invalid and you and your father took care of her." Graham drew upon the information he'd gotten secondhand and encouraged her to tell him more about what her life had been like.

Catherine wasn't reticent, once he made it clear he was interested. She answered his questions, as he'd answered hers. Occasionally some sad emotion crept into her account, but none of it was for herself. Her memories were good memories, overall. She saw herself as basically fortunate, she explained, because she'd had loving parents and a secure home.

By that definition, he was a lot more fortunate, since both his parents were still alive and well. His father's job with a big corporation had taken them to another state some years ago. Both his sisters were now grown and married and residing elsewhere, too. Graham had all the benefits of close family ties and the luxury of living his life exactly as he pleased.

"I have to admire you," he stated simply. "You deserve to be very happy."

"I am fairly happy. And I hope to be happier in the next year or two." She glanced at her watch. "Goodness, I didn't mean to stay so long. You have work to do."

"It'll get done." Graham reached over and caught her left hand before she could rise. The coffeepot was long since empty, but he wasn't ready for her to leave. He studied her bare ring finger. "What's going to happen to make you happier in a year or two? Are you planning to marry the older guy who picked you up in the big Lincoln last night?"

"Dale would be crushed to hear you describe him as an 'older guy.' He considers himself quite youthful." Catherine's fondly amused voice seemed to be an affirmative answer to Graham's question.

"He looks about fifty. That's almost old enough to be your father."

"He's forty-nine. I didn't see you outside when Dale came to get me," she commented.

Graham grinned. "I heard him pull into your driveway and checked him out, like a nosy neighbor." He was still holding her hand and gave it a gentle squeeze. It felt soft and feminine, and yet capable. "So, are you serious about him?"

"No, I'm not," Catherine said. "He's a very nice, dull man, and we have a lot in common. He was a classroom teacher and is a principal now. His wife died almost a year ago. He has grown children and several grandchildren. It's only a matter of time before he would probably ask me to marry him, if I were to stay here in Mandeville and kept seeing him regularly."

"If you were to *stay* here," Graham repeated, frowning. "You aren't thinking of moving away?"

"It's confidential, but, yes, I am."

He didn't try to hide his dismay at the unexpected news. "But I was looking forward to having you as my next-door neighbor. Where are you going?"

"Biloxi, Mississippi. You remember Lauren Piper. You dated her in high school," she reminded. "We've been friends since kindergarten. She has a small day-care center in Biloxi and wants me to go into partnership with her. I've decided to do that. As soon as school is over, I'll be putting my house up for sale."

"When did you decide this?" he asked, sounding as disgruntled as he felt. "Have you thought the matter through carefully?"

"Very carefully. Lauren and I discussed the pros and cons thoroughly at Christmas. I'm really excited about making the change," she said, not quite meeting his eyes.

Graham wouldn't let her hand go when she tried to pull it free. "So you really have your heart set on relocating?"

"Yes."

He sighed. "Well, I hope the move works out well for you."

"In the long run, it will. Once all the upheaval is over. I'm prepared for a transition period that has its problems and disappointments."

"At this end, you can count on me for a helping hand."

His casually sincere words brought a blush to her cheeks. "Beware of making offers like that," she warned, again not quite meeting his eyes. Looking flustered, she extricated her hand and stood up. "This was very pleasant. Thanks for the coffee and doughnuts."

Graham had stood up, too. He had to move fast to reach the back door first. It stood open. Fresh air, fragrant with the scent of lush spring vegetation, came through the screen door. Outside, the sun shone brightly. In the back of his mind, he had been aware that it was a beautiful day, but suddenly the knowledge was urgent information that he needed to act upon.

"What's your hurry?" he asked. "Do you have a lunch date with—what was his name?"

"Dale Stanton. No, I don't have a date with him. But I do have plans for this afternoon."

"Could I talk you into canceling them and spending the afternoon with me? I'm out of the mood for working indoors. A friend of mine who's out of town has a sailboat that I'm welcome to use. He left the key with me." Graham was thinking on his feet, immediately enthusiastic about his impromptu outing. "We could ice down some beer and soft drinks in a cooler, pick up sandwiches for lunch, and go out sailing on the lake."

The town of Mandeville was nestled along the northern shoreline of Lake Pontchartrain, a large brackish body of water twenty-four miles wide across the middle and longer than it was wide.

Catherine was shaking her head. "No, I'm sorry, but I really can't. I'm one of the hostesses for a baby-shower luncheon for a coworker who's on maternity leave this semester."

"How long will it last?" He wasn't ready to give up on the whole rest of the day.

"Probably until about three-thirty. Then I'm going to a matinee movie with another woman coworker who will be at the shower."

"Can you cancel out on that?"

She shook her head again, without even stopping to consider. "No, I wouldn't feel right knowing that she was left at loose ends. She doesn't have much of a social life, and this is an occasion for her. After the movie, we're going to a seafood restaurant for supper."

Graham was not only disappointed, but his pride was ruffled. She might have acted a little more sorry to have to turn him down for what didn't exactly sound like an exciting afternoon and evening.

"Are you usually this booked up in advance on a weekend?" he asked.

"I don't turn down opportunities to get together with friends on the chance that something better will turn up. It's been my experience that I would end up sitting at home." She put him in his place pleasantly and with dignity.

"How about next Saturday night? Are you free?"

She paused before answering, and she wasn't searching her memory, he could tell.

"Yes."

"Would you pencil me in?" Graham couldn't remember the last time there had been any suspense when he asked a woman for a date, but there was suspense now as she gazed at him questioningly. "I like to be spontaneous," he said, "but what I have in mind, generally, is dinner and spending the evening together, doing whatever we decide on."

"You don't have to be more specific." She smiled. "I'll write you in for Saturday night, in ink."

Graham's truck was parked in his driveway and lights were on in his house when Catherine got home shortly before nine. Had he taken some other woman out sailing that afternoon? she wondered. Or had he worked on his house?

Probably the former. Catherine sighed and went inside, knowing that it had been all for the best that she'd had plans today she couldn't break. She'd never set foot on a sailboat. In fact, her experience with any kind of boating was more limited than her experience with sex, which meant she was doubly unqualified to be Graham's female crew member. She could just picture herself, green with seasickness, clinging to her seat and wearing her modest one-piece swimsuit.

Any interest he'd had in her would have quickly died if she'd gone on the sailing trip. Of course, there was something to be said for getting the inevitable over with and done. Catherine fully expected that the date next Saturday night would be the first and last. Familiarity might not breed contempt, but it would breed boredom.

Any appeal she held for Graham was nothing more than novelty and would quickly fade. He would discover that she was just as unexciting as she appeared on the surface, just as unalluring.

Once he took her to bed—if things even progressed that far—that would definitely be the end. Making love to her one time would be enough. He would either give up on her as a lost cause or, if he were more successful than her few previous lovers had been, pat himself on the back and be content not to repeat the experience. Either way, how could Catherine possibly benefit?

If she learned the meaning of ecstasy from Graham, she still wouldn't have satisfied her deepest need: the need to nurture and love.

That afternoon at the baby shower, Catherine had been flooded by tender, wistful emotions when the gifts were opened and passed around. Along with the other women, she'd exclaimed over the tiny infant garments and nursery paraphernalia and felt her maternal longings well up stronger and sharper than ever before, to the extent of being painful.

Later, in the darkened movie theater, she'd been unable to concentrate on the plot of the movie, which was R-rated with bedroom scenes that left little to the imagination. Watching the hotly passionate scenes hadn't aroused her, but she'd found them disturbing and was left feeling restless and tense.

All in all, it hadn't been an enjoyable afternoon or evening. Although she didn't blame Graham, she held him responsible. He'd pushed himself to the forefront of her consciousness, however temporarily, and upset her emotional calm.

Normally she would have been ready to return to her house after an eventful day such as she'd had, change into her nightgown and robe, and contentedly read or watch TV until she was ready to go to bed. But tonight she was keyed up. The comfortable, perfunctory element was missing.

Catherine was mildly annoyed at her own awakened sensibilities. Undressing, she felt the shape of the buttons on her blouse, the difference between the nubby texture of her skirt and the filminess of her panty hose. When she'd stripped down to bare skin, she actually caught herself glancing in the mirror. Briskly she picked up her nightgown and pulled it over her head. The silky nylon slithered coolly over her nakedness.

She would have taken it off and put on a shabby old cotton nightgown, just on principle, except that Catherine owned only pretty nightgowns with matching robes. She indulged herself when it came to shopping for nightclothes and lingerie.

This particular set was a rich deep blue with red embroidery. Catherine buttoned the robe, thrust her feet into satin mules that were the same cranberry red, and was headed to the bathroom to cleanse her face and brush her teeth when she heard a knock at her back door.

Coming to a dead stop, she thought, *now who can that be?* and immediately knew that it had to be Graham. Her sense of anticlimax was suddenly gone. She wasn't going to have to wait until Saturday night, after all. *Okay, Catherine, let's act out this little drama and get back to life as normal,* she told herself, and went to let him in.

Sure enough, he stood on her back steps, big and tall and ruggedly good-looking, holding what appeared to be his English paper. Before Catherine had gotten the door wide open, he began to explain his presence, his deep, masculine voice as disarmingly sheepish as his smile.

"I rewrote this and wondered if I could impose on you to look through it again—" He broke off in surprise, taking in her attire. "I didn't think that it was too late to come over, but I see that you're ready for bed."

His tone, like his face, expressed apology and disappointment, but he obviously wasn't bowled over by the sight of her. Not that Catherine had expected him to be. She would probably be quite modestly clothed in his eyes if she were wearing only her nightgown, which was pretty and feminine, but hardly sexy.

"It isn't too late. I wasn't going to bed this early."

"Good. Because I'll be turning the paper in at class tomorrow night."

Catherine showed him into the small, cozy family room located off the kitchen. Among the comfortable furnishings grouped around the television set was a man-size recliner and an easy chair with a hassock. Graham glanced at them and took a seat on the sofa.

"You don't look wind-burned," she remarked, still standing. "Didn't you go sailing?"

"No, thanks to you I had a productive day working inside my house, and didn't talk to a soul." He grinned and waggled the paper in his hand. "When I heard you drive in, I hurried up and finished my excuse for a visit and rushed over."

"You don't need an excuse to visit other than the need to hear another human voice." Catherine sat down on the sofa at the opposite end and smiled self-consciously at his startled reaction to her open-ended invitation. His mouth had all but dropped open. "Come into my parlor, said the schoolmarm who lived next door to the handsome bachelor," she said with light self-mockery.

His recovery was quick. He smiled back at her and drawled, "Why, thank you, ma'am. You're more than cordial, but how about slipping into something less comfortable and sitting a little bit closer?''

"If I sit closer, I won't be any more relaxed wearing different clothes," she told him honestly.

"In that case, don't change—unless, of course, you want me to be more relaxed."

Catherine reached out her hand for the paper. "Maybe if I keep my distance, we'll both forget that I'm hardly decent in this skimpy, see-through negligee."

Graham leaned and gave her the paper, then moved over onto the cushion next to hers. "A robe doesn't have to be see-through to be sexy," he pointed out. "There's always the question of what's underneath it. A man's imagination is his primary sex organ."

"Underneath my robe I'm wearing a nightgown that is just as big a tease. Underneath it is a figure that leaves some leeway for an active male imagination." Catherine unfolded the pages of his paper with a businesslike crackle. Involuntarily she stiffened as he lifted his arm and stretched it along the back of the sofa.

"Easy," Graham chided. "I didn't come over here tonight with any thoughts of seducing you. Honest. I just want company."

She sighed, refolded the paper and put it aside. "What you mean is, without any thoughts of seducing me tonight. You do foresee getting me into bed eventually and freeing me of my hang-ups about sex. Isn't that right?"

Graham squirmed with his discomfort, but he met her gaze directly. "My feelings toward you aren't brotherly," he admitted. "But I don't *foresee* anything where you're concerned. Probably that's part of your attraction for me. I'm not confident I can get you into bed, and if I do, all I'm certain about is that it will be a unique experience."

"It's a novelty for you to have to seduce a woman."

"Yes, it is." He grinned. "And definitely a first to sit and discuss the matter like this and analyze my motives."

Catherine forced a wan smile. "Another old wives' tale proves to be true. It pays for a woman to play hard to get."

"You aren't playing hard to get. I can tell the difference."

"No, I haven't been using any feminine wiles, but mainly because I don't know how. If I thought that I could lure you into having an affair, I would. For my own reasons," she added in good conscience. "Let me take away the suspense for you, and maybe we can both save ourselves some disappointment. You *can* get me into bed. I don't have to be seduced, but will go willingly. The experience won't be unique, I can assure you, unless it's uniquely forgettable for you."

"And if I'm going to persist, you would just as soon go ahead and be done with it tonight," Graham stated with a perceptiveness that Catherine found unsettling.

She nodded.

"Taking away the element of suspense hasn't done the trick," he mused. "If anything, I'm even less interested in a platonic relationship now than when I arrived tonight. Since you don't want this thing hanging over your head, why don't we engage in a little foreplay here on the sofa and see what happens?"

"You're amused by this whole situation," Catherine accused.

"*Intrigued* is more the word. You just try to relax and cooperate a little. This is standard stuff. I'll put my arm around you. You scoot over closer. That's nice." He coached her playfully and smiled into her face.

It *was* nice, sitting with his arm around her, so nice that she was compelled to remark, "Tomorrow is a school day. We don't have all night, so you're working against a time limitation."

"I'm mainly working against a strong mental resistance," he said. "You say that you're willing, but you're really not."

"A minute ago you were keen on seducing me," Catherine pointed out.

"There's no hurry for me. I was only accommodating you. Let's talk for a while, and then I'll go. What movie did you see?" He sat a little farther away from her, letting his hand drop to her shoulder. While he waited for her to answer, he fingered the material of her robe, but there was no provocative intent, just a casual intimacy.

She drew in a breath, overwhelmed for just a moment by a sense of failure that drowned her immediate relief. "I'm not in a very talkative mood, I'm afraid. And I'm going to renege on Saturday night."

"I won't let you," Graham objected. He clasped her shoulder, the contact warm and strong. "Look, I won't make a pest of myself and show up on your doorstep every night, if that's what's worrying you. I'll call first from now on, and all you have to say is that you don't want to be bothered."

"You don't understand all that is involved. I'm on the verge of making a big transition in my life."

"I know you are. You told me this morning, remember?" His hand had moved to her neck, and he was massaging her tense muscles. "I'm not putting any pressure on you tonight or any other time to go to bed with me."

"But you came over here tonight prepared, didn't you?"

"Prepared?" His momentary puzzlement cleared away as he comprehended what she was asking. "Yes, I guess I am 'prepared' in that sense. I got in the habit years ago of carrying a condom in my wallet." He hesitated, mulling over a thought that gave him pause. Catherine's heart started to beat fast. "If it will help you relax, I'll take it out. That way you can rest assured that nothing can happen. Except at my house, of course," he added with a grin. "So beware of invitations, 'Come over to my house.'"

"I'll be on my guard." Catherine didn't dare look him in the eyes.

"How about a kiss to seal our good faith contract?" Graham leaned closer, resting his free hand along her cheek and turning her face toward him. He rubbed her bottom lip gently with his thumb, apparently waiting for her permission.

"Why not?" she said, focusing on his mouth. "A kiss will probably do away with any need for a good faith contract. I don't kiss very well. You might say that I never advanced beyond Kissing 101." His lips were twitching at the corners. She glanced up to see that his eyes were alight with amusement.

"It could be that you never stopped talking long enough to develop any technique," he suggested.

"No, my problem has always been that I can't seem to lose sight of the fact that I'm pressing my lips against another pair of lips and, when the kiss gets to the heavy breathing stage, touching my tongue to another person's tongue. No matter how hard I try, I don't get all inflamed and excited. Though I have faked it," she confessed.

"Well, we aren't going to get to the heavy breathing stage since this isn't foreplay for making love, just

friendly, get-acquainted kissing. Don't try to feel anything, and don't try to block out the basic reality of what
we're doing. For all I care, you can keep your eyes open."

Graham was bringing his mouth to hers as he talked.
The last few words were spoken almost against her lips.
The distraction in his voice and the warmth of his breath
on her face caused a stir of anxious anticipation.

"No, I'll close my eyes . . ."

"Suit yourself," he said, "but I would like for you to
put your lips together."

"Oh. Okay."

He kissed her, the contact light and brief. Then he
kissed her several more times, exactly the same way.

"That's nice," Catherine murmured.

"I'm enjoying it," he replied with his mouth nuzzling
hers. She could feel his smile as well as hear it in his voice.
"In fact, I can't remember the last time I found kissing
this enjoyable." He nipped her bottom lip with his teeth
and then rubbed the spot with his tongue. "Which goes
to prove that the pleasure doesn't have to be mutual."

The tingle in her lip was spreading through her body
and her heartbeat had picked up. She felt compelled to
make some reply and was embarrassed by the hint of
breathlessness in her voice. "I wasn't being polite or
damning with faint praise. This is very . . . nice."

He was tracing the outer shape of her lips with the tip
of his tongue. Once he had finished, he filled in the out-
line. Awash with pleasure, Catherine remarked, "That
was more than nice. It was somewhat erotic."

"It was for me," he said, drawing in a deep breath.
"You taste even better than I imagined." He covered her
lips with his, blotting the moisture he had put there. Then
he kissed her seekingly, as if searching out sweetness. Her
mouth softened and clung. When he pulled away ever so

gently without kissing her any harder or with more passion, Catherine had to contend with a sharp dissatisfaction.

She sat for a moment with her eyes closed. Opening them, she looked into Graham's face. His expression was so unexpectedly tender that Catherine stared, feeling utterly defenseless. He smiled, and her emotions became that much more confused.

"So much for the possibility that a kiss would do away with any physical attraction," he said. "Do you still want me to lighten my wallet, the way I promised?"

She sat back, her inner turmoil taking on a whole new character. "You said that you weren't in a hurry."

"What I meant was, I can be patient."

"Has that changed?"

"No. If anything, I can be more patient now." He sat back, too, seeming to mull over his own quietly reflective answer.

Why can you be more patient? Catherine wanted to ask him. Before she could, she blurted out truthfully, "I did feel freer because I believed that you didn't intend to make love to me tonight."

Graham reached over and laid his hand on her tightly clasped hands. He squeezed them gently and said, "Then that's the end of the discussion until you open it up again."

Chapter Three

Graham stayed another hour. Catherine read his English paper and approved the revision. Then they turned on the TV and watched a cable news channel. It was surprisingly companionable, though not totally relaxed.

She couldn't forget that she was wearing her nightgown and robe with nothing else underneath. Graham didn't help her to forget. His appreciative glances weren't directed just at her face, and he paid her casual compliments several times, right in the middle of conversation.

"That dark blue color is very becoming," was one compliment, and another was "You have such fresh, pretty skin."

Catherine had never felt any more attractive in the presence of a man, which was all the more amazing considering that Graham was a better-looking man by far than any she'd ever dated.

When he got up to leave, she walked with him to the back door. He bent and kissed her on the lips. His mouth felt familiar on hers during the sweet, all-too-brief meeting. Catherine had to suppress an urge to put her arms around his neck and make it last longer.

She leaned against the door after she'd closed it behind him, then strained her ears, listening. He was whistling a tune as he walked off, a love song.

The melodic sound touched a chord inside her and unleashed regret and longing. How she wished . . .

Catherine sighed and didn't complete the thought. She couldn't afford to fill her head with romantic hopes that couldn't possibly come true. It was better to wrestle with her conscience.

What you're planning to do isn't honest, Catherine.
I know. But I can live with my guilt.

Graham would never know about her duplicity, whether or not it was successful. More than likely it wouldn't be, and Catherine would end up with nothing but memories of him as her lover, her womb still empty.

From past experience those memories wouldn't make her feel good about herself. Despite her pleasure in his kisses, she had no confidence that she would be a satisfactory sex partner for him. Catherine still believed that one time in bed with her would be the beginning and the ending of an affair.

If she didn't believe that so strongly—

Once again, she cut off a futile line of thought. But clear-sightedness couldn't prevent her from a certain amount of wistfulness. It hadn't gone away the next morning when she got up at her usual time, had her breakfast while she scanned the *Times Picayune,* the New Orleans newspaper, and then got dressed.

Catherine gazed into her closet, and her wistfulness was tinged with depression as she noted the wide range of colors in her wardrobe. There were pinks and oranges and reds, as well as sedate browns and navy blue and forest green. But it was a subdued kaleidoscope, just like all the styles were tasteful and conservative.

Catherine dressed well, but without any flair. She was guided by practical instincts, never buying on impulse. Her wardrobe reflected her personality. She wasn't a vivacious person who thrived on attention. Though she no longer shrank from being noticed, as she had when she was a self-conscious teenager, she was perfectly happy to walk into a room and not have heads turn or eyes widen. It suited her temperament to blend in.

She couldn't blame her profession. There were as many styles of dress among schoolteachers as there were different personality types. Catherine had coworkers who were fashion plates, others who wore such loud colors and tacky clothes that she cringed. Her own style of dress reflected *her*.

You have many good qualities, but you're dull, Catherine.

Thanks for telling me something new.

Impatient with herself for her inner dissatisfaction, Catherine picked out one of her most understated outfits, a taupe skirt and a cream-colored blouse. She knew, of course, what had brought on the bout of self-criticism. The woman in her wished for a miracle. But she wasn't going to be a late bloomer at the age of thirty-two and knock Graham Macaulay off his feet.

Catherine would live out her days being herself, and she wasn't a bad person to be. She was a darned good teacher, a loyal friend, a patriotic citizen. In the past she'd been a loving, devoted daughter. If things had worked out differently and she'd ever fallen in love, she didn't doubt that she would have made some nice, dull man a perfectly good wife.

She wasn't lacking in the kind of self-esteem that really mattered. Otherwise she wouldn't be as certain as she was that she would make a better-than-average mother. Fortunately for her, glamour wasn't a prerequisite for motherhood or any of the essential roles in life.

On her arrival at school, Catherine soon put aside all thoughts about herself. Her duties as a teacher and her responsibilities to her small students required her full concentration. She knew by the end of first period that she had a new problem to deal with, or rather a new development in an existing problem.

Something had obviously happened over the weekend to upset Ted Anderson, the little boy who'd been placed in a foster home during the school year, partly as a result of her determined efforts to rescue him from his abusive father. Ted acted withdrawn and wouldn't participate in class activities. Catherine kept him in at recess and with gentle questioning got the story out of him.

He had been playing in his new neighborhood on Saturday afternoon when his father had driven up and gotten him aside to make drunken promises that Ted would be returned to his parents soon. The man had also voiced intentions to do harm to both Catherine and her principal, Eleanor Akers, the two he most blamed for losing his son. He'd forbade Ted to tell anyone about the unauthorized visit, threatening him with beatings. The poor child was anxious on his behalf and on Catherine's.

She did her best to soothe his fears and reassure him that he would continue to live in a safe environment. At lunchtime she had a talk with Eleanor and apprised her of the situation. Eleanor's main concern, like Catherine's, was Ted's welfare. Both women were of the opinion that they probably weren't in any real danger. They shared the view that Ted's father, like most bullies, was a coward at heart. Still, Eleanor intended to notify the police as well as the appropriate child protection agency and social worker assigned to Ted's case.

"It won't hurt for us to be a little more vigilant," she said. "You, especially, since you live alone, Catherine. You might want to ask your neighbors to be on the lookout for anyone suspicious lurking around your house."

"That wouldn't be a bad idea," Catherine replied, but didn't commit herself any further to following the ad-

vice. Just three days ago if she'd been having this same
discussion, she would have reacted differently to solicit-
ing neighborly watchfulness. The last thing she wanted
to encourage now was well-intentioned spying.

It gave her a secure feeling to know that Graham lived
next door. There was no doubt in her mind that he would
react quickly to an S.O.S. from her.

Graham knocked off work early, having gotten in his
full day as combination workman and foreman by getting on the job a half hour early and working through his
lunch hour. He and his crew were making good progress
on the major renovation of a large, lakefront house that
dated back to the era of steamboat transportation between Mandeville and New Orleans.

They were all dependable, skilled workmen and didn't
need Graham looking over their shoulders. His foreman
role was mainly seeing that materials were ordered and
reporting any problems to Cal Bordelon, the boss. Cal
had other jobs going and had turned this one over to
Graham almost entirely.

Graham thoroughly enjoyed his work. He had never
minded physical labor. He liked using his hands and getting exercise that wasn't part of a fitness regimen. Plus,
he was not only earning a livelihood, but was doing a
kind of paid apprenticeship, the way he saw it. Once he
had his architecture degree, he didn't intend just to park
himself behind a drawing table. Graham's goal was to be
an architect/builder, specializing in designing and building or renovating houses. He wasn't in the least interested in designing shopping malls or high-rise apartment
buildings.

His ambition was not to be rich, but to be able to afford a comfortable life-style for himself and a family.

Graham had always assumed that he would eventually marry and be a father. There had never seemed any hurry. It was only lately that he'd stopped to think that he *had* to wait. He *shouldn't* get serious about a woman now.

Possibly he was reaching that psychological state when he was tired of being a bachelor and ready to settle down into domesticity. If that were the case, he would have to content himself with a steady, companionable relationship. It was too soon to tell, but Graham wouldn't be surprised if a relationship of that nature with Catherine Baker turned out to be exactly what he needed for the next few months.

He'd thought about her often during the day. She was the reason he was taking off from work early. He hoped to squeeze in a visit with her before he had to head across the lake to his Monday-night class.

The local elementary school where she taught first grade wasn't much out of his way. On impulse Graham decided to drive past it. As he approached, driving slowly, a school bus loaded with youngsters pulled away. The school day had obviously ended for the children but, judging from the parking lot, the teachers hadn't left.

Graham spotted Catherine's car. What the hell, why not stop and see her? he asked himself, and made a hard right turn off the street. After maneuvering his big pickup into a parking space, he got out and strode for the front entrance. He had reached the door before it occurred to him that he was wearing his work clothes, which weren't filthy dirty but weren't clean and fresh, either.

His reception by half a dozen women milling around the school secretary's office put to rest any qualms about his appearance. Some of them, he surmised, were teachers. Graham introduced himself, explained that he was a friend of Catherine's, and got directions to her class-room.

On the way, Graham tried to remember his own first-grade classroom, but nothing in particular stuck out in his memory. It had been painted a pale neutral color, had had blackboards on two walls, wooden desks lined up in rows, a bulletin board that the teacher changed periodi-cally to depict a current holiday or season or theme. All in all, just your generic elementary school classroom.

The difference between it and Catherine's classroom was like night and day, he saw at once when he walked through the open door. There were no student desks. The seating was child-size chairs around low tables, and the walls were painted the vivid blue of a cloudless spring day. Graham postponed a detailed inspection of the cheery learning environment in favor of looking at Catherine. She was bent over, pushing a chair into place, and straightened up to acknowledge his presence, her cheeks becomingly pink. Obviously she'd been fore-warned, probably via an intercom, that he was en route.

"I drove past and saw your car," he explained, not too certain of his welcome. "I hope it was all right to drop in."

"Hello, Mr. Macaulay. How nice to see you," she greeted him pleasantly, glancing over at a small boy who was playing at a table sandbox.

Graham took the hint that the conversation shouldn't be too personal in the presence of her pint-size student. "Recently I've gotten more interested in our educational system in this parish," he stated in a pompous tone of voice. "I thought I'd like to see for myself how my tax dollars are being spent." He looked around, his hands on his hips, and eyed a carpeted area in one corner that had several small beanbag chairs in primary colors and shelves of children's books.

Catherine's lips twitched. "Your tax dollars don't go far enough, Mr. Macaulay. We teachers have to rely on fund-raising by our parent organizations to supplement the budget, and we also spend our own money to make our classrooms a place where children can enjoy learning." She nodded in the direction of the corner. "A reading center like this one makes reading recreational and fun."

"But what does it do for posture?" Graham inquired sternly, and was rewarded with her smile of amusement.

"I can tell that you're from the old school, Mr. Macaulay. Reading, writing and arithmetic in straight-backed chairs with desks lined up in rows."

"And science and history in the higher grades."

"We start with those subjects in kindergarten. This is a science project over here by the windows." She led the way to a long bench laden with individual pots of small plants. "My first-graders grew these from seeds and transplanted them."

"Was it an art project, too?" Each pot was decorated.

"Yes, it was. And also incorporated reading and writing skills. We read about gardening and wrote stories."

"You certainly seem to be a very creative teacher. My guess is that the children in your classes are in good hands." Graham had dropped his critic's pose and spoken sincerely.

"I do my very best. Teaching is such a worthwhile job." Looking pleased and slightly flustered under his admiring gaze, she glanced down at her watch and then over at the little boy. He was absorbed in his play at the low sandbox table, driving miniature automobiles up to the gas pumps of a toy service station. "Ted, it's time for you to catch your bus."

Her voice had a gentle note that caught Graham's attention, as did her sympathetic expression. He glanced more closely at the boy, who straightened with a show of reluctance. He was towheaded with a cowlick, a somber little tyke.

"Yes, ma'am," he said. "Bye, Miss Baker." Turning around, he started to trudge toward the door.

"Ted." Catherine stopped him and went over to kneel down and put her arms around him and give him a hug. "Everything is going to be all right. Your daddy isn't going to hurt you or Mrs. Akers or me. So don't worry."

Graham was watching the scene, thinking to himself that he hoped to be on the receiving end of some affectionate hugging himself. Hearing her words, he frowned.

"What was that business about the kid's father not hurting him or you?" he asked as soon as the boy had gone.

His frown deepened during her matter-of-fact explanation, which included some grim background information about Ted's family history.

"Poor little guy," Graham said, reacting with as much anger as compassion. "He's starting off with two counts against him, having a mean drunk for a father. I'd like to give that bastard a taste of his own medicine."

"I'm not a violent person, but I wouldn't stop you, not after the bruises I've seen on that little boy's body," Catherine replied. She had been moving about the room while she talked, tidying up.

"I have my class at N.O. tonight. I won't be back until nine-thirty, at the earliest." Graham was thinking aloud, his mind on her safety. "Is there a friend you could stay with during the time that I'm gone?"

"That won't be necessary. I'll just make sure my doors are locked. Eleanor was going to notify the police. She and I don't think that Ted's father has the guts to carry out his threats against us."

Graham persisted. "But you can't be sure of that. I'll be very uneasy leaving you alone. Humor me and spend a few hours with a friend. A woman friend," he added.

Catherine went over to straighten her desk. "I appreciate your concern, but I'm not going to let this man disrupt my life."

"Then I'll cut my class and stick around to keep an eye on you."

"Don't be silly!" she protested. "You'll do no such thing. You can't become my bodyguard. The Jacobs are always home across the street and so are the Culbertsons, next door. It's not as though I live in rural isolation."

Graham sighed, capitulating, but not happy about it. "I'll call during the break and make sure everything's okay. And check on you when I get home, for my own peace of mind."

"Why don't you plan to come over for a cup of decaf when you get home?"

"Sure thing." He accepted with alacrity, pleased at the invitation. "Right now a cold beer or a soft drink would taste good. Are you ready to leave, or is there a faculty meeting or something of that sort?" She had finished fussing with items on her desk and stood there, as if waiting for him to clear out.

"No, there's no faculty meeting on Monday. I can leave anytime."

"May I have the pleasure of walking with you to the parking lot then?" he inquired.

"I'll just get my purse." Appearing anything but delighted, she bent to open a drawer.

"Unless you're ashamed to be seen with me." Graham glanced down at himself to indicate that he was wearing his soiled work clothes.

"Just get ready to meet any of the women faculty that haven't left yet," she said, letting his remark pass without a denial. "I'm sure the news has spread like wildfire that you're on the premises."

"I have good manners," he replied mildly. "I promise not to embarrass you."

True to her prediction, they encountered at least a dozen females between her room and the parking lot. And it was evident to Graham that she was embarrassed to have to introduce him. He had never felt quite so tall and big and muscle-bound as he felt undergoing the polite, curious scrutiny of her fellow teachers while she managed not to look at him at all.

For the first time in his life, Graham experienced some pangs of male insecurity. Driving in tandem with her to their neighborhood, he tried to soothe his injured feelings with objective reasoning. Catherine would probably have acted the same way, introducing any visitor who was an eligible male. Her behavior didn't necessarily have anything to do with the fact that Graham was a blue-collar worker without a college degree.

There was one sure way to find out: ask her point-blank. She wouldn't lie to him. Graham could bank on her honesty, based on even his superficial acquaintance with her. All he needed was the courage to ask, courage that was surprisingly short in supply. Her answer mattered more than he would have expected. It mattered a lot.

He was parked and out of his pickup by the time she was pulling under her carport. He walked over and waited while she got out of her car, seeming to take a long time, long enough that Graham had to struggle against cowardly instincts that advised letting well enough alone for now. After he'd had a shower and changed into clean clothes, he would feel less vulnerable perhaps. And why pin her down anyway? If he forced the truth out of her, and it dealt a blow to his pride, what then?

Catherine smiled a bright forced smile as she finally joined him on her driveway. Graham didn't smile back.

"I warned you it would be like an obstacle course getting from my classroom to our cars," she said. She didn't quite meet Graham's eyes directly.

"If it hadn't been so uncomfortable for you, I wouldn't have minded," he replied.

"Tomorrow I'll get the third degree." She grimaced in distaste.

"What will you tell them about me?"

"The truth. That you're an old high school classmate and my next-door neighbor. With your permission I might lie and make up a story that you're engaged and soon to be married."

Graham ignored the request. He refused to make light of the situation. "Would it have been less embarrassing for you if I'd been wearing a suit and tie and didn't look like a common laborer?" he asked bluntly.

Catherine looked startled at the question and then concerned at what she evidently read in his face. "My embarrassment had nothing to do with your clothes, Graham." Her gaze traveled over him, measuring the breadth of his shoulders and taking in the rest of his brawny physique. "You would still be as—" Pink color stained her cheeks, and she started her sentence over

again, speaking briskly. "In a suit and tie, you would still
be as virile-looking as you are in work clothes. Surely I
don't have to tell you that."

Somehow Graham wasn't making any headway in
finding out exactly where he stood with her. "What does
my being virile-looking have to do with anything? I'm a
man. I'm supposed to look virile."

"There's a question of degree. Most men don't knock
women over with their sex appeal, like you do. You can't
help it," she assured him. "To make matters worse,
you're charming and have a deep, masculine voice. If you
were homelier and not so well built and had a speech im-
pediment, I wouldn't have been nearly so self-conscious
introducing you. Once a wallflower, always a wallflower, Graham."

"I'm afraid I don't buy that explanation," Graham
told her quietly. "There's more to it."

"Yes," she admitted, guilt written all over her face. "I
wish you weren't so perceptive. Everything I just said was
true, but it wasn't the whole truth. I was embarrassed by
my own thoughts when I was introducing you. I felt terribly transparent, as though it were all too obvious that
I'm perfectly willing to carry on an affair with you."

"Frankly I doubt that anyone was left with that impression," he said. His intuition told him that she still
wasn't being totally truthful. "Would you rather I didn't
visit you at school again?"

"Normally you don't get off work this early anyway,
do you?"

"No, not normally." Graham more than half wished
he hadn't taken off early today.

An older dilapidated car was passing slowly on the
street. He glanced at it, seeing that the driver was a man
who was looking straight at them.

"Anyone you know?" he asked, remembering the threat that had been made to do harm to her. Renewed concern for her safety took priority over his male uncertainties.

Catherine shook her head. "No one I recognize."

"Would you recognize the kid's father?"

"No, I've never seen him. I met Ted's mother once, and Ted resembles her."

"So the man could walk right up to you, and you wouldn't know who he was?"

"I'm sure some sixth sense would warn me. He's probably unshaven and shifty-eyed." Catherine shuddered with her disgust. "Besides, I doubt that he'll walk up and accost me openly. It's more in line with his character to make threatening phone calls or lie in wait behind a tree at night."

"Just because the man's a coward doesn't mean that he's not dangerous. I wish you'd take his threats more seriously," Graham urged worriedly.

"I'm not discounting the possibility that he could be dangerous," she assured him earnestly. "Once it gets dark, I'll probably be jumpy, especially knowing that you're not home. If anything at all should happen to alarm me, I won't investigate. I'll pick up the phone and call the police."

"You said your principal was going to alert the police," he reminded.

Catherine grimaced. "I meant to go by and talk to her before I left school. But then you showed up, and I got all flustered. She's probably still in her office. I'll call her as soon as I go inside." She smiled a pained smile. "I'm sure she's heard a full report on you and is dying of curiosity, too."

"Lock your doors and don't open them to any strangers." Graham lifted his hand in a farewell salute. He had reached his driveway when she spoke his name hesitantly. He turned and saw that she was standing in the same place, looking after him with an anxious expression.

"I really do apologize for not carrying the situation off any better this afternoon," she said.

"No harm done," he replied gruffly. "I'll call you from the campus and come over for that cup of coffee you offered when I get back from across the lake."

She smiled, visibly relieved, and made a beeline for her back door, a prim figure in her beige skirt and cream-colored blouse.

Graham watched her a moment, noting the twitch of her skirt. Then he turned and headed again toward his back door. Her apology had been sincere. He didn't doubt that. But the real source of her anxiety had been whether he was still coming over later on that night.

He'd never known a woman who was as baffling and elusive as she was, without even trying to be. She gave out such mixed signals, attracting him and pushing him away. On the one hand, she was possibly the most candid female he'd ever run across and yet possibly the most difficult to read.

Damn, he liked her, contradictions and all.

Chapter Four

"Yes, I guess you could describe Graham as a 'hunk,' Eleanor. There's a constant flow of women over at his house. He and I are just old high school classmates and next-door neighbors."

Catherine's phone had been ringing when she walked into her house. The caller was Eleanor Akers, who, sure enough, had heard the news of Graham's visit and wanted to know why Catherine hadn't brought him by her office to introduce him to her.

As soon as she could, Catherine directed the conversation to what she knew was Eleanor's real purpose in phoning.

"Did you report the business with Ted Anderson's father to the police?"

"Yes, I talked to the police chief himself, and he's assigning an officer to keep a surveillance on the Anderson man. Frankly, I wish Anderson would try something, the bum. I'd like to see him locked up in jail," Eleanor declared in a hard voice. "So, anyway, you can sleep easy tonight."

"I just hope poor little Ted doesn't have nightmares," Catherine said.

They discussed the steps that had been taken or set into motion to protect him from another similar incident. Before Eleanor hung up, she gave the conversation a personal turn again.

"I'm sick over losing you, Catherine. I'll swear you're lying if you quote me, but you're the best teacher on my faculty. I intend to wait until the last minute to hire a replacement for you, just on the chance that you might have a change of heart.''

Catherine was touched. ''Thank you, Eleanor. That's high praise, indeed, coming from you. I couldn't have asked for a better principal to work under or one who's a nicer human being. But it's time for a change.''

''I sincerely hope that it's a good change. The right change.''

''I hope so, too. And we'll keep in touch. Biloxi isn't the end of the world.''

After she'd hung up, Catherine stood a moment in the kitchen, where she'd answered the wall phone. She felt the way she had last night, arriving home after a full day—stirred up and dissatisfied.

Was she making the right change in her life? Suddenly she wasn't as certain as she needed to be.

I need to talk to Lauren and get everything back in perspective, she thought, going over to the kitchen table to sit down. Though the secrecy bothered Catherine, she hadn't confided her plans for becoming a single mother to any of her friends other than Lauren, perhaps fearing that they'd try to discourage her. Lauren admittedly had been a strong influence on her thinking, shedding pragmatic, if cynical light on the whole issue of single motherhood when the subject came up during one of their heart-to-heart talks this past Christmas.

Catherine had confessed what amounted to despair over her reduced odds for marrying and having a family. Missing out on being a wife didn't depress her nearly as much as resigning herself to remaining childless.

Lauren had posed the question, ''Why not be a single mother?'' and then begun to sell the more conventional Catherine on the idea. ''Married women who have children have more than a fifty-fifty chance of ending up single parents anyway," she'd argued. "I speak with the voice of experience." She herself was divorced and rearing two children with no financial or moral support from an ex-husband who had remarried and now had another family. He lived in California and didn't even send presents to his son and daughter from his first marriage.

"Skip the husband and save yourself the agony of divorce is one way of looking at it," Lauren had gone on to say, and then added with her caustic wit, "Of course, I have a jaundiced view on marriage, which was all I got out of the divorce settlement."

Catherine had played the devil's advocate, knowing that she hoped to lose the debate. "But the children of divorced mothers were at least conceived in love. They started out with two parents. They were the product of a relationship."

"A relationship that went sour and a love that, nine times out of ten, turned to contempt. In an ideal world, sure, a child *is* conceived in love and nurtured by a mother *and* a father who are committed to a marriage and to raising a family together. Unfortunately we live in a real world, not an ideal one. All too few children have happy, secure homes. That's a fact of life that you have to deal with every day as a teacher, Catherine."

"Yes. Of course, I do. But just because the majority of marriages don't work out, does that make it *right* for an unmarried woman to bring a child into the world to fulfill her needs? Isn't that selfish?" Catherine had asked, posing the troubled question to herself as well as Lauren.

"What better reason is there for a woman to get pregnant and have a child than because she really wants to be a mother?" Lauren had answered. "Women get pregnant accidentally and have their babies because abortion isn't an option for them. Woman have children hoping to hold their marriages together. Lots of women become mothers because it's the expected thing for them to do. Those are the wrong reasons, in my opinion. I was guilty of the first and second ones myself, as you know.''

They had talked over every angle, moral and practical, and the thrilled realization had grown inside Catherine: being a mother *was* in the realm of possibility for her. It wasn't a dream she had to forego because romance had passed her by.

Financially she was in a position to be a parent. She owned her house and her car and had no debt. For the past ten years she had been paying into the state teacher retirement fund. If she resigned from teaching, she could draw that money out in a lump sum and invest it. Plus she had a money-market savings account with a respectable balance.

"Sell your house and move here to Biloxi and go into partnership with me," Lauren had suggested. "We can expand my day-care center into a nursery school and enlarge my enrollment."

"And I could take care of my baby during the day while I'm at work," Catherine had put in, thrilled at her own words, my baby.

The two friends had looked at each other and then smiles had broken out. "I'm a genius!" Lauren had exclaimed. They'd both started talking excitedly at once, in agreement that Lauren's proposal, spoken off the top of her head, was indeed sheer genius.

It seemed mutually beneficial in every way. Lauren was strapped for the necessary funds to enlarge her day-care center. Catherine would have some money to invest. She also would bring her considerable teaching experience.

Lauren had her college degree in elementary education, too, but had only done student teaching. They would complement each other and work well together. Of that, neither had any doubts.

In making a career change, Catherine wouldn't be leaving the field she loved. She would still be using her training in early childhood learning and development. And the whole wonderful notion of being an unmarried mother seemed more feasible in a new locale among strangers. Yet she wouldn't have to lose touch with friends. Biloxi was only an hour and a half away from Mandeville and was an attractive location, situated right on the Gulf of Mexico.

Catherine had gone home after the Christmas visit, her mind more than half made up. By the end of January, she had decided definitely on the move and on becoming a single parent. Until now her only uncertainty about the latter decision was the means, whether she would have a baby or adopt an infant.

You aren't having doubts. You're just getting cold feet, Catherine.

Using a man to get pregnant is like stealing from him.

Nonsense. It's putting to good use what he discharges and wastes in the process of enjoying himself sexually. But maybe there's a more honest alternative here. Maybe Graham would agree to being a biological father, with no obligations.

Dream on, Catherine. He'd be shocked at the very notion. This is Mandeville, Louisiana, not Fantasyland, U.S.A. Here's some advice. If you should be lucky enough to get pregnant and have his baby, you would need to make very sure he never finds out. Or you just might have to share custody with him.

That's not such a horrible thought.

Catherine got up abruptly before her voice of logic could recover from the shock of that last admission from her conscientious but confused self.

She did have a case of cold feet. It was fine to theorize cold-bloodedly about using a man for stud service, but actually taking advantage of a totally unforeseen opportunity was a different matter. Her jitters weren't caused by doubts. They were caused by female insecurity. For proof all Catherine had to do was conjure up the imaginary hospital nursery with Graham's infant offspring. Her flood of tender maternal emotion washed away the uncertainty.

No harm would be done to Graham and a great deal of good could result for her. Resolute once again, Catherine rationalized her guilt.

Tonight would be the night, she decided. Her nerves wouldn't take stringing out the suspense. And biologically, this should be a fertile time for her. When Graham returned from his class that night and came over for coffee, somehow Catherine would lure him into bed with her.

To that end, she would be wise to capitalize upon his concern for her safety. That meant not disclosing the information that the police were watching the Anderson man. If Graham's fears were laid to rest before he left for his class, he might succumb to some better invitation than coffee with her. Catherine hadn't forgotten that Tina was in his English class.

Feeling fresh pangs of guilt along with renewed nervous jitters, Catherine plotted. The real test, if all else went well tonight, was whether she could lie convincingly and get him to have intercourse with her without using a condom.

It came as a relief to hear Graham's truck engine start up. He was leaving, thank heaven. Now her conscience couldn't get the best of her, and she couldn't pass along the gist of Eleanor's phone call, not until he phoned her during his break, as he'd promised. Catherine got through that hurdle, too.

"Nothing at all out of the ordinary has happened," she assured him. "I haven't had any kind of scare."

"You sound nervous," he commented.

"Do I? Well, I'm not," she denied. "I may be a little restless. I don't like being a prisoner in my own house."

"Don't get defensive," he chided gently. "It's all right to have some chinks in your armor."

"Okay, so I'm edgy," she conceded.

"Hold down the fort. I'll be there as soon as I can." But he seemed in no hurry to hang up. He chatted with her, his deep voice lowered confidentially and causing shivers of pleasure to run through her.

"This is long distance," Catherine reminded him.

"Did I interrupt you in the middle of a good TV program?" he asked, a smile in his tone.

She could visualize him so clearly standing at a pay phone, attracting glances from every female between the ages of eighteen and eighty who passed by. A smile curved her lips, and she suddenly felt lighthearted.

"Not exactly the *middle*. Actually it just started, and I'm really not expecting it to be that good."

"I get your point. A bad TV program is better than my conversation."

"Not at all. I was only concerned about your phone bill." She dropped the bantering tone. "You accomplished your purpose. I'm a hundred percent more relaxed. Thanks, Graham. You're an awfully nice man."

"And you're a smart woman, Catherine," he remarked, sounding exasperated. "But I'm beginning to wonder if you know anything at all about men. I'm not Sir Galahad. Now I had better hang up. Someone is waiting to use this pay phone."

Catherine was taken aback. After he'd broken the connection, she sat and gazed at the receiver for several seconds before she hung up. Why had he seemed almost annoyed? She sat with the TV set playing and a magazine in her lap. No sooner had she picked up the remote control to turn the volume back on than the phone rang again.

It was a wrong number, the caller obviously a drunken, uneducated man. "Is this Clara?" he kept asking insistently, and became surly when Catherine told him several times that there was no one of that name at this number. Finally she hung up on him.

He immediately called back, furious. Catherine hung up on him again in the middle of his profane threats to come in person and beat up Clara and everyone else in the house. When the phone rang again in less than a minute, she picked up the receiver to verify that the drunk was on the line. If he was, her next move would be to unplug the cord.

"I know the address," he snarled. "It's right here in the phone book." He read out Catherine's address, slurring the street name and numbers.

"Who are you?" she asked, a chill crawling down her spine.

"That's okay who I am. Just let me talk to that bitch, Clara."

"There isn't anyone here named Clara." Catherine enunciated each word in her sternest schoolteacher voice.

"As soon as I hang up, I'm calling the police and reporting you."

She hung up and waited, but the phone was silent. Was the man on his way to her house? she wondered, shivering with her uneasiness. Her name was listed in the phone book as C. Baker. Perhaps there was a Clara Baker who lived in Mandeville.

Another explanation was that Ted Anderson's father might have gotten her first name wrong. The drunk's voice fit her conception of him as crude and ignorant and mean. A policeman was supposedly assigned to him, but what if he slipped out a back door? Just because he was uneducated, that didn't rule out his being crafty.

Catherine went to double-check that the doors were securely locked. When she returned to the den, she left the volume of the TV off so that she would hear any sound. Time dragged. Her anxiousness had eased by the time she finally heard Graham's pickup come roaring into his driveway, but she was still relieved that he was back.

He came right over. At the sound of his knock barely a minute later, Catherine tensed with another kind of anxiousness. *This is it, Catherine,* she told herself on the way to her back door.

"Come on in. I've never been any gladder to hear a truck engine," she declared lightly. "How was your class?"

"It was long," Graham answered, looking at her closely as he stepped inside. "Was the rest of your evening uneventful?"

"Not as uneventful as I could have wished."

She explained about the phone calls as she led the way into the den, and they both sat down on the sofa.

"You should have called the police," he scolded her, his expression stern.

"My common sense told me that it was probably just a drunk looking up the wrong person in the directory."

"For God's sake, he knew your address, Catherine. Even if he wasn't the kid's father, he could have come here." Graham shook his head. Then he regarded her with a kind of frowning absorption. "I don't like the idea of your staying here alone in this house tonight."

"You're right next door."

"Yes, but I'm a sound sleeper, and, besides, I don't know if you'd have sense enough to be afraid if you woke up and someone was breaking in. You might wait to make sure it was really an intruder and then find out who he was."

"I'm not that foolish or brave," Catherine scoffed. She made a shamed face of confession. "Actually I never realized before what a scaredy-cat I am. At least I have more empathy with the deaf now. After those phone calls, I sat here tonight with the TV volume off."

Graham gave the sofa a critical inspection. "You must have a spare bedroom," he said. "This sofa isn't long enough for me to sleep on."

"I have two guest bedrooms. But you can't sleep over here," she protested so weakly that she could feel herself blushing to the roots of her hair.

He grazed his knuckles gently along her hot cheek. "Tell me you wouldn't rest better tonight."

"I might rest better with my eyes wide open. I doubt seriously that I'd sleep a wink."

"You'll soon relax when you hear me snoring loud enough to wake the dead," he predicted, his tone indulgent. He was earnest as he went on, "This is all strictly on the up and up. I'm not going to climb into bed with you. You have my word on that. Tomorrow morning I'll leave before daylight so the neighbors won't be any the wiser."

"I'm not worried about the neighbors."

"Well, I am. I have my reputation to consider," he said teasingly. "It's settled then. I'll just need to go over to my house and get a toothbrush."

"I have a brand new toothbrush," Catherine blurted out, and blushed hotly again as he smiled ruefully.

"Don't you trust me to get just my toothbrush?" he asked.

"You said yourself you weren't Sir Galahad."

"Me and my big mouth."

Catherine got up and went to the kitchen to make the coffee. Graham followed along.

"Are you hungry? Would you like a sandwich?" she inquired when he helped himself to a handful of cookies as she was preparing a plate of them.

"If food is to be my only gratification, a sandwich sounds great," he answered promptly. "All I had for supper was a couple of burgers."

"You're in luck. I made party sandwiches for the shower and have leftover cold cuts and cheese and chicken salad." Catherine took out packages and containers from her refrigerator and loaded up Graham's hands. He transported items to the table and refused nothing that she offered until practically the entire contents had been emptied out, lettuce and tomatoes, jars of pickles and condiments, the carton of milk.

"Are you sure you don't want this container of yogurt?" she asked, tongue-in-cheek. "It looks lonely on the shelf."

He grinned. "I wouldn't want to eat you out of house and home."

When she'd made the offer of a sandwich, she'd had in mind making him one, but instead she sat opposite him and watched with fascination and amusement as he proceeded happily to build himself a man-size sandwich.

"Aren't you eating?" he paused to inquire.

Catherine was surprised to realize that the food did appeal to her. She should be feeling much too tense and nervous to have any appetite.

"I was waiting to see if there was enough for both of us," she replied, reaching for the loaf of bread.

He put away two hefty sandwiches and two glasses of milk. Catherine brought up his English class, and he told her about the subject matter that had been covered and made comments about his professor.

"Was Tina there?" she ventured to ask.

Graham nodded, apparently not minding her inquisitiveness. "I didn't talk to her. She's miffed at me," he commented matter-of-factly. His next words indicated that he'd already forgotten the pretty, sexy blond woman.

With no ado, he helped Catherine clear the table after they'd finished eating, handing her what food remained and letting her store it in the refrigerator. Then he loaded the few dishes in the dishwasher while she wiped the table. So companionably did they move about the kitchen that he might have been a frequent visitor.

Graham had had much practice at making himself right at home in women's houses or apartments, Catherine reminded herself. His contented manner was no compliment to her.

"Why don't you take the plate of cookies into the den?" she suggested briskly, getting two mugs down from a cabinet shelf. "We can have our coffee in there."

"Yes, ma'am," he said from just behind her. Before Catherine had had any forewarning, his arms had closed around her waist in a big bear hug. "I'll do anything to be the teacher's pet." He held her against him in a strong, warm embrace, rubbing his cheek against her hair. "When you hugged that little kid this afternoon, I was downright jealous of him."

"I'll just bet you were," she jeered weakly.

"Do you ordinarily show affection toward the children in your classes or did your sympathy get the best of you?" he asked, sounding genuinely interested.

"I don't hesitate to give them a hug or a pat on the head or even a kiss on the cheek. And they feel free to come up to me and slip their hand in mine. Touching is very important to children."

"It's important to adults, too," Graham remarked. He squeezed her and then released her and picked up the plate of cookies.

The physical interlude was obviously a casual matter to him, but Catherine wasn't nearly so unaffected. She still felt the strength of his arms as she poured the coffee. Her whole body protested the loss of warm contact with his big rugged body.

In the den, much to her disappointment and chagrin, Graham didn't sit beside her on the couch, but instead sprawled comfortably in the recliner. Catherine had been counting on closer proximity. How was she supposed to entice him from across the room?

"Do you mind if I take off my shoes?" he asked, not waiting for her permission.

"By all means, make yourself at home."

"That's not hard to do in this house. It's so homey and lived in."

"And not as neat and tidy as you expected."

His broad smile told her that she'd read his mind. "You've been full of surprises," he said, his words somehow highly complimentary.

Catherine kicked off her shoes and curled up in the corner of the sofa. They sipped their coffee and watched the news. At this rate she'd be lucky to get a chaste good-night kiss, but it was so cozy and pleasant being there with him that she couldn't muster any strong regret.

"More coffee?" she asked, putting aside her own mug.

"No, I'm perfectly content. Well, not perfectly," he amended, pushing the chair to an upright position and standing.

"That was my father's chair, and he wasn't as tall as you are. You're welcome to the sofa." Catherine swung her feet down and sat up straighter, her complacency suddenly shattered.

"Does that offer include using your lap for a pillow?" he inquired lazily, coming over.

"Anything to be the perfect hostess."

The sofa wasn't really long enough to accommodate his full height. He had to hang his feet over the arm at the opposite end. And his shoulders were too broad to fit on the cushion. He hung over the edge several inches after he'd stretched out on his back, laying his head in her lap. But he sighed happily.

"If my head gets too heavy, just say so," he said, and closed his eyes.

Catherine's spine was ramrod stiff. She willed herself to relax. There was no place to rest her left hand except on him. Tentatively she lowered it, palm down, to his chest. He immediately picked it up and brought it to his lips, kissed it and then returned it to his chest, imprisoning it beneath his big hand. She could feel the weave of his knit shirt and underneath it, solid muscle.

The lamplight shone on his auburn hair. It had enough natural curl and wave to be unruly. She touched a lock and then grew bolder, using the tips of her fingers like a comb. He reached up with his free hand and captured that hand, too, and held it against his cheek.

"Was I tickling you?" she asked, a little put out.

"No," he denied. "But I'm very sensitive to your touch. I could get aroused easily."

"How do you know?"

He opened his eyes and tilted back his head to glance up into her face. "Just take my word for it. I know."

"I wasn't exactly groping you. All I did was touch your hair and lay my hand on your chest."

"The problem is that I want you to 'grope' me. You can touch my hair," he conceded, releasing her hand that was against his face. "Just don't be so delicate."

Catherine gave his hair a little playful pull. When she tried to free her other hand, he let her. "Your face must be a non-erogenous zone," she remarked, and tweaked his nose. The discussion had put her considerably more at ease. For her own pleasure, she stroked the rugged planes of his cheeks and his strong jawline and chin. When she touched her fingertips to his mouth, he bit them.

"This wasn't a good idea. I'm getting up," he said.

"What about touching you here?" Catherine goosed him in the ribs.

He yelped, grabbing her hands. With a lithe twist of his big body, he turned on his side and sat up in one motion.

"Don't!" she begged, holding her arms close to her body to try to protect her rib cage as he reached for her, his intent to retaliate plain. "Don't! Please! I can't stand to be tickled! I go wild!"

But he showed no mercy. Catherine shrieked and tried in vain to escape him, ending up eventually lying on the sofa with him half on top of her. It wasn't at all an unpleasant predicament when he stopped the punishment. She relaxed her arms, leaving his hands on her ribs, near her breasts.

"Let that be a lesson to you," he said gruffly. "Don't pick on someone bigger and stronger."

Catherine ruffled his hair and smiled up at him. "Bully."

Her heart was beating fast with the exertion. It seemed to skip a beat as he looked down at her, his expression changing and becoming intent. She could feel a gradual tensing in his body and an answering languor in hers. Her defenselessness against his physical dominance was suddenly a new kind of advantage. For the first time, Catherine experienced a thrilling awareness of her own feminine power. Using it was a different matter.

"How many times have we seen scenes just like this in a movie?" she demanded breathlessly. "A friendly skirmish between male and female suddenly turns into a battle of the sexes."

"We'd better fight on the same side of this battle, because I want to lose it," Graham said. "In the thick of our friendly skirmish, I managed to get a feel or two of your breasts, in case you didn't notice."

"I noticed, but I thought it was accidental contact."

He glanced down as he slid his hands up and covered her breasts. There was nothing in his gaze or in his touch to make Catherine regret that her bra size was only an A cup. "There's nothing accidental about this," he pointed out softly, squeezing. "I need to have my hands slapped."

"Consider them slapped," she murmured, closing her eyes in sheer enjoyment.

"You're not being much help." His voice was husky with satisfaction as he accused, "Your nipples are hard." Using his thumbs, he rubbed the offending proof that she wasn't cooperating.

Catherine gasped with weak pleasure and arched her back shamelessly. "I'm sorry. I guess I'm no different from the rest of the women lined up outside your house. I'll make a better effort. Take your hands off me this minute, or I'll... I'll— You didn't let me finish," she complained as he moved his hands down to her waist.

With one part of her mind, Catherine knew that she should be behaving with more feminine calculation and trying to inflame him sexually. But the truth was that she didn't want to risk doing or saying anything to spoil the delightful intimacy.

"I'm getting you in a better position so that I can kiss you without being a contortionist," Graham explained. He scooted her up higher on the cushions, with her wriggling her body and helping him. "There." He lowered himself, bringing his broad chest and shoulders within tantalizing reach and his face conveniently close. "I figure the best way to get this situation under control might be to disgust you with some French kissing. You know, wet and slippery with lots of tongue play."

Catherine feigned a shudder. "Just the thought is *almost* disgusting enough." She put her arms around his neck as he brought his mouth to within inches of hers.

"The more participation on your part, the more revolted you'll probably be," he suggested.

"It makes sense to me." Catherine licked her lips, wetting them. "I'm ready."

"How about wetting mine for me?"

"Anything to hurry this along..." She brought his mouth to hers, anticipation curling inside her.

He met the tip of her tongue with the tip of his own, then let her moisten his parted lips, a task she enjoyed so much that she did a thorough job. "Is that slippery enough?" she murmured.

"Yes, but now your lips are probably dry," he murmured, and remedied the theoretical problem with his tongue. "All set?"

Catherine made a sound in her throat for affirmation. Her body, not just her lips, was eager for the promised kissing. Her small breasts felt heavy and she was conscious of her hips and thighs.

She met the light pressure of his mouth and made warm, glancing contact with his tongue. He made a sound deep in his throat as they ended the brief kiss and then repeated it with a kind of leisurely hunger, then repeated it again. It was unlike any kissing that Catherine had ever done. The pace quickened, until they were both breathing audibly, and their tongues played a more and more active role, but Graham didn't take over and kiss her hard, as she began to want him to do with some urgency.

Finally Catherine's patience snapped, and she tightened her arms around his neck and initiated longer, harder kissing. He took her hint and crushed her mouth with his and became more aggressively male with his tongue, invading her mouth and insisting on a coupling with her tongue. At the same time, one of his hands was tugging her blouse free of the waistband of her slacks.

The caressing touch of his palm on her midriff was sheer heaven, but then came a fiercer pleasure as his hand moved up higher and took possession of first one breast and then the other. She moaned and moved restlessly to relieve a sharp ache of dissatisfaction in her lower body.

"Catherine." He spoke her name in a groan as he abruptly stopped kissing her and rested his cheek against hers, withdrawing his hand from beneath her blouse. "We have to stop." He raised his head and looked down at her. "I can't make love to you without a trip over to my house first. Has that slipped your mind?"

"Yes," Catherine was able to answer honestly. His tone of voice and the expression on his face thrilled her. Both said so clearly that he wanted her and hated to have to stop. "Just now I wasn't doing much thinking," she admitted guiltily, and saw how much her words pleased him.

He kissed her tenderly on the lips. "Why don't you change into that pretty nightgown and robe outfit you had on last night? I'll be back in less than five minutes."

Catherine parted her lips to speak the lie she'd rehearsed, but no words came out. In an agony of uncertainty, she gazed at him, her arms still up around his neck.

When he returned, he would have a condom. They would resume the wonderful foreplay and have intercourse that was purely for pleasure, his pleasure and hers. The sex very well might be good for both of them. She was, incredibly, almost confident that it would be. A short affair with him didn't even seem out of the question at this moment, all the more reason that she should tell her lie.

"What's the problem?" Graham inquired gently. "Are you working up your nerve to recommend that I take a cold shower?"

"No, I'm working up my nerve to make a confession," she replied. "There's something I haven't told you."

"Go ahead and tell me, whatever it is," he encouraged.

For just a split second, Catherine considered baring her soul and making a full confession: *I'd like nothing better than to get pregnant with your baby.* But the risks were just too enormous that she'd end up with nothing but a clear conscience, no affair, no baby, no brief relationship with him.

"You don't need to worry about birth control," she explained, and dropped her gaze as surprise flashed across his face. "I've been on the Pill since I was a teenager, to regulate my period."

Catherine summoned the courage for a questioning glance when he said nothing. His expression was thoughtful, but not doubtful. "I was truthful about not being sexually active," she assured him. "You don't have to worry about safe sex."

He dropped a kiss on her nose. "That was the farthest thing from my mind. I was just thinking that you've been on the Pill a long time. Your doctor would warn you, I suppose, if there were any serious side effects."

"I have complete faith in him," Catherine evaded.

His expression of concern about her health caused her to feel twice as guilty about deceiving him. But what she was doing couldn't hurt him and could make her so happy.

Chapter Five

"I wish we'd had this discussion beforehand," Catherine remarked wistfully as Graham levered his long body free of hers and then maneuvered himself into a sitting position on the edge of the sofa next to her.

"It's probably all for the best that we cooled off a little," he replied, taking both her hands in his and squeezing them. Graham was a little dazed. He couldn't quite believe he'd gotten that hotly aroused just kissing her and touching her breasts. There was more than sex involved here. Her response had aroused a sweet emotion that set off alarms. *Careful, Macaulay, you're getting in over your head.*

"Why do you say that?" she asked anxiously.

"Well, because there are some things I feel I need to state clearly." Not just for her hearing, but for his. "I have a lot of irons in the fire right now. It's just not feasible for me to get serious about a woman."

"You've already said as much during our conversation yesterday morning, over at your house."

"Did I?"

"Yes, words to the effect that you'd be pushing forty before you could get married."

"I guess I forgot," he lied gruffly.

"Are you afraid of hurting me? If you are, don't be. I have more sense than to let myself fall for you."

Graham winced. "That takes a load off my mind."

"I didn't mean that in any insulting way!" she protested quickly and sincerely. "My words were more a reflection on me than on you."

"It's okay," he said. "Who needs a male ego?"

"You'll make some lucky woman a very good husband one of these days. I have no doubt of that."

"But I'm not your idea of a good husband prospect for you."

"No, of course, you're not."

Graham bent over and kissed her to cut off the apologetic explanation he could sense coming. "Don't tell me. Let me guess," he said, hoping to cover his hurt pride with humor. "There's a backhanded compliment hidden in your words somewhere."

She pulled her hands free to slip her arms around his neck. "You're my idea of the best lover I'm ever likely to have."

"Well, that's better than nothing, I suppose." He gathered her up in his arms and stood, holding her. "How about some directions to your bedroom?"

"I can walk," Catherine declared with a hint of breathlessness. "You don't have to carry me."

"It's not going to affect my stamina," Graham said. He carried her toward the door, not waiting for the directions.

"Did I offend you by being so brazen just now?" she asked with a mixture of worry and embarrassment.

Graham had to smile at her perception of her own behavior as brazen. "I've had more explicit propositions."

"Don't feel that you have to be a gentleman. If you're really turned off, I certainly wouldn't want you to go through with this."

He could hear the nervousness in her voice and held her closer, a wave of tenderness washing away any remaining disgruntlement. "I'm not turned off," he said gruffly. "Do you want to go through with this?"

"Yes," she said guiltily, and hugged him tighter around the neck, much to his pleasure. "Here's my bedroom."

Graham entered the room sideways, walked over near the double bed, and set her on her feet. The bedside lamp shed soft light in the room.

"The time of reckoning, when the padded bra comes off," Catherine declared.

"You don't wear a padded bra." He reached to unbutton the top button of her blouse. "Yours is thin silky material with lace. It felt pretty and sexy."

"I'm sure you know more about women's lingerie than a lingerie sales rep."

"Why don't you concentrate on what kind of underwear I might be wearing?" Graham suggested.

"I would assume that they're jockey shorts, not boxer shorts. They're either white or a solid color, I would imagine. Maybe the style that rides down lower on the hips."

"Sounds to me like you've been browsing in the men's underwear department," he speculated, finished with unbuttoning her blouse.

She grasped the two sides of the front and held them together. "Is there any rule that the woman has to strip down first in these disrobing scenes?"

"No." Graham managed not to smile. He'd known that taking her to bed was going to be a new, different experience, and, sure enough, it was, delightfully so. "You know all the different scenarios. We each tear our own clothes off, in a great fever to get naked as quickly as possible. Or we tear each other's clothes off, actually taking longer. Or we take our time and make undressing a kind of foreplay. I undress you. You undress me. Or we just calmly get undressed and get into bed. With or without the light turned on," he added. "It's entirely up to us."

"I vote for the last option," she said, and sighed.

Graham unceremoniously stripped his knit shirt over his head. Next he kicked off his loafers and yanked off his socks. Then he unsnapped his jeans, unzipped them, and took them off. He was about to shed his dark blue briefs when he looked inquiringly at her. She had been watching him and hadn't made a move to undress.

A blush of pretty pink color rose in her cheeks, and she smiled, explaining, "I'm waiting for you to turn the light off."

"Uh-uh," he answered, shaking his head. "The light stays on until you're down to your underwear, too."

Without any argument she slipped her blouse off, treating Graham to the view of her small breasts nestled in the cups of her lacy bra. She was a picture of feminine modesty as she took off her slacks, revealing matching panties that weren't as brief as bikini panties, but revealing, with lace inserts. Her figure was slim and girlish.

"It would be a shame to strip down to that outfit in the dark," he remarked, his male appreciation in his voice. "I'll gladly help you take it off after I turn this light off."

"If you want to leave the light on, you can. I know it's more erotic with the added stimulation of being able to see one's sex partner."

"Tonight I'd rather make love in the dark." Graham clicked the lamp switch, plunging the room into darkness.

"You're hoping that I'll be less inhibited." She breathed a sigh.

Faint light filtered in from the hallway, and he could see her silhouette. "I'm hoping that you won't be so tongue-tied and will verbalize more," he said with gentle teasing. Stepping closer, he put his arms lightly around her waist. She rested her hands on his bare chest.

"That's a defense mechanism, stating everything."

"No kidding," he said. "Once I get my college degree, I'll be able to figure out these things for myself."

"You already have the equivalent of a Ph.D. in the workings of the female psyche." She explored his bare chest with her palms, then slid her searching fingers up to his shoulders, where she measured their width. Her delicate touch sent shivers of pleasure through Graham. "You also look perfectly gorgeous in your underwear."

"Good. You didn't notice the paunch."

"What paunch?" she scoffed.

Graham sucked in his breath as she took his cue and rubbed his stomach, her fingers brushing the elastic of his briefs. Already fully aroused, he felt a sharp ache of anticipation, waiting for her to venture farther down, but instead she lifted her hands and stroked his biceps.

"How about checking me out below the waist?" he urged.

She readily complied, bringing her hands down to his hips. Then she reached around and massaged his buttocks. "You're even all hard muscle here," she praised.

"Catherine, would you *touch* me?" Graham groaned.

Finally she made the intimate inspection he wanted. Her gentle fondling through the layer of knit cloth was almost more pleasure then he could stand, especially accompanied by her candidly appreciative feminine description of her findings.

Rather than call a halt, he put his own hands to work, caressing and fondling her body. She was soon clinging

to him, weak with her own pleasure and murmuring
compliments about his expertise as a lover. Graham finished undressing her and with both of them naked, got
into bed with her.

For all his urgent desire to be inside her, he was filled
with a patience greater than any he'd ever known before. He could wait indefinitely, until he'd already given
her the ultimate sexual pleasure that he wanted her to
experience with him. There was more than ego involved,
and Graham knew it. There was a tender caring.

Using his hands and his mouth and his tongue, he
raised her to a peak of desperate need and beyond it to a
release that left her spent and vulnerable. Cradling her in
his arms, he felt a fierce, sweet satisfaction of his own.
After she'd recovered, he made love to her again, this
time coupling his body with hers.

Entering her, he was fleetingly conscious that he wasn't
taking the usual precautions, but then the awareness was
gone in the excruciating enjoyment of being tightly
sheathed by her silken warmth. Her response and words
of pleasure tested his control, but he hung on by a thread,
wanting to prolong the sensations and the rhythmic one-
ness. When she reached climax again, it was an unexpected bonus and a tribute to his manhood. Tender
gratitude snapped the tenuous thread, and his control
shattered.

This is what sex is really all about! he shouted in his
mind before he succumbed totally to explosive joy.

Afterward, lying with her cuddled closely against him,
he was awash in deep contentment. "I'm glad we turned
the light off, baby," he murmured drowsily. "Because I
don't think I'd have the strength."

"Thank you, Graham," she said softly, and pressed a
kiss to his chest. "That was incredible."

"I thought so."

"For all practical purposes, I was a virgin before tonight. I had no idea that sex could be like this."

"Me, neither." He yawned, losing the battle against sleepiness. "Sorry, baby, but I'm fading fast. Good night," he mumbled, and didn't hear her answer.

Catherine lay there, listening to his even breathing and reveling in the fact that she was trapped in his heavy warm embrace. She remembered that they'd left lights burning in the den. Should she ease up and turn them off? she wondered idly, and decided against it.

Let them burn all night. She didn't want to risk disturbing him. She didn't want to move an inch away from him. All she wanted to do was drift off to sleep in this blissfully contented state.

Go to sleep, Catherine, she told herself. *You can think and analyze what you've done tomorrow and for the rest of your life.*

Tonight was hers.

Graham had gotten up and gone. Catherine knew that she was alone in the bed the instant she awoke the next morning, before she even opened her eyes. She had slept nude. That realization was almost instantaneous, too, triggered not so much by memory as by sensual awareness.

She *felt* naked under the light covers. She was conscious of her body, of her breasts and stomach and hips and thighs. A languorous movement of her hips verified that last night's lovemaking was no fantasy. The private twinges of soreness seemed somehow connected to her breasts, and her nipples tingled.

Catherine touched her breasts and only then did the thought occur to her that she might be pregnant with

Graham's baby. She pressed her hands to her abdomen, disturbed that she wasn't more thrilled at the possibility. After all, conceiving had been her main motive for going to bed with him, not sexual satisfaction.

You're afraid to get your hopes up, she told herself, throwing off the covers.

The consciousness of her body persisted as Catherine went through her morning routine. Rather than making her awkward, she moved with a new, *looser* co-ordination. Her walk was subtly different, more womanly. What was more, she even looked different to herself, striking a dignified pose before the mirror. The prim, tight, virginal quality was gone, and the change had nothing to do with whether she was pregnant or not.

Catherine, why don't you just wear a sign that says, I Had Wonderful Sex Last Night? The scathing advice brought a blush to her cheeks and a self-satisfied smirk.

No one else will see any difference, she assured herself.

But all day she received curiously appraising—and approving—looks from her colleagues. The news about Graham's visiting her at school the previous afternoon had been widely reported, and no one put any stock in her denials that there was a romance going on. Catherine didn't sound very convincing even to her own ears. She really didn't mind the teasing interest and only wished that speculation about a match between her and Graham had more substance.

It was a long day, and she ticked off the hours, alternately eager and anxious as she thought ahead to seeing him later. For surely she would see him and talk to him.

There was a faculty meeting after school that dragged on interminably. Catherine kept glancing at her watch, telling herself that she might as well kill time here as at home. Graham would still be on the job anyway.

Sure enough, when she finally got away from school and drove straight home, there was no sign of his truck. But then he turned into his driveway just as she was getting out of her car. He tooted his horn, drove in with his usual burst of speed, killed the engine and hopped out, giving the truck door a vigorous slam.

"What lucky timing!" he called, heading immediately over.

Catherine walked to meet him, hoping that her face didn't reflect her rush of gladness. Words failed her. She felt as tongue-tied and shy as she had felt at sixteen, passing him in the high school corridor.

"Hi, neighbor," he said softly, and for just a moment she thought that he might bend down and kiss her. Instead he reached with a big hand to touch her cheek. "How was your day?"

"Busy," she replied. "How was yours?"

"Mine was busy, too. And it isn't over. I want to get in a couple of hours of work on my house."

His note of regret helped Catherine to summon her poise. She guessed that she had made it plain as day that she was available for the rest of the afternoon and evening.

"Well, don't let me hold up progress," she said, stepping back.

"It's a big temptation to put everything on hold for a few months, while you're living right next door to me, but at the same time I'm more geared up than ever to achieve my goals that I've set," he explained earnestly. "I intend to amount to something, Catherine."

"Please don't think that I expect you to modify your life in any way, because I certainly don't. You're as much a free agent as you were before what happened last night . . . happened.''

''This cramps my style, laying my cards on the table out here in sight of all the neighbors,'' he complained with a rueful glance around. ''Not to mention that I'm in my sweaty work clothes.'' He looked down at himself.

Neither circumstance would have mattered to Catherine if he'd wanted to take her in his arms and hold her to soften the blow of the truth: last night was nothing special for him.

''In case you were worried about me, I just wanted you to know that I'm not eating my heart out over you because I discovered ecstasy in your arms last night,'' she declared.

He shoved his hand through his hair, seemed to be debating with himself about what to do or say, and sighed over whatever conclusion he'd arrived at. Catherine swallowed hard at a lump of total despair.

''Speaking of eating, would you have supper with me tonight?'' he asked. ''I thought I'd get in a couple of hours of work, clean up and go pick up some fried chicken dinners.''

It wasn't a spur-of-the-moment invitation. The knowledge changed misery to happiness.

''I could just as easily go pick them up,'' she pointed out, trying to sound as casual as he had sounded.

''Would you mind?''

''Not at all.''

''You're a sweetheart.'' He held out his hand for her hand. When she gave it to him, he squeezed it, and she felt both the gentleness and the strength of his callused fingers. ''Remind me to give you a big hug and a kiss later on.''

"Don't think that I'm too shy to jog your memory. How many pieces of chicken would you like? White meat or dark meat?" Anticipation was shamefully audible in her voice.

He told her his preference and agreed promptly to her suggestion that they have supper at her house, rather than at his. With the plans made, he said as he turned to leave, "See you later on. If you want to visit, feel free to come over."

"I'd only be in the way," Catherine replied, absurdly pleased at the offhanded invitation.

At 6:45 she went to get the dinners. On her return, she stuck the carton of coleslaw in the refrigerator, wrapped the piping hot chicken in foil and stuck it in the oven on a low temperature to keep warm. The table was already set. Graham had asked for red beans and rice as a side dish, and she was having Cajun rice. Before they sat down, she would reheat the servings in the microwave.

Should she just wait for Graham to come when he was ready? she asked herself. The alternative was just too tempting, and Catherine walked over to his house with the handy pretext of making sure that he hadn't lost track of time.

There was no response to her knock. She opened the back door, stuck her head in and called his name. He didn't answer. Perhaps he was in the shower, she thought, entering the kitchen. His tools were scattered on the floor of the dining room, where he'd evidently been removing ceiling tile. Catherine picked her way through and called out, "Hello. Is anyone home?" This time he answered.

"Catherine? I'm in the bathroom."

She boldly took the words as instructions of where to find him. He was toweling off, and glanced at her with a welcoming smile, giving no indication that he minded the invasion of his privacy.

"I've been slaving over a hot stove, and supper is cooked," she said from the doorway, enjoying her vantage point and looking him over none too discreetly. Naked and partially aroused, he was definitely male centerfold material.

"I'm starved," he declared, draping his damp towel over the shower rod. "It'll only take me a minute to put on some clothes."

"Does a hot shower have the opposite effect of a cold one?" Catherine's curiosity got the best of her.

Graham grinned, glancing down at himself. "Are you writing a book?" he asked teasingly. "If you must know, I was indulging in some male fantasy and thinking about how nice it would be if you were taking a shower with me."

She crossed her arms, feeling her nipples tightening as her whole body responded positively to the idea. "Men are so unself-conscious about their bodies. Of course, you have good reason to be," she added.

He pulled down the damp towel and wrapped it around his hips. Catherine stood aside and let him pass her. "Don't go," he said over his shoulder. With only a moment's hesitation, she followed after him, the temptation to watch him dress more than she could resist. He took a pair of burgundy briefs from a bureau drawer and quickly put them on under her interested gaze before gesturing toward the bed and inquiring politely, "Would you like to sit down?"

"No, thank you," she refused, looking at the bed. A picture of the brunette flashed clearly in her memory. Catherine felt a sharp stab of jealousy, reflecting that not only had the brunette slept with him, but she'd probably watched him getting dressed. The woman may even have showered with him.

"It's a new bed," Graham volunteered. "I bought it when I moved in."

He'd obviously guessed the general direction of her thoughts even if he hadn't read her mind. Humiliated, Catherine said primly, "I'll wait for you in the kitchen."

"Stay and keep me company," he cajoled. "Another thirty seconds and I'll be ready."

"Oh. In that case."

He had pulled on jeans and left them unzipped. Now he walked over to the closet and took a striped knit shirt off a hanger. As much as she enjoyed the ripple of muscles in his back as he put the shirt on, she wished that he had turned around to tuck in the shirt tail and zip and fasten his jeans. Carrying his loafers, he got a pair of socks from a dresser drawer, sat down on the edge of the bed, donned the socks and thrust his feet into the shoes.

"That was fast," Catherine commented as he stood and went over to the bureau to give his wet hair a quick combing.

"I was in a hurry to say hello properly." He covered the distance to the door in a few long strides, slipped his arms around her and picked her up, holding her against him with her face on a level with his. "Hi, neighbor," he said softly. "How about that friendly hug and kiss now I'm fresh from the shower and we don't have any audience?"

She wound her arms around his neck and complied with pleasure, inhaling his clean scent and reveling in his strength and masculinity.

"You can leave the TV on. It won't bother my concentration," Graham said.

"Are you sure?" Catherine pressed.

"Positive." He smiled at her and then opened the textbook on his lap. They'd had supper and were settled in the den, him at one end of the sofa and Catherine at the other. "Oh, before I forget, though, I want to give you some money."

"I don't want you to give me any money," she protested, but he was reaching for his hip pocket.

"Damn," he cursed mildly. "I left my wallet over at my house. I'll have to reimburse you tomorrow."

He turned several pages and began reading. Catherine picked up a magazine from the end table near her and curled sideways so that she could sneak guilty glances at him. The mention of his wallet had brought to mind the condoms that he had stopped carrying, because of his pact with her.

What was Catherine going to do? Let him go on believing that she was on the Pill, or tell him the truth, that she had lied and tricked him into having intercourse with her?

As if searching for the answer, she flipped through the magazine, stopping to gaze at fashion ads with glamorous models. The ads awoke a kind of hopelessness. There wasn't any real chance that Catherine could hold Graham's interest for very long. Last night had been magical and tonight he had been attentive and affectionate, seeming to enjoy her company as much as she enjoyed his. She felt attractive in his eyes and thrilled to his most casual touch, but common sense told her that this wasn't anything lasting. It was too good to be true.

Wasn't her wisest decision just to have a short, wonderful affair with him and, with luck, conceive in the process? Could that be wrong?

But I hate being dishonest with him, she thought, glancing over and seeing that Graham was rubbing his jaw absentmindedly, absorbed in his reading.

He looked up as the extension phone on the table at her end of the sofa pealed into life, making her jump. The caller was Lauren Piper.

"Catherine, I haven't heard from you in a coon's age. How are you?"

"I'm fine, Lauren. How are you and the kids?" Catherine could hear her own note of constraint, and Lauren picked up on it immediately.

"Have I called at a bad time?"

"Actually, I do have company."

"Male or female?" her good friend was quick to inquire.

"You remember Graham Macaulay. He's bought the house next door." Catherine smiled nervously at Graham, who didn't smile back. He was making no pretense of not listening.

"Graham Macaulay has moved in next door to you!" Lauren exclaimed. "Of course, I remember him. What girl who ever saw him doesn't remember him? Catherine, God must be giving you the go-ahead sign on having a baby au naturel. Is he divorced?"

"No."

"Since you didn't mention a Mrs. Macaulay, he's still single, I take it."

"Yes. Lauren, could I call you back in the morning?"

"Oh, ho! He's spending the night! Catherine Baker, you're having an affair with Graham Macaulay! Good for you! You've gone and found yourself a biological father, I do believe! Just say yes or no."

"It isn't a clear-cut matter," Catherine evaded, horribly uncomfortable with the conversation.

"I'm dying of curiosity to find out all the details. Is he a fantastic lover? I'll bet he is."

"That's a safe guess. Thanks for calling, Lauren."

"Have a good evening, my friend, and say hi to Graham for me."

"I will. Goodbye." She hung up the phone. "Lauren said to tell you hi."

Graham closed his book.

"Sorry about the interruption," Catherine said. "Did you finish your chapter?"

"No, I didn't," he replied quietly. "You know, I can't help wondering what Lauren could have been saying to make you feel that awkward about answering in my presence."

Catherine couldn't meet his eyes. "When I didn't suggest calling her back tonight, she jumped to the conclusion that we were having an affair and you were spending the night. Among other things, she wanted to know if you were a fantastic lover."

"Was that the one definite yes?"

"Lauren and I have been friends since kindergarten. She knows my whole background, including the fact that I never dated popular guys like you. Naturally she was amazed at the turn of events, your moving in next door to me and so on." Catherine made a defensive explanation, telling a portion of the truth with all the earnestness that she could muster. "I could hardly sit here and discuss my rare good fortune in having you as a neighbor when you could hear every word."

"Believe me, I wouldn't have minded," he said.

"I could call Lauren back right now and rave about you," she suggested, but the attempt to lighten the heavy atmosphere fell flat. Catherine sighed. "But then that might backfire on me. Knowing Lauren, she might in-

vite herself over to Mandeville for a visit. The very
thought brings out all my insecurities. One look at her
and my little Cinderella story would probably be over.
Lauren hasn't lost her figure after having two children,
and she's still just as pretty as she was in high school
when you dated her."

Catherine was appalled at her own jealous emotion as
she tortured herself with a picture of Graham and Lauren together.

"If I can't afford a wife, I certainly can't take on a
ready-made family," he pointed out.

"That's some reassurance, I guess," she said with
wistful irony.

Graham waited as though giving her an opportunity to
say more. When she didn't, not knowing what he wanted
her to say, he opened his textbook again, found his place
and resumed reading, his jaw set and a little frown of
concentration on his face.

Catherine reopened her magazine and gazed unseeingly at the lead paragraph of an article. She wished that
Lauren hadn't called and yet it was all for the best that
she had. There was no doubt what her pragmatic reaction would be if Catherine poured out all her doubts.

*Don't blow it, Catherine. So you suffer a few conscience pangs. Sure, Graham's a nice guy, but he's getting what he wants, sex and companionship. When it's
over, he'll go on to the next woman and never be the
wiser. You still do want very badly to be a mother, don't
you? That hasn't changed, has it?*

*No... yes, it has changed. Oh, I still want to be a
mother every bit as much, but—*

But what, Catherine?

*But now I'm not so sure, the way I was, that being a
mother is enough to make me completely happy.*

What's to be unsure about? Of course, it won't. Happily ever after doesn't exist except in fairy tales.

You don't understand what's happened.

Spell it out for me, Catherine.

I think ... I think I probably love him.

Oh, God.

Catherine gnawed on her bottom lip, her heart heavy. And yet she wanted to smile. It was the strangest feeling she'd ever had, a kind of despairing happiness.

Chapter Six

Graham snapped his book closed and tossed it onto the coffee table. "Did Lauren assume right?" he asked. "Am I spending the night?"

Catherine had been in a fog. "I don't know," she stammered, flustered. "Are you?"

"It's up to you. I could use some encouragement."

"Encouragement?" Her magazine slid to the floor as she sat upright. She bent down, picked it up and placed it on the end table. "My feelings must be very transparent. Of course, I want you to spend the night. Very much," she added.

"Is that it? Am I to consider myself encouraged?" His rueful note brought a rush of relief. The threat of his going home was gone.

Catherine smiled at him. "If you like, I'll try my hand at some nonverbal encouragement."

He shifted a little sideways and crooked his arm on the back of the sofa. "I do like."

"Are you the same man who was complaining about women's liberation going too far?" she remarked, moving over to sit next to him.

"Not exactly the same man," he replied. "You've altered my thinking somewhat."

"Not as much as you've altered mine, I'll bet."

"We'll have to compare notes one of these days."

Catherine had too much of a serious nature to confess to be comfortable with the repartee. "Are you planning to just sit there calmly?'' He hadn't made a move to kiss her or touch her.

''Wasn't that the idea? I'm feeling very responsive,'' he assured her with a smile.

''Why don't you talk me through this and tell me what you'd like me to do?''

''I'd like you to do whatever you feel like doing. Don't worry about pleasing me. Please yourself.''

''You want me to be more forward.''

''That's one way of putting it.''

''Here goes.'' Catherine laid her hand on his knee and slid her palm along his thigh. ''Too forward?'' she inquired when he caught her hand and stopped her before she reached his groin.

''Too soon,'' he corrected, smiling.

She freed her hand and rubbed his flat, muscled stomach, then slipped her fingertips beneath the waist of his jeans. He caught her hand again and carried it up behind his neck.

''I guess I am going to have to talk you through this, after all, or else bypass any preliminary hugging and kissing. I forget. You don't like kissing, do you?''

''I never liked it much before, but I do now.'' Catherine put both arms around his neck and kissed him on the mouth, letting her lips cling to his. ''You can take over anytime,'' she murmured, touching tongues with him.

''You're doing fine,'' he murmured, his arms closing around her tightly.

The kissing quickly became passionate and led to intimate caressing. Last night's lovemaking seemed to have made Catherine more susceptible to the pleasure of his hands on her body. Much of her inhibition about touching him had gone. When he started unbuttoning her blouse, she tugged his shirt free of his jeans, eager for the sight of his bared upper torso. They were both naked to the waist before they went to her bedroom.

There was no discussion of procedures for undressing. Catherine brazenly unsnapped his jeans and unzipped them, while he unfastened and unzipped her slacks.

"What? No conversation?" he inquired with a teasing indulgence. "Surely there are thoughts running through that head of yours."

"I was thinking about how man-hungry I've become, thanks to you. I wanted to take these jeans off you as soon as you had put them on."

"Next time don't suppress any urges like that."

"If I don't, you might end up naked out in the yard and get arrested for indecent exposure."

"It must have been fairly obvious to you that I didn't want to put on clothes in the first place."

"No, you know how obtuse I am when it comes to sex. You seemed in quite a rush to get dressed." Catherine spoke abstractedly. He had helped her shed the slacks and she had him down to his briefs now and was intent on easing them down. "It's a good thing these are stretchy knit," she commented. "You need a lot of stretch."

Graham was finessing her panties down past her hips. Catherine paused to absorb shockwaves of pleasure as he postponed moving her one remaining garment while he caressed her and discovered unerringly intimate evidences of her desire for him.

The conversation became frank, urgent lovers' talk, a new language for her. He didn't seem to mind in the least her trace of shyness in speaking it. Tonight, if possible, he made her feel even more seductive and utterly desirable than he had the previous night.

Catherine gave no thought whatever to her lie that she was on the Pill until their lovemaking had reached the point where he entered her, joining their bodies in a deep, complete union that took her breath away. She suffered a guilty moment, regretting her dishonesty. Then she gave herself up to the intense physical pleasure.

Deceiving him was the only wrong. With her knowledge that she loved him like a joyous song in her heart and mind, nothing seemed more right than allowing her body to be a fertile receptacle to his life-giving sperm.

Afterward, though, the guilt came back. He'd turned out the light, and she lay nestled against him, sated and blissfully content except for her nagging conscience.

"Graham?"

"What, baby?"

His use of the casual endearment in a tender tone of voice made her heart swell with love. She had to wait a second while the poignant mixture of pain and happiness subsided.

"I was thinking. Maybe we should take double precautions, to be on the safe side. No method of birth control is foolproof."

Catherine didn't have the nerve to make a full confession, but she could stop deceiving him without his knowing that she had deceived him in the first place.

"The Pill is practically foolproof." He sounded totally unconcerned. "I'm not that paranoid. Are you?"

If she said yes, it would be another lie. "Well, no, not really. I thought you might have some uneasiness."

"Normally I would. You're the first woman I've ever trusted to take care of birth control. I'm old-fashioned enough that if I got a woman pregnant, I'd have to marry her."

Oh, God, don't tell me that, Catherine thought. *I'm only human.*

"I know you're too responsible a person to be careless," Graham went on. "And there's no danger that you'd want to trap me into marriage. In that honest way of yours, you've eased my mind on that score." He yawned and hugged her tighter before remarking in a drowsy, satisfied voice, "If our sex gets any better, I'm not sure double precautions will do the job anyway. Nature might win out. Baby, before I go to sleep on you, how about keeping tomorrow night free for me?"

Catherine agreed and lay wide awake after he'd fallen soundly asleep. *What was she going to do?* Loving him introduced a whole new complicating factor: no longer did she want just any man's child.

She was starting her period. The telltale heaviness and aching discomfort alerted Catherine immediately upon waking and finding herself alone in bed, as usual. Graham didn't leave before daylight now. She had convinced him of the truth, that she wasn't concerned about gossip.

He got up at five-thirty and went over to his house to shave and dress for work and have his breakfast. By the time Catherine rose, he had already left for work. He was highly disciplined, she'd discovered, packing his day full. With working full-time, being a part-time college student, and renovating his house, he didn't have much spare time, and he spent all of it with her.

Since that first night they'd made love two weeks ago, he hadn't slept in his own bed. They'd had supper together every night on weeknights and most of their meals together on weekends. For all practical purposes, they were living together. It was anything but claustrophobic for Catherine. It was sheer happiness except for her emotional dilemma. On the one hand, she prayed that she wasn't pregnant, then, on the other hand, became anxious, worrying that she might not be fertile enough to conceive before the affair was over.

Now the suspense was ended temporarily. She wasn't pregnant. *Now what, Catherine?* she asked herself when she'd gone to the bathroom and confirmed what her body had already told her.

More in love with him than ever, what was she going to do? Tell him the truth or continue the deception? She had a few days to decide. Other questions weighed heavily on her mind. With the interruption of the physical relationship, would he want to be with her? Was her company enough? Would he want to sleep with her when it was just sharing a bed?

It was Monday, and he had his English class that night. One of his class members was Tina, the pretty, sexy blonde. Catherine depressed herself with the reminder as she got dressed for school after finally making her selection of clothes from a wardrobe that had suddenly become offensively dull again.

Graham got home that afternoon with just enough time to shower and change and come over to say hello and good-bye to her. Catherine could hear his cheerful whistle as he climbed the back steps. "Hi. It's me," he called as he entered without knocking, a big, good-looking, virile man.

His hug and kiss were every bit as affectionate as she'd come to expect. She clung to him tightly, her love surging up strong.

"Hmm. That's a nice welcome," he said. "It makes me wish that I weren't such a conscientious student. By the way, I won't be coming straight home after class tonight. A group of us are having a study session."

"Oh," Catherine said, feeling her face falling. "Then I guess I'll go ahead and have supper by myself." She waited and had a late supper with him on the nights he had class.

"It completely slipped my mind until today. I started to come by at lunch to tell you, but I didn't know if that was a good idea. The thought crossed my mind that you might want to make some plans for tonight that didn't include me for a change. I've been pretty well monopolizing your free time."

"I wouldn't have minded if you'd come by the school." She didn't trust herself to reply to anything else. Was this the first sign that he was starting to feel hemmed in?

"Are you feeling okay?" he asked. "You look a little pale and peaked."

"Actually I'm not feeling all that great. I'm having my period."

"That's good news." He gave her another hug and a quick kiss. "Take it easy. I'll call you either during the break or after class, if you're going to be here."

"I'll be here. I'll be fine," she added because his expression was so kind and sympathetic. "There haven't been any new threats from irate fathers."

The police had dealt with the Anderson man. They'd hauled him in for drunken driving. While he was in jail, he'd confessed to the threats against Catherine and Eleanor and was now receiving counseling.

"I'll call you anyway."

He was whistling as he walked across her backyard. The cheery sound drifted through the screen door. Catherine heard the slam of his truck door and the roar of the engine. The noises of his departure were vigorously male. The silence, after he was gone, was like a vacuum.

This is just your emotions going wild, Catherine, she told herself to combat the sensation of being utterly abandoned.

True to his word, he called shortly after nine o'clock. She could hear voices and laughter in the background. "Hi, how are you feeling?" he asked.

"I'm okay," she said.

"Don't think you have to wait up for me. Just go on to bed, if you're tired."

"I may do that. Don't feel like you have to rush back across the causeway and check on an invalid. It might even be a welcome change for you to sleep in your own bed." Catherine bit her lip, hoping for a quick denial.

"Is that a tactful hint?"

"No."

"Hey, Graham, enough love talk!" a male voice in the background yelled out.

"Come on, you big hunk," sang out a female voice. "I want a ride in that pickup truck of yours."

"You're going to get Graham in hot water with his honey," another female chided.

"My study group is giving me a hard time," he said, and she could hear the sheepish grin in his voice.

"I heard. How many of you are there?"

"Four."

"That's a nice even number. I won't keep you. Have a good study session," she said and hung up, tears of jealousy stinging her eyes.

At eleven o'clock Catherine went to bed, tired, but too tense and miserable to go to sleep. At eleven-thirty she heard Graham driving into his driveway. Every muscle rigid, she strained her ears and waited. With the sound of his quietly entering through her back door, she went limp with relief and joy and then tensed again with a new dread.

She was going to tell him the truth.

He eased into her darkened bedroom and began undressing. She heard him unsnapping his jeans and unzipping them, the rustle of denim.

"I'm not asleep," she said.

"Did I wake you up, baby? I'm sorry," he apologized softly and yawned. "I'm beat."

He got into bed, took her into his arms and hugged her tight, not commenting on the fact that she had on a nightgown and he had kept on his underwear. Catherine hugged him back fiercely, struggling to control her emotions.

"I didn't know whether you'd want to sleep with me tonight," she confessed.

"Is that why you suggested that I might like to sleep in my own bed? You were giving me an out?"

"Yes, hoping all the while that you wouldn't take it."

"I was a little worried that you might be telling me in a gentle way that you didn't want me as just a bed partner."

"How could you wonder that? I love having you sleep with me."

He kissed her hair. "You never said anything to that effect. You were used to having your bed to yourself and for all I knew, you were thinking, 'I wish that big lug would make love and go home.'" His teasing, indulgent tone was full of warm affection.

"For all I knew, it was just less effort for you to stay than to get up and put on your clothes and go home. Or maybe you were acting out of consideration for my feelings."

"Well, now you know that I like sleeping with you. I like being with you, in case you have any doubts on that score. Going without sex for a few days is no problem for me." He rubbed her back, his touch strong and yet gentle. "You're all tense, baby. Relax."

I wouldn't have to tell him, Catherine thought. *I could go to the doctor and get a prescription for birth control pills.*

"Is there anything else troubling you?" he asked.

"Yes."

"Tell me what it is."

"Graham, I haven't been honest with you."

"Go on," he encouraged.

"I lied to you when I said that I was on the Pill," Catherine blurted, and felt his arms go slack around her as her words sank in.

"You aren't on the Pill?" He sounded stunned.

"No, I'm not. It's a long story. I can explain."

He sat up. "Before you do, you'd better tell me whether you're having your period. That wasn't a lie, too, was it?"

"No, that was the truth," she said miserably. "I'm not pregnant. Please don't jump to the wrong conclusion. I didn't have in mind trapping you into marrying me."

"Just what the hell did you have in mind?" he asked with a kind of angry disbelief. He snapped on the lamp and swung his legs to the floor, sitting on the edge of the bed with his back to her.

Catherine sat up behind him. Tentatively she reached and touched his shoulder, and then dropped her hand when he flinched.

"I guess I should start at the beginning," she said, sighing. "My reason for resigning my teaching job and moving to Biloxi was that I had decided I was going to become a single mother.''

''Oh, God, I'm not believing this,'' Graham muttered, leaning forward to rest his elbows on his knees. His head hung down and he shook it slowly. ''I can figure out the rest, but I need to hear it from your mouth what a complete sucker I've been.''

''It isn't like that!'' she protested. ''There was no scheme. But let me try to make you understand. Realistically my chances were slim to none that some wonderful man was going to come into my life and want to marry me and give me children. I could accept being unmarried. I'd never had any relationship with a man that made me want to be a wife. But I've always loved children. That's why I became an elementary school teacher. I couldn't bear the thought of never having my own baby.''

''Lauren knows and approves, I assume,'' he put in grimly.

''Without her supportiveness, I never would have had the courage to make such a decision,'' Catherine admitted. ''As crazy and desperate as the whole notion may seem to you, it really wasn't. I considered every angle. As Lauren's partner in a nursery school, I would be doing work I was trained to do and be able to have my baby with me. With the equity in this house, my savings, and my teacher retirement, I could afford to be a parent.'' He was listening, showing absolutely no signs of softening. She went on, hearing the hopelessness in her voice.

''The big question mark was how to make my dream of having a child come true. My options were going to a clinic and being artificially inseminated, or adopting a baby. Lauren and I discussed my simply having an affair and getting pregnant, but it was never really a viable means.''

"Until I came along and unknowingly volunteered for the job." He raised his head, but still sat slumped forward. "Let me get this straight. You were going to have my kid and keep me totally ignorant of the fact."

"*Yes.*" Catherine whispered the damning truth. "Except that there was so little likelihood of my getting pregnant at first. I never believed that you would stay interested in me long enough to have an affair."

"Lord help me, I was interested in more than having an affair," he said with bitter self-contempt. "I've never been so taken in by a woman or so wrong in my judgment about a person. I thought you were the greatest thing that ever happened to me, sweet and fun and intelligent and honest to a fault. Here I find out that you're capable of doing something so unscrupulous, so damned *wrong* for everybody concerned."

He stood abruptly and went over to pick up his jeans from her vanity bench, where he'd draped his clothes, and began putting them on. "Just what the hell were you going to tell this kid of mine in a few years when he or she asked, 'Who's my daddy?''"

"I would have had to come up with some story that was a lie," Catherine admitted with shamed despair. "What I was willing to do was wrong. I see that now. From the start, my conscience bothered me terribly. If you remember, the second night we slept together I suggested that we might be doubly careful. By then, though, I knew that I was falling in love with you, and it didn't seem immoral to want your baby."

He was finishing getting dressed, jerking his shirt down over his shoulders and chest. "Were you telling the truth when you said you weren't sleeping with the principal guy you were dating?" he asked harshly.

"I never want to bed with Dale. The only lie I've told you, I swear, is that I was on the Pill."

"What was the matter with him that you didn't try to use him to father a kid?"

"There was no physical attraction on my side. I didn't even like kissing him. Also—" Her voice faltered as Graham's gaze bored into her. "He'd had a vasectomy."

He sat down on the vanity bench and jerked on his socks with angry movements, thrust his feet into his loafers, stood up and headed for the door, obviously leaving without another word.

"Graham, please!" Catherine pleaded. "Don't go like this." He stopped and braced his hand on the doorway, but didn't turn around. "Is this the end of our relationship? Can't I do something to reinstate myself with you?"

"We didn't have a relationship, Catherine," he said. "We were a couple of people completely at cross-purposes. I'm not only mad as hell over being duped, I'm disappointed and hurt. And at this moment I don't think it's something I'll get over. I can't imagine that I would ever trust you again. It's a real kick in the gut to learn that I was totally oblivious to the fact that you even had this deep need to be a mother."

"I didn't dare confide in you."

He sighed heavily. "No, I don't guess you could. Here's some parting advice, for whatever it's worth. Don't sell yourself short. You don't have anything to apologize for as a woman. You have looks and personality. I'll put your house key in an envelope and shove it under your back door."

He left without a backward glance at her, walking out of her house and out of her life.

Catherine sat there, tears blinding her and blurring her vision of the empty doorway where he'd stood.

Chapter Seven

The unhappiness was easier to bear than the loneliness. Catherine missed Graham so much that the longing to see him and hear his voice was like an ache inside her. She shamelessly watched for him, peering out a window through the blinds.

When he glanced over at her house or at her car, his reproachful expression made her heartsick. The happy-go-lucky man had disappeared. The cheerful whistling had stopped. He looked sober and didn't give the appearance of being any happier than she was.

A few times they'd encountered each other in their driveways, going and coming. He spoke, but that was all. Catherine tried to prepare herself for the inevitable, knowing that sooner or later he would bring a woman home with him, but two weeks passed and the dreaded occurrence didn't happen.

From all indications, he was devoting the bulk of his spare time to working on his house. Catherine observed him unloading sheets of drywall and lumber and materials that he brought home in his pickup. On weekends he was home and indoors, for the most part. The same was true of evenings, except for those nights that he attended class.

Was it possible that he was as lonely for her as she was for him? Catherine wondered wistfully. There was one way to find out. She could go over and ask him, if only she had the nerve.

Don't sell yourself short, he'd said, despite being angry and disappointed in her. *You have nothing to apologize for as a woman. You have looks and personality.*

A lesser man would have attacked her and said things to hurt her, the way she'd hurt him. The fact that he hadn't, only made her love him more and wish with all her heart that she had another chance with him.

Her main hope rested in his words that he'd blurted out, *Lord help me, I was interested in more than having an affair.* Had he meant that he loved her?

"Come in, Catherine," Eleanor Akers invited warmly. "Don't you look pretty today! Is that a sundress underneath that jacket? Take the jacket off and let me see."

Catherine complied and turned around, miming a fashion model.

"That's snazzy," Eleanor declared. "I like that coral color on you. And you found sandals to match."

"You're looking at the new me, Eleanor. Get ready for brighter colors and more stylish clothes. I'll be replacing my dowdy wardrobe bit by bit."

"I wish I wore your size. I'd gladly accept some of your castoffs."

"Actually I'm too practical to clean out my closets," Catherine admitted. "I can do a lot with accessories and some new blouses. Mostly it's a change in attitude."

"What on earth has happened? You looked like you lost your best friend for a couple of weeks there. And now this week you've perked up."

"I've made some important decisions and have set some personal goals that I'm very excited about. One of the decisions is that I would like to sign a new letter of intent."

"Catherine, I'm delighted! You're planning to be back next year after all!" Eleanor rose and came around her desk to give Catherine a hug. "Have a seat. I want to get your signature on the dotted line."

When the document was signed, the two women chatted about several school matters, including the annual end-of-the-year faculty picnic that weekend. This year it would be a crawfish boil, and Eleanor had volunteered the use of the camp that she and her husband owned on Bayou Lacombe.

"You can bring a guest," Eleanor reminded when Catherine got up to leave. "Why don't you invite that good-looking neighbor of yours that I've never gotten to meet?"

"Actually I plan to do that this afternoon," Catherine said, donning her jacket. "Whether he'll come is another matter."

"I recommend that you take off the jacket when you invite him."

Catherine had already planned to do that, too.

She waited fifteen minutes after he'd gone into his house. *Here goes, Catherine,* she told herself and set out on the long journey from her back steps to his back steps.

The pungent scent of paint came through the screen door, but Catherine couldn't hear any movement or activity. She knocked briskly on the doorframe.

"Come in," he called after a moment's silence. "The door's unlatched."

"It's me, Catherine," she called, stepping inside the kitchen.

There was no answer.

Her sandals made a tapping sound on the linoleum floor. "Smells like paint," she observed in a loud conversational tone, and then felt foolish when she reached the doorway and saw that he was working in the dining room, painting wood trim. There hadn't been any necessity to raise her voice. "Here you are," she said.

He was bent over slightly, painting a horizontal molding that ran along the wall. Turning his head, he glanced over at her, did a little double take and looked her over from head to foot.

"Do you like my new dress?" she asked.

He resumed his painting. "Is that what you came over to find out?"

"I bought it, hoping that you'd like it. But I came over to try to make up with you. Are you still furious at me?"

"Fury can last just so long," he replied.

"In the meantime, you certainly have been making headway, I see. This room looks great," she complimented sincerely. "I like the pale mauve color on the walls. Don't you?" She had helped him select the color.

"As long as a prospective buyer likes it, that's all that matters. I'm well pleased with the way the house is shaping up on the inside," he added.

"I've decided not to sell my house. I'm staying in Mandeville and keeping my teaching job," she announced.

He absorbed the news in silence and straightened to flex his broad shoulders. "At the rate I'm going, I should have a For Sale sign up by the end of June."

"So soon? You had allowed yourself a year." Catherine didn't make any attempt not to sound dismayed.

"Well, I've stepped up my schedule. This fall I'm planning to take a full course load. I'm applying for the G.I. Bill." He dipped his brush in the can of paint he held in his left hand and resumed his painting.

"Will you be moving across the lake?"

"I'm considering it. I can live cheaper over here, but I have the longer commute and more travel expense."

Catherine sighed. "Then you'll only be my neighbor for a few more months."

"That's about the size of it. The house will show better empty than poorly furnished, so I'll move out when it's ready to put on the market."

"This is a perfect opening for you to make a crack about leaving the coast clear for another unsuspecting bachelor," she pointed out.

"It was on the tip of my tongue."

"I would certainly have deserved the insult. It's wonderful talking to you, even carrying on a restrained conversation," she remarked, sighing. "I miss our conversations as much as I miss anything. Would you mind if I sat on that little stepladder and talked to you while you work? I have quite a bit that I would like to say. I've been rehearsing, so I have my thoughts organized and won't ramble on."

The small stepladder in question had only three rungs. He'd evidently used it to paint the higher molding. It stood near the wall just several yards away from him.

Without a word in reply, he balanced his paintbrush on the top of his paint can, turned and walked to the stepladder, picked it up and brought it to the center of the room and left it there, the farthest possible distance from him as he returned to his spot.

"Thank you," Catherine said, and arranged the stepladder so that when she perched on the top rung, she was facing him. She would have been perfectly happy just to sit there in silence and gaze at him. He was wearing old, paint-stained jeans and one of his dark, plain T-shirts. "I wonder about the origin of the expression 'a sight for sore eyes,'" she mused and smiled with flustered apology when he straightened and glanced around as though to say "Get on with it." But then his gaze lingered on her a moment.

"I promised to be concise, didn't I?" she said as he turned around, presenting her with his back again. "It's just so good to look at you at close quarters like this. I've been peeking through the blinds, hungry for a glimpse of you, and on pins and needles—that's another odd expression—for fear that you'd have a woman with you."

"I've sworn off women for the duration. However long that is," he added.

"I was about to ask. That's very painstaking work, isn't it? For having such large hands, you handle that paintbrush so delicately— I'm sorry." She apologized when he straightened, drawing in a deep breath. "I'll quit stalling and prolonging my visit. I can tell that your patience is wearing thin."

"What did you want to tell me, Catherine? Let's hear your prepared speech."

She rested her feet on the bottom rung of the ladder and clasped her knees. "First, I want to say thank God that you came along and saved me from making a grave mistake. I realize now that I would have been selling myself short, to use your words, if I'd given up on having a husband and a home and children. In today's society, sure there's a high incidence of broken marriages, but I believe in the traditional family and I'd like to take my shot at making a marriage work. I want to be a wife to the man I love, not just a mother to a fatherless child."

He had stopped painting and stood there, listening, his back to her. "There's no reason you can't have the whole package," he said. "Lots of men hit the marrying age in their thirties."

Catherine went on. "I'd convinced myself that I could be both mother and father. The truth was that I wasn't nearly as qualified as a mother as I thought I was. There was—is—so much I needed to experience as a woman first in order to be a more complete person. I figure I have a few years before I need to worry about being past the child-bearing age. It's time that I stop fading into the woodwork and become a late bloomer. You said yourself that I have nothing to apologize for as a woman. You did mean that, I hope, and weren't just being kind."

Graham set down his paint can and brush and turned around, wiping his hands on his jeans. "You know damned well I meant it," he said. "Here's another statement you can quote me on. What you don't know about men would fill several books."

"I can't argue with that," she replied. "If I gave the impression that I'm about to embark on some manhunt, I'm not. This visit today is the beginning of a campaign. I intend to chase after you so shamelessly that Tina will seem shy by comparison."

He glanced down at his hands and wiped them again. "You figure you have a few months to waste before you get down to the business of finding yourself a husband?"

"No. I may not know a lot about men, but I recognize an eligible male when I see one. When I told you that I thought you'd make some woman a good husband, I wished that I might be that woman. I just didn't dare hope that I could be so lucky. Maybe I won't be, but I'm going to try my best to land you."

Catherine rose and smoothed down her skirt. "Having given you fair warning, would you possibly consider going with me as my date to a faculty party on Saturday afternoon? It's a crawfish boil. There'll be kegs of beer.

I realize that it would be asking a lot for you to take the time off—"

"I'll go with you," Graham said.

"Anything to get rid of me, I suppose," she speculated wistfully. "Don't you have anything to *say* about all the things that I've said?"

His expression softened. "Of course I have things to say. Why don't you go back to your house and give me fifteen minutes to clean up and organize my thoughts? Then I'll come over, and we'll talk."

"But your reaction is generally positive?"

"Yes," he said gruffly. "Strongly positive." Then a smile tugged at his mouth, and Catherine felt her own smile turning up the corners of her mouth. "I don't think you'll encounter much resistance reeling me in."

"But there's still a lot of hurt pride and disappointment that you have to overcome?"

"Not a lot."

"You think you'll be ready to kiss and make up, literally speaking, soon?"

"Probably in about the same fifteen minutes that it'll take for me to shower and change."

"Then I would be rushing it if I walked over brazenly and threw myself into your arms?"

"You might get paint on that pretty dress—"

Catherine was on her way toward him, and his arms were opening wide as he issued the warning. He hugged her tight against him, lifting her feet off the floor.

"I missed you like hell," he said. "I've never been so damned miserable."

"I was twice that miserable," she insisted happily, hugging him back with all her strength. "I was so terribly lonely, I thought I would go crazy."

"You smell so nice and feel so good in my arms. And I'm dirty and sweaty."

Catherine raised her head from his shoulder and smiled dreamily into his face. "About this fastidious streak of yours..."

They kissed, the meeting of lips poignantly sweet. "I love kissing you," she murmured, and the confidence seemed to explode hunger in him. Catherine returned the bruising pressure of his mouth, coupled her tongue with his, soft moans of desire coming from her throat.

Graham groaned her name as he turned his head aside, breaking the seal of their lips. He hugged her harder, a shudder of passion running through his body. Then he set her down.

"Give me ten minutes," he said.

"Five minutes," she bargained.

"Baby, I'd have to sprint over to your house in a towel."

"Why do we have to go to my house?"

"We don't, except that this place is a mess. And I didn't know if you'd want to make love with me in my bed."

"I might suffer some jealous pangs, but your bed is more convenient than mine." Catherine took his hand. "Not to appear overeager, but could I escort you to the bathroom?"

He squeezed her hand and held it in a tight clasp, going willingly. His voice was warm and indulgent and happy as he said, "My life has been deadly dull these last couple of weeks without you, Catherine."

Serious talking was postponed until much later. There was too much physical intimacy to enjoy after what seemed like an eternity apart. In the bathroom, they carried on the provocative conversation of lovers while he stripped off his clothes and got into the shower. Catherine was ready with a towel when he stepped out, fully aroused.

The period of abstinence lent an urgency to their lovemaking. There was an overwhelming need to couple that rushed them through the preliminary kissing and fondling and caressing that they both wanted, but found far too pleasurable. An added element was the emotional communication that made words unnecessary, but nonetheless thrilling to speak and hear.

"I love you, Graham," she told him.

"I'm crazy about you, Catherine."

Satisfaction was cataclysmic and then sweet, but not lasting. They made love again a second time, at longer length. Afterward, they talked, lying in a close, warm embrace.

"I'll never *ever* lie to you again," Catherine promised fervently.

"Good. Because I have several tough questions and I want honest answers. First, how do you feel about marrying a thirty-two-year-old guy who's working on a college degree?"

"Easy question. I'd marry him in an instant if his name is Graham Macaulay."

"We could live together, but that might be a problem for you as a teacher in a small town."

"Next question. I've already answered that one."

"Can you be happy postponing being a mother for several years?"

"Yes. Especially if the marriage proposal hinted at in Question One materializes. But I do have my heart set on eventually having a little auburn-haired, blue-eyed baby."

"All I can promise is that I'll do my best to give you one." Graham hugged her.

Catherine nuzzled her cheek against his chest. "I have no doubt whatever that your best will be good enough."

* * * * *

Carole Halston

I have no firsthand experience with being a mother, since I don't have children, but I didn't hesitate when my editor called and extended the opportunity to write a story for the 1992 Mother's Day collection. As the oldest girl in a family of six, I've changed my share of diapers and done a lot of "mothering" as a big sister. Maternal instincts are no mystery to me or to most women, whether or not we ever give birth.

When I was ten years old, my mother had a baby especially for me. Or that was the way I regarded the event when she brought my little brother Gary home from the hospital. Once interfering Grandma went back to her house, I appropriated him as my own adorable live baby doll. All in all, I was a responsible nurse, but I'd seen a photograph in a magazine—a doctor holding a newborn infant upside down by the heels—that had, for some reason, made a deep impression. One day when I was tending to Gary in his crib, my mother conveniently out of the house taking clothes off the clothesline, I seized my opportunity and carefully held him up by his heels for a few seconds until he turned purple with outrage. Years later I confessed the now-amusing anecdote to my mother, and she went pale even as she laughed.

Michelle came along when I was seventeen. I was her second mother. She had three mothers altogether, counting my fourteen-year-old sister Linda. We hurried to pick her up when she whimpered and changed her into a clean cute little outfit about every thirty minutes.

Brian, the baby of the family, but definitely not the runt—six feet four inches tall at last measurement and 210 pounds—was born when I was a freshman in college. He was a fussy baby, and my mother had her hands full with him and a two-year-old. I came home on weekends and took my turn holding and rocking him and entertaining Michelle, who strongly favored sending him back to wherever he had come from.

Now they've grown up into interesting individuals—Gary and Michelle and Brian, those babies I bathed and changed and rocked to sleep. I enjoy knowing them as people and take pride in their various accomplishments. Best of all, they're parents now and live close enough that I can have all the fun of being an aunt to Matthew and Rebecca and Brittany.

By the time this is published, Rebecca, who's nine, will have a little brother or sister. Her mommy, Michelle, is having a baby for her!

Jilly's Secret

LINDA
SHAW

A Note from Linda Shaw

Once upon a time, in November 1938, a girl was born in El Dorado, Arkansas, and she was named Linda Louise McCullough. (The Shaw was added eighteen years later!)

Soon after that, this baby girl, who was, I'm told, a most difficult infant, was given to her grandmother—a poor, work-worn woman who had only completed three years of formal schooling.

This grandmother's responsibilities were heavy. She had already raised four children, her husband was now crippled, and their meager, fixed income was supplemented only by what she could earn baby-sitting.

Of course, I was that baby girl, and I have a feeling that I'm just as difficult now as I was then. One of my fairy-tale dreams when I grew up with this hard, stern woman was that my life wouldn't be as grim if I had a "real" mother. I wanted a mother like all the other girls had, one who wasn't tired most of the time and who knew how to dress up and fit in with the other mothers. I imagined that a "real" mother would say the words I never heard in my grandmother's house, such as *I love you*.

It's amazing how much a woman learns about mothers when she becomes one. As the years passed and my own children grew, my grandmother died. Even then, I didn't really know about the sacrifices a mother makes.

Eventually the blinders fell from my eyes. I began to see the price this weary woman had paid to take me and how much it cost for her to open up her heart, while in middle age, to an infant who would bring built-in burdens that no one else wanted to bear.

Mothering began to take on an entirely different meaning. With older eyes, I can look around today and see many, many children who are without mothers in one form or another. Many women raise children who were borne by another, and I ask the question: When it comes to a mother's love, does blood really matter? Love is a thing of the heart, and sometimes even the words *I love you* are not as important as the act of faithfully being there when you're sick, sewing clothes in the night, doing without so you can have a pair of new shoes. What do genes matter when it's the love that speaks?

So *Jilly's Secret* is my way of saying "thank you" to a woman now gone, who never had an inkling that I would ever write a single story. I consider it my deepest honor to thank her, for she gave me the very best she had. What more can a mother give?

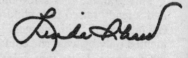

Chapter One

"But you should be *thrilled,* darling!" Arnetta Bowers's round, pudding face anticipated a soggy sneeze. "It's like the Academy Awards, don't you think? And you—so pretty in your long skirt. Do you have your acceptance speech ready? Oh, I do wish Mr. Bowers was here to see his beloved foundation honored so...so... achoo!"

Jillian Winston arranged the same smile for her employer that she gave most anyone who offered compliments, and she resumed the strangulation of her evening bag.

"Tonight's a milestone, all right," she politely lied, and glanced at her watch. "It makes me want to cry."

"I know, darling, I know." Arnetta blew her nose with one hand and patted the vicinity of Jilly's back with the other.

It was a quarter to nine, unduly warm for an April evening. Jilly and Betty Clay, her hyperactive young assistant at the Bowers Foundation, were waiting with Arnetta behind a folding partition in Boston's Parker House. Arnetta and Betty had been afraid the ceremony might not make the late television news. Jilly was praying fervently that it wouldn't.

The entrenched Eastern money crowd was making one of their rare appearances tonight. Middle-age matrons in sturdy jackets and modest spring hats sat beside their husbands, whose impeccable credentials made them the invisible power base of the country. They were recognizing those whom the Boston city fathers had declared were deserving of commendation.

On the dais, Senator Phillip Chamberlain was bracing a hand on each side of the podium. He had made some ad-lib remark that brought applause from the audience.

He was a striking man, Jilly thought, and rather interesting as politicians went. He had interrupted his term to fulfill an obligation to the military in the Persian Gulf—an extremely clever political move—and he had returned darkly tanned and trimmed to a hard, virile leanness.

Seated behind him was Mayor Dean Hadley, less lean and less virile.

Three television minicams were aimed at their smiles, and Jilly plucked at her satin blouse where it was clinging. She blew down the neck and smoothed back her short red curls where they were tightening mistily at her temples and her nape.

"It's too bad they couldn't have gotten Billy Crystal for the master of ceremonies," Arnetta was snuffling.

"What's wrong with Senator Chamberlain?"

"Nothing." Shrugging, Arnetta geared up for another sneeze. "It's just that Billy's so funny."

Looking like a wise little owlet in her horn-rim glasses, Betty twitched away Arnetta's tissue and replaced it with a cotton handkerchief.

"Paper tissues are a no-no, Mrs. Bowers," Betty whispered gravely. "Wood particles. I mean, they leave all those teeny, weeny microscopic splinters in your nose."

Smothering a smile, Jilly met Arnetta's bleary surprise. *It's much simpler just to take the handkerchief, Arnetta. Believe me.*

"Thank you, child," Arnetta said, and sneezed resoundingly.

Arnetta and Betty were the same petite height, but Arnetta, at fifty, had an edge of thirty pounds. Arnetta also covered every conceivable surface with diamonds, while Betty enhanced her hundred-eighty IQ with cropped black hair, hightop Kaepa sneakers and a cocktail dress. Betty not only marched to a different drummer, she wasn't aware there was a drummer.

Between the spraying of each nostril with decongestant, Arnetta added chidingly, "And you, Jilly girl, should stop being so nervous."

"For the dozenth time, Arnetta, I'm perfectly calm." Jilly struck one of her most self-assured poses. "Don't I look calm?"

Arnetta dropped the atomizer into her Gucci handbag. "You look beautiful, and you lie beautifully. But never mind, I forgive you. I really have no choice, do I? The foundation would collapse without you."

Laughing, Jilly shook her head. "Now who's lying?"

But Arnetta was right about lying beautifully. For thirty years Jilly had been perfecting her dissembling skills, and when she threw back her head and stood to her full five feet ten inches, her eyebrows aloofly arched and her smile cool, no one suspected that her hauteur was all a sham.

"Actually," she told Arnetta, "it's *your* money and *your* foundation. Why don't *you* accept the award?"

"Pooh! If you didn't want recognition, you should've remained callous and self-serving like the rest of us."

Laughter rippled through the room in response to something Chamberlain said. Jilly peered around the partition.

Not since John Fitzgerald Kennedy had a man so young captured the national affection as Phillip Chamberlain had done. His critics claimed he had climbed the ladder by virtue of who his parents were, but he wore his privilege with modesty. "A fine legislator to watch out for," the *New York Times* had tagged him.

The photographers were charmed by his twelve-hundred-dollar suits, naturally, and the counterpoint of his disarming smile. His salt-and-pepper hair didn't hurt, either, making a becoming frame for the dimples in his cheeks.

Beneath his brilliance and sophistication, however, was something more primal—a harnessed force that made it easy for Jilly to imagine him wearing a pith helmet and having an M16 slung over his shoulder.

The question was, why was he still single? He should have been married long before now. Some fatal flaw must be hidden away.

He was removing a pair of glasses from his tuxedo, and he put them briefly on to read from an index card, "Our next honoree . . ."

Jilly's own cards contained biographical statistics that had been provided by Arnetta—mundane things about the Peace Corps and working with the homeless.

"We met once," she murmured offhandedly.

Arnetta's watery eyes widened. "You never told me that."

"He was a small-time city politician then, traveling with some fact-finding group that was making the rounds of South America."

"Darling, you should've said something. I would've put it in your biography. Oh, look, he's unbuttoning his jacket. Mmm. Do you think he's a good lover?"

"For crying out loud, Arnetta!"

"Don't be such a prude, dear. Senators do make love. At least, in my day they did."

"Really?"

They smothered their laughter at Arnetta's slippery reference to the past. Though they had worked together for four years, there were still many unknowns on both sides.

The sound system blasted an earsplitting feedback, and Chamberlain reared back with a comic ferocity. He took advantage of the laughter to put away his glasses.

As Jilly was laughing with Arnetta, he caught sight and mistook the object of her amusement.

Ash-colored eyebrows lifted above clear, sandy-irised eyes. "Well, hello there," his expression seemed to say.

"Hello, yourself," Jilly fired back before she thought.

His smile warmed several degrees as he looked her up and down. Too late, Jilly remembered to slip into her arrogant mode, but his spell had taken effect and she was momentarily paralyzed. Her feet were nailed to the floor, and she was holding her breath, swimming in the glow of his smile.

The audience, sensing Chamberlain's absorption, turned to seek its source, and their stares struck Jilly like hurled javelins.

Snapping sharply into focus, Jilly stepped behind the partition and pressed her heart to keep it from leaping from her breast. She looked down at her herself, half expecting to find that someone else was wearing the long tapestry skirt, the green satin blouse. What had happened? Had she dreamed it?

"Jillian?"

Over her shoulder, she gaped at her employer in dull surprise. "What?"

"What's the matter?"

"Nothing's the matter." The sound of Jilly's voice had the effect of clearing her senses. She shook her head and touched her forehead. "Nothing, really. I just..."

She waved at space, indicating nothing and everything.

Senator Chamberlain had begun speaking again, but Jilly didn't dare watch him. All the negatives for being here—her fear that Veronica sight see her on television, that all her old, built-in phobias about her mother would surface—made her want to run away.

There was nowhere to run.

"You're upset because he didn't come, aren't you?" Arnetta quizzed as she sensed things she didn't understand.

"Who?"

"Him."

"My *father?*" Jilly laughed. "Jess Winston? Come out of his burrow over at Harvard? Not likely, Arnetta."

"Well, it's his loss, sweetie. This is your night, and since your mother's not alive, I'll stand in for her. Tonight, I'll be your mother, and I'll be as proud as if you really were my very own daughter."

So shocked that she forgot all about Phillip Chamberlain, Jilly dropped her jaw. How could Arnetta, after four years, have made such an erroneous assumption?

"My mother's not dead, Arnetta," she said, dismayed. "What made you think that?"

Arnetta dabbed the handkerchief to her reddened nose. "But—"

Jilly dismissed her friend's good intentions. Talking about Veronica was not a thing she wanted, especially not now. "It's my fault. Don't worry about it."

"But I feel terrible, darling. It's just that you're always talking about Mattie... Mattie having been your nanny, Mattie being your roommate, I naturally assumed... oh-dear-oh-dear-oh-dear."

Though Veronica's beautiful face was the last thing she wanted to see, Jilly found herself automatically peering around the partition in search of her mother. How many times had she walked down streets of another country and found herself startled by the sight of her mother's head, her walk, a sliver of profile?

She hugged Arnetta. "Please don't feel bad. Someday I'll tell you all about it. And Mattie's here, so I'm fine. Really. Believe me, you wouldn't like having me for a daughter."

At the podium, the senator was saying, "So it gives me great pleasure to introduce one of the most extraordinary women I've ever met."

"That's you!" Arnetta gave Jilly a brisk shove.

To Jilly's astonishment as she moved from behind the partition, her hem lifted to keep from tripping, Phillip Chamberlain began to announce facts about her past that she had forgotten—her grade-school essay on seals, her merit badges in the Girl Scouts. He knew about the Peace Corps, yes, and the homeless, but also about her present involvement with the nutrition of preschoolers.

Baffled, she found Arnetta over her shoulder. "Why did you write all that stuff?"

"I didn't!"

The Senator was beckoning her forward. "The first time I met this young woman," he said as he captured her eyes and refused to let them go, "she was on her hands and knees, planting trees in Brazil. For the past five years, she's been with the The Bowers Foundation, which is probably one of the most user-friendly sources of social assistance in the city. Much of that to Jillian's credit, I'm told. Her name is also well-known to abused women in the Boston shelters. We received a number of endorsements from women whose lives are better now, thanks to this woman."

No, no, no, Jilly wanted to beg. *Don't say nice things. Don't make me rush to explain why I have to fight and struggle and stare the world down, for the control, because of who I am, because of her.*

"Ladies and gentlemen, it is a privilege for me to present this plaque on behalf of the city of Boston to Miss Jillian Burke Winston. Congratulations, Jillian."

He was waiting for her at the top of the steps like a groom awaiting his bride. Rubies winked in his cuff as his hand reached for hers. His palm was hard and dry and surprisingly callused. From playing polo, Jilly thought with a sharp lack of charity.

"Don't be nervous," he murmured, and drew her smoothly up the steps.

Don't be nervous? Was he insane? Jilly could only thank heaven for the hours Mattie Corday had drilled her like a sergeant major: "Stand up straight, Jillian... Walk like a princess, dear... Slow down. Never touch your face... Uncross your legs... Don't fidget...."

"How do you know all that about me?" she murmured through a smile as tungsten filaments exploded before her face.

He grasped her left hand and lifted his own to silence the applause. "Shh, this is a live mike, Jilly. Enjoy your moment of glory. Believe me, they don't come that often."

He could not understand, of course, how meaningless the plaque was.

"You should be very proud," Mayor Hadley was saying as he rose and shook her hand with a politician's vigor.

"Thank you." Jilly's voice sounded absurdly high-pitched and brittle. "It's a privilege to work for the Foundation, sir."

"Congratulations, Miss Winston," someone called from behind a viewfinder. "Hold it? Smile? Perfect!"

Jilly had no idea what she said to the audience. Not that it mattered all that much. She even forgot to worry if Veronica would watch the evening news.

Phillip Chamberlain was leaning gracefully upon the side of the podium, waiting for her to finish. Beneath lowered lashes, she could see the slim cut of his trousers, the satin strips down the side.

"Thank you very much," she mumbled, and with the plaque tucked under her arm, she concentrated on leaving.

Lift skirt, extend foot, take step, heel-to-toe, repeat. Don't make a fool of yourself before this man.

She was astonished when Senator Chamberlain reached behind to snag her skirt with trailing fingers. So deftly was she reeled back, it was as if she had merely stepped aside so he could step forward.

"Stay," he murmured in the act of turning.

Stay? On the platform? But that wasn't part of the plan.

She strained against his grip, but because they had a history, fragmented though it was, it could have been a matter of moments since he was looming over her, watching her plant trees in the Amazon Basin.

So she sat down. Not that she remembered taking the chair beside the mayor, but she had to have done it because here she was, staring at Phillip Chamberlain's wonderful back.

The audience came to its feet when the program was done, and it moved toward the platform. Jilly also rose, uncertain about what would happen now. She clutched her bag and attempted to collect words and arrange them into some passably sensible order.

But she could have saved herself the trouble. People were forming a human net around the senator and the mayor. She was pushed farther and farther back as Phillip was taken farther and farther beyond.

"Senator Chamberlain, can you comment on the latest fallout from the Middle East?" someone shouted, and thrust a wanded microphone above the crowd. "Will there be lasting peace?"

"Will your name be on the '96 presidential ticket, Senator?"

"Has your bill on budget reform been shot down?"

Many times in the past, Jilly had been left behind, but she couldn't remember a time when it had confounded her more. Now she knew why Phillip wasn't married. *A high price to pay, eh, Senator?*

Disappointed in a way she could never have predicted, she left the dais. She told herself not to look back, but she was no more able to resist than Lot's poor wife had been.

To her surprise, Phillip was waiting for her gaze over the heads of those who crowded him.

Now you know, his sad smile said. For all his privilege, part of him was as victimized as she was. The very essence of what he was had become his prison.

I understand, she told him as she imagined herself bizarrely taking him into her arms and stroking the back of his silvery head. *I wish I could help you, Phillip, I really do.*

But she didn't know him well enough to help. She hardly knew him well enough to sympathize.

She tried to shake off her strange, troubling empathy and turned to search for Mattie among the guests. In Mattie, she could find solace. Mattie always understood.

At forty-seven, Mattie Corday was one of the few people Jilly trusted without qualification.

"I'm so proud of you," Mattie said as she moved forward to place a filmy shawl around Jilly's shoulders. "You don't suppose they'd give us one of the photographs for my scrapbook, do you?"

"Put this in your scrapbook," Jilly said, grimly thrusting the plaque into her friend's hands.

As was her habit, Mattie was dressed in gray. With long, thin fingers, she touched the cameo pin fastened to her prim collar. "Dear me."

"I've got to get out of this place," Jilly said, and gratefully dropped her pretenses.

"Shall we say goodbye to Arnetta?"

Arnetta was standing near an exit with a man wearing a clerical collar.

"I meant *really* out of this place," Jilly said.

"I was sort of hoping we could queue up to speak to the senator."

Rarely did Mattie joke, and Jilly gave the woman's arm a pinch. She elbowed them a path through the Parker House and blazed a swift, clicking trail across the parking area to her car. Not until she reached it did she collapse against the door and drop her head upon the roof.

"Hang on, hang on," she told herself, and expended another drop of precious energy to locate her car keys, only to drop them to the tarmac with a clatter. "Darn!"

Other guests were seeking their cars now, their voices drowned by revving engines and bleeping horns, radios and a nearby siren.

She finally unlocked her door. "I thought it would never end," she said over the roof to Mattie.

"What happened up there on the stage?" Mattie asked.

Ordinarily Jilly would have been eager to share her frustration with Mattie. She would have sputtered a few complaints and gripes and drawn a few misguided conclusions, then gotten on with her life. Now she covered her face and sighed.

"I'm sorry, Jilly."

"Don't be silly." Jilly gathered her tattered composure. "To tell the truth, Mattie, I'm not sure what happened. It was crazy. I felt in him—and I'm aware of his influence, his ambition—I felt in him a terrible need, I suppose, for lack of a better word. Yes, need. I suddenly found myself wanting to fill that need. Isn't that insane?" She laughed unhappily. "Some deprived maternal instinct, no doubt. A symptom of my deprived past."

"There's something to be said for maternal instincts, Jilly."

"Well, what the heck? He probably wanted to upgrade his Rolodex." She pulled a grimace that contained more disappointment than she was willing to admit. Under her breath, she mumbled, "He probably wanted a warm body for the night."

Mattie was too attuned to Jilly's despair to be horn-swoggled. "You don't believe that."

No, Jilly didn't believe it, and she willed herself to laugh. "I'm starved. Let's go home and eat until we can't squeeze into our nightgowns.

The older woman laughed, too. "The cheesecake is mine."

"Says you."

They climbed into the car, and Jilly had no sooner inserted the key into the ignition than a knuckle rapped on the window.

"Oh, God!" With lightening reflexes, she struck the button that locked all the doors.

"Miss Winston!" a voice called, and the rapping became insistent. "Miss Winston, Miss Winston!"

Outside stood one of the perfectly shorn, perfectly manicured, perfectly pin-striped young men who'd been part of Phillip's cadre. Behind his glasses, his intelligent eyes were large with concern, and in his hand was a small black book, fat with pages, a place in it being marked by his inserted forefinger.

"Good grief, man!" Jilly rolled the window down and poked her head outside. "You took ten years off my life."

Stooping, the aide brought his head down on a level with hers. "I'm sorry, Miss Winston. My name is Clifton Holmes. Could I have a word with you?"

Jilly drew her eyebrows together in a scowl. "Does this have anything to do with the limousine parked over there?"

Her remark directed their attention to where a long, sleek car crouched at an exit, its headlights holding their tight circle on the tarmac and a small poof of vapor bubbling from the tail pipe.

"Actually," the young man explained, "Senator Chamberlain wonders if you would mind having a word with him."

"He does, does he?"

"Yes, ma'am."

"Well, tell the good senator that I—"

Mattie's hand upon Jilly's was a discreet urgency, and Jilly twisted on the seat. "Mattie..."

"Maybe you should listen to what he has to say, Jilly."

"You're not serious!"

"What could it hurt?"

Mattie hadn't seen the burn in Phillip's eyes, Jilly wanted to counter. She hadn't had her defenses broken through as if they were so much cardboard.

She gave Clifton a lie-detector scrutiny. Rising, Clifton sent a signal to the waiting car. The back door opened and Phillip climbed out.

He cut a tall silhouette against the light-spattered city. His tie had been undone and his collar unbuttoned—a prince with the accoutrements of battle laid aside. With both hands, he raked through his silvery hair.

What a simple gesture, Jilly thought as an old emotion rose as if from a grave inside her.

"You can understand the need for precaution," Clifton said, and added something about security.

Jilly and Mattie shared a strange awkwardness. Of all the things they had talked about, this was not one of them.

Mattie had the impression they were standing at a crossroads, and her impulse was to turn and retrace her steps along a more familiar path. Jilly had no way of knowing what people saw when they looked at her, and she certainly couldn't conceive of Phillip Chamberlain comparing her to the women in his world and finding her more rare than all of them.

Mattie didn't relish sharing Jilly with the man, but to try to hold on now would be selfish.

"Listen to your heart, Jilly," she said, and lovingly arranged a flyaway red curl. "Listen to the now, not to the past."

Staring blankly through the windshield, Jilly presently let out her breath in a slow resolve. She covered her face with her hands and gradually let them slide away. She glanced at Clifton Holmes, who had gently opened the door and was reaching for her hand.

As Jilly was climbing out, Mattie realized how much she had been hoping that Jilly would refuse to go.

But Clifton shut the door and stooped to peer inside. "Will you be all right, ma'am?" he asked.

No! Mattie wanted to shout as she sat numbly, her hands folded in her lap. *I'll lose her to him!* But it was a loss every mother suffered. It was the natural order. The child moved on and the parent was left behind.

Parent? The word echoed: parent, parent, parent.

"You're a sentimental fool, Mattie Corday," she said aloud as Jilly walked across the tarmac with Clifton Holmes.

The wind caught Jilly's long skirt and tossed it out like a sail, her shawl floating about her shoulders. When she reached the car, Chamberlain moved forward and took her hand, drawing her into his side.

How lovely they were, taken together. They brought to mind a more romantic age when men of power made proud women their queens. He said something, and Clifton Holmes took a discreet position at the front door. Then the senator drew Jilly into the intimacy of the car. She was gone.

Hot tears of loss collected on Mattie's lashes, and she covered her mouth with her hands. So many of the ways of men were lost to her, but she did know the strange ways of the rich. Men like Phillip Chamberlain wouldn't do a thing for fun. He would have a reason.

Do be clever, my precious girl. Do know the priceless opportunity you hold in your hands. Be careful, be careful.

Chapter Two

As he watched Jillian Winston walk toward him, Phillip was not surprised when his senses catapulted. This woman was different from the women in his world. As she came toward him, she didn't sway daintily from side to side like a Gypsy temptress. She took the ground with the organic stride of a vigorous, healthy woman.

She seemed oblivious to the cars that passed and nosed onto the street. People were craning to make the connection between her and the waiting limousine. The whispering campaign would begin now, he guessed, oddly not resentful.

Finally she stood before him, breathing a bit quickly and flicking her tongue across her lips, her cheeks stained with the same fiery color as her curls.

"You have to forgive the sturm and drang," he said, and grinned as Clifton discreetly took his position beside the front door. "Security's a serious business with these guys."

She was briefly distracted by her own car passing, and he didn't watch the car but watched her. She was tall and her waist was so narrow, he could have spanned it with his hands. Her perfume was a subtle torment, making him want to move closer, to get drunk on it.

"You were with someone," he said.

"My roommate," she said, distracted for a moment but then facing him sharply, lifting her head and looking at him with eyes that were the color of dark, raw honey and as liquid. "I think we should come straight to the point, Senator Chamberlain."

"I couldn't agree more."

"Good." Her smile, though delightful, was not completely successful. "Well, what d'you want?"

Laughing, he wiggled his eyebrows at the waiting door. "For you to get in the car."

Stooping, she studied the car's interior like a pretty witch considering a boiling caldron. "I suppose I'd be following a grand and glorious tradition if I did."

"You flatter me, madam."

Her eyelids dropped to half-mast so that she was measuring him obliquely from behind their thick fringe. Would she refuse to come, even after all this? he wondered, and sighed with relief when she finally scooped up her hem and rippling shawl and made the awkward climb inside.

He received a glimpse of flashing legs and sleek knees. Her rear was sculpted by the folds of skirt.

Oh, Lord! He curled his fingers into loose fists.

The interior of the car was filled with Beethoven's First Symphony, and Jilly glanced around as she settled in—at the wet bar that offered refreshment, the silver ice bucket open beside bottles of sparkling mineral water, a decanter of whisky.

Jilly could have told him that she was no stranger to the luxury of limousines. Each morning, as a child, the butler had placed her into one, and Veronica's chauffeur had whisked her off to school. The Winston limo hadn't come equipped with bookcases, of course, or notebooks and volumes of law, video tapes and a battery of telephones, legal pads and scattered pens.

Nor had it come equipped with a magnificent Alaskan malamute that was perched politely on the opposite seat, wagging its tail.

"Oh!" Jilly gasped as her reserve fell away, and she leaned across the space, enchanted. "My, my, aren't you a beauty! And you shake hands, too." Laughing, she grasped the sleek paw. "Hello, I'm glad to make your acquaintance."

The dog's tail wagged furiously, the black markings on the white face giving the animal the look of a crafty masked bandit. As Clifton Holmes opened the front passenger door and took his seat, however, the dog jerked his head around with a low growl.

"Ohh, what's the matter?" Jilly purred, and consulted Phillip, who had shut the door and was leaning back to cross his legs, "don't you like Mr. Holmes?"

"About as well as Mr. Holmes likes him, I'm afraid."

"Well, I think he's beautiful." Forgetting about why she had been summoned, Jilly perched on the edge of her seat and scratched the dog's ears. "And you know it, too, don't you?"

"His name is Ranger, and I ought to warn you. Ranger's kisses have a history of dislocated collarbones."

"Then it's a good thing I'm not much for kissing, isn't it, sweetie?"

Ranger's ears perked as the engine rumbled and the big car slewed into the street, headlights lurching as they left the Parker House behind. Once they were on the straightaway, Jilly was acutely aware that she was on foreign turf, and she sat more properly. She folded her hands in her lap as Phillip rapped on the slide and asked Clifton about a speech he was scheduled for.

After consulting his black book, Clifton said, "A week from today at the State House. One o'clock."

Phillip consulted the calendar on his wristwatch, satisfied himself and settled back as the slide whisked closed again.

"Not ever?" he said, and Jilly frowned, confused.

"Pardon?"

"You do kiss occasionally, don't you?" He snapped his fingers as casually as if he had just mentioned the weather and gave an order to the dog. "Sit, boy."

Ranger obediently dropped to his haunches and laid his head upon his master's thigh. He stared across at Jilly with black, soulful eyes.

I know what you mean, she thought, but said aloud to Phillip, "That's a rather bold question, Senator."

"I'm a bold man."

"I guess I should consider myself forewarned, then."

"What you're supposed to do—" he stripped the loosened tie from his neck to toss it to the opposite seat "—is to admit that you don't really know a great deal about kissing."

Mercy! Jilly crossed her legs as a burst of peppery sensations made her shiver. She wasn't skilled at this kind of repartee, and her fingers found a loose bead on the tapestry skirt and plucked erratically.

The stitch broke with an audible snap, and the bead lay in her hand like some warning of bad things to come.

Capturing her wrist, Phillip turned up her hand, opening her palm and removing the bead. "I have a bad effect on people sometimes."

Jilly couldn't bring herself to look at him again, and she stared at her reflection in the darkened glass. "You didn't tell me what I'm doing here, Senator," she said, and was surprised at the sting in her timbre.

In the reflection of the slide, she watched him adjust his creases and chew his lip, his dimples winking. She was afraid that her voice revealed the fearful cadence beating in her. She had not expected to fear his answer, yet panic was coursing through her like blood, leaving her damp and chilled.

When she finally twisted around, he was rubbing the top of his cummerbund with his thumb.

"I have a habit of moving too quickly," he said, and ran his right hand through the loose mass of his hair. "I apologize. Life doesn't afford me the luxury of time. When I see what I want, I have to make my move."

So, she'd been right after all! He wanted nothing more than a warm body!

"Then I think you'd better tell your driver to turn around," she said angrily. "I wasn't into one-night stands when I was young and foolish, Phillip Chamberlain, and I'm even less young and foolish now."

When his expression was devoid of emotion, she lunged toward the glass slide. She would alert the driver herself.

But Phillip grasped her waist, burying his fingers into her sides. He hauled her back so swiftly, she lost her balance and ended up on his lap like a barroom wench with her face crushed into the tiny, starched ruffles of his shirt, his knees pressing shockingly into her buttocks.

"Don't be so quick to cut off your nose, darling," he whispered into her hair as his embrace tightened.

"I'm not your darling, Mr. Chamberlain," she said against a ruby stud as panic uncoiled inside her.

"Forgive me." Mockery was a rumble in his chest like pent-up laughter. "*Miss Winston.* And just for the record, one-night stands aren't my style, either."

She sat very still, the purity of her logic bruised by the provocative smell of spice and the hard textures of his body. She could feel the pull of muscles under his taut skin.

Why weren't her arms around his neck instead of shoving against his chest? He was, with his forthright male ego, simply letting her know his intentions. Wasn't that what she had always asked for in a man? The truth?

With senses reeling, she scrambled from his lap and shrank into a knot against her door. She bent her head to maul her curls.

From behind her hand, she glimpsed the twinkle of a smile, and the bottom dropped out of her stomach.

Leaning forward, Phillip said to the driver, "Drive us up to the Sound, Ron."

The car left School Street and zoomed up Highway One. It streaked north past Bunker Hill and the naval shipyards. Boston was a twinkling blur of lights as they drove past. Overhead, jets were roaring their descent into and ascent from Logan airport. Beyond, the Charles River rolled between its banks.

For the first time in weeks, Phillip leaned back and relaxed. He could spend the rest of the evening simply watching this woman. She was like a kaleidoscope, constantly changing—at the moment, thoughtful and still and serious, a little afraid, reminding him of a transparent glass animal, a swan or a doe, ready to leap away at a cracking twig.

Yet that was a deception. Even now, as her profile was silhouetted against the window and she watched the dark night fly by, clutching her shawl to her bosom, she appealed to him. He could imagine her soft breasts with their impudent freckles.

After crossing the river, Ron veered onto Shore Road. A half hour later, they were speeding through the cluster of beach houses that fronted Massachusetts Bay.

Presently the car jerked to a rocking stop, and Ranger rose up, his ears cocked as if he knew things that humans were not ken to.

The headlights brushed an arc of brilliance against a pavilion that once had been a summer attraction but was now crumbling in decay—a place whose ghosts had danced to Glenn Miller and Cole Porter.

"Want to walk?" he asked her.

She considered her long skirt and a shoe that was dangling precariously from the tips of her toes. "I'm not exactly dressed for it."

"A minor inconvenience."

Her grudging smile was there, then gone. The tiny lines at the sides of her eyes tightened. "Phillip, I don't know why, but every time you open your mouth, I feel like Eve being offered the apple."

"I don't have the faintest notion. Maybe you're hungry."

"I don't think so. I just had an apple."

Grinning, he opened the door so that Ranger leapt over his legs and shot into the darkness. They laughed without planning to, and Jilly reached out her hand to be helped from the car. As they stepped to the sand and straightened, she was very close to him, unplanned laughter still warm on her face.

She swayed slightly, and Phillip leaned toward her, wanting to kiss her laughter, but she recoiled, not out of frustration but because she was wiser than he.

"I keep running clothes in the trunk," Phillip said as Ron unlocked the back. "I come here to run. It's quiet, private."

"Not so very private." She dipped her head at Clifton, who was moving out onto the beach to make his reconnoiter.

Phillip shrugged. He had grown accustomed to having people around him all the time—an occupational hazard. She walked a distance beyond to ponder the pavilion. With her heels buried in the sand, she hugged herself and sympathized with the gaunt timbers.

From the trunk, Phillip fetched a zippered nylon duffel and tucked a Frisbee beneath his arm. He removed a jogging suit of wine-colored velour that was passably clean, and when Ranger returned with a flurry of barking, he hurled the toy, sending the dog speeding into the darkness again.

He moved closer to drape the suit across Jilly's shoulder. With an artlessness that continued to dazzle his senses, she held it out at arms' length.

"Well, Phillip—" she looked from the suit to him and back to the suit "—they do say the clothes make the man."

Phillip played out his smile. He was hungry for the taste of her now, for the silk of her skin. He wanted to bury his hands in her hair and, like some starving adolescent, pull her beneath him.

Good going, Chamberlain. You've sunk to an all-time low.

Ron doused the headlights of the limo, and they were left in darkness. The front doors were left opened, and music drifted from the stereo speakers.

Phillip slapped two pairs of clean gray socks into Jilly's hands. "Slip these over your pantyhose. They'll sub for shoes."

"Dear me." She studied the socks. "You're a knowledgeable man, Mr. Senator."

"What?"

"Knowing about pantyhose and all that."

She wasn't even good at flirtation, but he couldn't remember when a woman had made him so reckless. He tapped the top button of her blouse and was pleased when her breath caught audibly in her throat.

"You're playing a little close to the fire, Jillian Winston."

To his disappointment, she drew back into herself—a sensitive blossom closing against the invader. "Don't you find it all a little sad?"

"Pantyhose?'"

She laughed. "No, silly, the pavilion. So much is lost."

"Buildings decay."

"The dreams, I mean." Her eyes moved wistfully over the ghostly ruins. "Men going off to war, not knowing if they'll return, dancing with their sweethearts."

His answer was uncharacteristically peevish. "I went off to war and you didn't dance with me."

Her intensity was a branding iron, and she presently shook her head. "You didn't ask."

"Would you have waited for me? If I'd asked?"

And did she have any idea, Phillip wondered, how swiftly his world begun orbiting around hers? Did she feel the gravitational pull as he was feeling it? Was he losing his mind?

A tremor passed through her and she focused on the pavilion again. He drew a fallen curl from her eye and couldn't help flinching when she looked at him directly. There was nothing coy in her now, and he knew that she was looking far into the future as she debated her response.

Admit that you feel it, too, he wanted to demand as he was drawn inextricably into her gravity. *I won't ask any more of you.*

But she stepped back and he dropped his hand, allowing it to fall along the contour of her body. She knew how much he desired her, but she would not let herself be made his prey.

"I'd better change now," she said.

Chapter Three

Where they walked, waves gulped at the shore and the night air was splintery with the smell of salt. The moon spilled its white fire upon the bay, and sand dunes lay like shadowy, beached whales, spires of grass brushing the great underbelly of the wind.

Jilly had to laugh at Ranger racing up and down when Phillip sent the Frisbee spinning, charging into the surf and returning with it between his jaws, proud as a new parent.

Their footprints created a topographical map on the wet sand behind them.

"No sense of history, footprints," Phillip observed.

"They need a Robinson Crusoe."

"And he would find us, hollow eyed and ragged."

She laughed. "Dripping and sexually starved."

"Well . . . maybe not the last."

She shot him with a quill of pointed silence, and he said quickly, "maybe we can get Clifton to play stand-in and save ourselves."

But they had left Clifton behind, and Jilly wondered if the aide had been given his marching orders.

Phillip reared back to send the Frisbee spinning again, his crouch all sharp angles and gathering tension. He stretched in a lyrical symmetry that took Jilly's breath, and Ranger streaked into the sloughing foam to bring down the dangerous missile.

When he returned, Phillip grabbed the Frisbee and dodged, feinting and cavorting, laughing with such rowdy boyishness that the dog tripped him, pouncing and planting his great paws on his chest.

"I give up!" Phillip howled. "I give up, you monster!"

Jilly dropped to the sand and wiped foolish tears from her cheeks. Somewhere she'd made an awful mistake with her life. The searing irony wasn't that she'd made the mistake, but that she was learning about it now, at thirty.

Crawling toward her on all fours, Phillip arranged himself alongside and made a production of mirroring her pensive pose—arms wrapped about his knees, his cheek laid upon them as he grinned across the inches at her.

Galvanized into a sudden, desperate action, she leapt up. "Let's race!" she cried.

"Now? Aww, I'd just beat you, Jilly. It would be unsportsmanlike. Anyway, you don't wanna race. Come back and sit down."

She pranced sassily before him in his floppy socks and baggy sweats, chanting, "Fraidy-cat, fraidy-cat."

He pulled up onto an elbow. "Sticks and stones."

"The trouble with you, Phillip Chamberlain, is that you're spoiled." She kicked sand onto his sneaker. "You should experience losing sometime. It builds character."

He heaved himself up, and Jilly skittered away before he could swat her. For half an hour, they ran, side by side, arms and legs churning in unison, their breaths a heaving duet.

Jilly's first miscalculation was in believing she was in decent shape. She was one of those who fell out of bed in the morning and groped for her clothes and Pumas sneakers and hit the stairs running. She took vitamins, she didn't eat red meat. She read labels and avoided food additives.

But running at the crack of dawn and running in the exhaustion of midnight with a battle-hardened six-footer were two different things. Her legs were no match for Phillip's scissored stride.

"Tell me when you've had enough," he taunted, and added insult to injury by blithely dancing around to jog backward as she labored to plow forward. "There's no nine-one-one Service out here."

"Speak for yourself," she wheezed, praying she wouldn't have a seizure. What had possessed her to suggest this? "I'm just getting started."

"A woman after my own heart."

He maddeningly picked up the pace. Jill doggedly hiked up the pants she wore as the crotch persisted in drooping to her knees. The night was no longer beautiful. She hated him.

"Here, Ranger!" he yelled, and split the air with a cheerful whistle. "Here, boy!"

Gasping, she stumbled to a stop and buckled, dropping to the sand and folding up like a jackknife. She bent her head to her knees.

"You win, you sadist!" she groaned. "I can't go another step!"

"Poor baby," he said, and clasped her skull in a wide hand.

She struck feebly at him. "Touch me and you die!"

Laughing, he dragged her up by the shoulders and curled an arm about her waist, reeling her into his side. "Jeez—" he pretended to stagger "—how much do you weigh?"

"Enough to break every bone in your body." She stabbed a murderous elbow into his ribs.

"Ugh! I get the message, but you still have to cool down."

"Let me die in peace." She was a rag doll, disconnected at her joints. "Bury me in the sand. Don't even put up a marker."

"Just what I admire—grace under pressure—but you'll have a heart attack if you don't cool down, Jillsy-Willsy."

"I want a heart attack. I like heart attacks."

"Look, Ranger's come to sympathize."

"If it takes the rest of my life, I'll make you pay."

After a few minutes of foot-slogging torture, he aimed her at the rise of a nearby dune. Jilly lifted her eyes to heaven in gratitude as she stumbled toward it and fell, her arms a windmill, over the whale's hump and into a dry, sandy hollow.

Phillip dropped down beside her as she heaved up to sit and wrestle with the soggy socks.

"I've ruined my pantyhose," she wailed as she bared one foot. "And I can't feel my feet! Oh, God, I can't feel my feet!"

He poked a finger in a laddered run of nylon. "Yep, they're ruined, all right."

"Agggh!" Jilly dropped back and flung her arm across her face.

Presently, as her breathing leveled and her chest stopped hurting, she focused at the clouds tearing into rags overhead.

Phillip wasn't watching the raggedy clouds racing across the face of the moon; he was watching her. "Don't get *too* comfortable," he said serenely. "You're crazy if you think I'm carrying you back to the car."

She stuck out her tongue. "I've managed to get around under my own steam for a long time, thank you very much."

"Which is one of the reasons I want you in my life."

Why was it that the most lethal missiles came from out of the blue, giving a few seconds of warning, but not enough time for escape?

Jilly slid a look to see the moonlight pouring upon Phillip's face. Did he think she was a fool that she would actually believe such a remark? Could he not see that she knew the vast shadow his life cast? That she *knew* the powerful circles he moved in?

"That was a stupid thing to say," she said quietly.

They were close enough that he could have been holding her, but a thousand miles stretched between them.

"It's said now. I can't unsay it."

Which was, of course, the truth. Things never go back the way they had been.

She could not look at him. She drizzled sand through her fingers. "Do you think I don't know what you want from me? That I haven't known since the moment I got in the car?"

"You think I brought you here to seduce you?"

"I may be naive by your standards, Phillip, but I do know what men want from women."

"If I'd wanted sex, I could have found it easier and a hell of a lot faster than you, Jillian Winston."

Phillip had to admit that she hadn't read him all that wrongly. Through the flash of her temper that blazed at him, he could see himself undressing her. His body reacted to the excitement such visions entailed, and his pulse was strong and hot in his throat.

But she had seen his ambition, too, and he would have
to confess that young men of his social ilk invariably grew
up spoiled and full of themselves. He'd been no excep-
tion. His sexual triumphs at Harvard were as predictable
as the reasons why he'd stopped having them. He hadn't
even protected himself because of a moral conscience but
from a self-centered ego. Early on, safe sex became a
political expediency.

Time was the enemy now, though, not sex. He was
forty years old. The ambition that had kept him young
and expectant was wearing thin. He had to make his
move for happiness quickly or lose his chance.

When she scrambled up and started walking away, the
anger of that young Harvard dandy flashed like gun-
powder. Damn it, no one walked away from him!

Lunging, he caught her about the ankles, and his head
struck her hard behind the knees. Like an Imperial
Walker from *Return of the Jedi*, she weaved precariously for an instant, then crashed facedown into the
sand.

She was easy to conquer, and when he threw himself
upon her, her wriggling only underscored the surging lust
he had just vehemently denied.

"You're so predictable, Phillip," she hissed.

Grinning, he moved against her, grinding against her
bones.

She struck his shoulder hard with a fist. "Damn you."

"I probably will be." His grin was gritty and unpleasant. "But not this very minute. Till then…" He dropped
a swift kiss upon her lips, uneasy with the path he was
taking, but finding no other way to say that he was suddenly afraid he didn't know how to touch her and draw
her into his world. What bigotry kept him from asking to

be admitted into hers? What self-absorption drove him to use this primordial meeting ground rather than approaching her intellect? Because hers was more fastidiously crafted than his own?

It didn't matter, for she had already slammed doors shut inside, and he was left outside like a fool.

Lifting his weight, he slid off her and received her wounded silence.

"All right," he said hoarsely. "All right, I'm sorry. Look, Jilly, I just wanted to talk."

Her sharp censure challenged him as no one had challenged him.

"Can't we communicate like two sane adults?"

"We could." She continued to lie perfectly still. "If both of us were sane."

The hysteria of laughter saved them. It occurred to Phillip, as he rolled onto his back and let it build like steam, first a chuckle that life was so backward and insane, that human beings invariably screwed things up by hurting the ones they wanted to keep safe, by loving the ones they should have left alone. Then gut-deep hilarity that rolled out like music and thunder and tears.

Even if she laughed, too, because of the contagion of his own, what difference did it make? They were sharing something, mutually and at their own expense. It was the most satisfying sensation he had known in years, and he realized that she had been wanting to empty herself this way for a long time, too.

Presently, though, they were confronted by the restoration of sanity, and they sat wiping tears from their eyes and letting the craziness dwindle into afterthought. They repaired their composure and stole curious looks—at each other, then away, then back, then up at the arrogant moon.

Returning, Ranger dropped down to cover his nose with his paws, as if what he had long suspected was true: Human beings were indeed a lower species.

"I guess this means that skinny dipping is out," Phillip quipped dryly.

That sent them both off into gales again, but the equilibrium achieved its balance more quickly. By now the battle zone between them was cold. Finding the socks, Jilly shook the sand from them and arranged them neatly on the sand to dry.

"You asked me a question earlier." Phillip unnecessarily smoothed a wrinkle from one sock, watching his hands instead of her. "About how I knew all those things from your past."

He squinted at the perfection of her profile. Her silence was not an invitation to continue, but neither was it a rebuff.

"It would be romantic if I could say that I'd been thinking about you all these years," he told her, "but the truth is, I never gave you another thought until they handed me the program a few days ago. Your name was on it."

"Who worked up the introduction? Clifton?"

"Yes, but don't think I didn't remember you. You leaned back on your heels that day and squinted up at me like I was a poacher. Remember?"

"I remember perfectly."

"You pushed your hair out of your eyes and left a streak of mud on your cheek. I remember thinking that it would've made a great poster for the Peace Corps."

As she digested his words, he wanted to ask if she believed him. Instead, he walked straight to the edge of a precipice in his mind and stepped off.

"I'm forty years old, Jilly," he said.

With an unplanned lightness, she took his hand, but realized immediately that it was a giant step toward something undeclared—an admission of something that did not yet exist.

"That's really old, Phillip," she said, forcing herself to continue the mood. "I'm surprised you didn't keel over on the beach."

"You're going to make me say the whole damned speech, aren't you?"

"Speeches are what you do best." She would have drawn her hand away, but he caught it and placed it upon his knee. He felt her acknowledgement of the lightning speed with which things were moving.

"I do other things. The point is, my family has, for twenty-five of those forty years, been investing heavily in my future. *My* future, not that of my brothers and sisters. I've been the one who's going to put our family name in the history books, and in case you're thinking how lucky that is for me, it hasn't left a great deal of room for failure."

"You think it's worth the cost, don't you?"

"Would you?"

"Of course. I voted for you."

He had traveled much farther with her than he'd meant to, but it was too late to turn back now.

"The time has not only come—" he watched her breaths, her moves, her sighs "—past time. I should've married years before when there was some choice about the matter. If I had, my children would be old enough

now that my life wouldn't scar them. Now I find myself
in the unpleasant position of collecting mental dossiers
on all women I meet. That's why you're so perfect, Jilly.
No, let me finish. You have everything. You come from
an excellent family. I realize there're others who come
from good families, but you have something they don't.
You're your own woman. You said it yourself. You
haven't been seduced by this materialistic rat race we're
caught up in. I could look the rest of my life and not
come up with anyone more perfect than you."

Phillip felt his blood beating at his skull as if he had
risen too suddenly. All those words. What position had
he placed her in? How badly had he screwed up? Who
did he think he was?

She had laid her hand across her breast, and her cheeks
were pale as the moonlight. He could read her mind as
she absorbed the implications—the style of it, the sexual
implication of it, the childbearing, the outward posture.

"Say something," he said quietly, desperately.

Say what? Jilly wanted to scream at him. What could
she say to such things?

Not the part about marriage and children, for she had
very, very foolishly imagined herself coming to him in
that way already, yielding her most intimate secrets, even
those that she was ill at ease with, prepared to learn how
to please and even to take pleasure in him. She could even
see herself falling in love. He had earned her respect already, and how many men could she say that about?

But he was presuming things about her family that
couldn't have been more wrong. It *wasn't* an excellent
family! It was the most unexcellent he could imagine, and
to ignore that would not only earn the disgust of those

who had sacrificed, it would, in the end, trigger his own contempt.

"You're talking about a marriage of convenience," she said, deliberately letting him believe that the concept horrified her because it was simpler that way.

"A lot of good marriages begin with much less."

She stared blindly at the sand. She had to save this moment from disaster.

"You're asking me to forego the dream, Phillip," she said gently, very gently. "Don't you know that every woman dreams of being Cinderella? Waiting for her prince?"

"Love!" He handled the word too roughly. "You wouldn't believe me if I said the words. I *like* you, Jilly, I respect you. We would be...good to go."

He was right. They *would* be "good to go."

But she had no time to justify the crystallization of her feelings. He had turned and was coming up onto his knees before her, spanning her waist, pulling her against him so his face was on a level with hers. For long, breathless moments, he looked deeply through the windows of her soul. No man had ever looked at her so.

His kiss, when it came, was with deliberation. He bent his head—carefully, with stops and starts and delicate savoring, as if giving notice that she had plenty of opportunity to stop him.

But paralysis had struck her limbs. She could not move. She was standing at the edge of a quicksand swamp, and she could not step back, nor could she go forward.

Slowly, he slanted his mouth across hers. "Please say I'm right," he muttered as he captured her more deeply. "Don't let me make a bigger fool of myself."

"Phillip—"

But he gathered her, holding her wonderfully tight, reaping her and turning her golden and ripe. She was being absorbed into his flesh and bones. She was no longer in her own body but was a spirit—a mist that could curl up inside him and be safe.

Her one brief affair was no help to her now. It knew nothing of the magnetism of this man when he clasped her hips until they fit perfectly to his, to his rock-hard tension that merged perfectly with her softer femininity. She could be forgiven, couldn't she, for yielding?

"Jesus," he whispered as she wrapped her arms around his neck and melted into his sweet assault.

They were, suddenly, an urgent, straining shaft of humanity. Thrill after thrill shot through Jilly as, with her fingers, she searched along his neck, sliding to his face, tracing the place where their lips connected. She could not taste as deeply as she wanted, and she knew if she yielded, he would bend her knees and print his body upon hers so that they would no longer be two, but one.

His mouth abandoned hers and found its way across her bosom, lingering over the curves and hollows as his hands found her beneath the clinging shirt. The sandpaper of his chin brazed her skin, and when his teeth closed upon the eager swell of flesh, she groaned, having forgotten that a man could make a woman feel such things.

Yet she saw, too, a bloodred aftermath of such recklessness. She didn't care so much about hurting herself, but if she hurt him—he was honest, he only wanted to do the right thing—she could not live with that.

Pushing free, she eluded his grab for her. "This is my fault!" she choked out and held him at bay with outstretched hands. "I'm sorry, Phillip. This is too fast, this is too... Please don't hate me."

When she crouched down in a tight little knot, Phillip bent over her as uncertainly as a man who has discovered an infant on a doorstep. He felt drugged, unable to clear his head. His hands were trembling.

"Jilly?" He wanted to touch her, but her misery compelled him to hold himself suspended, hovering.

"It's not you," she confessed grievously to her knees. "I—I can't deal with this now. I'm lost. I don't know... Please... I just... *can't.*"

She couldn't? She couldn't? But he had tasted hunger upon her lips and felt it in her shiver, heard it in her breaths. She had reached out for something and had abruptly slammed a door, not only in his own face, but upon her heart, and the sound of its crash had nearly killed him.

But how could he blame her? He had done it to himself. He was blown up with his own inflated importance. He had been trying to convince her that she was good enough for him, but the truth was that he wasn't good enough for her. If he had been in her place, wouldn't he have shut himself out?

He could have slapped her. He could have shaken her. But he rose and walked toward the sea where the wind could lash his hair and he could formally receive the sullen night. She did not call out to him, nor did he expect her to. He was alone and abandoned, unsure of where to go from here, only that he must go somewhere.

He had a great sense of being exposed, of teetering upon the future. But it, like the sea that spoke in the darkness, was dark and very cold.

Chapter Four

Jilly's first memory was of Mattie seated at a piano. She was curled on Mattie's lap, sniffling and mewling and clinging. Mattie was kissing her curls and singing "Itsy Bitsy Spider" as she accompanied herself with her left hand upon the keys.

In the recollection, Mattie coaxed Jilly to smile through her baby tears, and she tucked Jilly's chubby hand inside her own. She guided the tiny finger so that it sounded the notes of the melody.

Only later did Jilly connect her memory to the reality of her mother's violent tantrum. The timbers had shaken that night as Veronica ordered her second husband from the house. Jilly could recall viciously slammed doors and earsplitting shouts, threats to kill her stepfather if he ever came back.

There were other scenes, of course: Jess Winston, Jilly's father, coming to the house and fighting bitterly with Veronica over Jilly; Veronica in her bedroom with compellingly mediocre men who drove handsome cars; Veronica's rages and petulant silences because Jilly—always awkward, always clumsy and doing the wrong things— was in the way of an affair that could change their lives for the better.

Jilly's escape was inevitably to the nursery. There, she would hide beneath the bed and gather her dolls into her arms, kissing their plastic hair while she tearfully sang "Itsy Bitsy Spider." Like a faithful mother hen collecting her one beloved chick, Mattie would gather Jilly beneath her wings.

Veronica's one gift to Jilly was to keep Mattie in her employ. During Jilly's teens, Mattie took over the running of the large house, and Veronica was given the freedom to find and marry her fourth husband, Robert Mills.

It was after her mother's marriage to the corporate titan that Jilly found her own position unexpectedly usurped. Blythe Mills was the apple of Robert's eye, everything that Jilly was not. She was the blond, shining daughter whose smiles cast an irresistible spell upon adults. She was also the granddaughter of multimillionaires whom Veronica was desperate to please.

Early on, Jilly realized that her contest with Blythe was no contest. The lovely face Blythe showed in public was not the determined one she showed to Jilly. Jilly's escape was to drop out of college and join the Peace Corps.

With Jilly gone, Mattie had no desire to remain on Veronica's staff. She took the job of superintending a three-story brownstone owned by a West Coast corporation.

On the afternoon following the awards ceremony and her evening on the beach with Phillip—which she still wasn't able to think about without panic—Jilly stood on the front stoop of the brownstone and shifted the grocery sacks as she went through a series of acrobatics to unlock the door.

Once inside, she bumped the door shut with her behind. Echoing the slam, Mattie's voice called out to her, not from the chic little garret upstairs, but from the basement. "Jilly? Is that you?"

Puzzled, Jilly ventured toward the back stairs, where a door opened onto the musky basement below ground. "Mattie?"

"I'm down here."

Jilly placed the sacks outside a glossy white door and rapped sharply on the facing. "Mr. Fanelli, I'm leaving some things outside your door for a minute."

The door jerked abruptly open and a wiry-haired man with the face of a terrier screwed up his expression. He considered Jilly and considered the bulging sacks. "Are those for me?"

"No, Mr. Fanelli." Jilly raised her voice to the half-deaf man. "They're mine. I'll be back...no, no, they belong to me. To Mattie and me. Forget it. Take what you want."

"Take what?"

Lifting her eyes to the gods in supplication, Jilly shook her head and went down the steps and into the basement, where the furnace was housed along with the renters' electric meters and plumbing. A bare electric bulb dangled from a cord at the foot of the crude stairs, yet it did little to rake the shadows from the corners.

"Ugh!" The smell made Jilly stop on the bottom step and tucked her nose into the bend of her arm. "What're you doing down here, Mattie?"

Her answer was the sound of splashing. "No one has hot water. Mrs. Restick's very upset. She's positive it's terrorist sabotage and wants to call the FBI."

From the step, Jilly laughed at the mention of their strange, second-floor tenant. "Did you pay the bill, Mattie?"

Mattie stepped from behind a wall where the beam of a flashlight moved from the electric meters into Jilly's face. Over gray slacks, Mattie had pulled on knee-high rubber boots, and the sleeves of her sweater showed beneath a smock. Her hair was turbaned with a scarf.

"No wonder you have no hot water," Jilly quipped. "It's all over the floor. Would you shine the light somewhere else?"

"Sorry. Well, what I did was call a plumber. He promised to call me back, but I'm beginning to suspect that he lied."

"All plumbers say they'll call you back. Maybe we could fix it ourselves."

The light returned to Jilly's eyes. "You're either temporarily insane, my dear, or your lack of sleep has caused brain damage."

Jilly stuck out her tongue. "I honestly considered waking you up when I came in."

It was half-true. When Phillip's car had brought her home and he'd walked her to the door, they had stood beneath the misty porch light and hadn't known what to say. He had, at the end, lifted her hands to his lips and kissed their backs. Then, with a tenderness that still made her want to weep, he had placed a kiss upon her forehead and had bidden her a sad good-night.

Jilly had lain awake until dawn, trapped in her own misty bubble of confusion. When she finally had managed to crawl out of bed, her body aching and her eyes filled with sand, she was relieved to find Mattie's note that she'd gone shopping.

Now, after an interminable day at the foundation, she was simply too weary to explain.

"Try again," Mattie gently chided. "Maybe I'll be fool enough to believe that one."

Jilly giggled. "Quit griping and let me have the light for a minute."

Mattie plunked and splashed to the steps.

"Give me the boots, too," Jilly said.

Frowning, Mattie climbed up to sit on a step and removed her boots. "Anything else of mine you want?"

"You're such an arrogant woman, Mattie."

Mattie waited patiently as Jilly inspected the water heater. After several minutes, she asked, "Are you accomplishing anything or just having fun? If you promise to stop what you're doing, I'll call the plumber again and threaten him."

Jilly tromped back to the steps. "Smile, Mattie." She made an impish face. "It's your lucky day!"

The older woman's look, Jilly thought, would have pulled nails.

"The water," Jilly cheerfully explained, "is coming from the connection at the steam vent. I can fix it myself. Unfortunately, we'll have to drain the thing."

"Look around yourself. It's not a problem."

"Give me a few minutes to change clothes and run down to the hardware store. Meanwhile, tell everyone we'll have hot water by bedtime."

"You're not being overly optimistic, are you?"

"This happened once at the compound in Brazil. I helped fix it. Stop frowning, Mattie. Your face'll freeze that way."

Squishing her way up the steps, Jilly left the older woman standing on the island of the step.

"Jilly?"

Jilly knew the question, yet knowing it, she could not bring herself to turn round. "I know what you're going to ask, Mattie," she said from the threshold and waited, not moving, not really breathing.

"What did he want?"

"A wife, as it turned out."

Jilly flinched at the sound of Mattie's surprise. Echoing in the corridors of her past, she could hear the fragile child's voice singing "Itsy Bitsy Spider."

"What did you tell him?" Mattie asked in hushed wonder.

"I told him no." She would not weep, Jilly promised herself. The decision was made. There was nowhere to go but forward now. Phillip would be the first to agree.

As Jilly's steps sounded down the front hall and the front door opened and closed, Mattie dropped down to sit upon the steps. She drew the scarf from her hair and wiped her hands upon it.

"Oh, my dear," she whispered as she stared dully into the water at the foot of the stairs. "What have you done? What have you done?"

Hours later, lamplight was spilling through the cozy, slant-walled garret that Mattie had spent the past years decorating with charming wallpapers and delightful chintz-slipcovered furnishings.

Though small, the apartment extended an invitation to those who entered. Footstools squatted before chairs made dainty with needlepoint coverings. Spidery lace curtains fluttered at the dormer windows. Handmade afghans draped promisingly over the arms of the rockers.

Mattie looked up from her knitting and smiled. Everyone's apartment now possessed steaming hot water.

She said, "When you didn't return last night, I occupied myself with terrible scenarios of what was happening."

Jilly was curled on the love seat, swathed in a terry robe as she blotted her wet hair. "Yes, Mattie..." She laughed because their habit of shorthand conversation was so predictable. "Phillip did kiss me, and yes, I did like it. But that's not the reason I told him no."

Mattie placed the knitting into a basket at her feet. "Do you get the feeling that this discussion calls for a nightcap of cappuccino?"

Jilly smiled unhappily. "I just hope you didn't eat all the cheesecake."

Their slippers slapped reassuringly as they moved about the kitchen. They made no attempt to talk as Mattie filled the tea kettle and Jilly laid out the linen napkins that matched the Blue Willow cups. Next she debated the perfect place to equally divide the last piece of cheesecake.

Not until they were seated and Mattie had poured did Jilly begin to explain the remarkable events that had transpired between Phillip Chamberlain and herself.

For some moments after she described the horrible way she had ended things, Mattie sat drawing a fingertip round and round the rim of her cup. "You know, I sometimes think there's something to be said for the old ways."

"No touching below the waist?"

"No. When arranged marriages were the norm. Both parties knew long before that it would happen, and they went into it certain of what was expected. The husband wanted his wife to continue with her life, and he planned to build on his own."

"Most people wouldn't find that very romantic, Mattie."

"Marriages had less to do with romance—not whether Phillip was sexually attracted to Jilly and Jilly was attracted to Phillip. The question was whether or not they could feed and clothe the children and keep a roof over their heads."

Jilly's spoon clicked against her saucer as she compulsively stirred. "There has to be love between two people, Mattie. Goodness!"

Shrugging, Mattie rose and began collecting the dishes. "I didn't say there wasn't love. We were talking about sex."

"No, not sex—love. Love. You know, romance."

Rising, Mattie placed her cup and saucer in the sink. She shook her head. "Love isn't sex, Jilly. Love is two people giving their whole lives, all their beings to a marriage that will last, to something bigger than both of them. Love is doing the job together, paying the bills and raising the children. Love is getting it done. Romance, well, romance is... an orgasm."

Gasping, Jilly dropped her cup with a clatter. Her cheeks were hot and she swallowed with effort. "I don't believe I've ever heard you use that word, Mattie."

"You think I don't know what it is."

"Why... no, I don't think that!"

"My point is, if you're very, very lucky, you can have both—love and the orgasm. But you can't build a marriage on an orgasm, Jilly. Not if you don't want to wind up in a divorce court in a few years."

Mattie indicated Jilly's cup. "Are you finished with that?"

Jilly blinked. "Yes." She laughed self-consciously. "Frankly, I couldn't swallow another bite."

After Mattie finished tidying, Jilly sat folding a pleat in her napkin, then another and another. "It wouldn't have been as simple as Phillip loving Jilly and Jilly loving Phillip," she said, keeping her eyes lowered to her hands. "What you have to understand is that his life is complicated. It's all mapped out and has been for years. It really doesn't even belong to him. Phillip's problem is that he has to look at a wife in the light of who she is and where she came from, how much she will bring to the marriage." She looked up, her mouth twisting. "Rather feudal, don't you think?"

"But you have background," Mattie said. "You could bring all those things to a marriage."

Jilly's honesty flashed in contradiction. She shook her head so violently, her turbaned towel slipped askew.

"He has all kinds of misconceptions about my family, Mattie. He looked at me and saw a scientist and a social butterfly. How could I tell him that I haven't spoken to that social butterfly in years and that she doesn't want me?"

"That isn't true."

Tears clotted Jilly's voice. "And as for my father..."

Mattie waved the words away. "Yes, why don't we look at your father? He's a good, decent man, Jilly. He's reclusive, yes, but he's good, respectable stock."

Jilly's fist came down hard on the table. "The point of all this is that Phillip would suffer a major disillusionment when he found out who I really am! I don't want to see that betrayal on his face!"

"Poppycock!"

With a sigh, Mattie touched a light switch and darkness dropped into the kitchen. Jilly sprang to her feet and bumped the table with her hip. They walked, as they had walked a thousand times before, to the living room and opened the doors to their bedrooms.

The lamps were turned out until only one remained, and Jilly slumped morosely against the frame of her door. When Mattie touched her brow, she went into the woman's faithful arms as willingly as the child who had always gone.

But her Mattie was changing. The years were taking their toll. Mattie's breasts were not as high as they had once been, her arms not as hard. Her flesh not quite as firmly knitted upon her bones. Her beloved Mattie was beginning to age. One day she would be gone, and then what would happen to poor Jilly?

"Jilly," Mattie whispered, and leaned back so they could see each other's faces, "you know what you have to do."

Jilly shook her head stubbornly. "No."

"You have to repair the breach between you and your mother."

Thrusting away the arms that she trusted above all others, Jilly placed space between them. "I can't, Mattie. And even if I could, I wouldn't."

"Do you think the Chamberlains don't have a few skeletons in their own closet? Do you think they wouldn't understand if they looked up one day and found that Veronica was a selfish, self-absorbed woman? Darling, it isn't an isolated instance. Veronica, even with her mistakes, is a recognizable name, and that's what you need. Her heritage, your heritage, is sound. Believe me, if Veronica knew about this, she would want to reconcile."

Jilly struck angrily at the emptiness between them, not only a physical space, but the space that fate had placed between them. "She's not my mother, Mattie."

"She is, Jilly."

"*You're* my mother, not her."

Jilly moved into her doorway, stooping beneath the weight of a decision that she had convinced herself she had escaped.

"I'm a maid, Jilly," Mattie was arguing behind her. "I was your teacher, not your mother. Now you need the blood and the name. I wish to heaven I could give them, my dear, but I can't."

The truth struck Jilly squarely in her back. She walked into her room and shut the door, but the hard truth had followed her inside. She did want to try to see if something real, something lasting couldn't be found between Phillip Chamberlain and herself.

But what if, in wanting Phillip and the life he represented, she somehow lost more than she could ever hope to gain? What if she lost Mattie? Without Mattie, she would have no past. Mattie *was* her past.

Chapter Five

Jilly's night with Phillip was a week old now; hindsight created vast and detailed lists of her regrets.

To compensate, Jilly threw herself into a tailspin of work. She was the first to arrive downtown in the mornings and the last to leave. Her days were spent beneath an avalanche of projects, the more problematic, the better.

The Bowers Foundations occupied a corner on the fourth floor of the Handley Building, a musty Victorian relic whose only redemption was that it offered a fantastic view of South Boston. On Thursday, Arnetta returned, her cold so improved that she had justified all her excuses for smoking.

Now, in Jilly's office, she was searching for an ash tray. Not finding one, she flung herself into the only empty chair and thumped a cigarette end on end, end on end.

"Arnetta—" Jilly looked up from a stack of case histories of homeless families "—you can't smoke in here. Die of cancer in your own office."

"Oh, it's that LaMott person!" Arnetta huffed a grumbling sigh. "I've had it with her. Four phone calls and all for nothing. She's out of her mind if she thinks she'll get another penny of my money!"

"You've already made the offer," Jilly blandly reminded, and gave a start as she stared down at her blotter. She had unwittingly traced Phillip's name dozens of times.

She furtively slid her hand over the scribbling and mumbled something about it being bad form for Arnetta to go back on her word now. "Think of the children." Like a criminal, she tore off the sheet, folding it to the size of a post card.

"Bitch!"

Jilly jerked up her head.

"No, no, not you, dear." Arnetta waved away her words and replaced her Virginia Slims cigarette in its gold case. "Tell me, Jilly, if a Foundation offered *your* school an after-hours facility, wouldn't *you* arrange transportation to get the children to it?"

"I'm not Madeline LaMott." Jilly discreetly slipped the folded, spindled and mutilated blotter page into her wastebasket.

"Well, straighten it out, will you, dear, and get back to me?"

"Arnetta, handle Madeline LaMott yourself."

"She makes me crazy."

"She makes me crazy, too."

"But you're strong."

Jilly watched dismally as the woman chugged out of her office under a full head of temper. Betty lingered in the doorway for a moment, watching.

"She must've forgotten to take her estrogen again," Jilly said. "Find out. But tactfully."

Later that evening, Jilly sat in the garret with Mattie and flipped through the same magazine she had been flipping through all week. Mattie had stopped offering advice on the subject of Phillip Chamberlain. She kissed Jilly good-night and went to bed.

Alone, with a half dozen people going peacefully about their lives below, Jilly paced the garret floor as quietly as possible. She turned the television on then off, tried to read and slammed the book shut, then migrated to the kitchen.

She ate an entire crumb cake by herself. With her stomach refusing to forgive her, she dragged herself to bed and huddled beneath the blankets, shivering and craving a woman's satisfaction that would ever be.

But it wouldn't have worked, she told herself as lost chances for happiness rattled the bones of her skull. *He was wrong. You wouldn't have fit into his world. Veronica would have betrayed you just as she always does. Phillip's mother would have seen through you. He would have hated you for that.*

Sometime before dawn, she slept.

In her office the next day, Jilly had dragged the telephone to the full limit of its cord so she could stand before her office window and gaze out at the peninsula.

As a sort of combination punishment and protest, she had worn her least-favorite pair of brown gaberdine slacks today and a sports jacket that should have been tossed into the Goodwill box years before.

"I understand perfectly, Miss LaMott," she was droning as she rubbed her eyes that were full of grit.

In response to Betty's harried tap on the door, Jilly waved her inside, holding up a hand for silence.

"But what *you* have to understand, Madeline," Jilly said, "is that many of these children are returning to empty houses until a parent can get off work... No, I don't think it's unusual, but it isn't safe, either. I think you should meet us halfway. One can't put a price tag on safety."

Not being one to waste time, Betty sped around the office and made swift work of solving the Gordian knot of Jilly's desk. She gathered files and straightened furniture, watered the African violet. She picked up the wastebasket.

"Ahh, would you hold a moment, Miss LaMott?" Jilly cupped the mouthpiece and hissed, "Betty, whatever you're doing, stop! What did you want to see me about?"

Betty hugged the wastebasket, her chopped hair bouncing. "I was trying to tell you. The problem is solved. I mean, it was solved for us. I told them flat out that we would only consider... I mean, you know because we worked all that out, and then they walked through the door. I've already made a cursory interview and taken some notes."

From her pocket, Betty drew out a sheaf of pink papers and stuffed them into Jilly's hand as if they would clarify all confusion.

Jilly held her hands up in a time-out signal. "Start from the beginning, Betty. What problem? Who came and where did they come from?"

"Transportation. Three high school seniors—Jack Meritt, Ellen Dent, Steven Herzog."

"What?"

"They have valid driver's licenses. They said they'd been told to transport grade schoolers for Miss LaMott as part of their student work program. I can check out their driving records through the Department of Motor Vehicles if you'd like me to."

"But who sent them?"

"Senator Chamberlain."

As if she had slammed into a wall head-on, Jilly slumped against the window and crushed the telephone receiver against her stomach. *"Who?"*

"Chamberlain, forty, Harvard Law, two terms, Captain, U.S. Marine Corps. Reserve, Saudi Arabia—"

"I know that, Betty, I know that." Phillip was closing his arms around her, making her burn as he pulled her down into the sand.

"But how did he know what we needed?" she whispered.

"He called Arnetta yesterday after you left. He could've talked to her. But that's speculation. I'll try to reach him if you want me to, for specifics. Let's see... State House, one o'clock."

Jilly shivered with a vague sense of déjà vu. "How do you know that Phillip... Senator Chamberlain, I mean, is going to be at the State House at one o'clock?"

"The *Globe*." Betty tapped her chin as she called up information from her vast memory banks. "Op-ed, Hastings, ten years on staff, previously stringer for state—"

"All right, Betty, all right."

Now Jilly remembered Phillip talking to Clifton about the speech. Phillip's ghost wasn't supposed to invade the day! Nor was the treacherous, liquid rush of her own longing.

"Madeline!" She glanced down at the telephone, her apology a throaty rasp. "I'm very sorry. Yes, my time is valuable, too. Could I call you back, Madeline?"

The receiver clattered as she dropped it into its cradle. Jilly strode past Betty and out into the reception room. Here, near the door, waited a trio of squeaky-clean teenagers, two boys and a pink-cheeked girl. Their smiles brightened when they spied her, and they glanced nervously at one another.

The receptionist leaned over her desk. "Jillian, Miss Cantonelli needs a lawyer."

"Call Delia." Jilly's thoughts were swirling like leaves in a dust devil. Phillip wasn't out of her life. He hadn't taken her at her word. He had called Arnetta. Was she glad? Yes, yes!

"Miss Cantonelli swears she never signed the living will," the receptionist insisted as Jilly moved past. "Her son-in-law has seemingly forged it."

"Call Delia. Tell her the Foundation will pick up the retainer."

Before Jilly could speak to the students, the outer door opened and a uniformed man with a ponytail poked his head inside.

"Is there somebody named Winston in here?" he yelled.

Jilly frowned at the students. "Don't move a muscle." She transferred the frown to the ponytail. "I'm Miss Winston."

"Sign here."

Jilly scrawled her name on the sheet, and the man disappeared, returning almost immediately with a large bouquet of fresh flowers.

"Where d'you want 'em?" he asked from behind the baby's breath.

"Are you sure you have the right office?"

His smile was small, as if the band about his ponytail was too tight. "Bowers Foundation?"

"Yes."

"Winston?"

"Yes."

"There you go." He disappeared as abruptly as he had come.

Though the students were grinning, Jilly found the florist's envelope. She glanced at the high schoolers, then at the card.

Scrawled boldly were the words, "I can't stop thinking about you. Please? Tonight? Your place? No strings. Phillip."

Jilly was aware of dying and coming to life again in a different body. She was in a different warp of time. The students who were watching weren't students at all, but the Scarecrow, the Cowardly Lion and the Tin Man drawing the curtain aside to reveal the Wizard of Oz. Only the Wizard wasn't the one working the machine behind the curtain, Veronica was.

Veronica—the hurdle Jilly could not circumvent now. Mattie was right: she could not dream her mother away or pretend her away or lie her away. To reach Phillip's family, there was only one way—through Veronica. Did she want to reach them? To face her nemesis?

She did, but, dear Lord, if she were being gullible, if she were playing the fool again, if she were being tricked, please don't let her ever find out.

Dazed, Jilly tucked the florist's card into her pocket. She thanked the students for coming and placed them into Betty's capable hands and breathed a prayer of sympathy for poor Madeline LaMott.

Then she announced she was taking an early lunch.

She didn't go to lunch. She went to the House chamber of the State House. As she walked, the world was amazingly sane and beautiful. A shell slithered through the cobalt blue of the Charles River and, farther out, sailboats rode the wind. Catching the sunlight, the Bulfinch gold dome of the State House glittered, and gulls darted and wheeled as if they knew why Jilly had come and approved.

She went straight to the balcony where family and friends of the Court were allowed to sit. Once there, she searched the mahogany-lined chamber.

Senators and representatives of the Commonwealth of Massachusetts were finding their desks. Clerks and pols were lining the walls, along with journalists, who were scanning the balconies for anything of interest.

The chairman called the meeting to order and announced the visiting U.S. senator, a home-grown, native son. Applause cracked through the chamber and hung in the high, domed ceiling.

Leaning forward, Jilly's breath caught as Phillip mounted the platform. He stood for a moment, receiving the admiration—so silver, so handsome and princely. When he began to speak, Jilly didn't remember the private things they had shared. Instead, she found herself listening to his words and the ideals behind them.

Mattie had been right. The love growing inside her was much deeper than sex. She wanted Phillip to be the absolute best, and when he was appreciated, she warmed with pride. Could she, by marrying him, make his life better, and thereby her own?

Startled, she twisted round to find Clifton leaning over her shoulder from the seat behind. "Man, you'll be the death of me yet!" she gasped, and was, in a rush of feminine vanity, aware of her slacks and jacket and walking shoes.

He smiled politely. "I saw you from the floor. Do you mind?"

He gestured to the seat, and she shrugged lamely. "I just . . . came to hear the speech."

"I understand."

When he had settled, she leaned toward him and asked under her breath, "Are you going to tell Phillip I was here?"

His smile left no doubts. This purposeful young man would be a fixture in her life when she and Phillip were together.

She had made her decision, hadn't she? She would meet Phillip halfway. More than halfway. Could she manage the difficult role of a senator's wife? Perhaps the wife of a president?

"All right, Clifton," she murmured, and had no doubts that the aide would understand exactly what she was talking about. "This evening, at seven."

Jilly had never been one to worry about a life-style that was more conducive to Guess? jeans and Reebok sneakers than Laurel suits and Henri Bendel evening gowns. Glamour, though not undesirable, had not been high on her list of priorities in the rain forest.

At half-past six o'clock, she was standing before a mirror in her bedroom, criticizing the tangerine-colored silk chiffon palazzo pants that clashed with her red curls. The shawl neck of the gold-sequined silk crepe jacket had obviously been designed with cleavage in mind. No bustier on earth could create a bosom where nature had been only modestly generous.

"Maybe a pin," she debated, and poked about in her collection of costume jewelry, holding up one, then another. "Drat!"

She dusted her cheeks. She lipsticked her mouth and ruffled her curls. By the time she fastened the jet earrings in her ears, her legs felt like a baby's preparing to take their first, wobbling step.

"I might as well tell you this now," she called out to Mattie as she peered over her shoulder to critique the view from the rear. "I made my decision about Veronica."

Mattie didn't respond, which was odd, because it had been her idea.

"It took a lot out of me, too," Jilly said less enthusiastically as she stared at herself again, full-front. "You know, I think I dread Blythe more than Mother. How does that girl make me feel like an orphan holding out a begging bowl?"

Blythe, as far as Jilly knew, had moved back into Veronica's house after returning from college. Why should she leave? She and Veronica fed on each other. Their continuity was among themselves.

Mattie still didn't reply. Frowning, Jilly stepped through her door and looked around the living room. "Mattie?"

Nothing.

Puzzled, Jilly attempted to fasten a bracelet as she walked through the quiet garret. "Mattie?"

She peered into the kitchen, but it was eerily empty and foreboding. She retraced her steps, her concern escalating. "Mattie? Where are you?"

Again, nothing.

Jilly's throat knotted with alarm. Oh, no! She ran quickly to her friend's bedroom, sending the door crashing back on its hinges as visions of Mattie lying unconscious burned her mind.

"Mattie!"

On the night stand beside Mattie's bed was propped a powder blue envelope. Snatching it up, Jilly ripped the paper and sank upon the foot of the bed.

In neat, precise penmanship Mattie said:

Jillian,

What I want for you, my dear girl, is beyond my ability to put in words. Tonight could change your life. I think you know that. I ask one thing of you, dear, and perhaps you'll disagree. But even if you do not understand, please don't elaborate to Senator Chamberlain about my place in your life. We can talk about this another time, but please, do this one thing for me. I hope you have the most wonderful evening of your life.

Mattie

Jilly crushed the paper into a tight, frustrated ball. "You don't give up, do you, Mattie? Don't you see, you've made it more difficult?"

If she and Phillip built any kind of existence together, it had to be built on truth, not a lie.

What a mess! Disheartened, she peeled off the crepe jacket and hurled it to her bed. From a bureau drawer, she laid out a plain knit sweater. She pulled off the earrings and dropped them, clattering, onto a tray. The lace teddy that she'd slithered into so dreamily was now a mockery of champagne-colored silk.

The sound of the knocker on the front door brought her round with a start. Mattie had decided to stay after all! She would meet Phillip. They would work it out.

She hurried to the door and threw it open before her logic caught up with her legs. Mattie wouldn't have knocked; she would have used her key.

She caught Phillip in a deliciously off-guard moment when he was stooped, his head on a level with the polished brass of the name plate as he made a last-minute inspection of his teeth.

Grinning, he straightened—slowly, so Jilly received the full benefit of his dovegray suit, his shirt, white as a cloud, his pleated trousers that were held up with whimsical paisley-printed suspenders.

He whistled softly against his teeth. "Well, well," he drawled, "when I said the other night that I'd waited too long, I was wrong. It was worth the wait. Very worth the wait."

The teddy!

"Senator," Jilly said coolly, promising that if she gave so much as one tug to the top of the damnable teddy, she would hang herself from the coat tree, "you're late."

He drew a cuff from a wafer-thin gold wristwatch. "Me? Nah. I'm the early bird."

Without a trace of smile, she gave his paisley suspender a bold snap. "So now you're calling me a worm?"

Lines tightened at his temples as he studied her and wrapped himself around the door frame to peer into the apartment. "We're being recorded, right?"

"A classic nonanswer, Senator."

His laughter, when it rolled richly down the stairwell, threw a net over Jilly's senses. She couldn't think of a single reason why he shouldn't stroll inside and shut the door as if he had come to stay.

"Boy, I can't fool you, can I, Jilly?"

He glanced around before drawing a small box from his pocket, wrapped in gold paper and tied with a gold satin bow. "Because I'm such an all-round nice guy, I came bearing gifts."

At a complete loss, Jilly brought steepled fingers to the tip of her nose. "That's for me?"

"Nooo." His dimples flirted madly. "It's for the worm."

He drew her hands from her face and placed the box in her palms. Leaving her to deal with her mounting dread, he wandered through the apartment, pausing here and there to appreciate Mattie's perfectly tailored slipcovers, the fringe on an afghan, a silver box on a table beside a lamp. He picked up a snapshot of Jilly as a baby, one that Mattie had made when they were feeding the ducks at the park. Squatting, Jilly had her chubby hand outstretched, her little rear jutting in a padded curve of pink ruffles.

He baldly compared the infant's behind with that of the adult. "It got better with time."

Blushing, Jilly shifted her attention to the bow of gold satin. "You have no shame."

Shrugging, he moved to one of the dormer windows, where he parted the curtains with the hook of a finger. "This is nice. You have a decided domestic streak, Jilly."

Mattie, I've a good mind not to do this. Yet, she murmured the half truth, "I h-have a roommate. She's the clever one."

"Ah."

He had shoved a hand into a pocket and braced his shoulder on the wall. Jacket was drawn aside, framing his spare hips with folds of silk.

"Open it, Jilly," he said without turning round. "It's not an engagement ring."

"I wasn't thinking that!"

"No, you were thinking that I'm an opportunist. Did you think I was talking through my hat the other night?

Well, I wasn't. And I won't apologize for something that to me feels very, very right."

Before Jilly could construct a barrier against such madness, he was moving toward her with a stride of a man out to prove something.

"I still want to marry you, Jilly," he said, taking her face in his hands, "and there's nothing you can do or say to change my mind."

Chapter Six

He hadn't told her the whole of it, of course. About how he hadn't had a good night's sleep since he had left her that night. Or about how he couldn't eat. Or that he couldn't work, or how an hour hadn't passed when he hadn't indulged in a sullen fit of self-bashing.

"But I have to tell you, Jilly—" honesty clotted his voice "—I didn't want to be here. I told myself a dozen times I wouldn't come. Hell—" a smile flickered self-effacingly "—I even read my horoscope. Romance was definitely out of the picture."

Phillip didn't think that Jilly meant to appear at the door half-naked. But the delight of it, the rippling melody of it was somehow healing and arousing and almost made the days and nights worth the torment.

"What do astrologists know?" She giggled as he took advantage of her lapse and caught her close, leaning her back in a whispery ellipse.

Their legs were juxtaposed, and her wide pants swirled about their feet like a sunset. Phillip felt the same danger as when he and his buddies had sweated through the buried land mines of Desert Storm.

"Yeah. They don't even know how to dance the tango." He dipped her recklessly low so that she laughed and clutched his lapels. "Do you know how to dance the tango, Jilly Winston?"

She had dropped the gift, and it toppled to the floor, not even brushing the margins of their minds.

"No," she gasped out as her eyes turned to liquid pools he could have drowned in.

"Dear me. I'll have to teach you."

The remark implied a future, and their nonsense was mislaid. Slowly, he placed her on her feet, yet they didn't move apart. She didn't drop her hands from his jacket. They were caught in the powerful, swirling undertow of mating—all the prescribed patterns and approaches, circumventions and retreats. She opened her mouth to speak, but closed it again.

"Well, you *are* going to kiss me, aren't you?" he challenged huskily. "You aren't going to make me do it, are you?"

"Maybe." Her smile had spent itself. "Maybe not."

"Oh, we have to kiss, Jilly. It's the rule."

"On the mouth?"

"It's an awfully nice place."

She laid a hand upon his lips, and he nibbled the tip of her finger. "In *Pretty Woman,*" she said demurely, "Julia Roberts didn't kiss Richard Gere on the mouth."

"At the end, she did."

"And look what happened."

"They lived happily ever after."

"Let that be a lesson to you, Phillip."

His face was very close to hers now, so close, they couldn't focus. His heart was an anvil. "Are you casting a spell on me, Jilly?"

"I'm no witch."

But her breasts lightly grazing his chest were mesmerizing him, and her breath mingling sweetly with his was drugging his senses. With the slow motion of one who has already surrendered, he drew the straps of her teddy over her shoulders and stood gazing at the stunning loveliness of her curves.

In a self-consciousness that struck flint to tinder, she gasped softly and grabbed his hands. "Wait!"

He shook his head. "There's a time to wait, my darling. This isn't it."

She stepped swiftly against him so that her breasts were crushed to his shirt. Phillip's breath tore as her cheek found the pillow of his shoulder.

She wrapped her arms around his waist and held tightly. "Phillip," she whispered. "Oh, Phillip."

Wondering how he had managed to live this long without her, Phillip squeezed his eyes tightly shut and prayed he wouldn't do something stupid and lose her. "Can you begin to imagine how much I need you," he whispered desperately into her curls.

"Please don't need me."

"How can I not?"

"Because I'm not good at your kind of life. I'm not good at ... what you want."

Humility had never loomed large in Phillip's repertoire of experiences, but as he breathed in the sweet fragrance of her hair and felt the rush of blood beneath her skin, he knew he didn't deserve her. She was a rarer jewel, found one day in an unexpected place. Never again would there be this simple innocence between them, never again the discovery of love's breathless rush. He wished it would last forever.

"I think," he said huskily as he tipped her dewy face and reached for her lips, "that I can't believe my good fortune."

Again and again he kissed her, like a boy whose curiosity of women was being sated for the first time, plac-

ing starved, impetuous kisses all over her face and behind
her ears. As they held each other, listening to their sounds
of breathing and the heartbeats of the other, Phillip
wanted to force her answer, but fear was packed down
hard in his chest. What if she was simply too wise to become embroiled in his difficult life?

So, for lost stretches of time, they simply held each
other, not speaking, not engaged in seduction, just reveling in the amazing miracle of this moment.

Presently she stirred. "I think I'd better open the gift
now," she said, and stepped back, holding the teddy in
place and slipping her arms through the straps.

So aroused was Phillip, he was in pain. "Maybe you'd
better."

"It's such a pretty box," she said as she retrieved it and
found a place on the love seat, her cheeks and lips pin-
kened by his assault.

"You're not going to be like my grandmother, are
you?" he said, forcing himself to sound normal. "Sav-
ing every piece of wrapping?"

She was self-absorbed. "They're part of the gift."

"Oh, brother."

She took so long to remove the bow, Phillip could have
torn the wretched thing open a dozen times. Finally, she
succeeded in removing the bow intact and placing it me-
ticulously upon the table.

But her hands were trembling and the tiny strips of
transparent tape baffled her. She picked at them with her
fingernails. With a whimper, she finally tore off the paper and flung it to the floor like petals of some strange,
golden flower.

Wide-eyed, she lifted out the heartshaped amethyst
that was surrounded by tiny diamonds and attached to a

thin, gold chain. When she looked up, her resiny eyes spilled great tears.

"Jilly." Phillip knelt beside her legs as she let the chain slide through her fingers to her palm in a tiny pool of gold. "Don't cry. I didn't give it to you to make you cry."

But tears flowed in rivers from her eyes and her lashes were sparkling wet clumps. "I can't help it."

"If you don't stop crying, Jilly, I'll cry, too. Believe me, it isn't a pretty sight."

"But I can't accept this. Can't you see? You don't love me, Phillip. You ask me to marry you, but you don't love me. I mean, I understand that, but how can I accept something so...serious?"

"Do you love *me*, Jilly?"

Jilly hadn't been prepared for such an honest question. She had no words and certainly not the truth. So how, she asked herself, could she protest when he laid her back upon the seat and pulled himself upon her? She no longer wanted to protest. She knew fully well what he intended to do, and between them, she could distinguish his shape, hard and massive, beneath his trousers.

Did he say her name? It really didn't matter, for the fuse had played itself out and neither of them could put the explosion back into the powder. If he had stripped her naked, she might have held on to her reason better than she did, but he only kicked off shoes and shrugged out of his jacket, like a boy in a parked car who had dreamed of the moment so long, he was now out-of-control.

Like a flash fire, his urgency became her own urgency, and their breaths were struggling. Their hands collided but were amazingly efficient as they negotiated with his zipper and buckle and a lace barrier between her legs. She lifted herself, eager to be taken as his kisses burned her.

But the more she urged him to take her, the more he played her out—seeking her readiness, taking pleasure in all the aspects of her body that were of no interest whatsoever to her.

"You have to marry me," he whispered as she was floating through some erotic corridor.

She captured his hand and pressed it to her, moving against it in stately circles, her breath catching as the spasms burst in a free-falling anguish.

"Marry me," he said again and, in his own way, saved her from the answer by filling her quickly and searching for his own thrusting truth.

There was nothing in her experience to compare with the thoroughness with which he possessed her. She had never been filled so completely or watched so knowingly. She could not conceive of what it would be like to be adored by him for the rest of her life, to have responses literally drawn out of her with no thought for skill or performance or egos—only the pleasure they could express to each other. She wanted to know things about him that she had never wanted to know of any man, and when he finally lay upon her breast, his chest laboring as she stroked his head, it came to her how completely she had fallen in love.

She grew shy and attempted to slip from beneath him, but he turned on his side and kept her imprisoned in his arms.

"Not so fast," he whispered, and kissed her lashes. "We're not expected for a while, yet."

Her mind cleared suddenly like water when the silt has settled. Rearing back, she blinked at him in astonishment, as if he were more of an errant husband than a winsome lover.

"What?" She was all whipping steel. "What did you say?"

Closing his eyes, Phillip cursed himself. "We're expected for dinner at the Harvard Club," he admitted. "My parents..."

"Your parents! Oh, great, Phillip!" she cried, and thrashed free of him. "That's just great! Oh, let me up! Why didn't you say something? How could you let me...how *could* you... Look at me, I'm ruined."

Grinning, he moved his eyes over her charming dishabille. "Yes, you are."

"You—"

"Wait a minute!" Fastening his pants as he swung off the loveseat, he caught her wrist. "We have a decision to make first."

Jilly wanted to hit him. She wanted to blacken both his eyes. She whirled on him. "Why do you keep pressing me, Phillip?"

"Because you keep pussyfooting, Jillian."

"Didn't it ever occur to you that I might have reasons for not jumping into this? Oh, I know you're the world's greatest catch—"

"All the women want to marry me. And I'm rich, too."

"That's what I'm talking about!"

"Enough. Come here."

He was much stronger than she gave him credit for, and after he had dragged her back down to sit beside him, Jilly had little choice but to confess, in a strained and jerky narrative, the basic skeletons in her closet—Veronica, her father, Blythe and her stepfathers. She told him all the reasons why she was not the kind of woman he wanted to spend the rest of his life with. She told him about everything except Mattie.

"That's it?" he said when she was done.

Rising—this time he made no move to stop her—she scooped up her palazzo pants and hurried to her bedroom. He came after her, and she wanted to shut the door in his face. Sex could only go so far, couldn't it? Now she needed to be by herself to think.

She snatched a handful of tissues and padded her teddy, turning to find him watching with a silly, groomish look. She slipped on her pants and picked up her hairbrush to furiously brush her hair, but his silence was like a quirt laid to her temper.

She flung the brush viciously onto her bed. "Now what?"

He unzipped his pants and blandly tucked in his shirt and zipped again. He straightened his collar and tie and put on his jacket, adjusted his cuffs.

From her seat on the bed, she slumped lower and lower. He dropped down beside her.

"I heard what you said, Jilly," he said, "and I think I understood most of it. But my life is half gone. I can't afford to waste a single day. I would deem it a great honor if you would let me spend the rest of it making up for some of the things that were stolen from yours."

Jilly didn't try to stem the tears that flowed down her cheeks. "Here I go again."

"So I'll say it first. I'm falling in love with you, Jilly Winston. I know I haven't paid the dues you have, but I promise I'll always be here for you. If you'll have me."

"Oh, me," she wept, and covered her head with her arms. "Oh, me."

Rising, he pulled her into his arms and found a handkerchief and wiped her tears. "If you don't stop crying, I'm going to get a complex."

He hugged her more like a friend than a lover, and into the curve of his neck where it was safe, she whispered, "Do you really think we could make it?"

"Absolutely."

Sniffing, she moved away to repair the damage as swiftly as she could, slipping into her jacket and searching around to locate her earrings, lipstick. As she squandered one last second to peep at the mirror, he fastened the amethyst necklace about her throat.

"See?" He slipped his arms about her waist and let his chin rest on the top on her head. "We make a perfect team."

"We're Mutt and Jeff," she mumbled. "And you're messing up my hair."

Laughing, he let her gather her evening bag and head for the front door. "Frick and Frack," he agreed to her back.

"Abbott and Costello."

"All right. You win." As they left the room, he turned off the light, chuckling as they hurried down the stairs.

Jilly stepped beneath the bridge of his arm on the door and felt strangely outside her own body. The limousine was parked near the curb. What had Clifton and the driver talked about when she and Phillip hadn't come down immediately?

"Adam and Eve," she said as she climbed in the car. "David and Bathsheba."

He sprawled on the seat beside her. "Amos and Andy, Ken and Barbie, Lewis and Clark, and Samson and Delilah. Now—" he held up a warning finger "—if you say one more word, I'll make love to you again here in the car and dinner be damned.''

Not for a second did Jilly doubt him, nor did she challenge him again. But in her mind she thought, *Phillip and Jillian, Phillip and Jillian.*

Chapter Seven

When she was a girl and Jess Winston was still brave enough to defy his ex-wife's rages, Mattie would dress Jilly in her Sunday best and Jilly would go with her father to the Harvard Club for lunch.

Then, the club seemed like a forbidding stronghold of granite and brick and made her imagine stern gentlemen of letters—much like her own father—who tucked silk top hats under their arms and retired with expensive Cuban cigars to discuss Wall Street and how to handle women.

Today, when her foot touched the curb and Phillip drew her hand through his arm, Jilly was surprised to find the Harvard Club was simply a granite-and-brick building that bore no intimidation whatsoever.

"Now it's the Chamberlains," she murmured cryptically.

"What?"

"Nothing."

Phillip drew her closer. "They're only people, darling. They won't eat you."

"Don't be too sure about that." Jilly recognized her paranoia for the dark creature it was and pushed it back into its cage. "There's no accounting for taste, they say."

"I love the way you taste."

He pretended to gobble her fingers voraciously, and Jilly thumped him sharply on the jaw.

"You're right." He was immediately as grave as an undertaker. "Dangerous business, meeting my parents. I'm a little terrified myself."

"Would you do me a favor?"

"Anything short of having a pig as a pet."

"Please introduce me as a friend?"

He stopped her on the sidewalk before they reached the entrance. Behind them, Clifton, ever discreet, also stopped and pretended to be absorbed with the lattice-work of the trees.

"You're serious," Phillip said, amazed.

"If they ask when you met your fiancée, do you really want to tell them a few days ago?"

His fingertips painted a feathery caress across her cheek. "I don't know who you think we'd be kidding. Love shows, darling."

"Don't give me that radiant business."

"Okay. You look like a hag."

But he was more right than wrong. With a family like the Chamberlains, form was almost more important than substance. Phillip could not understand that, for he was on the inside and style was as natural to him as the air he breathed.

When they walked inside and were instantly assailed by mouth-watering aromas and voices harmonizing with the bustle of waiters, the maître d' hurried toward them and Jilly flinched at the memories.

Menus were tucked importantly in the man's arm. "Senator Chamberlain," he enunciated with brisk precision, "so good to see you again, sir."

"Thank you, Mr. Eggers."

As the man inspected her, a flick of eyes with no opinion finding its way into their wooden courtesy, Jilly knew she had just been compared to other women who had had their moment upon Phillip's arm.

"Jilly," Phillip said, "I'd like to introduce Mr. Eggers. He doesn't bring you water, he walks on it."

A prissy smile delicately stained Eggers's lips. "Sir..."

"I'm acquainted with Mr. Eggers." Jilly couldn't help taking a secret pleasure in the tiny groove that appeared between the haughty waiter's eyebrows.

"Madam." He stiffened in disbelief that he had failed to remember someone who had once graced his presence. "I do beg your pardon most humbly."

She deliberately wrapped her smile around him and murmured, "My father used to bring me here." And she added, to restore the poor man's equilibrium, "You weren't supposed to remember me, Mr. Eggers. I was only ten years old at the time."

"Ah." He was suffused with relief. "And your father was..."

"Professor Winston. From the university. But you're not suppose to remember him, either. He hides behind a very stern gray beard and speaks in monosyllables about quantum physics."

Did a smile actually break through the man's crust?

"I understand perfectly, madam." He snapped his heels with Teutonic precision. "May I show you to your table?"

He led them efficiently through the jungle of sparkling tables.

"You handled that very well," Phillip murmured. "You'll probably get better service now than I do."

They were halfway to the Chamberlain's roped off area when a matron boomed in a voice as powerful as Pavarotti's, "Oh, look, there's Senator Chamberlain!"

As if a shot had been fired, heads lifted from Caesar salads and shrimp cocktails. Forks lowered to plates and looks were exchanged.

"Oh, please," a buxom woman gasped, and sprang from the nearest table, her ample hip bumping and setting the glassware to chattering.

With her flesh aquiver, she hurried forward and shoved Mr. Eggers aside as if he were a shiny piglet. She thrust a pen and paper at Phillip. "It's for my mother, Senator," she gushed. "She watches you on cable news all the time. And I vote for you. All my friends—" she gestured to the table "—all my friends vote for you. Don't we, girls?"

Jilly was amazed by the energy that was rippling through the club. But why not? Phillip was on his own turf. At nearby tables, men of middle years and silvering hair began rising and moving forward to speak.

A sensation of déjà vu swirled around her. Not again.

This time Phillip caught her hand and pulled her firmly to his side. *We're together,* the gesture said. *One doesn't come without the other now.*

Having murmured something about "fetching Liam," Clifton was weaving through the tables. He returned with a small, elegant man who flicked hawk's eyes over the crowd.

In a Southern drawl too thick to pour, the man intoned, "Why, hello theah, Milford, how're you gettin' along these days?" A slap to a man's back. A handshake, here, a nodding head, there. "Ah spoke with yore lovely wife the othuh day, James. Hollis, I decleah, that son of yours will be president some day."

As Liam blithely dropped names and called out to people, Clifton deftly cleared a path for Phillip and Jilly.

"Ma'am," Liam told her as he caught up and gallantly hollowed a circle with his arm, "if you'll kindly follah me..."

Jilly felt as if a surgeon had just opened her up, leaving her very being exposed to examination. Who is this woman? What is she to Phillip? Asset? Liability? Proper pedigree? Why haven't I been told?

"Phillip," Jilly said, wishing that Liam could not hear her words, "a woman is taking a picture of us."

Phillip's scrutiny swept over the tables. "Zelda MacAlpine."

Liam's laughter was rich and honeyed. "When Max Cordell presented his *in*famous proposal on the budget, Zelda polled the Senate an' wrote a memo that left pore Cordell's proposal bleedin' to death on the floah."

"Gored to death by a memo," Phillip quipped.

"May Ah introduce mahself, ma'am..." Liam folded his hands piously. "I'm Liam Brighton, Phillip's campaign manager, at your suhvice."

Phillip's presence at her side suddenly infused Jilly with strength. "Phillip is lucky to have you, Mr. Brighton." Then as the manager moved on, she said to her escort, "Yes, Phillip."

He didn't make the connection immediately but turned in the remaining seconds before they reached their table and captured her trailing fingers. "I'm sorry, darling."

Jilly met his wide eyes that she had come so to appreciate for their honesty. Her pulse was a drumroll in her ears. This was the rest of her life, not without risk, but she wanted him more than she had ever wanted anything, ever.

"Yes," she repeated softly. "I'll marry you, Phillip."

If Liam overheard, he was too professional to let them see. There was no time for more, and Jilly knew there would never be time enough. She would share Phillip with more people than she could ever imagine.

"I love you," he said, understanding.

"I know."

Phillip's family merited special privilege at the club. In their corner, their tables were especially lovely with their starched napery and polished silver, the red roses and silver ice buckets of Dom Pérignon.

Even without introductions, Jilly had no trouble identifying Phillip's sisters. They moved among the young debutantes who were invariably part of any political campaign as stuffers of envelopes and answerers of telephones.

The Chamberlain women's long dresses were not faddish, but stylish and terribly expensive. These were a privileged clique of well-bred women, one that Veronica and Blythe belonged to, but not Jilly. They had "the look."

Phillip's father was an older, more silvery replica of Phillip, and when Liam moved ahead to speak to him, his shining head bent. Then he looked up to focus on Jilly.

"You look like him," she said nervously.

"Except he's nicer than I am," Phillip said with a twist of affection. "And he'll adore you, I promise."

Did she sense a strain in Phillip now, a more cautious timbre in his voice?

"Your Mr. Brighton is one of a kind," she blandly observed.

Chuckling, Phillip was dividing his attention between her and the people who were vital to his career.

"The strange thing is," he told her as he conducted telegraphic conversations made up of nods and smiles and lifted fingers, "Liam is very good at what he does. If you'll look to the left, the tall woman wearing the mauve gown is my mother. My father's name is Andrew, by the way, hers is Delphine. A word to the wise— my mother adores Liam."

There it was—the reminder that of all the people at this dinner party, Delphine Chamberlain was one with whom she must make friends.

As if some signal had alerted her, Delphine lifted her head even before Liam reached her with the news. Delphine Chamberlain was a woman of enormous vitality, not as tall as Jilly and not truly beautiful, but she had retained her girlish slimness, and her porcelain skin gave evidence of lifelong tending.

More important was her air of destiny. Delphine was a woman of vision, and it was a quality that could not be taught; a person either had it or she didn't. Jilly had no illusions about her own lack. Had she made a mistake, wearing pants?

Don't be silly, Jillian Winston. If you're accepted, it will be because of Veronica, not because of tangerine palazzo pants.

"My mother," Phillip was saying as he simultaneously carried on a Morse code with Clifton, who stood a distance away, "was a Bower. Her father was Jonathan Bower of Bower Brothers Banking. My strength is that I'm not really a Chamberlain but a Bower. However—" he drew her reassuringly closer "—I wouldn't say that to my father if I were you."

Delphine's gaze connected powerfully with Jilly's.
Though people were moving back and forth between the
line of vision, their contact held.

"Phillip..."

Phillip's arm around her waist tightened. He didn't
look at her as he spoke. "You're worth ten of anyone
here, Jilly. You are what matters to me, not them. Later,
why don't you remind me to tell you about my Aunt Virginia's scandalous affair with General Whitehouse?
Hello, Dad."

For the rest of her life, Jilly would be grateful for Andrew Chamberlain's smile. It enclosed her like a warm,
safe coat. His handshake started a gathering around, of
course, and much before she was ready, Phillip was presenting her. Life would never be the same again.

"Mother—" his faintly irreverent smile included everyone who had migrated toward them "—I would like
to introduce my—" he gave Jilly a mind-shattering look
and a faint wink "—my friend, Miss Jillian Winston.
You remember, don't you? She received an award last
week. Marvelous work at the Bowers Foundation."

"Ah, yes, yes." Delphine grasped Jilly's hand. "Of
course. Mayor Hadley told me all about it. Miss Winston, we are so honored you've come."

Jilly didn't believe a word of it. Her knees were
threatening to dissolve. She was sweating. Her stomach
was knotting. She was a butterfly caught in a net. Yet
things moved on. The introductions blurred, and a glass
of champagne was placed in her hands. Names were
tossed at her like silver coins, and she smiled until her
face felt ready to crack.

Inevitably, perhaps purposefully, she and Delphine were left standing alone. The older woman's mouth turned up slightly, but not in a smile.

"Jillian, dear, would you indulge an old woman by sitting? Never again will I wear new shoes to one of these things. My feet are absolutely killing me."

Despite the woman's likable human frailty, she was cool and untouchable, as serene as a painting. Around her neck were pearls, and the only jewelry on her hands was a plain gold wedding band.

"I can't think of a better idea," Jilly said weakly, having to glance at her own feet to make certain they were still at the end of her legs.

When they had sat, Delphine slipped off her shoes with a sigh and spread caviar on a wafer, making sure it came precisely to the edges. She took a small, refined bite and dabbed her lips with a heavy linen napkin, as if it were all the nourishment she needed.

Jilly had the sensation of having failed miserably.

"How is your mother, Miss Winston?" Delphine said as she reached for a glass and sipped. "I haven't seen Victoria in ages, simply ages."

Panic unraveled. *Head up, Jillian, don't fidget, don't touch your face.*

"Veronica? She's doing very well, Mrs. Chamberlain. Excuse me, would you pass the hard rolls, please?"

"Wouldn't you like caviar, dear?"

"No, thank you."

"You don't like caviar?"

"I never really developed a taste for it, actually." Smiling lamely, Jilly busied herself with dipping and spreading, the placing of a knife and the blotting of a crumb.

Delphine's maternal eyes followed Phillip as he moved among the guests, pausing here and there to bend his head, to shift his weight, to place a hand in a pocket and listen.

"Nothing can be left to chance," she said softly, as if she were alone. "One tiny thoughtless detail, something not worth a thread can end up destroying a career—a trip to Bimini, a Chappaquiddick, a medical history."

She blinked the thought away, became a different woman with a different smile. She focussed on Jilly. "Veronica once chaired a committee I was on. She and Robert Mills were such a great help when Phillip was running for the senate. Your mother has an amazing sense of the past, Miss Winston, absolutely full of those wonderful stories about the Lowells and the Bundys, but then I'm sure you've heard them many times."

No, Jilly had never heard Veronica tell stories about the Lowells and the Bundys. She said brittlely, "You know Mother. Her stories are never boring."

Delphine sipped her champagne and blotted her lips again. "And your father, is he well? We never see him anymore."

"As a matter of fact..."

"Oh, I understand how it is when you're doing important research. Andrew, bless his heart, sometimes has to be reminded that he's still a part of the planet earth. When Liam told me who you were, it occurred to me that I should call Veronica and ask her to lunch. Do you think she would be too busy to come?"

Jilly's smile was worthy of all the years of Mattie's drilling. She said blandly, "It never hurts to ask, does it?"

* * *

In her mind, like snapshots, Jilly carried unhappy images of growing up in Veronica's great Gothic mansion on Bay State Road.

There it sat, three chilly stories of ornately carved stone and glittering leaded windows and Veronica's dining room table that seated thirty-six. Her mother liked to serve Chicken Vallee d'Auge from her Royal Worcester bowls, then take her guests on a tour of the portraits in the front rooms, each of them mounted in an ornate, gilded-wood frame and illuminated by a small picture light.

When Jilly rang the front doorbell, nausea rose in her throat.

An eye appeared at the tiny peephole. "Yes?" a man's voice haughtily intoned.

She waved to the faceless voice. "Are you going to let me in, Coster, or must I stand out here running up a taxi fare?"

A pause. Then heavy locks sounded and the door opened on a chain. Between the door and frame, a tall, thin, uniformed man appeared. He drew a pince-nez from his pocket and balanced it upon his nose, his bushy white eyebrows beetling above it.

His jaw dropped. "Miss Jillian!" The pince-nez slid off his nose and swung by its ribbon. "Is it really you? Why didn't you call first? I would have had Mr. Bridges drive you in the car."

Jilly wanted to laugh. Coster's whole day would be ruined. "It's all right, Coster, but I do need to pay the taxi driver."

The morning breeze played with the hem of Jilly's pleated yellow skirt as she returned from paying the driver herself, and she worked snowy gloves onto her fingers.

Coster was approving of her new suit. What he didn't know was that she had changed clothes three times before making a decision. She had risen at three o'clock in the morning and gone into Mattie's room, waking her and demanding that she promise on her Bible that everything would be all right.

Now, nothing was left to chance. Her black patent pumps matched her clutch. Her Hermes scarf was caught on her left shoulder with a pin. Veronica was very big on coordination.

Beneath her blouse, Phillip's amethyst lay between her breasts for good luck.

"I must say, Miss Jillian," Coster said as he escorted her to the back of the house where Veronica kept an office, "that you've turned out commendably well."

"Goodness, Coster, did you think I wouldn't?"

"Oh, no, miss." The old man blushed. "I only meant—"

"I know what you meant." She embarrassed him by hugging his frail shoulders. "You turned out commendably well, yourself, Coster. Why don't I wait here in Mother's office while you fetch her down?"

Veronica had spent a fortune decorating her office with eighteenth-century Chinese wallpaper, a cornflower blue rug and a priceless mahogany secretary.

"Darling!" she cried as she swept dramatically into the room a few minutes later.

It was eleven o'clock in the morning. Veronica was still dressed in her silk nightclothes—a caftan and high-heeled bedroom slippers. Her mane of hair was the same fiery color as Jilly's, but it showed Veronica's visits to the fashionable salons of Europe. Her skin was flawless; no freckle would *dare* show!

"Why didn't you let us know you were coming?" she demanded as they played kissy face.

And that was that. As if the past two years of silence did not exist.

A door slammed at the back of the house. Jilly was left with a faint scent of Shalimar when Veronica moved away.

"I simply *adore* your suit, darling," her mother confided, and stepped into the doorway and peered down the hall. "I always said that yellow is *absolutely* your color. Isn't Jilly *pretty,* Blythe?"

Though Jilly knew perfectly well that Blythe lived at the house on Bay State Road, she had forgotten to prepare for the young woman's resemblance to Ann-Margret in her most glamorous days.

It was incredulous! Blythe was wearing gray sweats and running shoes, though not an ounce of cellulite was on her anywhere. Her headband was soggy, and her vibrant blond hair was hanging in ringlets instead of her usual demure pageboy. A towel was draped over her neck, and in the hand was a glass of sparkling orange juice. Yet she made Jilly feel, quite unexpectedly, like a Barbie doll.

"Whatever you're doing, Jillian," Blythe said with a slight British lilt that would have both been affected on anyone else, but was perfect for her, "keep doing it. I've never seen you so pretty."

"You, too, Blythe," Jilly mumbled. "I'm surprised someone very famous hasn't snatched you up by now."

Laughing, Blythe dragged her headband from her hair. "You know how it is, Jillian. All the good ones are taken."

Not all, Jilly thought, and wondered if she could go through this, even for Phillip.

Frowning, Veronica walked across the room and tilted her head. "What is it, Jilly? Is something wrong. Tell us why you've come."

Embarrassed, Jilly tried to avert her mother's X-ray scrutiny. "Nothing is wrong."

"No, no." Veronica was adding up what little she knew of her natural daughter. "There is. Come, sit down."

"No!" Jilly was now delirious to get her task done and leave. What did it matter anyway? What would she lose? Only everything.

"I mean," she added hastily, as she stripped off her gloves, "I'd rather do this standing."

Veronica's lovely office grew so still, Jilly could hear the frightened flurry of her past. It wasn't right, she wanted to blurt out, that she had always been afraid to talk to her own mother.

Jilly stood severely tall, as Mattie had taught her, head back, shoulders down. She forced a perfect smile. "I came to invite you, Mother," she said with measured diction. "I've met someone, and now his family wants to meet you."

Veronica's penciled eyebrows inched together, and her smile grew wooden. Jilly flicked her tongue across her lips and resisted the temptation to twist her gloves.

"You mean," Veronica gasped, "they want to give *me* the once-over?"

To hell with it! Jilly suddenly wanted to set Veronica back on her heels, but this time not by doing unacceptable things like joining the Peace Corps and refusing to be on the team. She wanted to beat Veronica at her own game.

"I'm the one getting the once-over," she baldly explained. "Delphine and Andrew Chamberlain are giving a dinner party for Phillip and me. Delphine's as nervous as a mother cat for fear something might wash up someday in the future and damage his career, so she's checking birth certificates and doctor's bills. She wants very much for you to be there because she doesn't know me from an imposter, but she does know you, and she knows of Daddy who, I think, will come if I ask. There, that's the long and short of it. You'll do me a great favor if you'll make the effort."

The silence that followed was, to Jilly, like the final moments that a convicted criminal must feel when the sentence is coming down. Her soul had been laid bare, for pity's sake. She was exposed, naked!

"Jillian," Veronica gasped out at last, and moved away to find a cigarette and flick a lighter, blowing smoke at the ceiling and picking a shred of tobacco from her tongue with trembling hands. "You really can surprise me, sometimes, darling. You really can."

Jilly bent beneath a tangled length of memory.

"Now, what I want you to do," Veronica said, "is to come sit down right here and tell me everything. Don't leave out a single detail. When did you meet Phillip Chamberlain? Oh, my dear, you do realize that you have pulled off a small miracle, don't you? Actually—and I know you won't believe this, but Blythe will tell you it's true—I was thinking about calling you the other day and asking you over for lunch. But it's never too late. Let me ring for Cook—"

"Mother..." Feeling an overwhelming need to cry, Jilly twisted the cotton fabric of the gloves around her fingers. "That's all I came to say. I need to get back to work now."

"I won't hear of it! It's completely out of the question. Mercy, look at me. Not dressed and the day half gone. You are an example to us both, isn't she, Blythe?"

Jilly looked down at her tortured gloves and put them in her purse. She moistened her lips, which were suddenly parched. Blythe was staring coldly as she watched Veronica stubbing her cigarette and passing by a mirror to fluff her hair.

Veronica attempted to take Jilly's hand, as if by a tiny squeeze of it, nearly thirty years could be erased.

"You say Delphine asked specifically?" she murmured.

If her mother had said—or even intimated—that she wanted Jilly and Phillip to be happy, or if she had said that she wanted them to be friends now, Jilly thought she could have forgiven everything.

But she smiled at her mother's beautiful face and said, "Yes, Mother, Delphine was specific. I'm sure you'll be getting a personally written invitation."

"I know exactly what I'll wear. But enough about that. You will stay for lunch, won't you? I have it—we could go shopping!"

"I really need to go. It's been nice seeing you again, Blythe. You could do me one favor, though, Mother."

"Anything! You name it."

"Could you have your driver take me back downtown? I'm afraid I sent my taxi away."

Chapter Eight

When Phillip gave Jilly an engagement ring the first week of May, they were sitting behind the brownstone with the sun beating through the boughs of a birch and the fragrance of daffodils teasing their senses.

The ring was very old—a perfect cultured pearl mounted in diamonds, the gold band nearly worn through.

"Oh, Phillip," she whispered, and slipped it on, turning her hand to the sun and then to him.

"It belonged to my great-great grandmother," he explained as he delicately sought her lips. "Our first son will give it to his bride."

After Jilly finished crying, he pulled her to her feet and they walked along the sidewalk where sunshine spilled on the cracks and their shadows danced alongside.

"I swear, Jilly, I'm going to have to lay in a stock of linen handkerchiefs just for your tears," he happily teased, and went on to explain how their engagement must be kept a private matter until he could tell his family. "They would never forgive me if I cheated them out of such a perfect photo opportunity."

Almost every day, they saw each other, a fact that Arnetta wasn't particularly joyous about, but Jilly reminded her friend that she had stockpiled hundreds of extra hours, many of them donated, and never once had she taken a vacation.

"You're such a stickler for detail," Arnetta said, growling. "When do Betty and I get to meet the man?"

"You're invited to our party." Jilly presented both women with handwritten invitations, which they promptly opened.

Arnetta was interested that the occasion was to be held on the Chamberlain lawn. "I've never been to the Chamberlain house." She turned the card to identify the creator on the back. "Will you keep working after you're married?"

"Phillip wants me to do whatever I want to do."

"Hmm, then you must be lovers."

"Arnetta," Jilly warned as Betty's owlish eyes widened in astonishment, "you're shocking Betty."

Jilly never ceased to be amazed at her blossoming love for Phillip. Everything about him was delightful—his hands, his long, supple fingers, his wrists, his ears, his voice, his dreams. He told her things he had never shared with anyone about his family and his life. He opened her understanding to a scope of history that had passed her by, to a world that lay beyond the windows of her own mind and to his own private fears that he might not be good enough to help the country he loved. All he asked, he said, was to leave the world better than when he'd entered it.

She was struck by the honor of his dreams. She couldn't believe that he wanted her to play out her destiny at his side. She would have been swept up in his selfless ambitions even if she hadn't fallen in love with him.

"I want children right away," he told her one balmy night when he pulled over to park beneath a streetlight where the miller moths were battering at the lamp and the crickets were fiddling away. "Would you think I was a total mongrel if you got pregnant?"

"Maybe I'm pregnant already," she mocked, and leaned back upon the seat where his arm stretched along her back.

He tweaked her nose. "I have to warn you that my mother will mark our wedding day on her calendar."

She cupped her hand about the back of his gleaming head and drew it close so that she was whispering into his kiss. "Then you should stop sneaking into my bed."

"We-ell—" he slanted his face so it fit more neatly to hers "—maybe she won't find a pencil."

It was amazing how the most ordinary things became a celebration when one was in love. Sitting in the balcony of a movie and munching popcorn was a holiday. Eating hamburgers at a fast-food place was an event. She and Phillip were like children, and the world fell away as they amused themselves by looking at houses, walking Ranger, bicycling, driving for hours in the country. He took her to Washington for a television taping and introduced her to some of his important friends. They ordered out for pizza after being guests at terrible dinners. They took long, leisurely showers and went to sleep listening to Brahms and Sibelius.

"This is ridiculous," Jilly protested during another argument with Mattie. "I want to tell Phillip the truth. You're my family, Mattie. Why we're going through this charade, I can't understand. You met him, he met you. You liked him, he liked you. Everybody liked everybody. Why can't we just come out and say the truth about Veronica not being able to change her spots?"

Mattie stubbornly refused to budge. "Because I was your nanny. I was your mother's *maid*, Jilly. Let the Chamberlains get used to you and Veronica together. Let Veronica... We'll talk about it then."

Was Mattie slipping away from her? Was the time past when the whole truth could be told without wrecking things?

Jilly was far too much in the clouds to believe that everything wouldn't be perfect. The glass slipper would fit and her fairy godmother would descend, wand in hand, and she would be transformed into a princess capable of taking her place at Phillip's side and having Mattie, too.

When Phillip took her sailing in the long Chamberlain schooner, he had to teach her everything. He took her on a tour of the cabin below and explained how the compass worked, and the mainsail and jib.

The *Prince* was a splendid craft. Its polished brass fittings gleamed reassuringly. The weathered teak, trimmed with white, was well cared for. The lines were coiled perfectly. The Chamberlains were sailors, but Jilly had to admit that knowing an engine was belowdecks was comforting.

As she was standing before the wheel, her face turned to the wind, he wrapped himself around her and kissed her ear. "I love you, Mrs. Chamberlain."

"And I love you, Mr. Winston," she whispered as she held fiercely to the handles and lifted her lips to his.

"Are you pregnant yet?"

"Am I marked on your mother's calendar yet?"

"God knows."

"Then I don't know."

"Why didn't you just say that?"

"I thought maybe you might get discouraged."

"Look into this face. Is this the face of a man who discourages easily?"

A small squall had passed through earlier in the day, and now the air was exhilarating and clean, and the sky was full of blazing thunderheads and streaks of purple and turquoise and gray. When they dropped anchor some miles out, the *Prince* bobbed like a cork on the bay.

"Let's go below," Phillip said as the waves slapped the hull.

He dropped down into the cabin and held up his arms for her. Hardly had her feet touched down when he pressed her against the wall and captured her mouth.

Jilly had never felt fire as she felt it now, so isolated were they, rocking so seductively and life achieving its most perfect state. She battled frantically with his clothes, and when she'd torn them off, she greedily kissed his shoulders, his back, his waist.

"Damn it!" he muttered as he bumped his head.

She could not discard her clothes quickly enough.

"Come here," he whispered, and she turned to him. "Come here."

Desire rose up in him more fiercely than ever before. He was starving for her, and she was as ravenous as he. They didn't make it to the bunk, but dragged covers to the floor. He horrified her by licking her from her head to her toes.

With her head dropped back, she gave herself up to excruciatingly delicious sensations. When he filled her, she buried her nails into his back. Again and again, he drove into her until the pleasure became a pain, but one that she could not stop demanding. She locked her legs

around his waist and her arms about his neck. Over and
over she said his name, and when he was poised to spill
himself in that most vulnerable act of man, his mouth
sought her ear.

"Promise that you'll never stop loving me," he choked
out.

What did he mean, stop loving him?

She held him as tightly as her arms had strength.
"Until the end of time, Phillip."

"Promise."

"I promise."

Jilly and Mattie selected the pattern for Jilly's wedding gown.

"I wouldn't dream of letting you marry in something
made by a factory," Mattie said in horror.

Lovely hours were spent deciding between the silks and
satins and filmy layers of chiffon and delicate lace. They
debated over beading and buttons and seed pearls and
boning. Then they brought their parcels home and hurried up the stairs to the garret.

Jilly put on some music, and Mattie poured two glasses
of wine. They sat in the middle of the floor, surrounded
by yards of billowing satin.

They lifted their glasses as the sunlight shone through
the golden liquid.

"To the bride," Mattie said mistily, smiling.

"To the mother of the bride," Jilly said before she
thought.

When the limousine arrived to carry Jilly to the
Chamberlain party, Jilly had her first serious fight with
Mattie. The woman, so lovely and slim in gray crepe, her

hair arranged in its artful twist at her nape, insisted on driving her own car.

"Sometimes I really think you enjoy making me miserable!" Jilly shrilled unfairly, and burst into tears.

Unable to remember ever raising her voice to her beloved friend, Jilly hurled herself into Mattie's arms, begging forgiveness. "I don't know what's wrong with me," she grieved. "I'm losing my mind over this engagement. I'm going crazy."

Mattie, as she stroked Jilly's back, smiled sadly. She had guessed the truth the moment Jilly emerged from her room, dressed and beautiful in her shimmery blue frock. The style was off-the-shoulder, and Jilly's breasts were lusciously full, and her waist fit the dress, for once. Her hair beneath the wide-brimmed hat trailing streamers of filmy blue lace glowed with vibrant health, and a becoming glow had lightly stained her long throat that was completely bare of jewelry. Jilly was pregnant.

"All brides lose their minds," Mattie said comfortingly, and kissed Jilly's rosy cheek. "You'll feel better after this ordeal is over."

"I know, I know. But my nerves are shredded. I'm turning into a loony bird."

Mattie laughed. "I don't see a single feather, but you may turn into one if you keep the car waiting downstairs."

Riding in a limousine alone made Jilly remember the large seats of Veronica's car when her feet wouldn't touch the floor. She didn't speak to Ron until he swept the big car up the long drive to the Chamberlain estate that overlooked the bay. She was too shocked by the green-and-white-striped tent that had been erected on the expanse of lawn.

Here were private, tree-lined estates of the very rich. A force of security guards patrolled, and any unauthorized vehicles were turned away. This afternoon they were out in full force. Dozens of automobiles were parked in lines that reached to adjoining properties.

"An orchestra?" she gasped in horror as she spied violins, a cello and a harp beneath the tent.

"The Chamberlains go all out, ma'am."

"Oh, murder," Jilly groaned bleakly as Ron parked beneath the front canopy with its terra-cotta urns and brass appointments.

He hastened around to open her door and walked her up the steps as if she were a visiting diplomat. If Jilly hadn't immediately spotted Arnetta, smoking just inside the door, she guessed she would have climbed back into the limo and ordered Ron to take her home.

"Darling!" Arnetta cried, and rushed to open the glass panel, tossing her cigarette into Delphine Chamberlain's gardenia bush. "Don't you just adore this house? It makes me want to remodel immediately."

Jilly took in the whole of the vast, marble mezzanine with its Waterford chandelier hanging on a gleaming chain from the ceiling, the upstairs wings and descending stair, the ivory paneling that glowed with midmorning light, great bouquets on two-legged tables that lined the walls.

"Smile, Arnetta," she said, nodding, "a minicam is aimed straight at you."

Swiveling, the woman smoothed her non-existent waistline and whispered from the corner of her mouth, "I've been here ten minutes and still haven't seen him."

The caterers were emerging from the kitchen and leaving by a side door. Jilly drew her employer behind one of the ficus trees. "Who?"

"You know. *Him*."

"Well, don't feel bad, I haven't seen *him*, either. Where's Betty?"

"Around. Oh, look, it's that horrible man from the welfare office. Wouldn't you know he'd drive a Chevrolet? I must go and say hello."

To the horror of the doorman, Arnetta chugged through the front door and down the steps and out into the driveway.

"Whatever makes you happy," Jilly quipped, laughing as she watched.

"My sentiments, exactly," Phillip whispered as he slipped up behind her, wrapped his arm about her waist and nibbled her bare shoulder, bumping her hat askew.

"You!" Turning, Jilly clapped a hand to her head and stabbed the front of his shirt with her fingernail.

She stepped back to give him a thorough inspection. He was splendid in navy blue trousers with a buff-colored waistcoat that was impeccably tailored to show off his broad shoulders, narrow waist and long, long legs.

"Why didn't you warn me that this was going to be a holocaust?" she accused, and received his smile only to realize that he was, at the same time, sending a signal over her shoulder.

"Hello, Clifton," she drawled without turning round.

"Hello, Miss Winston."

Grinning, Phillip said, "Tell my mother to give me five minutes, Clifton, and see if Mrs. Mills has arrived yet."

"I believe she has, sir." Clifton consulted his black book and gravely pushed his glasses higher onto his nose.

"With her husband, Robert, and her stepdaughter, a . . . let's see, yes, Miss Blythe Mills."

Blythe? Jilly, alarmed, backed into one of the bouquets.

"Easy." Phillip caught her wrist.

Jilly wanted to bang her fist against something. How could Veronica have done this? How could she trap her into sharing her one moment of triumph with Blythe?

"Are you all right?" Phillip was already guiding Jilly to a nearby doorway and thrusting her through.

The room was lined with books and possessed four television sets. It was ornately decorated but amazingly filled with light. The moldings of the ceiling were hand carved, and the furnishings were covered in dark tapestry. French doors opened onto the lawn where the tent was set up, and Jilly could see dark-suited men strolling with their glamorous Elizabeth Arden women.

"Sit," Phillip ordered as he pushed her into a wing chair and strode to a hostess cart where he filled a glass with water. "When did Ron bring you?"

"Just now. Is Blythe really here?"

"If Clifton says she is, she is."

Phillip was kneeling beside her, solicitous as a man awaiting news of paternity. "What difference does it make? This is the day when my family meets your family."

"Don't pay any attention to me," Jilly said, and consoled herself by telling part of the truth. "Mattie insisted on driving her own car. We quarreled. The woman drives me crazy."

"Yeah, women can do that."

"You know Mattie."

"No, I don't. Not really. Shall we go find your mother and get this thing done with?"

The water Jilly had just drunk struck the bottom of her stomach and made everything she'd eaten for the past month threaten to turn on her in revolt. She pressed her fingers to her lips. Her nerves couldn't get the upper hand. Not today.

She eked out the words, "I need to go to the bathroom, Phillip. Why don't you go on? I'll be out in a minute. Please?"

For a moment he frowned, pondering her, then he rose and stood over her to brace a hand on both arms of the chair. "Are you sure?"

She nodded vigorously. "I'll be out shortly."

"I don't know . . . you look pretty . . ."

"Yes?"

"Pretty darn good," he said, and laughed, kissing her lips and starting for the door. "Don't be long. There're a lot of boring people out there I can't wait to introduce."

"Some of them are my family," she mumbled dourly.

Phillip wasn't keen on leaving Jilly alone. After a swift reconnoiter of the mezzanine, he stepped out to give Clifton a nod. "Where did you say Miss Winston's family is?"

"With your parents, sir. At the gazebo. The photographers are taking a few shots."

"Look, Miss Winston will be coming out in a few minutes. Wait here. When she's ready, walk her over."

"Yes, sir."

As Phillip strode across the lawn, his tails flapping and the midmorning sun beating down upon his head, he

could see his parents chatting with Veronica and Robert
Mills. Mills wasn't unknown to Phillip but he'd never
been on a first-name basis with the corporate mogul.
Knowing Delphine, she was probably putting her bite on
the man this very minute, which meant that Phillip would
soon find himself getting squeezed by another special-
interest group.

A cheer of laughter went up from the gazebo, and one
of his sisters called across with a wave. "Hurry up, Phillip, we're waiting on you."

Cameras swung round as he approached. Politics got
so complicated sometimes.

Veronica Mills stepped forward as he climbed the steps;
she was as pretty as Jilly had described her, especially
considering that she was in her fifties. But in a five-
thousand-dollar Chanel dress, who wouldn't be gorgeous?

"Senator Chamberlain," she said with a throaty purr
as her eyes fastened on his mouth, "we've never met,
have we? I'm Veronica, Jilly's mother, and this is my
husband, Robert. And—" her eyes didn't match her
dazzling smile "—the best for last—our daughter,
Blythe."

With half his mind still in the library with Jilly, Phillip shook hands all around. One of the things most important to a politician was his ability to go through the
amenities with style and keep another train of thought
running.

He was happy to let them chatter, and judging by the
way Veronica ran on, first to Delphine and to his ever-
diplomatic father, nothing much would be required of
him except to give the photographers their money's
worth.

After a dozen or so shots, he started to beg his leave.

Veronica slipped her arm boldly through his. "One more shot for the mother of the bride?" she whispered softly beneath the level of chatter.

She vampishly clapped her hand over her mouth. "I'm not letting the cat out of the bag, am I? I would so like a pose with Blythe. For posterity? It'll be one of those I-knew-him-before-he-went-to-the-White-House shots. Darling, stand here with Senator Chamberlain. Did you know, Senator, that Blythe took top honors at Smith? Maybe you could find something for her in Washington. Nothing big, mind you. But she can do everything well."

Phillip had heard the words before, yet there was something troubling about the young woman whose eyes were twice as old as her face. When she slid beside him, Veronica took Blythe's hand and looped it through Phillip's arm.

With a lame smile, he removed the girl's arm and his censure was aimed not at Blythe, but at Veronica. *Who do you think you're trying to kid?*

For one instant Veronica's honeyed eyes hardened and he saw her hand clutch into a fist that was swiftly tucked into the flowing Chanel dress.

Once the photograph was taken, Phillip bowed with a polite terseness and said, "I'll be at the house, Mother, if you want me."

Delphine was deep in conversation with Robert Mills. She shot him a look of disapproval and realized that he was leaving alone. "Darling, where is Jillian? Shouldn't she have arrived by now?"

"I was going to fetch her."

"I'll come with you, Senator," Veronica exclaimed.

Before Phillip could stop her, she had descended the steps and attached to his wrist. The insistence of her grasp dared him to remove her hand as he had removed Blythe's.

Her smile was underpinned with warning. "You don't mind if I trail along, do you?"

Neatly trapped, Phillip reminded himself that Veronica was the mother of his bride-to-be. Things said in haste now could create problems for years to come.

"I would be grateful for the company, Mrs. Mills."

But he purposely made his stride difficult to keep up with. He had to admire her grace as she managed her high heels and chattered skillfully about her hopes for the future, about her pleasure when Jilly had taken her into confidence, how she had never doubted for a moment that her daughter would one day make a grand showing.

"We really are quite close, you know," she said huskily. "Though we did have that dreadful falling out when she dropped out of college to go traipsing off to South Africa."

"South America," Phillip corrected, too polite to call her a liar to her face.

"Whatever. I only want you to know that I approve wholeheartedly of your engagement to my daughter, Phillip. You will allow me to give her a splendid wedding, won't you?"

"Actually, Mrs. Mills, we had planned on something very quiet and private."

"Please," she purred like a well-fed cat, "call me Veronica."

The library itself was Phillip's first warning that something was wrong. As he shut the door behind Veronica and invited her with flicking fingers to take any chair she wished, he looked around with the instincts of a hunter who has heard a snapping twig. Or perhaps, he thought, he heard only a silence when there should have been stirring.

"Jilly?" he called as his heart twisted in an illogical fear.

Voices came from the bathroom and a toilet flushed. "Coming."

But Jilly's voice was muffled and her hesitant tread on the tile floor prompted Phillip take a step to meet her.

As she returned to the room, she was touching her lips with a cloth. Her eyes were teary and her high, porcelain forehead glistened with moisture. With an intuition that neither of them questioned now, they started toward each other.

Dead in her tracks, Jilly stopped. Phillip followed the startled path of her bewilderment.

"Mother!" she said on a catching breath.

"Jilly!" Veronica exclaimed in what Phillip thought was the first genuine emotion he had observed since meeting her. "What is wrong, dearest? What's happened? You look terrible!"

Jilly gave a matter-of-fact shrug.

"It must be the excitement," Veronica said, and shooed Phillip aside to clear a path. "You never could take things being all topsy-turvy. Here, darling, put your feet up a minute. Oh, your lovely dress, you've soiled it. Sit, sit. I'll fetch—"

It was, Phillip thought, one of those moments when a person overempathizes to the point of sheer pain. Veronica's dramatic overkill was uncomfortable enough, but as she stepped to the bathroom door, before anyone could do anything, Mattie Corday appeared, Jilly's hat and purse in her hands.

"You!" Veronica gasped as her head went back in anger, nostrils flared. "What're you doing here? What have you done? What have you done to this child?"

"Mother!" Jilly was aghast as she lunged from her chair.

But Mattie Corday showed nothing. With a majestic poise, she stood tall and slender. "How do you do, Mrs. Mills."

"Oh, my God!" Veronica whirled around, then back, then threw up her hands. "How *dare* you come here today? This is a day for family. You have no business here. Get out. Just . . . go!"

"Mother . . ." In agony, Jilly stepped toward the two women.

"Oh, sit down, Jilly," Veronica snapped, "and be quiet. She knows better. Oh, I really have to say, Mattie Corday, that you do run true to form. You couldn't keep your nose out of it then, and you keep can't your nose out of it now."

"Mrs. Mills—"

"Shut up! I don't want to hear anything you have to say. Look, just get your things and go. We'll forget this gross incident. If you don't have transportation, I'll get you a cab. You, Senator, could you have your butler send for a taxi? I really apologize for this. As you can see, this personal matter goes way back." Again, a glare for Mattie. "Years and years back."

As accustomed as Phillip was to the capriciousness of fate, he thought the gods were carrying things a bit too far when the door behind him opened and his mother and father walked in.

One look told them that something was terribly wrong, and Delphine, who could not abide any situation beyond her control, consulted with Andrew.

"Oh, dear," she said simply, while Andrew discreetly shut the door.

With an instantaneous deftness, Veronica arranged a superior smile. "Delphine, Delphine. I really must apologize. I seem to have a small domestic crisis on my hands. Though it does happen, I'm told, even in the best of families. Actually, I had rather it hadn't happened in mine, especially here and on this particular day, but it's easily remedied. Mattie, you may leave now, and we'll put this behind us. We'll forget that it ever happened."

"No," Jilly said as the stillness of the morning settled like a cloud upon the library. "Mattie will not leave, Mother. I want Mattie here with me. I need her with me."

"Darling, I'm here with you."

"Mattie stays."

Jilly was positive that everyone in the room, had they known of a graceful way out, would have left. So intense was the discomfort, she could have sworn she heard the orchestra on the lawn playing "an itsy, bitsy spider climbed up the water spout..."

But there was no bed to crawl beneath now. There was no barricade to shut out the flood of wailing memories of standing at the second-story window and screaming as below, in the courtyard, Veronica was putting her luggage into the limousine and leaving again.

The tears in Mattie's eyes were because of those memories, and a fierce, feral protectiveness rose up in Jilly's breast. They were all looking at each other with the dread of what would happen next. Veronica's beautiful, lipsticked smile began to weaken around the edges as she viewed Jilly's own outrage.

Then she wasn't smiling any longer.

"Darling!" Phillip said softly as he took a step toward her.

With a thrusting hand, Jilly held him at bay. This wasn't his heartache. He hadn't asked for it. He hadn't even known about it, and that was her fault. She had had too many opportunities to confide and had let this slip past.

"Please…" She sought his understanding with a look. "I know I should have explained before…."

Dullness slid across his face as they spoke without words. The flesh seemed stretched too tautly upon his bones.

Finally he muttered, "Explained what?"

Jilly touched her fingers to her lips and, regret swimming, apologized to his parents. Then to Veronica she said as evenly as possible, "You owe Mattie an apology, Mother."

"What?" Veronica fell back, her hand clasped to her heart. "Me? You're not yourself, Jilly. Sit down."

"I'm better than I've ever been. Please, just tell Mattie you're sorry."

"My God!" Veronica swiveled round to implore of the Chamberlains that this scene was truly a mystery. "Jilly isn't normally like this. It must be some virus, some … this woman—Miss Corday…this woman is my maid! *Ex-maid!*"

"You're lying," Phillip said savagely as his eyebrows slashed bluntly across his forehead.

Veronica's smile glowed with triumph. "Ask Jilly if I'm lying."

Phillip faced Jilly as if they were the only two people in the room, and she knew that the truth would not hurt him. But her lack of trust could. Now he would wonder what other important things she had not told.

She wished she could faint. Or die. But there was no escaping so easily. "Mattie," she said to her mother, lifting her head to an angle Veronica could not possibly have duplicated, "Mattie is *not* a maid. She was my teacher."

"Teacher!"

"She raised me, Mother. As you did not. Mattie loves me. She's more of a mother than any blood could make her. She—"

"Ohhh." Veronica pressed the back of her hand to her forehead and staggered to one of the chairs, waving away Delphine's concerned interest.

"Oh, Mother, come on." Jilly shredded her mother's theatric. "We've played this game for thirty years. Surely you can do better."

"Oh, dear," murmured Delphine in bafflement. "Perhaps I should send for some coffee."

"Sit down, Delphine," Andrew said dourly. "And stay out of it."

"It's all right, Jillian," Mattie said with quiet dignity. "I should never have come. I tried to explain."

As Jilly stared, the whole truth came to her, of what Mattie had borne to befriend the tiny, helpless child of a woman like Veronica. What wrath she must have borne from Veronica, what accusations, what disdain.

"Mattie!" She rushed into the familiar arms and held with all her might. She tightened her arms around the stern, straight back and pressed her face against the crisp, staid collar. "It's all right, Mattie. I understand now, I understand."

A groan came from where Veronica had buried her head in her hands. "Spare us, Jilly. No one cares about this."

In a blaze of fury, Jilly whirled, her blue skirt the color of a storm.

In a voice devoid of the love she had once had, she said, "Mother, out of deference for this family, you and I will go through the charade. You will come to my wedding and take your place as the mother of the bride. You will, if you're so inclined, pretend to your friends that you are my mother. But do not, not ever, pretend that you love me. And if you ever raise your voice to Mattie again or treat her with the slightest disrespect, I will spend the rest of my life seeing that you regret it. Deeply regret it."

A thin smile of hatred spread across Veronica's face as she rose to her feet, one that Jilly had seen many times. "You are quite confident that this man still wants to marry you. Have you thought about that . . . ? I thought not."

Jilly was as sure of Phillip's love as she was of Mattie's. The only thing she did not know was if it could sustain the future.

But one look at the tiny lines crinkling his eyes relieved her. He was beside her in two strides, taking her into his arms. "Dear me," he drawled, and glanced at Delphine. "Remind me, Mother, to introduce Mrs. Mills to Aunt Virginia. I have a feeling that they'll get along famously."

He then signaled his father, who had a history of smoothing over nasty incidents such as this one.

With a loud clearing of his throat, Andrew strode to Veronica and grasped her hand. "Mrs. Mills, I think we should slip into the kitchen for some brandy before the rest of the guests arrive, don't you?"

Still, Veronica wasn't certain until she saw the distance in Delphine Chamberlain's eyes that they, in all their elegant good manners, had believed Jilly, not her.

"Come," Delphine said with toneless formality. "Andrew is right. Jillian needs a few moments of privacy."

When the door of the library shut with a click, Jilly collapsed into a chair and held her hand over her mouth, rocking gently, alone with herself. Over her head, Phillip looked at Mattie, a sad smile of understanding on his face.

"Thank you, Mattie," he said, "for taking care of her for me all those years."

Queenlike, Mattie accepted what he was offering.

"It was my privilege, sir," she whispered as her voice broke, prompting Jilly to reach up her hand, which Mattie took and held tightly. Lifting Jilly's fingers to her lips, she added, "It was the best thing I ever did."

Jilly's happiness spilled over into tears, and she was half laughing, half crying when she curled her other arm around Phillip's waist and laid her head wearily against his waist.

"I don't suppose I could interrupt you two and say that I've got to throw up again," she groaned.

"What?"

"You idiot! I'm pregnant, can't you tell? Can't you look at how green I am and tell?"

Not knowing whether to laugh or find a chair and sit down, Phillip buried his fingers in her sparkling curls and tipped up her face. His breath whooshed out in surprise as he shook his head. "Are you serious?"

"No." She made a grotesque face. "I always get deathly nauseous at engagement parties."

"Dear me." Laughing, Phillip winked at Mattie, who was much too private a person to look on as he pulled Jilly to her feet and kissed her with an appalling thoroughness. "Then I think we'd better get you a glass of ginger ale to settle your stomach. We'll have to tell my mother right away."

"I know," Jilly sighed. "She'll have to mark it on her calendar."

"I doubt that. You have no idea how good my mother is at turning an engagement party into a wedding on a moment's notice. It's really a wonderful photo opportunity. Tell me you brought the ring!"

*   *   *   *   *

Linda Shaw

A biography? Yes, well, I'm afraid mine doesn't include a glitzy, high-rise apartment, or tooling around in a smart little foreign car, or beautiful sculptured nails. I was raised in blistering East Texas where you rode your bicycle on melting oil-field roads, and if you were foolish enough to go barefooted...

A not-too-glamorous beginning for a writer, eh? But, then, perhaps I haven't strayed too far from those melting oil-field roads. Thirty-four years of married life, three children and three grandchildren have brought Bennett and me full circle to the north-central part of this hot state. We live out our days on sixteen acres, which I hurry from my desk to care for, mostly by myself, since Bennett drives into Fort Worth each day to General Dynamics. (If you want to know what I need for my next birthday, it's a new tractor!)

Writing has brought a certain "broadening" to my life, but it really began when I went back to school at thirty-three, after fifteen years of homemaking. What an education! A farm girl going through a tough university like North Texas State?

University life taught me one thing: I could survive *anything!* Yet I would never have written at all if Bennett hadn't given me the freedom to find out what I was made of. Truth is, though, I was *not* meant to be a writer. It's been the hardest thing I've ever done. It still is!

What I'm most proud of is what writing has allowed me to do—to help make all our families self-sufficient here on this hill. *Ballad in Blue* bought that first acre behind us, *December's Wine* and *All She Ever Wanted* my Buick—yes, it's *old* now! All the Special Edition and Intimate Moments titles have helped purchase the surrounding acreage, built our houses and planted the trees that Bennett and I are demented enough to keep coddling. (Listen, a Texas tree is a triumph. I hug my trees, and they *know*.)

I only wish I'd begun my writing career at twenty instead of at forty. My career of choice, actually, was teaching music. That's what my fancy degree is in: music. Little did I know when I graduated at thirty-eight that an older woman could be discriminated against even in education. One of the positions I wanted went to a twenty-eight-year-old man who had been fired from his last job!

A blessing in disguise, as the saying goes. I was so angry, I wrote my first book. Is it any wonder that my heroines are fighting tough odds and really come from behind?

None of my heroines are in their fifties, however, nor do they have the privilege of seeing the noses of rosy young grandchildren pressed to my atrium doors and voices calling out, "Grandma, have you got your pages yet?"

When that happens, I know it's time to give my characters a rest and go out to play!